Pirate Queen

THE LEGEND OF GRACE O'MALLEY

Pirate Queen

THE LEGEND OF GRACE O'MALLEY

WRITTEN BY
TONY LEE

ILLUSTRATED BY
SAM HART

COLORED BY
TARSIS CRUZ WITH **FLAVIO COSTA**

LETTERED BY
CADU SIMÕES

CANDLEWICK PRESS

he Irish Rebellion against Henry VIII led by Silken Thomas, the Earl of Kildare, has failed, and the leaders have been executed.

Henry VIII is now the uncontested king of Ireland — the lords of Ireland are now expected to surrender their lands to the throne in the hope that those lands will be returned in exchange for their loyalty.

Many never see their lands again.

The Irish are forced to follow the English Tudor rule, under which their churches are ransacked, their language ignored, their people oppressed. English lords are given Irish lands, and Irish clans find that their claims of succession fall on deaf ears.

But there is a storm coming.

In Connacht, Ireland, the chieftain Eoghan Dubhdara Ó Máille, known in legend as Dubhdara O'Malley, has a daughter named Gráinne Ní Mháille — better known as Gráinne Mhaol, or Granuaile. And this girl will one day bring the fight to the English, become a thorn in the side of Queen Elizabeth herself, and become a legend in the process.

For there is indeed a storm coming — and her name is Grace O'Malley, the Pirate Queen of Ireland. . . .

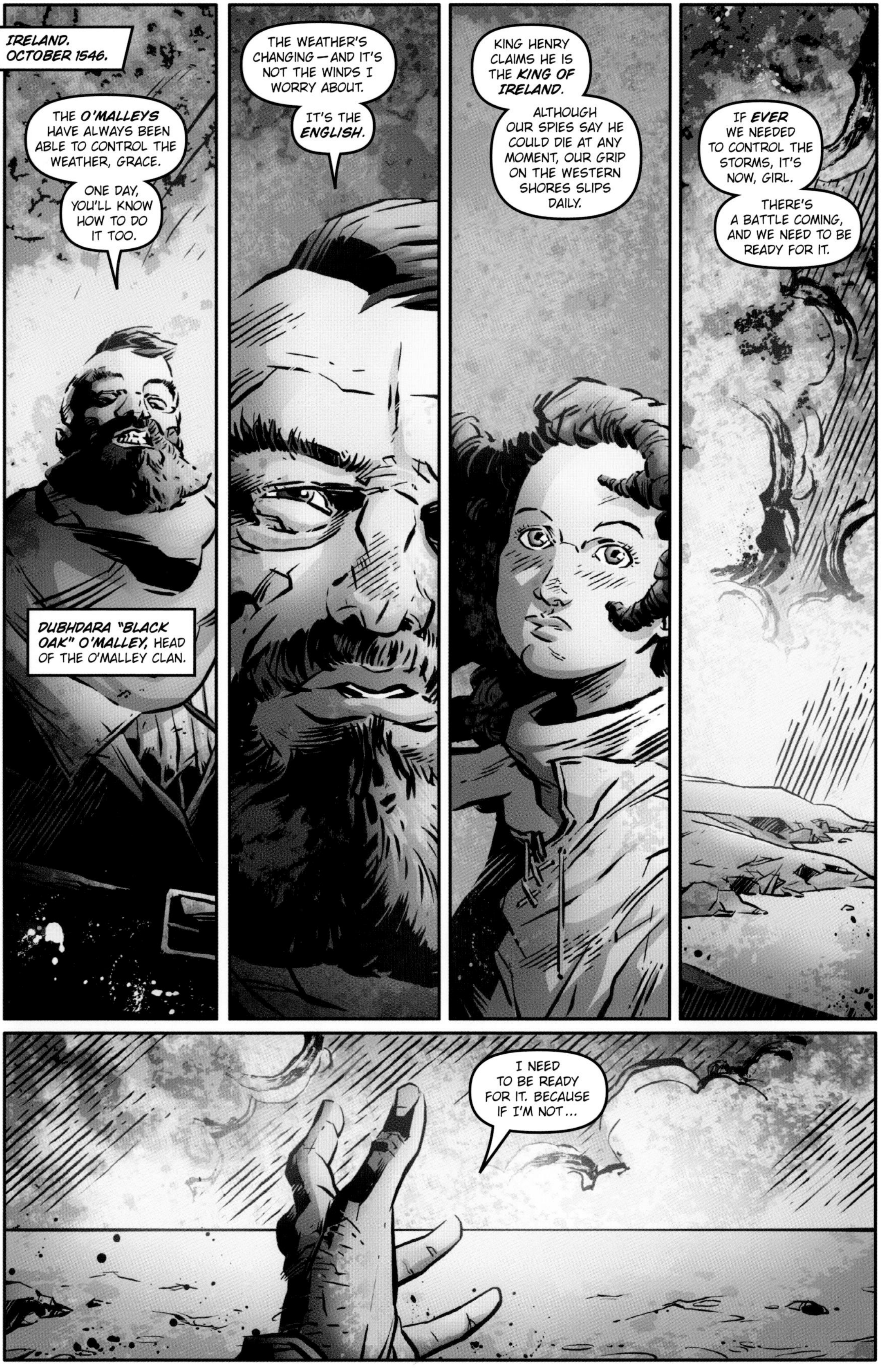
IRELAND. OCTOBER 1546.
THE O'MALLEYS HAVE ALWAYS BEEN ABLE TO CONTROL THE WEATHER, GRACE.
ONE DAY, YOU'LL KNOW HOW TO DO IT TOO.
DUBHDARA "BLACK OAK" O'MALLEY, HEAD OF THE O'MALLEY CLAN.
THE WEATHER'S CHANGING—AND IT'S NOT THE WINDS I WORRY ABOUT.
IT'S THE ENGLISH.
KING HENRY CLAIMS HE IS THE KING OF IRELAND.
ALTHOUGH OUR SPIES SAY HE COULD DIE AT ANY MOMENT, OUR GRIP ON THE WESTERN SHORES SLIPS DAILY.
IF EVER WE NEEDED TO CONTROL THE STORMS, IT'S NOW, GIRL.
THERE'S A BATTLE COMING, AND WE NEED TO BE READY FOR IT.
I NEED TO BE READY FOR IT. BECAUSE IF I'M NOT...

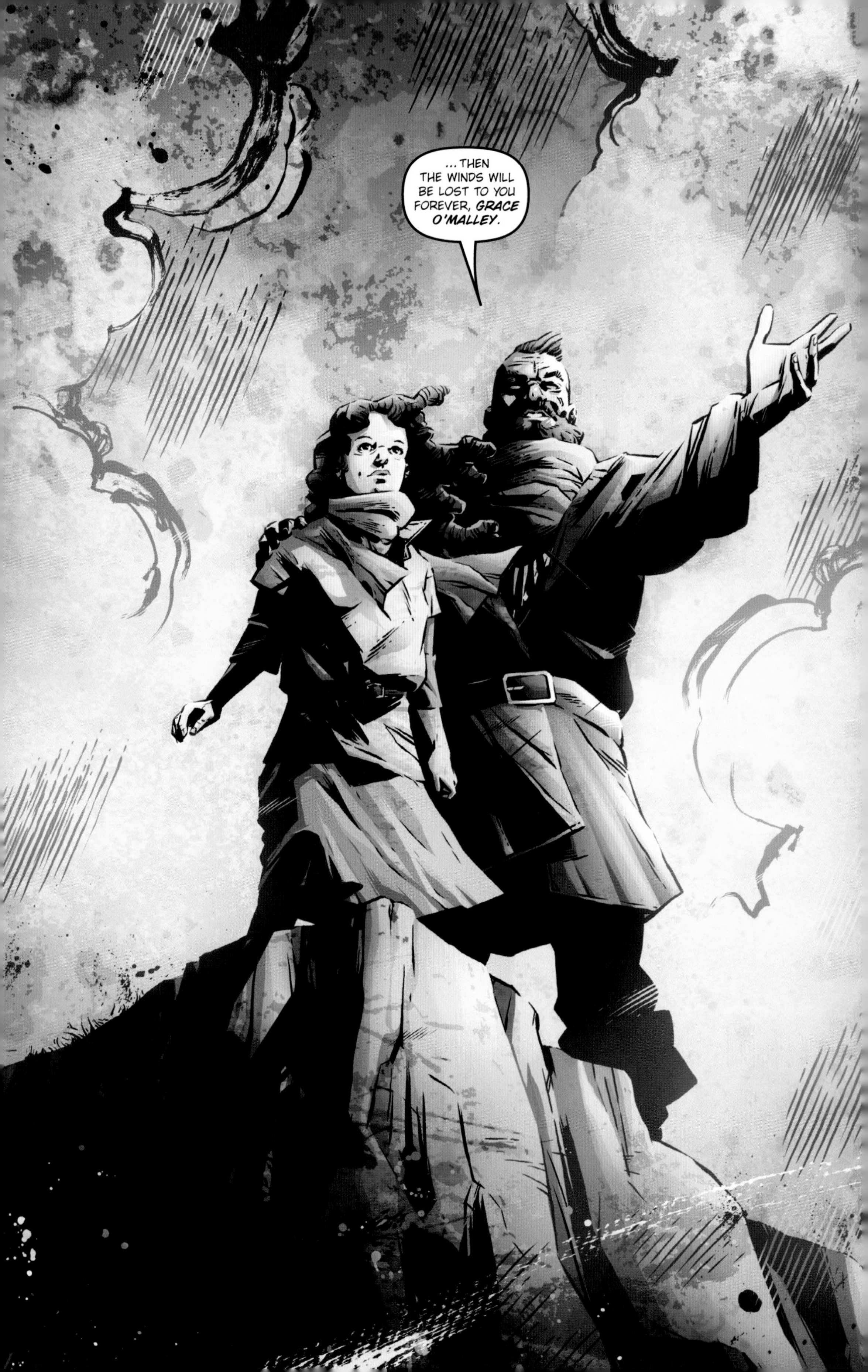
...THEN THE WINDS WILL BE LOST TO YOU FOREVER, GRACE O'MALLEY.

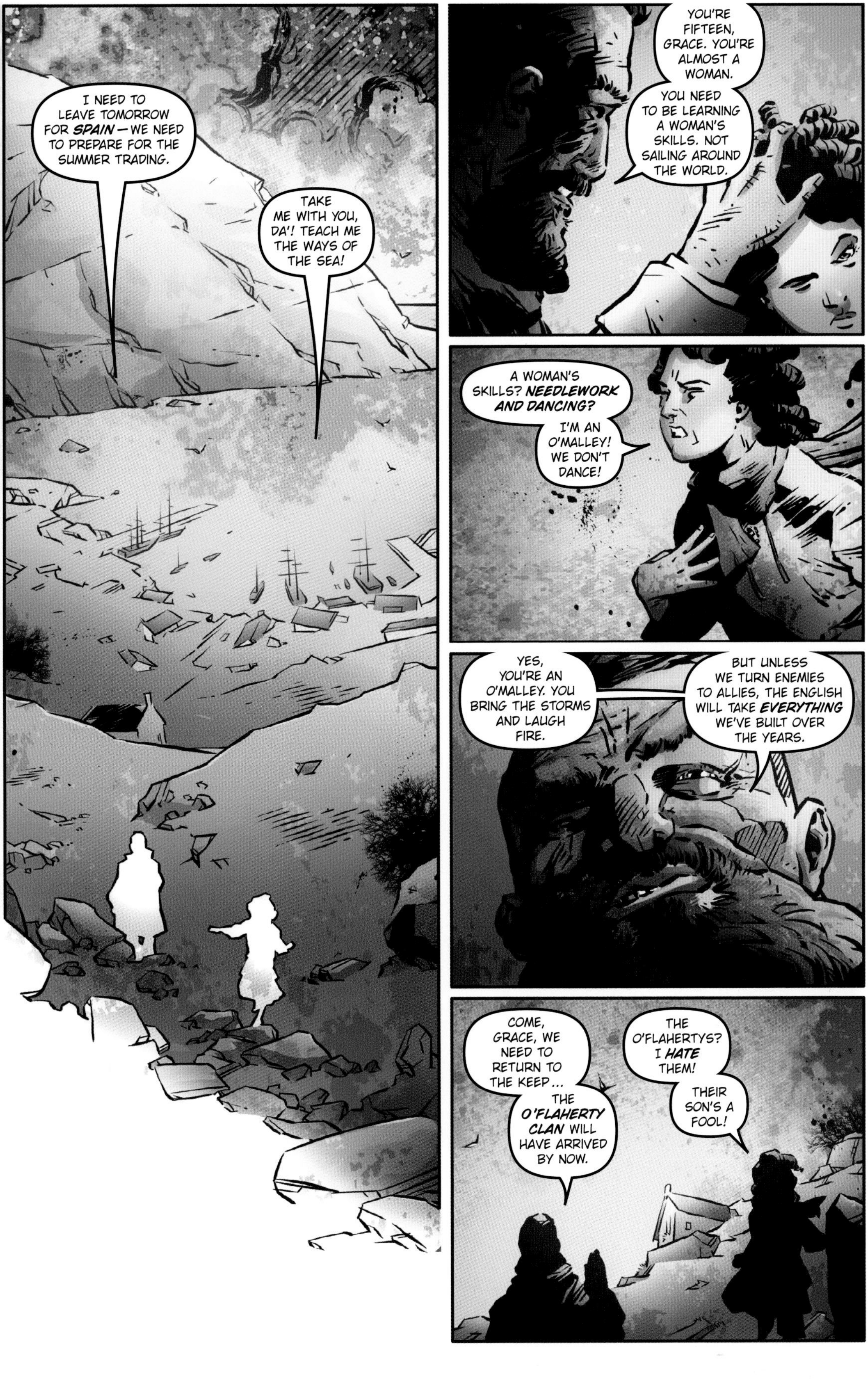
I NEED TO LEAVE TOMORROW FOR SPAIN — WE NEED TO PREPARE FOR THE SUMMER TRADING.
TAKE ME WITH YOU, DA'! TEACH ME THE WAYS OF THE SEA!
YOU'RE FIFTEEN, GRACE. YOU'RE ALMOST A WOMAN.
YOU NEED TO BE LEARNING A WOMAN'S SKILLS. NOT SAILING AROUND THE WORLD.
A WOMAN'S SKILLS? NEEDLEWORK AND DANCING?
I'M AN O'MALLEY! WE DON'T DANCE!
YES, YOU'RE AN O'MALLEY. YOU BRING THE STORMS AND LAUGH FIRE.
BUT UNLESS WE TURN ENEMIES TO ALLIES, THE ENGLISH WILL TAKE EVERYTHING WE'VE BUILT OVER THE YEARS.
COME, GRACE, WE NEED TO RETURN TO THE KEEP...
THE O'FLAHERTY CLAN WILL HAVE ARRIVED BY NOW.
THE O'FLAHERTYS? I HATE THEM!
THEIR SON'S A FOOL!

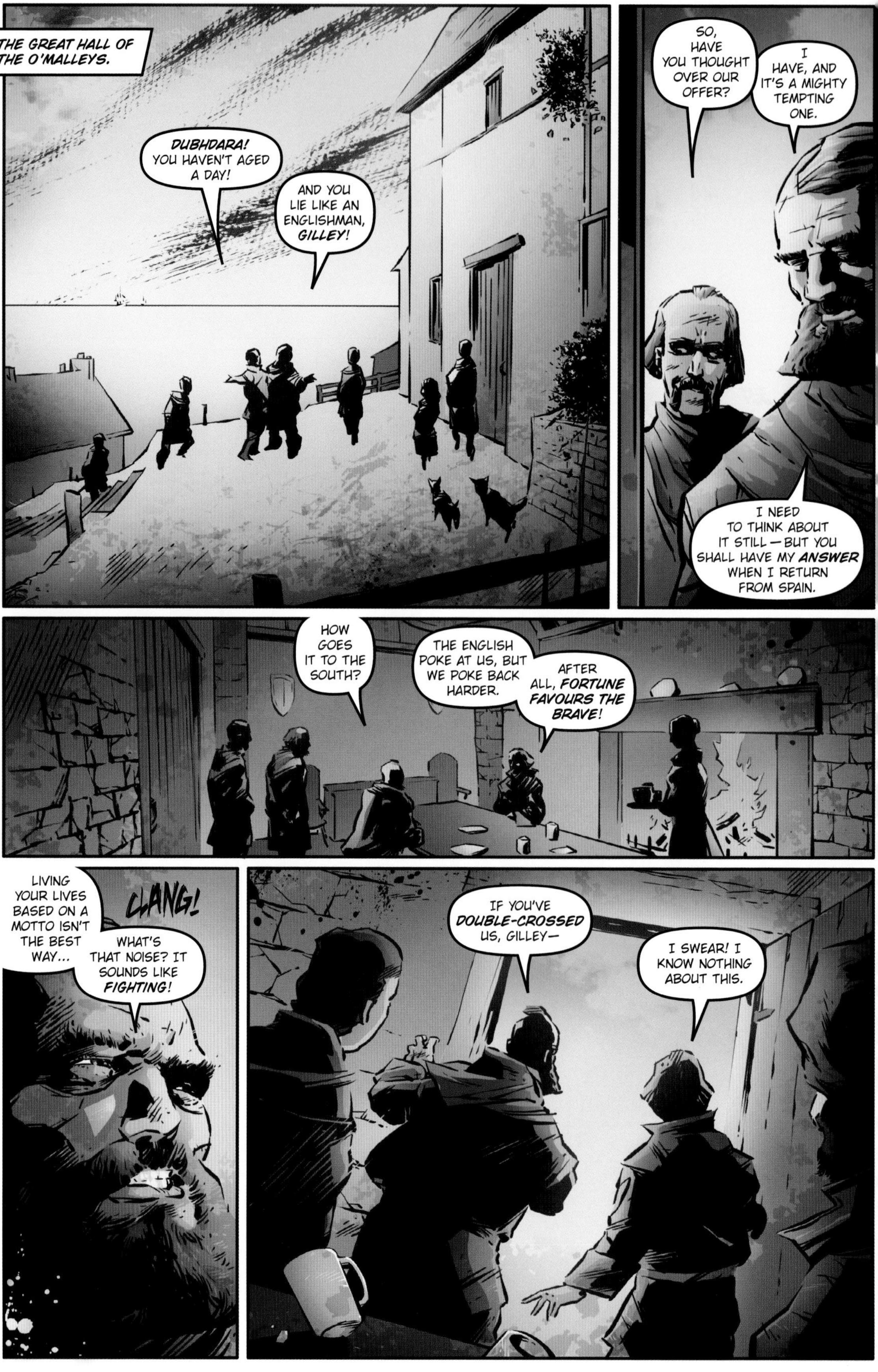
THE GREAT HALL OF THE O'MALLEYS.
DUBHDARA! YOU HAVEN'T AGED A DAY!
AND YOU LIE LIKE AN ENGLISHMAN, GILLEY!
SO, HAVE YOU THOUGHT OVER OUR OFFER?
I HAVE, AND IT'S A MIGHTY TEMPTING ONE.
I NEED TO THINK ABOUT IT STILL—BUT YOU SHALL HAVE MY ANSWER WHEN I RETURN FROM SPAIN.
HOW GOES IT TO THE SOUTH?
THE ENGLISH POKE AT US, BUT WE POKE BACK HARDER.
AFTER ALL, FORTUNE FAVOURS THE BRAVE!
LIVING YOUR LIVES BASED ON A MOTTO ISN'T THE BEST WAY...
CLANG!
WHAT'S THAT NOISE? IT SOUNDS LIKE FIGHTING!
IF YOU'VE DOUBLE-CROSSED US, GILLEY—
I SWEAR! I KNOW NOTHING ABOUT THIS.

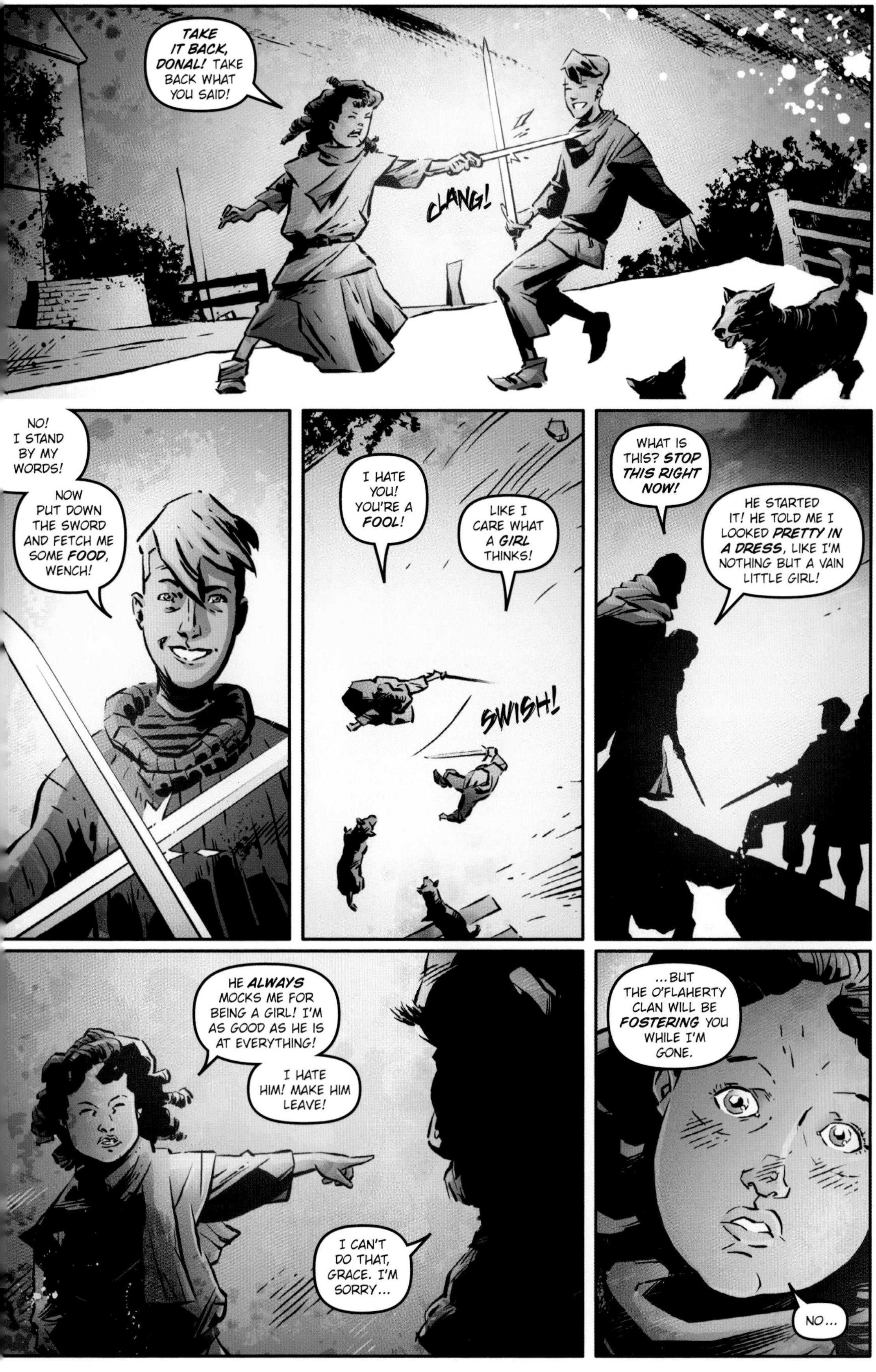
TAKE IT BACK, DONAL! TAKE BACK WHAT YOU SAID!
CLANG!
NO! I STAND BY MY WORDS!
NOW PUT DOWN THE SWORD AND FETCH ME SOME FOOD, WENCH!
I HATE YOU! YOU'RE A FOOL!
LIKE I CARE WHAT A GIRL THINKS!
SWISH!
WHAT IS THIS? STOP THIS RIGHT NOW!
HE STARTED IT! HE TOLD ME I LOOKED PRETTY IN A DRESS, LIKE I'M NOTHING BUT A VAIN LITTLE GIRL!
HE ALWAYS MOCKS ME FOR BEING A GIRL! I'M AS GOOD AS HE IS AT EVERYTHING!
I HATE HIM! MAKE HIM LEAVE!
I CAN'T DO THAT, GRACE. I'M SORRY...
...BUT THE O'FLAHERTY CLAN WILL BE FOSTERING YOU WHILE I'M GONE.
NO...

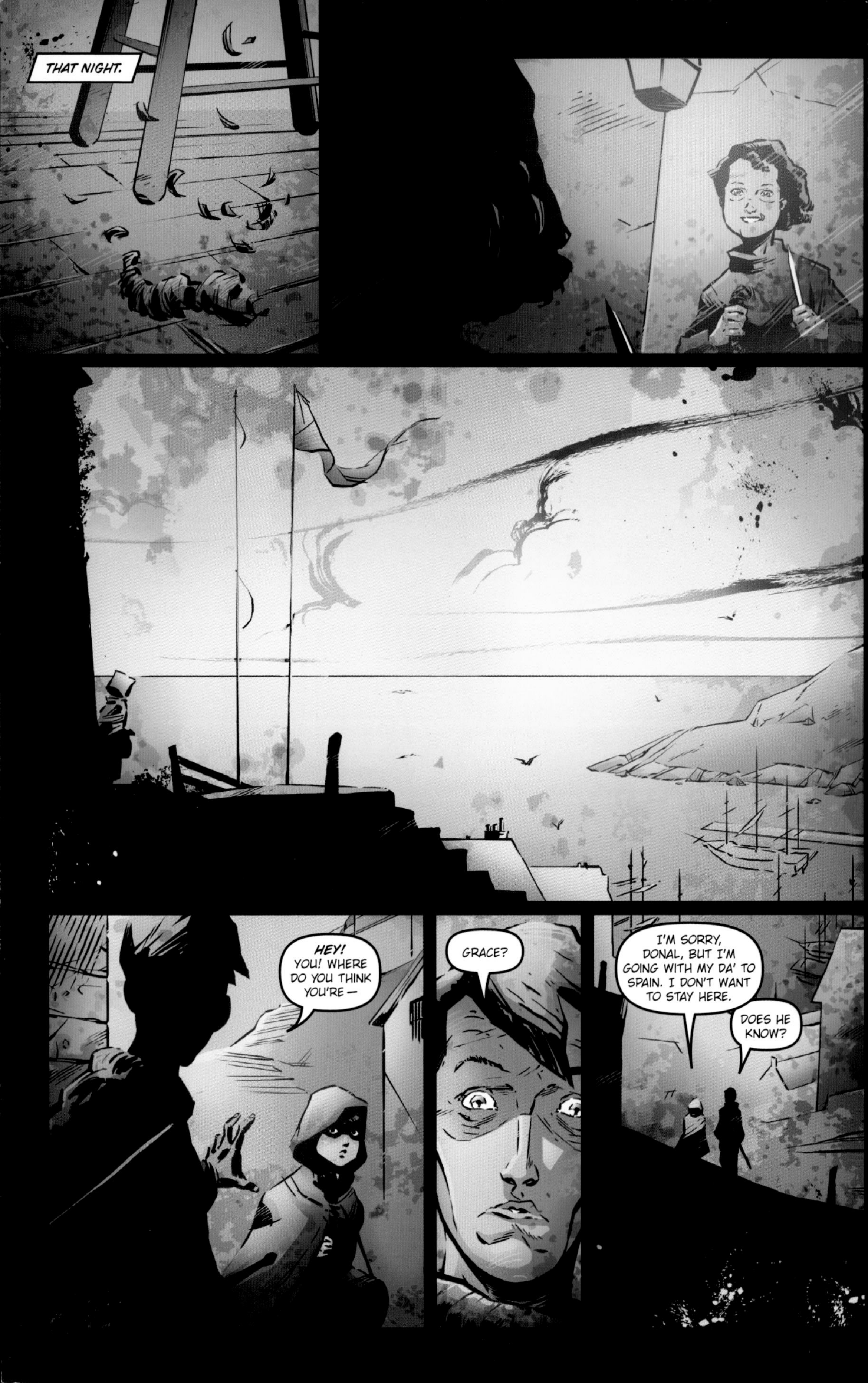
THAT NIGHT.
HEY! YOU! WHERE DO YOU THINK YOU'RE—
GRACE?
I'M SORRY, DONAL, BUT I'M GOING WITH MY DA' TO SPAIN. I DON'T WANT TO STAY HERE.
DOES HE KNOW?

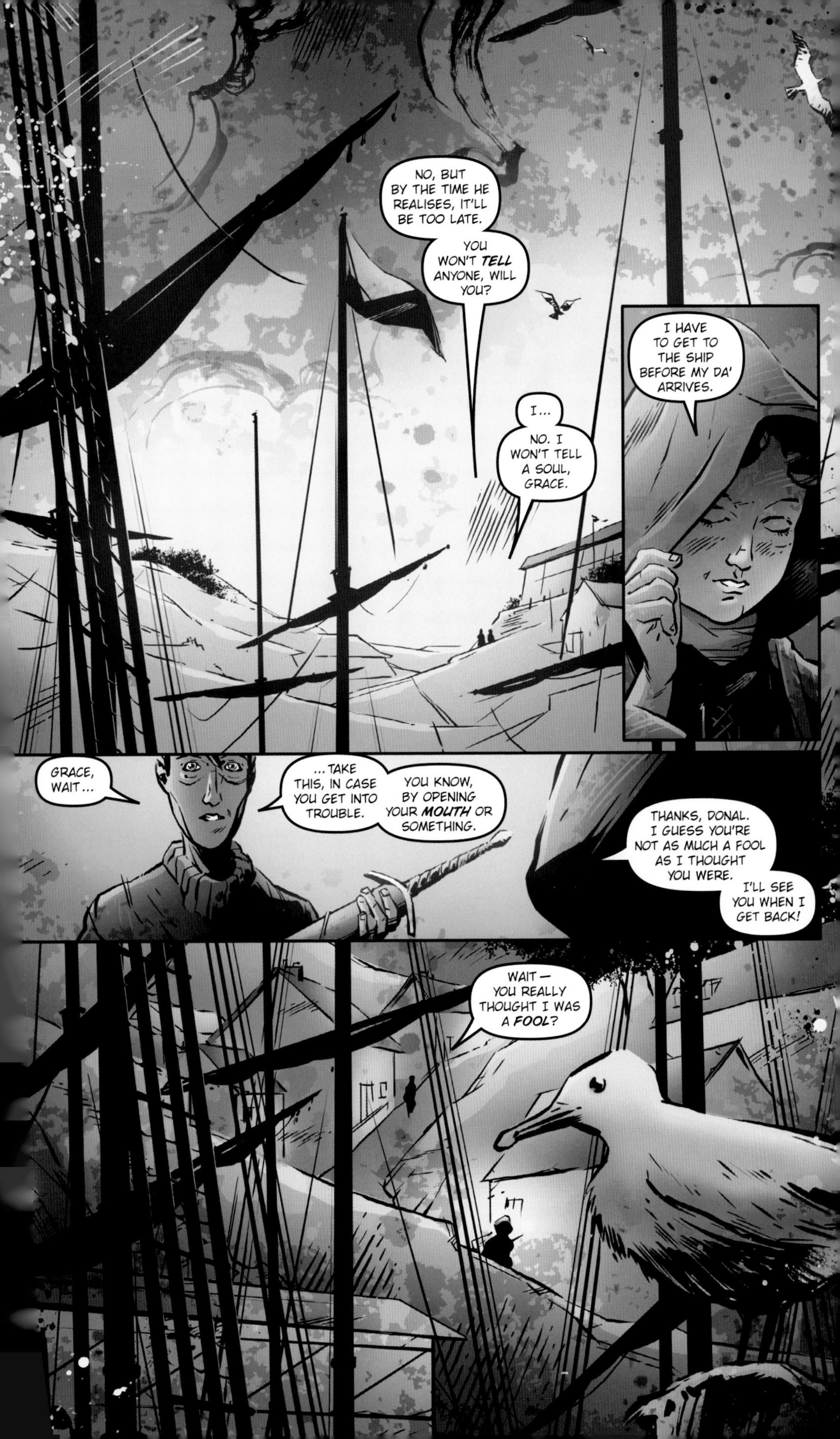
NO, BUT BY THE TIME HE REALISES, IT'LL BE TOO LATE.
YOU WON'T TELL ANYONE, WILL YOU?
I HAVE TO GET TO THE SHIP BEFORE MY DA' ARRIVES.
I...
NO. I WON'T TELL A SOUL, GRACE.
GRACE, WAIT...
...TAKE THIS, IN CASE YOU GET INTO TROUBLE.
YOU KNOW, BY OPENING YOUR MOUTH OR SOMETHING.
THANKS, DONAL. I GUESS YOU'RE NOT AS MUCH A FOOL AS I THOUGHT YOU WERE.
I'LL SEE YOU WHEN I GET BACK!
WAIT — YOU REALLY THOUGHT I WAS A FOOL?

WELL, WELL! WHAT DO WE HAVE HERE?

LOOKS LIKE A *STOWAWAY!* MAYBE I SHOULD THROW YOU OVER THE SIDE!

FINN! IT'S ME! GRACE!

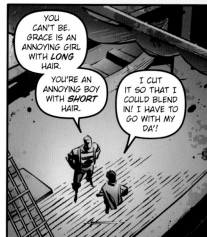

YOU CAN'T BE. GRACE IS AN ANNOYING GIRL WITH *LONG* HAIR.

YOU'RE AN ANNOYING BOY WITH *SHORT* HAIR.

I CUT IT SO THAT I COULD BLEND IN! I HAVE TO GO WITH MY DA'!

I HAD A DREAM. I SAW MY DA' IN *DANGER* AND NOBODY WAS THERE TO HELP HIM.

AND IT'S *NOT* BECAUSE YOU DON'T WANT TO STAY WITH THE O'FLAHERTYS?

WELL... THAT TOO.

GO ON, GET DOWN BELOW BEFORE YOUR FATHER CATCHES YOU.

AND WHEN HE DOES, *I DIDN'T SEE YOU,* OK?

THANKS, FINN!

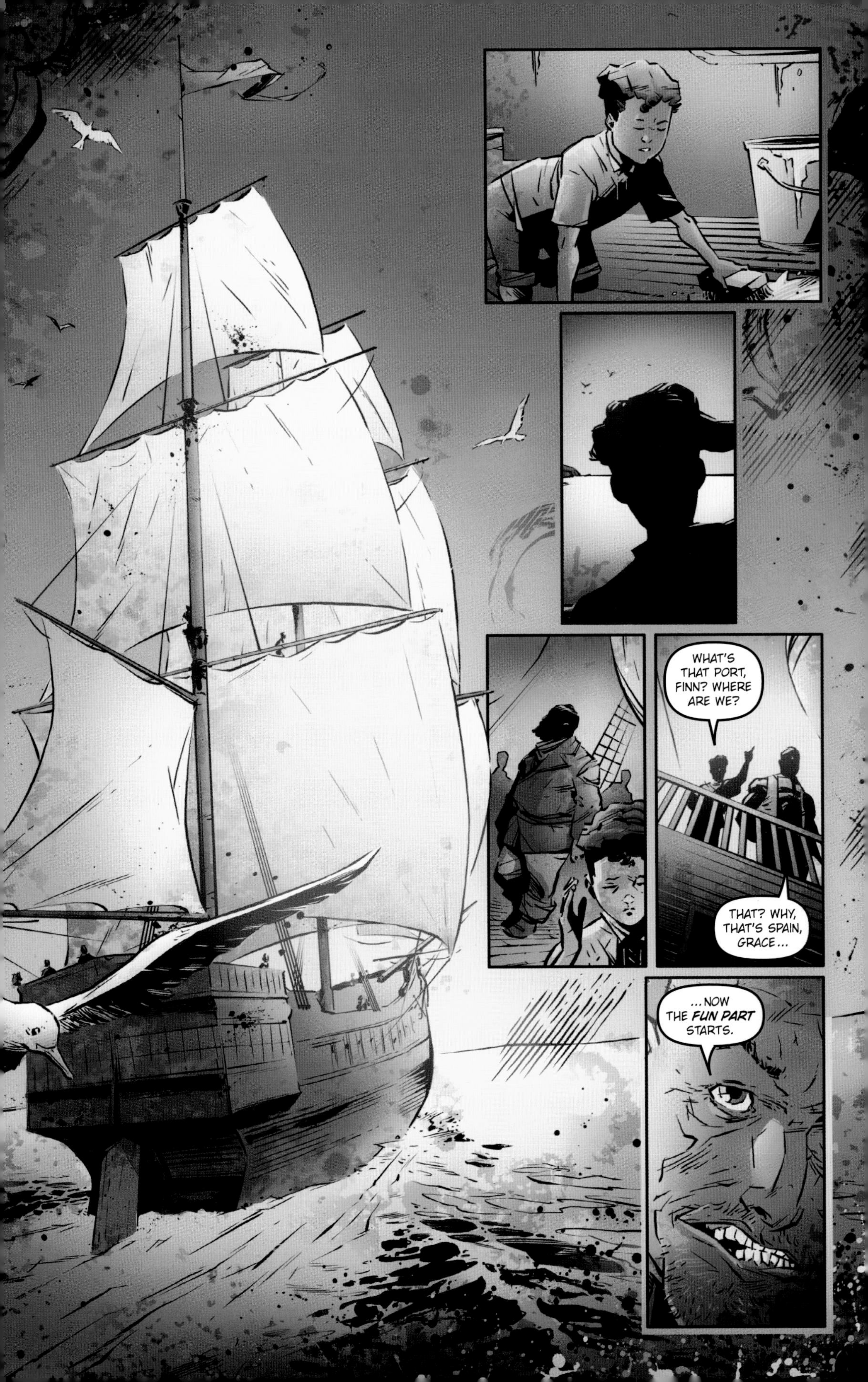
WHAT'S THAT PORT, FINN? WHERE ARE WE?
THAT? WHY, THAT'S SPAIN, GRACE...
...NOW THE FUN PART STARTS.

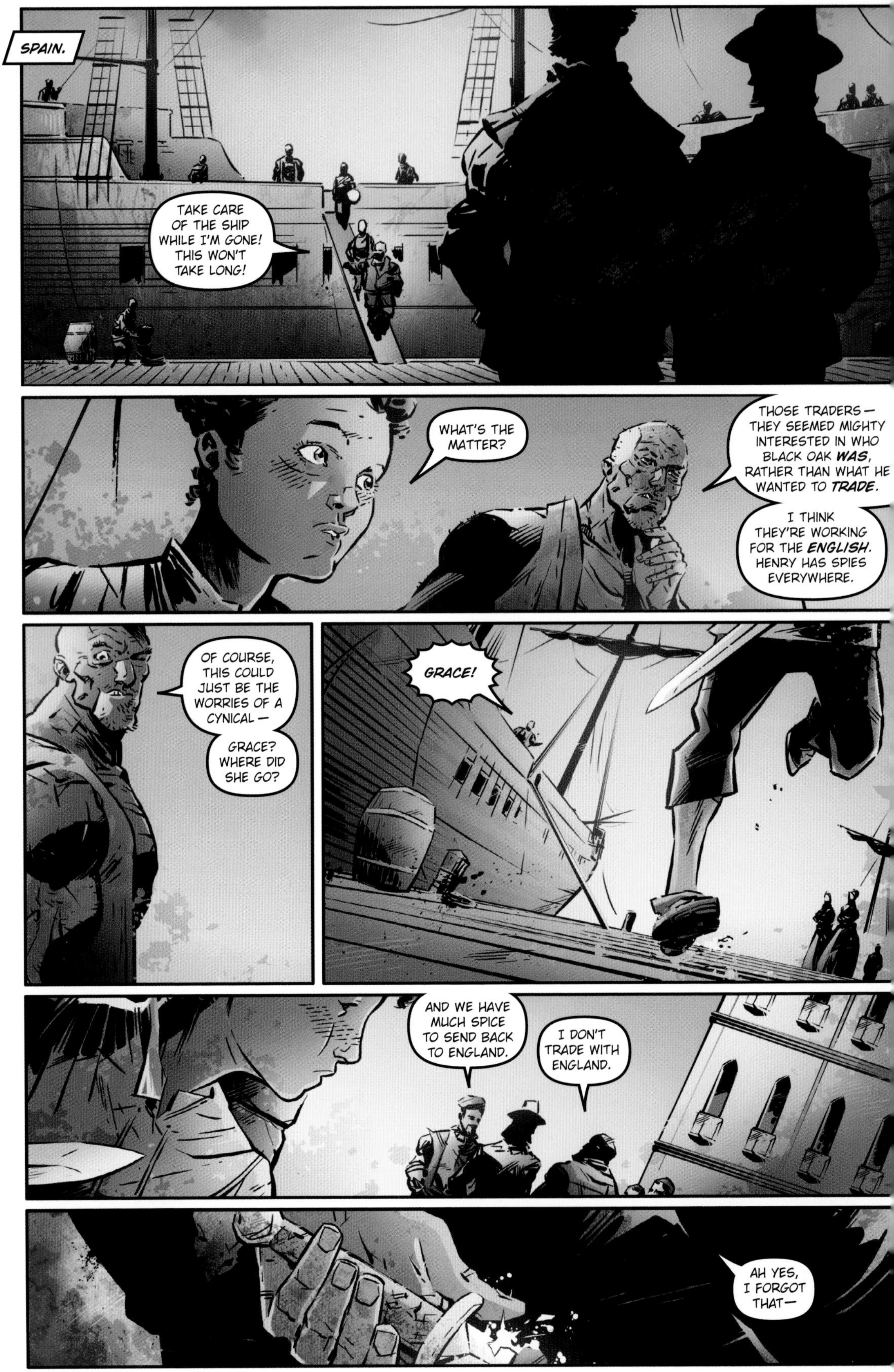
SPAIN.
TAKE CARE OF THE SHIP WHILE I'M GONE! THIS WON'T TAKE LONG!
WHAT'S THE MATTER?
THOSE TRADERS — THEY SEEMED MIGHTY INTERESTED IN WHO BLACK OAK WAS, RATHER THAN WHAT HE WANTED TO TRADE.
I THINK THEY'RE WORKING FOR THE ENGLISH. HENRY HAS SPIES EVERYWHERE.
OF COURSE, THIS COULD JUST BE THE WORRIES OF A CYNICAL —
GRACE? WHERE DID SHE GO?
GRACE!
AND WE HAVE MUCH SPICE TO SEND BACK TO ENGLAND.
I DON'T TRADE WITH ENGLAND.
AH YES, I FORGOT THAT—

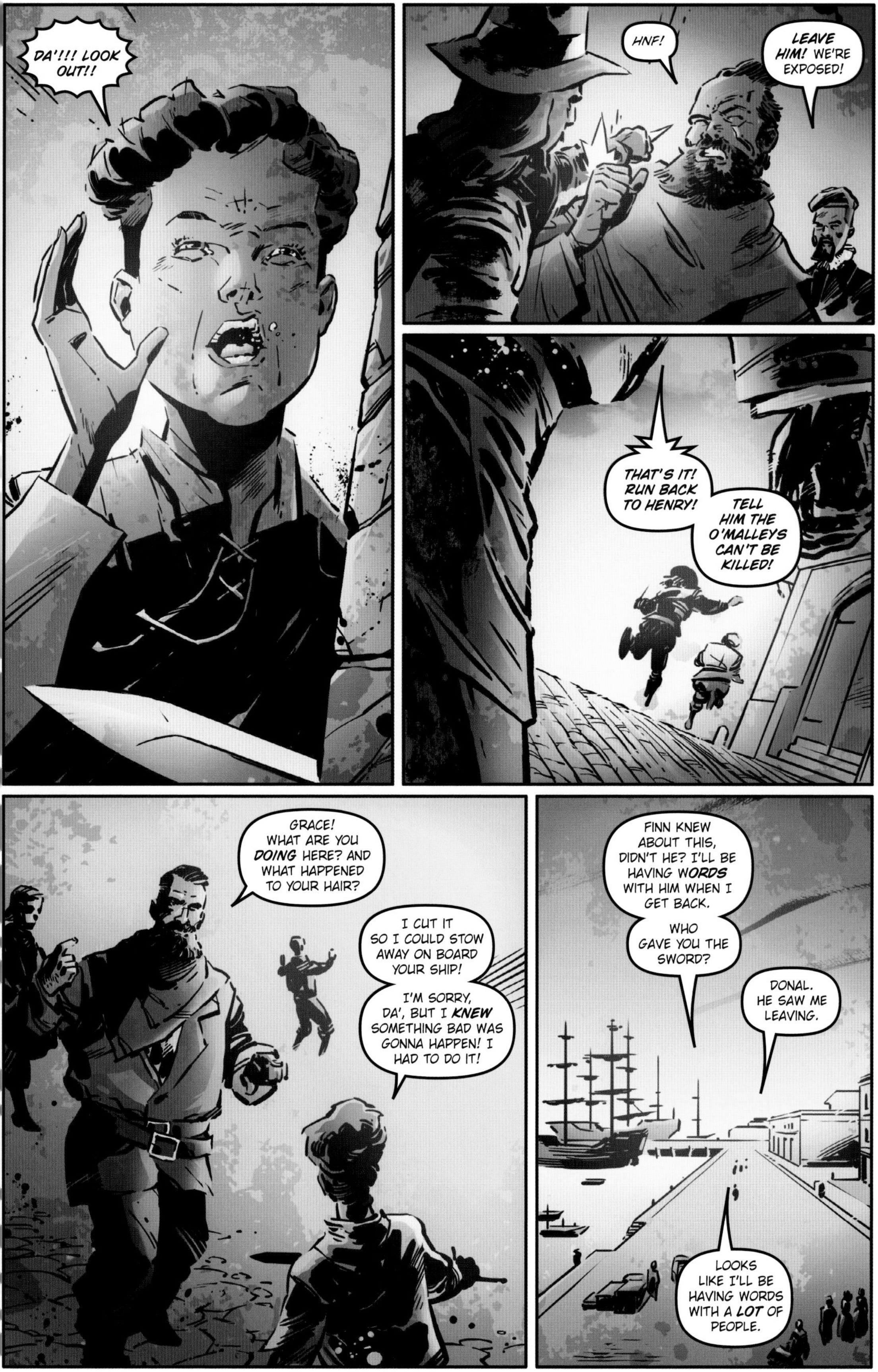
DA'!!! LOOK OUT!!
HNF!
LEAVE HIM! WE'RE EXPOSED!
THAT'S IT! RUN BACK TO HENRY!
TELL HIM THE O'MALLEYS CAN'T BE KILLED!
GRACE! WHAT ARE YOU DOING HERE? AND WHAT HAPPENED TO YOUR HAIR?
I CUT IT SO I COULD STOW AWAY ON BOARD YOUR SHIP!
I'M SORRY, DA', BUT I KNEW SOMETHING BAD WAS GONNA HAPPEN! I HAD TO DO IT!
FINN KNEW ABOUT THIS, DIDN'T HE? I'LL BE HAVING WORDS WITH HIM WHEN I GET BACK.
WHO GAVE YOU THE SWORD?
DONAL. HE SAW ME LEAVING.
LOOKS LIKE I'LL BE HAVING WORDS WITH A LOT OF PEOPLE.

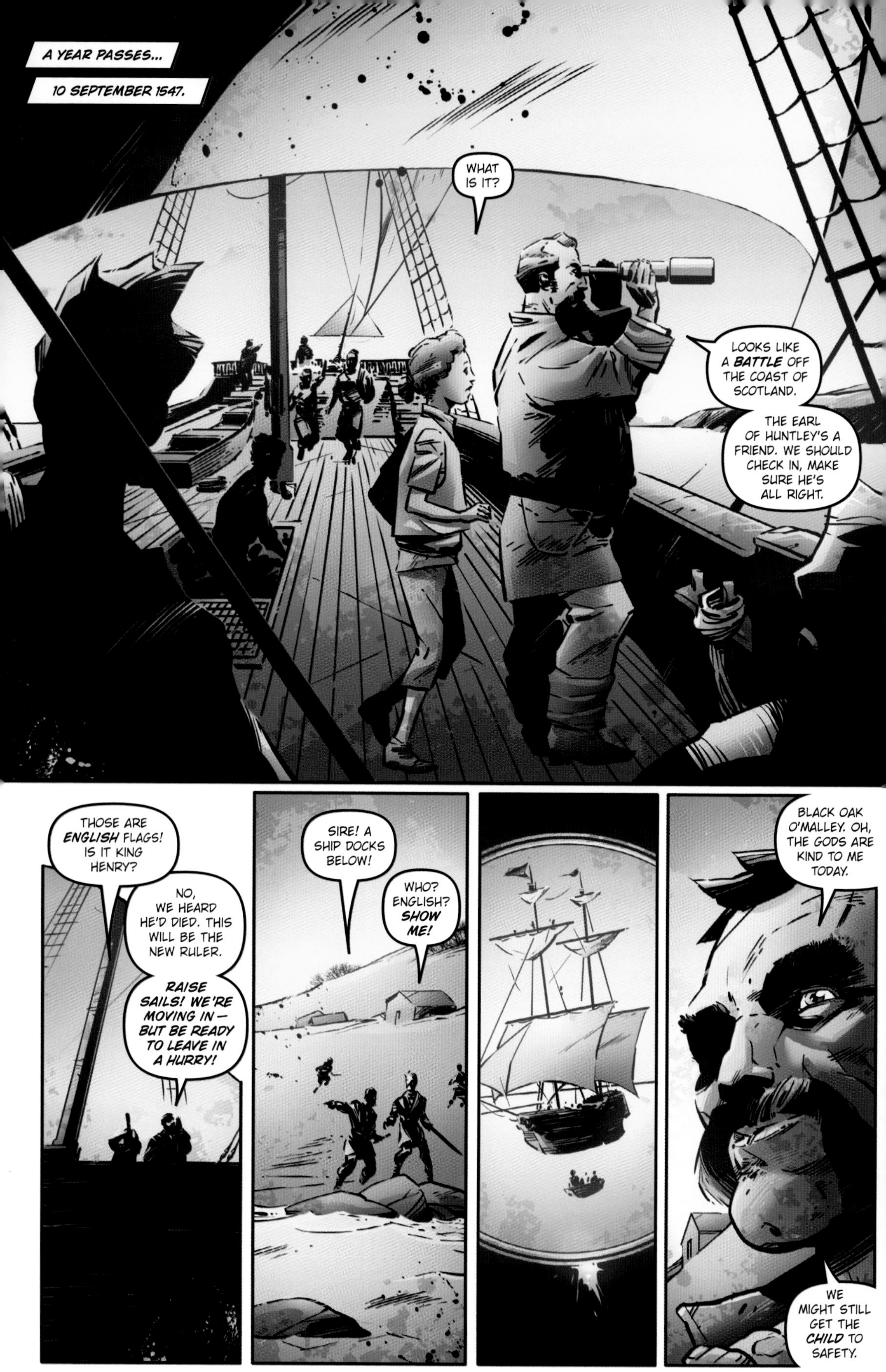
A YEAR PASSES...
10 SEPTEMBER 1547.
WHAT IS IT?
LOOKS LIKE A BATTLE OFF THE COAST OF SCOTLAND.
THE EARL OF HUNTLEY'S A FRIEND. WE SHOULD CHECK IN, MAKE SURE HE'S ALL RIGHT.
THOSE ARE ENGLISH FLAGS! IS IT KING HENRY?
NO, WE HEARD HE'D DIED. THIS WILL BE THE NEW RULER.
RAISE SAILS! WE'RE MOVING IN— BUT BE READY TO LEAVE IN A HURRY!
SIRE! A SHIP DOCKS BELOW!
WHO? ENGLISH? SHOW ME!
BLACK OAK O'MALLEY. OH, THE GODS ARE KIND TO ME TODAY.
WE MIGHT STILL GET THE CHILD TO SAFETY.

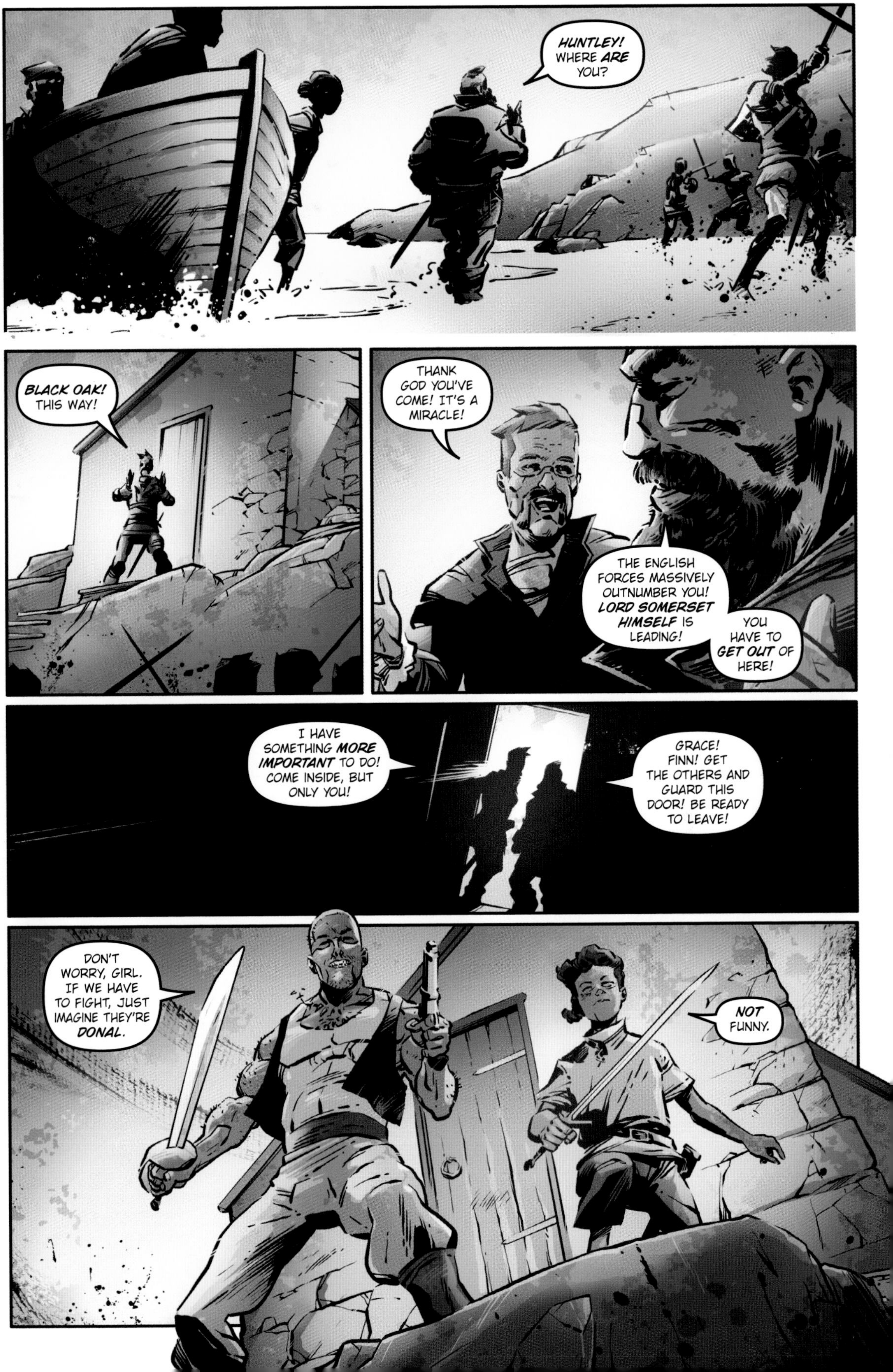
HUNTLEY! WHERE ARE YOU?
BLACK OAK! THIS WAY!
THANK GOD YOU'VE COME! IT'S A MIRACLE!
THE ENGLISH FORCES MASSIVELY OUTNUMBER YOU! LORD SOMERSET HIMSELF IS LEADING!
YOU HAVE TO GET OUT OF HERE!
I HAVE SOMETHING MORE IMPORTANT TO DO! COME INSIDE, BUT ONLY YOU!
GRACE! FINN! GET THE OTHERS AND GUARD THIS DOOR! BE READY TO LEAVE!
DON'T WORRY, GIRL. IF WE HAVE TO FIGHT, JUST IMAGINE THEY'RE DONAL.
NOT FUNNY.

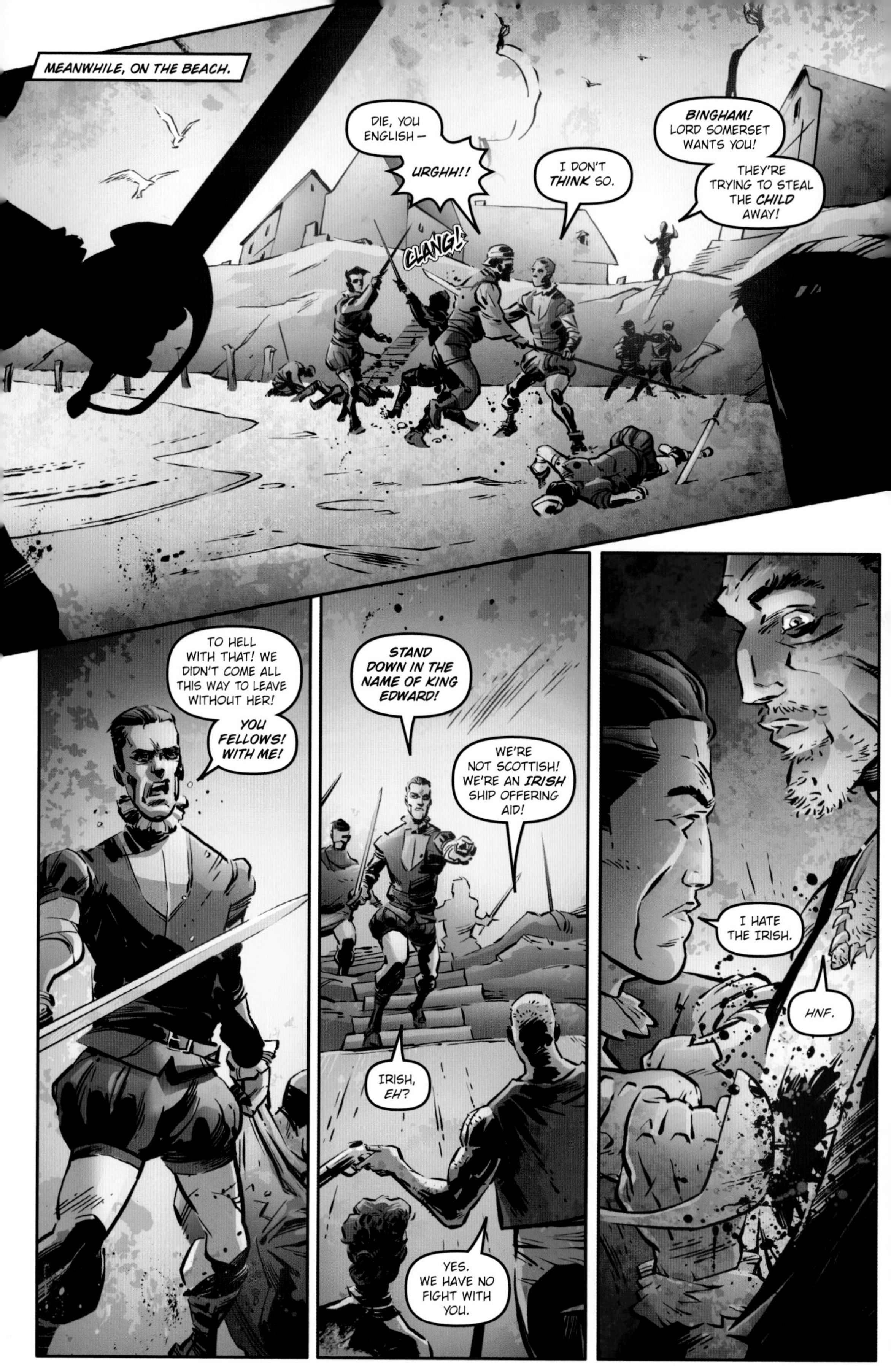

MEANWHILE, ON THE BEACH.
DIE, YOU ENGLISH—
URGHH!!
CLANG!
I DON'T THINK SO.
BINGHAM! LORD SOMERSET WANTS YOU!
THEY'RE TRYING TO STEAL THE CHILD AWAY!
TO HELL WITH THAT! WE DIDN'T COME ALL THIS WAY TO LEAVE WITHOUT HER!
YOU FELLOWS! WITH ME!
STAND DOWN IN THE NAME OF KING EDWARD!
WE'RE NOT SCOTTISH! WE'RE AN IRISH SHIP OFFERING AID!
IRISH, EH?
YES. WE HAVE NO FIGHT WITH YOU.
I HATE THE IRISH.
HNF.

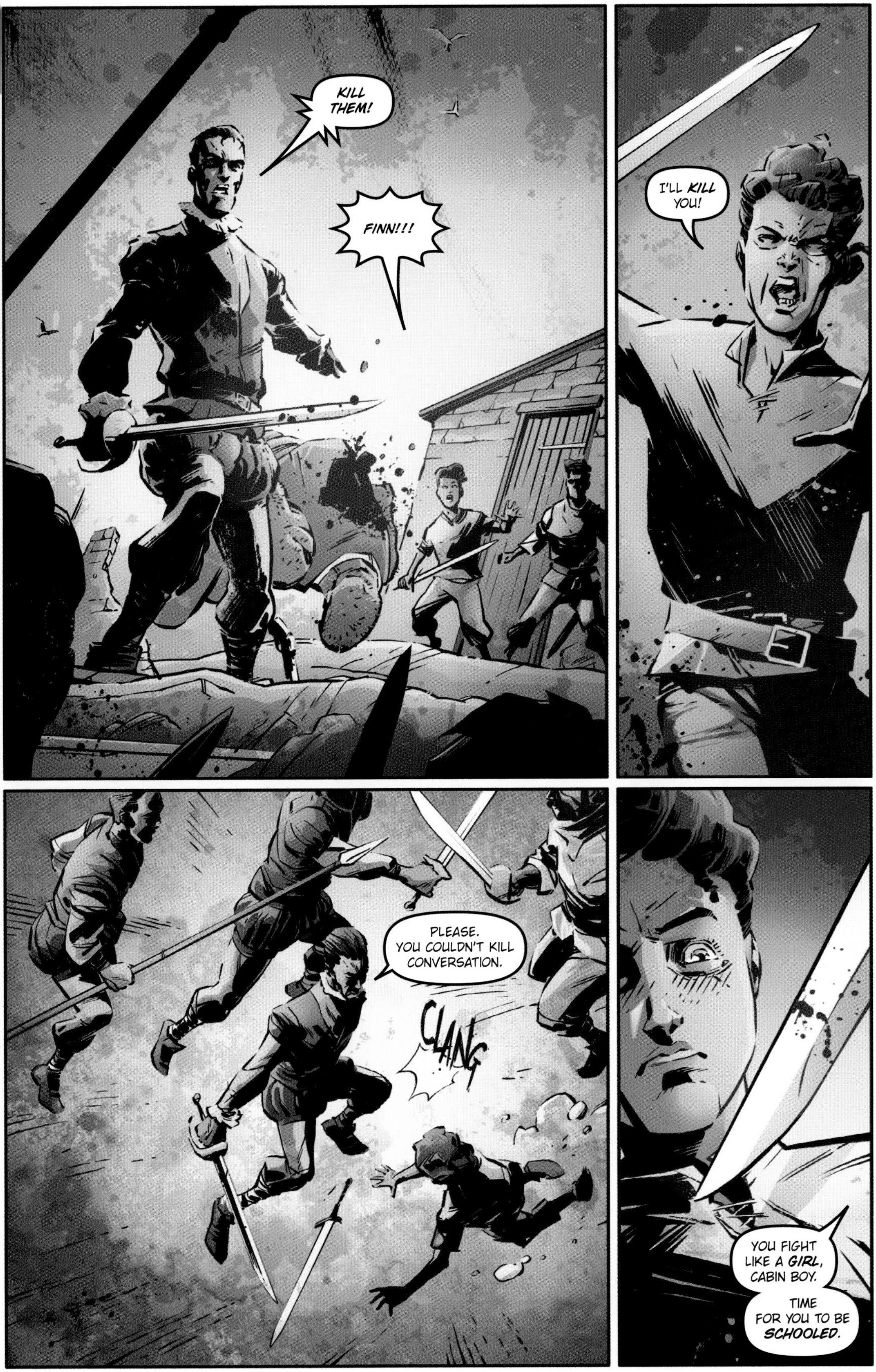
KILL THEM!
FINN!!!
I'LL KILL YOU!
PLEASE. YOU COULDN'T KILL CONVERSATION.
CLANG
YOU FIGHT LIKE A GIRL, CABIN BOY.
TIME FOR YOU TO BE SCHOOLED.

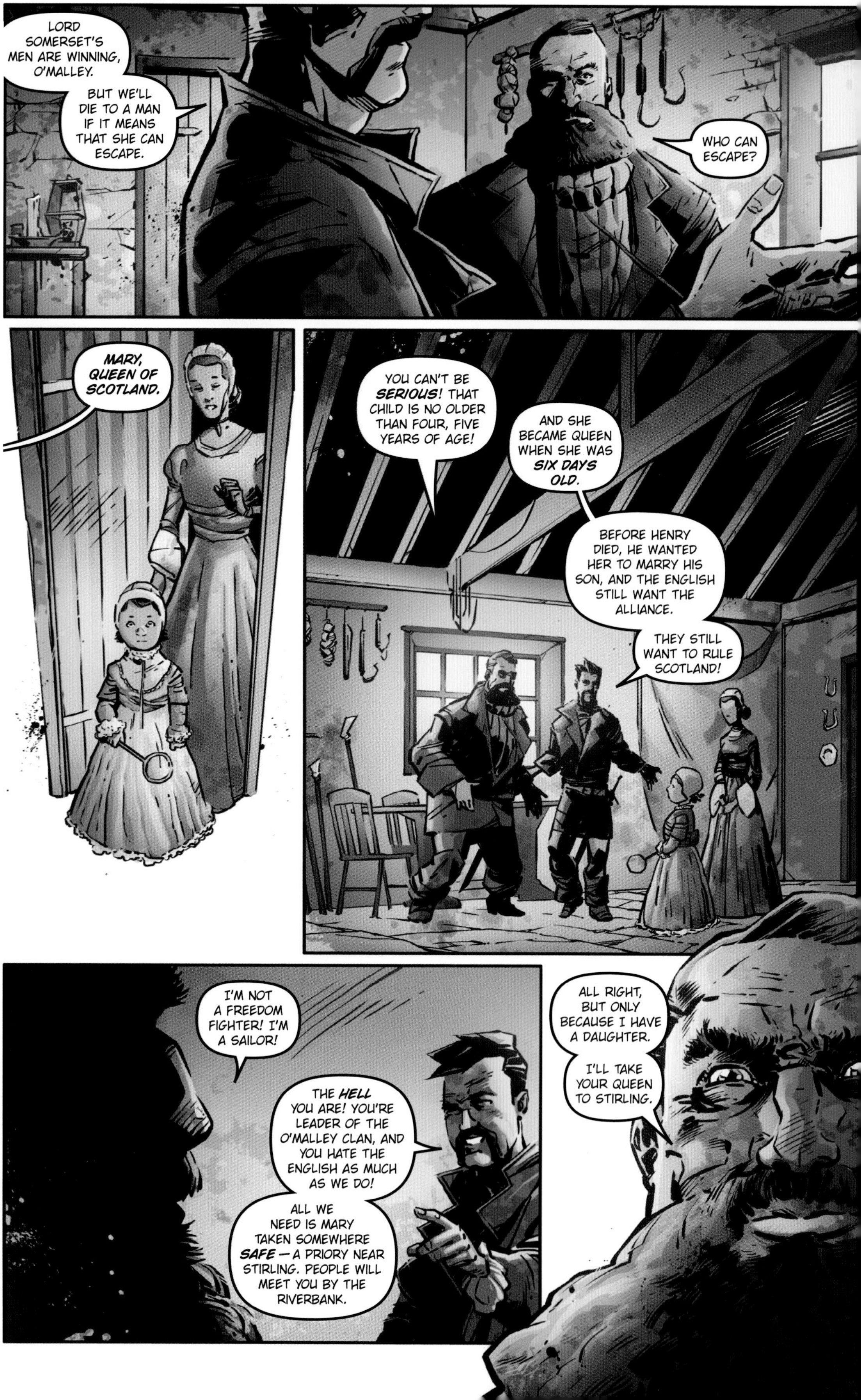
LORD SOMERSET'S MEN ARE WINNING, O'MALLEY.
BUT WE'LL DIE TO A MAN IF IT MEANS THAT SHE CAN ESCAPE.
WHO CAN ESCAPE?
MARY, QUEEN OF SCOTLAND.
YOU CAN'T BE SERIOUS! THAT CHILD IS NO OLDER THAN FOUR, FIVE YEARS OF AGE!
AND SHE BECAME QUEEN WHEN SHE WAS SIX DAYS OLD.
BEFORE HENRY DIED, HE WANTED HER TO MARRY HIS SON, AND THE ENGLISH STILL WANT THE ALLIANCE.
THEY STILL WANT TO RULE SCOTLAND!
I'M NOT A FREEDOM FIGHTER! I'M A SAILOR!
THE HELL YOU ARE! YOU'RE LEADER OF THE O'MALLEY CLAN, AND YOU HATE THE ENGLISH AS MUCH AS WE DO!
ALL WE NEED IS MARY TAKEN SOMEWHERE SAFE — A PRIORY NEAR STIRLING. PEOPLE WILL MEET YOU BY THE RIVERBANK.
ALL RIGHT, BUT ONLY BECAUSE I HAVE A DAUGHTER.
I'LL TAKE YOUR QUEEN TO STIRLING.

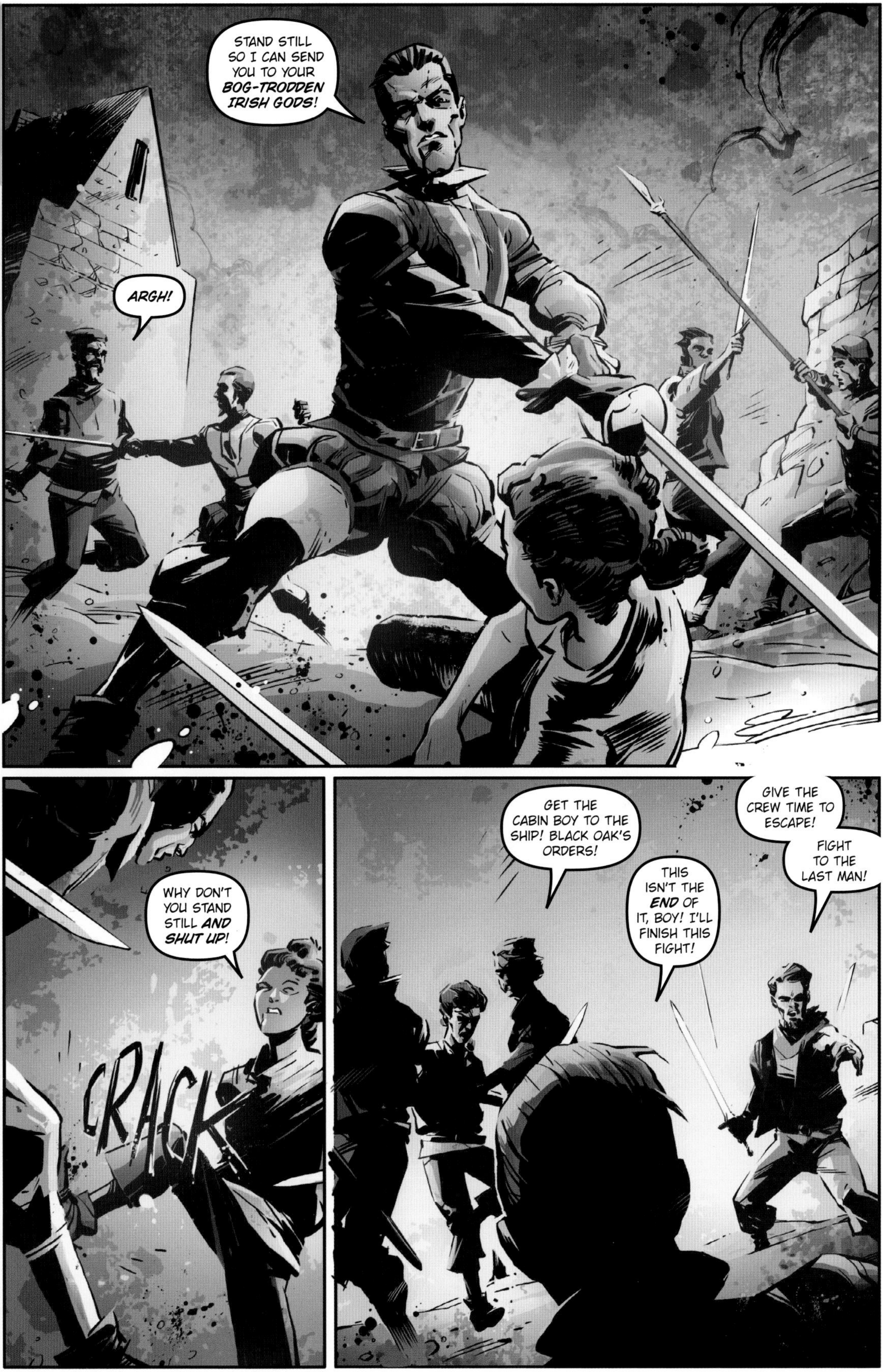
STAND STILL SO I CAN SEND YOU TO YOUR BOG-TRODDEN IRISH GODS!
ARGH!
WHY DON'T YOU STAND STILL AND SHUT UP!
CRACK
GET THE CABIN BOY TO THE SHIP! BLACK OAK'S ORDERS!
THIS ISN'T THE END OF IT, BOY! I'LL FINISH THIS FIGHT!
GIVE THE CREW TIME TO ESCAPE!
FIGHT TO THE LAST MAN!

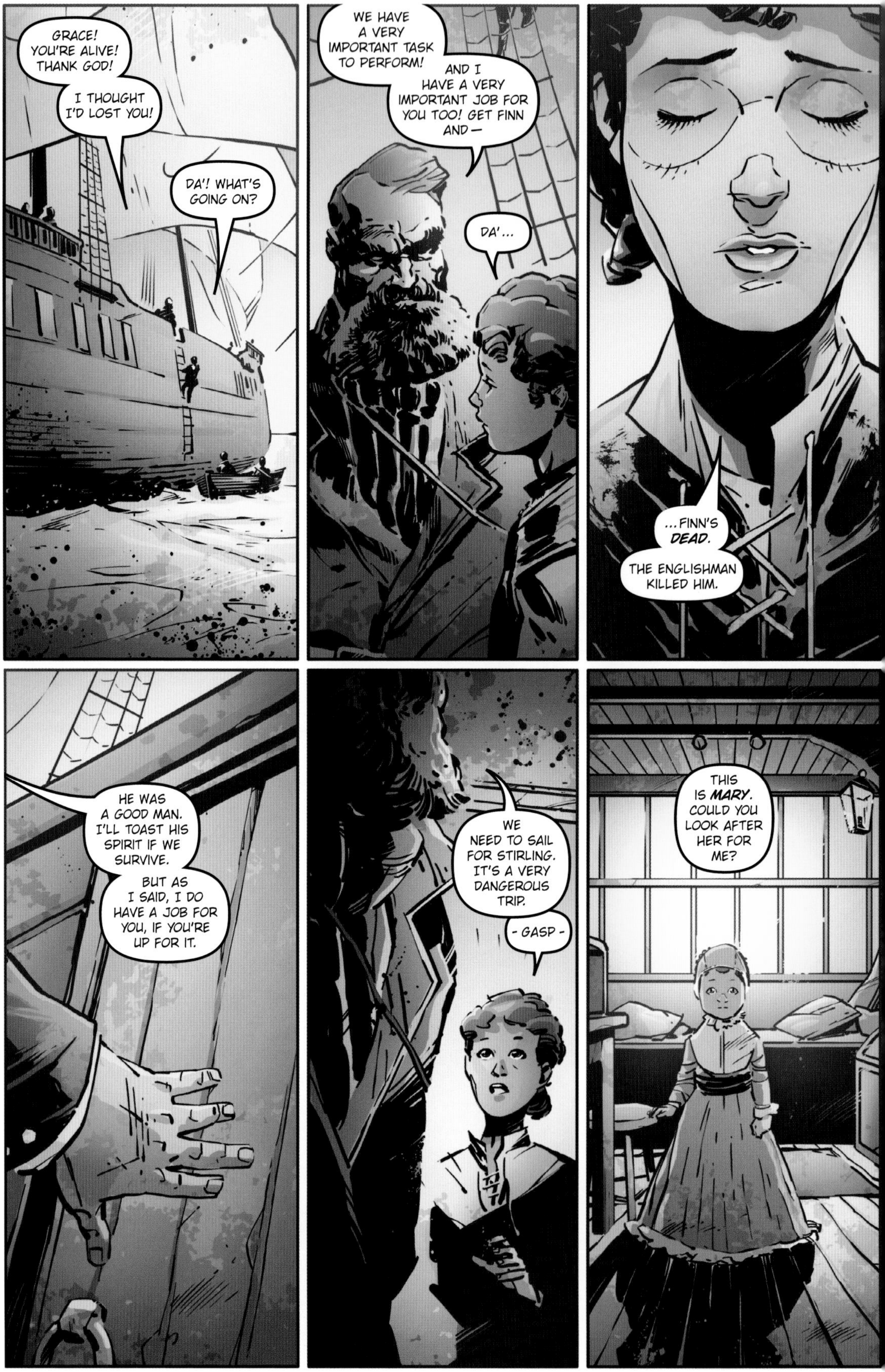
GRACE! YOU'RE ALIVE! THANK GOD!
I THOUGHT I'D LOST YOU!
DA'! WHAT'S GOING ON?
WE HAVE A VERY IMPORTANT TASK TO PERFORM!
AND I HAVE A VERY IMPORTANT JOB FOR YOU TOO! GET FINN AND—
DA'...
...FINN'S DEAD.
THE ENGLISHMAN KILLED HIM.
HE WAS A GOOD MAN. I'LL TOAST HIS SPIRIT IF WE SURVIVE.
BUT AS I SAID, I DO HAVE A JOB FOR YOU, IF YOU'RE UP FOR IT.
WE NEED TO SAIL FOR STIRLING. IT'S A VERY DANGEROUS TRIP.
- GASP -
THIS IS MARY. COULD YOU LOOK AFTER HER FOR ME?

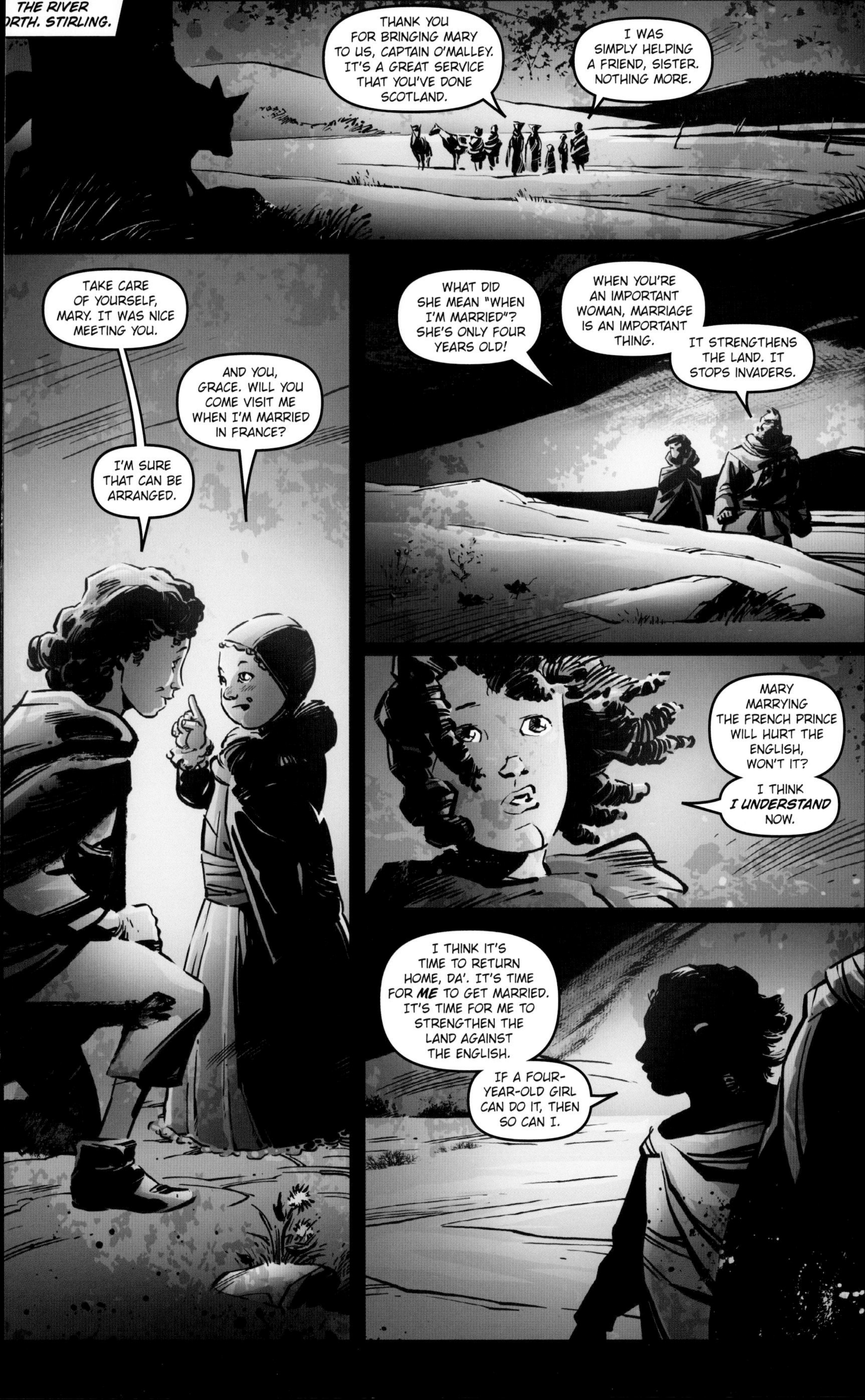

THE RIVER ...ORTH. STIRLING.
THANK YOU FOR BRINGING MARY TO US, CAPTAIN O'MALLEY. IT'S A GREAT SERVICE THAT YOU'VE DONE SCOTLAND.
I WAS SIMPLY HELPING A FRIEND, SISTER. NOTHING MORE.
TAKE CARE OF YOURSELF, MARY. IT WAS NICE MEETING YOU.
AND YOU, GRACE. WILL YOU COME VISIT ME WHEN I'M MARRIED IN FRANCE?
I'M SURE THAT CAN BE ARRANGED.
WHAT DID SHE MEAN "WHEN I'M MARRIED"? SHE'S ONLY FOUR YEARS OLD!
WHEN YOU'RE AN IMPORTANT WOMAN, MARRIAGE IS AN IMPORTANT THING.
IT STRENGTHENS THE LAND. IT STOPS INVADERS.
MARY MARRYING THE FRENCH PRINCE WILL HURT THE ENGLISH, WON'T IT?
I THINK ***I UNDERSTAND*** NOW.
I THINK IT'S TIME TO RETURN HOME, DA'. IT'S TIME FOR ***ME*** TO GET MARRIED. IT'S TIME FOR ME TO STRENGTHEN THE LAND AGAINST THE ENGLISH.
IF A FOUR-YEAR-OLD GIRL CAN DO IT, THEN SO CAN I.

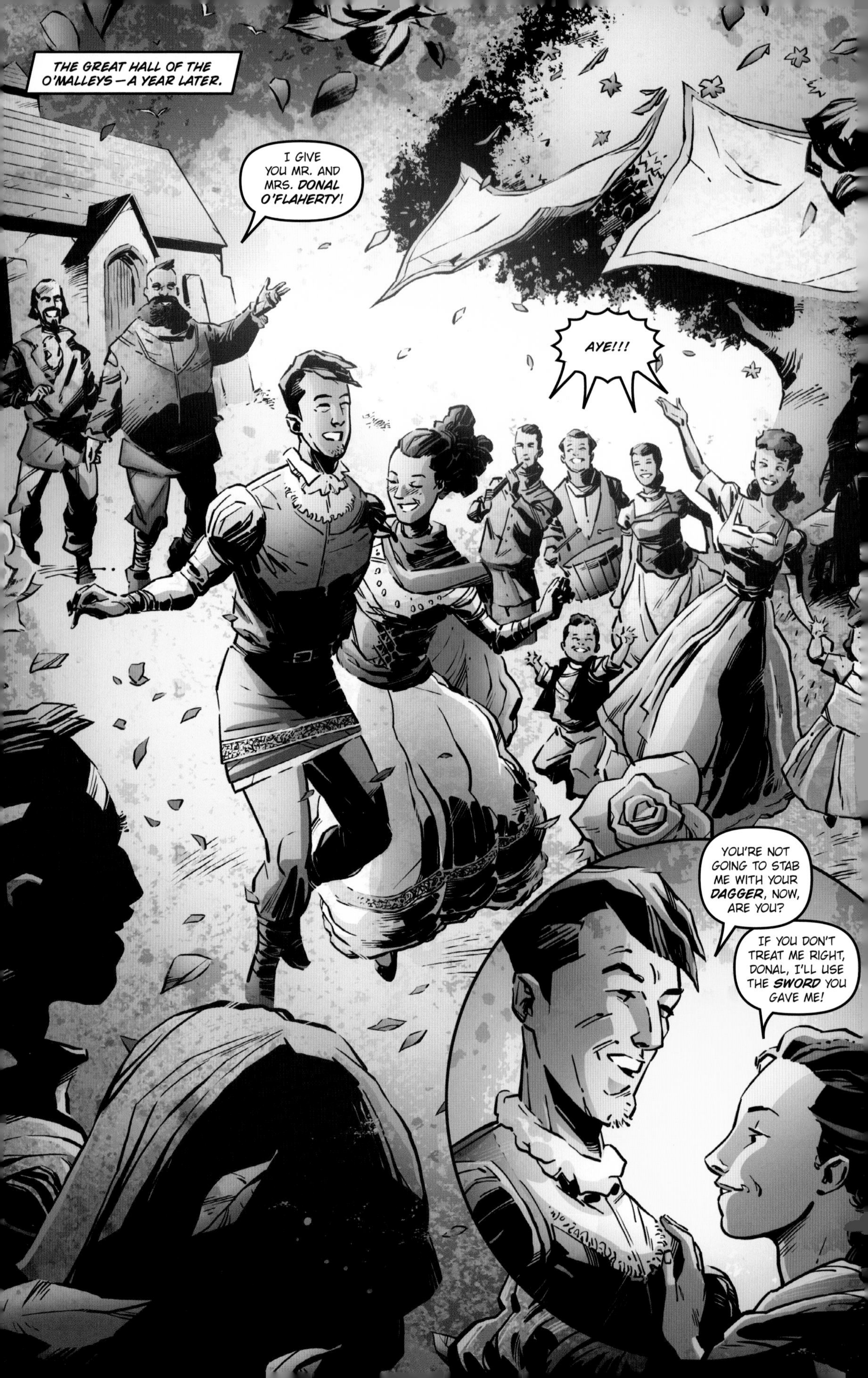
THE GREAT HALL OF THE O'MALLEYS—A YEAR LATER.
I GIVE YOU MR. AND MRS. DONAL O'FLAHERTY!
AYE!!!
YOU'RE NOT GOING TO STAB ME WITH YOUR DAGGER, NOW, ARE YOU?
IF YOU DON'T TREAT ME RIGHT, DONAL, I'LL USE THE SWORD YOU GAVE ME!

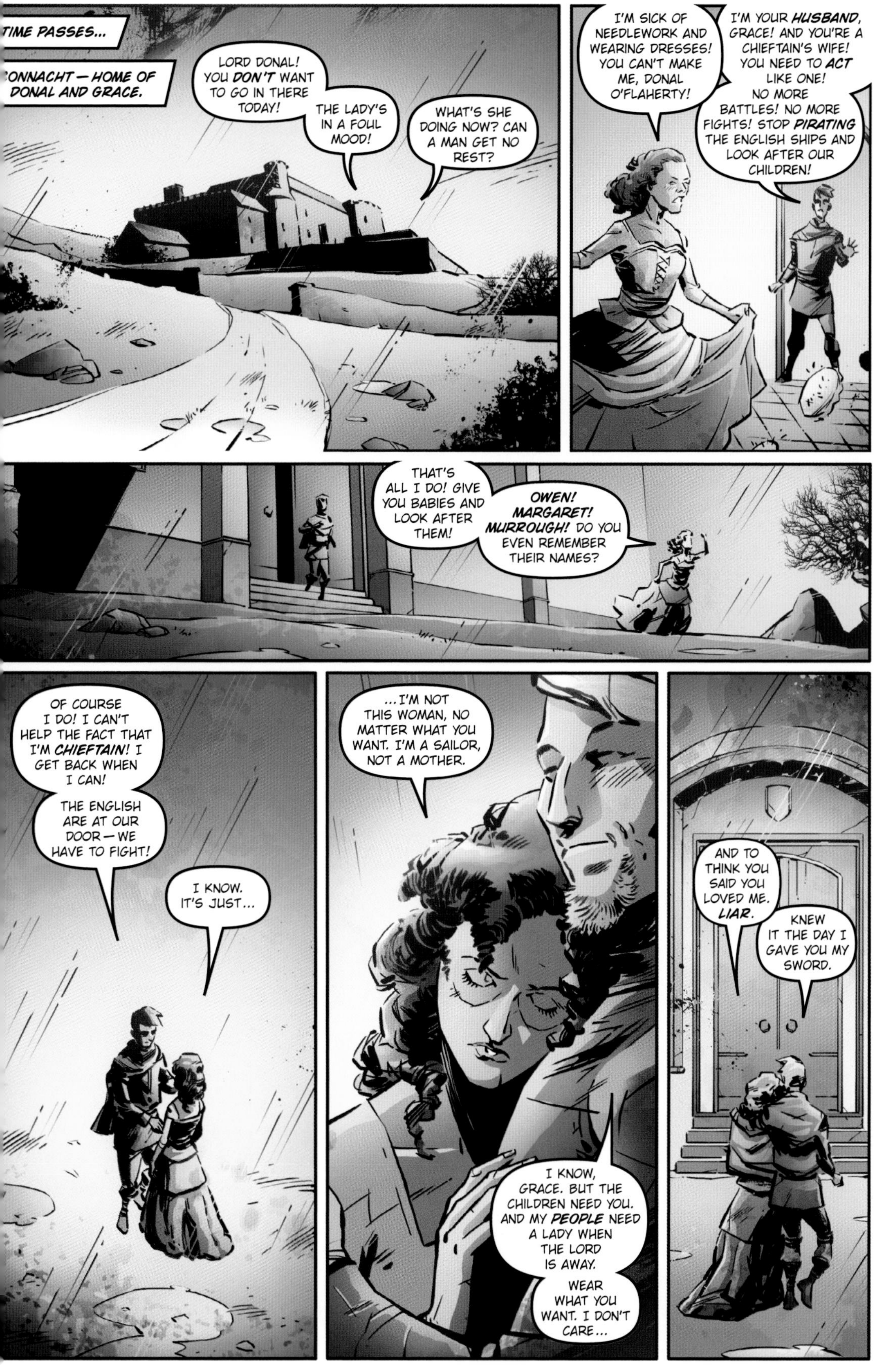
TIME PASSES...
CONNACHT—HOME OF DONAL AND GRACE.
LORD DONAL! YOU DON'T WANT TO GO IN THERE TODAY!
THE LADY'S IN A FOUL MOOD!
WHAT'S SHE DOING NOW? CAN A MAN GET NO REST?
I'M SICK OF NEEDLEWORK AND WEARING DRESSES! YOU CAN'T MAKE ME, DONAL O'FLAHERTY!
I'M YOUR HUSBAND, GRACE! AND YOU'RE A CHIEFTAIN'S WIFE! YOU NEED TO ACT LIKE ONE!
NO MORE BATTLES! NO MORE FIGHTS! STOP PIRATING THE ENGLISH SHIPS AND LOOK AFTER OUR CHILDREN!
THAT'S ALL I DO! GIVE YOU BABIES AND LOOK AFTER THEM!
OWEN! MARGARET! MURROUGH! DO YOU EVEN REMEMBER THEIR NAMES?
OF COURSE I DO! I CAN'T HELP THE FACT THAT I'M CHIEFTAIN! I GET BACK WHEN I CAN!
THE ENGLISH ARE AT OUR DOOR—WE HAVE TO FIGHT!
I KNOW. IT'S JUST...
...I'M NOT THIS WOMAN, NO MATTER WHAT YOU WANT. I'M A SAILOR, NOT A MOTHER.
I KNOW, GRACE. BUT THE CHILDREN NEED YOU. AND MY PEOPLE NEED A LADY WHEN THE LORD IS AWAY.
WEAR WHAT YOU WANT. I DON'T CARE...
AND TO THINK YOU SAID YOU LOVED ME. LIAR.
KNEW IT THE DAY I GAVE YOU MY SWORD.

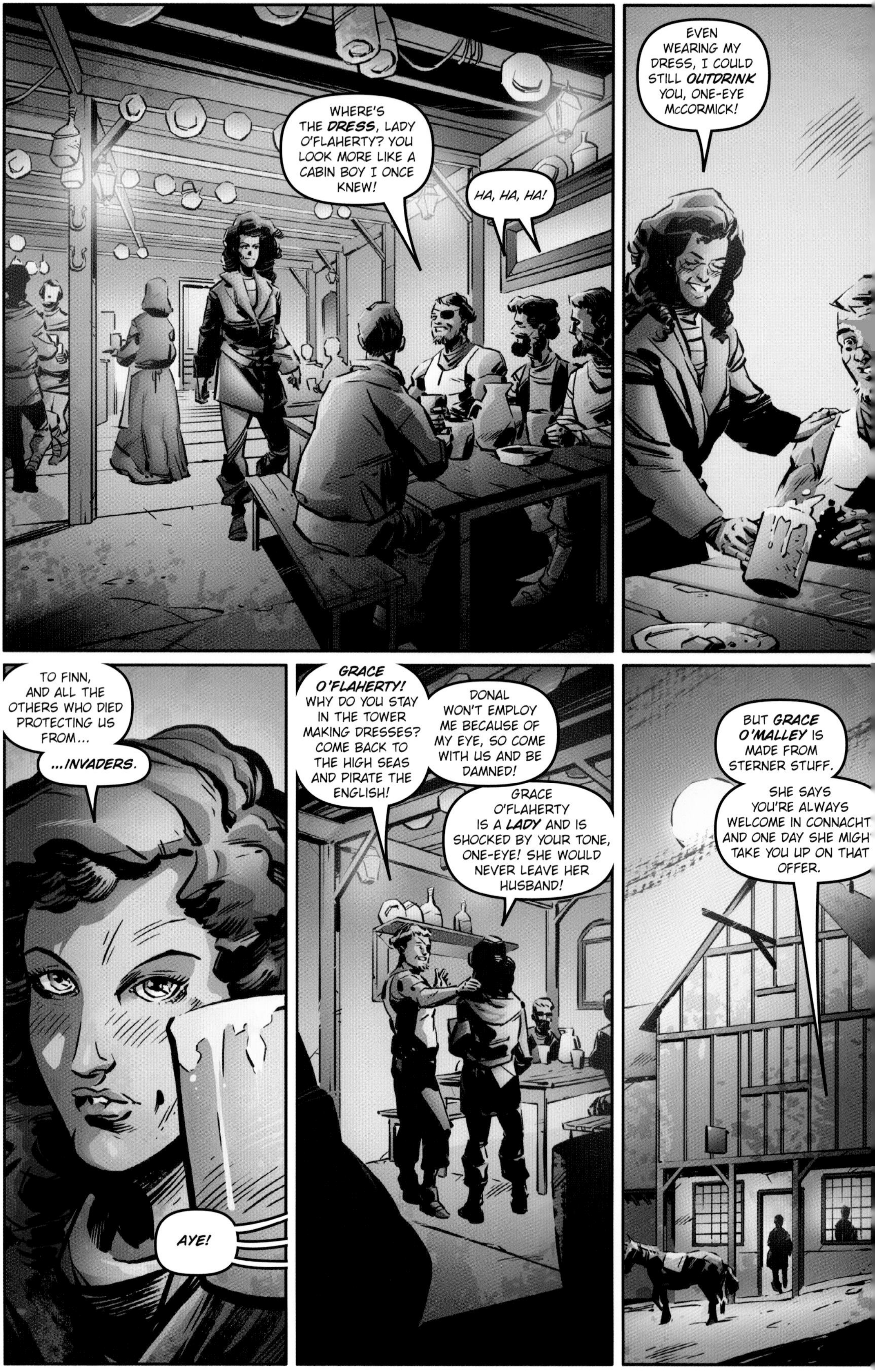
WHERE'S THE DRESS, LADY O'FLAHERTY? YOU LOOK MORE LIKE A CABIN BOY I ONCE KNEW!
HA, HA, HA!
EVEN WEARING MY DRESS, I COULD STILL OUTDRINK YOU, ONE-EYE McCORMICK!
TO FINN, AND ALL THE OTHERS WHO DIED PROTECTING US FROM...
...INVADERS.
AYE!
GRACE O'FLAHERTY! WHY DO YOU STAY IN THE TOWER MAKING DRESSES? COME BACK TO THE HIGH SEAS AND PIRATE THE ENGLISH!
DONAL WON'T EMPLOY ME BECAUSE OF MY EYE, SO COME WITH US AND BE DAMNED!
GRACE O'FLAHERTY IS A LADY AND IS SHOCKED BY YOUR TONE, ONE-EYE! SHE WOULD NEVER LEAVE HER HUSBAND!
BUT GRACE O'MALLEY IS MADE FROM STERNER STUFF.
SHE SAYS YOU'RE ALWAYS WELCOME IN CONNACHT AND ONE DAY SHE MIGH TAKE YOU UP ON THAT OFFER.

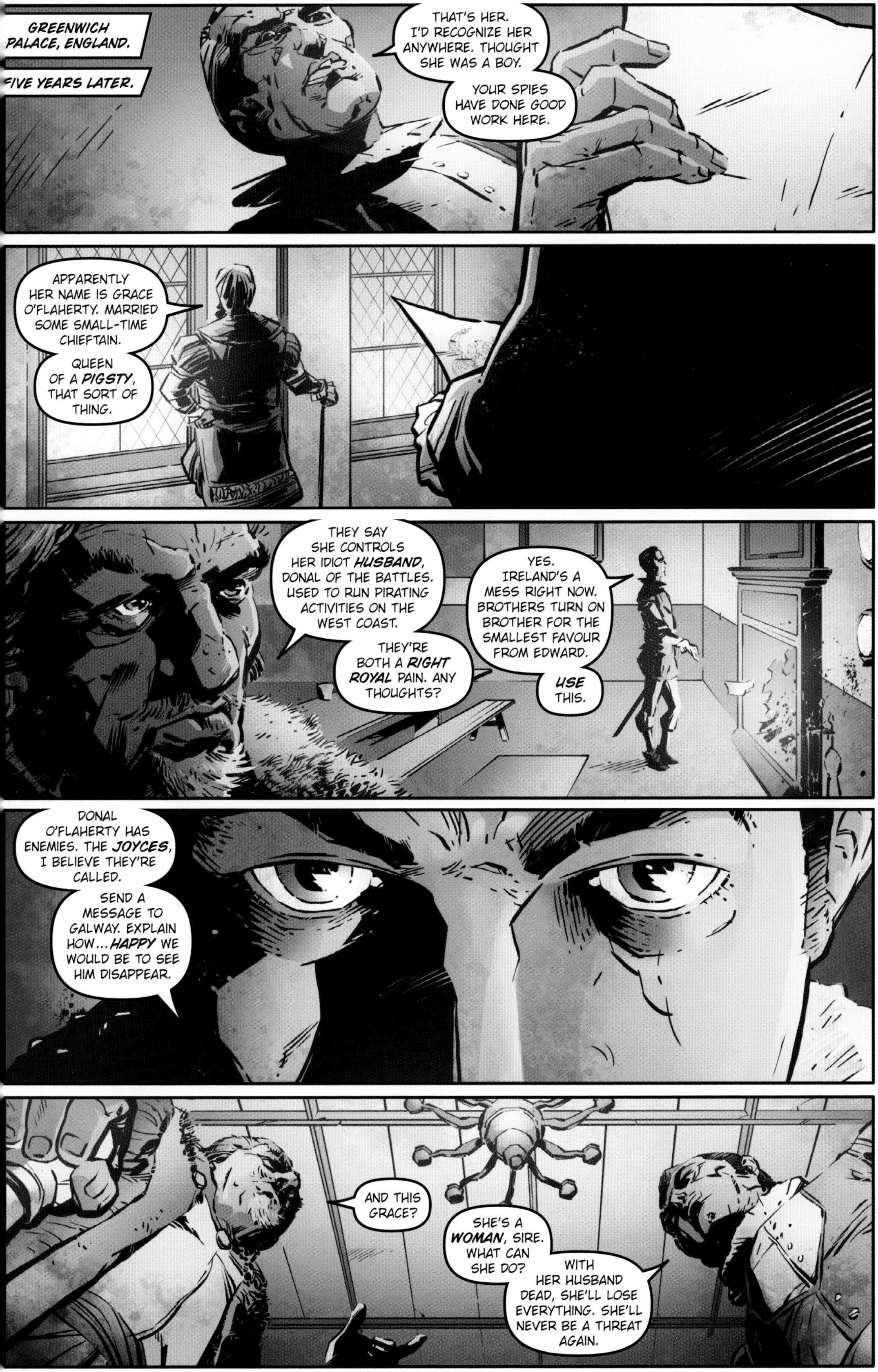
GREENWICH PALACE, ENGLAND.
FIVE YEARS LATER.
THAT'S HER. I'D RECOGNIZE HER ANYWHERE. THOUGHT SHE WAS A BOY.
YOUR SPIES HAVE DONE GOOD WORK HERE.
APPARENTLY HER NAME IS GRACE O'FLAHERTY. MARRIED SOME SMALL-TIME CHIEFTAIN.
QUEEN OF A PIGSTY, THAT SORT OF THING.
THEY SAY SHE CONTROLS HER IDIOT HUSBAND, DONAL OF THE BATTLES. USED TO RUN PIRATING ACTIVITIES ON THE WEST COAST.
THEY'RE BOTH A RIGHT ROYAL PAIN. ANY THOUGHTS?
YES. IRELAND'S A MESS RIGHT NOW. BROTHERS TURN ON BROTHER FOR THE SMALLEST FAVOUR FROM EDWARD.
USE THIS.
DONAL O'FLAHERTY HAS ENEMIES. THE JOYCES, I BELIEVE THEY'RE CALLED.
SEND A MESSAGE TO GALWAY. EXPLAIN HOW... HAPPY WE WOULD BE TO SEE HIM DISAPPEAR.
AND THIS GRACE?
SHE'S A WOMAN, SIRE. WHAT CAN SHE DO?
WITH HER HUSBAND DEAD, SHE'LL LOSE EVERYTHING. SHE'LL NEVER BE A THREAT AGAIN.

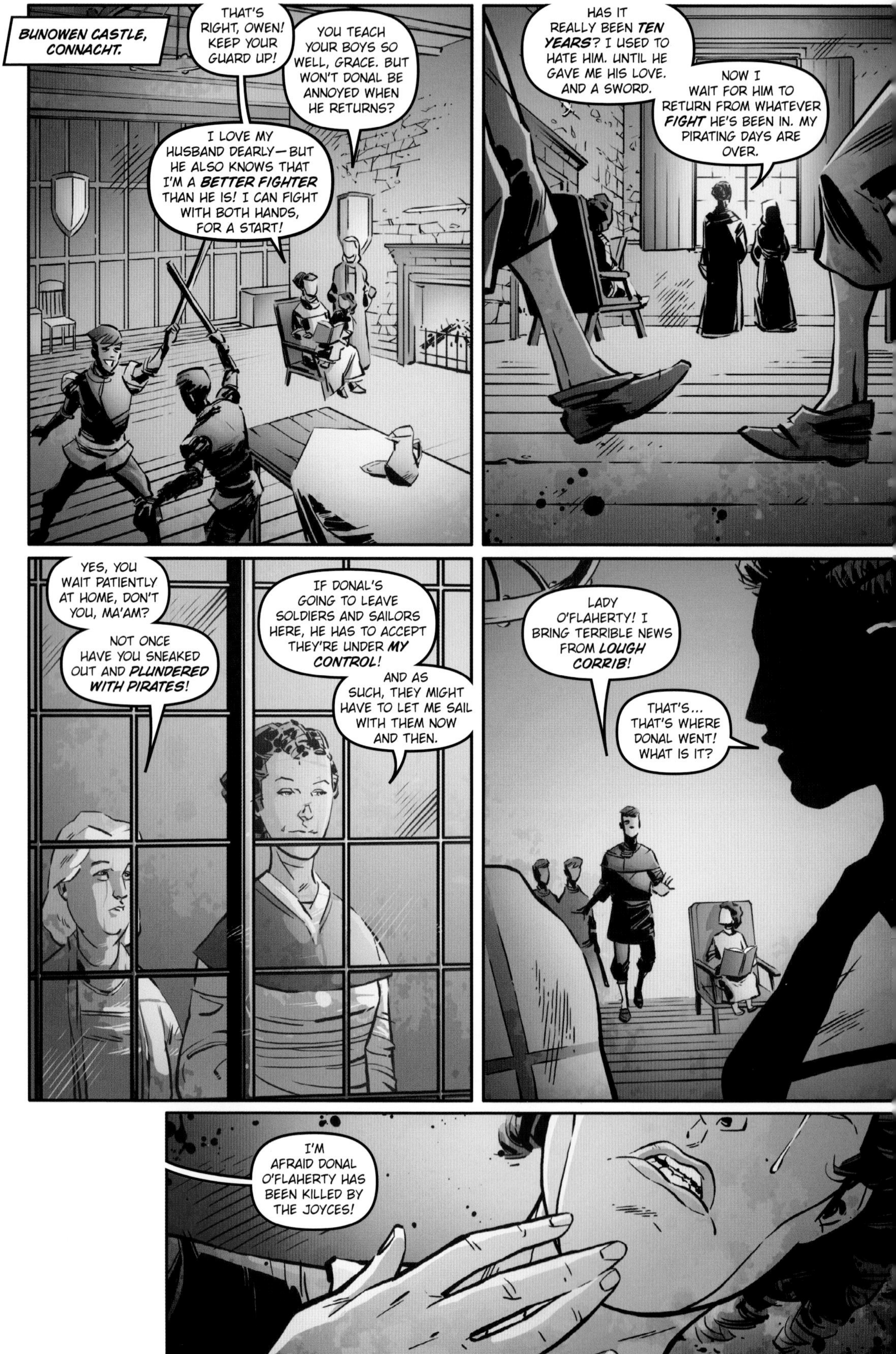
BUNOWEN CASTLE, CONNACHT.
THAT'S RIGHT, OWEN! KEEP YOUR GUARD UP!
YOU TEACH YOUR BOYS SO WELL, GRACE. BUT WON'T DONAL BE ANNOYED WHEN HE RETURNS?
I LOVE MY HUSBAND DEARLY—BUT HE ALSO KNOWS THAT I'M A BETTER FIGHTER THAN HE IS! I CAN FIGHT WITH BOTH HANDS, FOR A START!
HAS IT REALLY BEEN TEN YEARS? I USED TO HATE HIM. UNTIL HE GAVE ME HIS LOVE. AND A SWORD.
NOW I WAIT FOR HIM TO RETURN FROM WHATEVER FIGHT HE'S BEEN IN. MY PIRATING DAYS ARE OVER.
YES, YOU WAIT PATIENTLY AT HOME, DON'T YOU, MA'AM?
NOT ONCE HAVE YOU SNEAKED OUT AND PLUNDERED WITH PIRATES!
IF DONAL'S GOING TO LEAVE SOLDIERS AND SAILORS HERE, HE HAS TO ACCEPT THEY'RE UNDER MY CONTROL!
AND AS SUCH, THEY MIGHT HAVE TO LET ME SAIL WITH THEM NOW AND THEN.
LADY O'FLAHERTY! I BRING TERRIBLE NEWS FROM LOUGH CORRIB!
THAT'S... THAT'S WHERE DONAL WENT! WHAT IS IT?
I'M AFRAID DONAL O'FLAHERTY HAS BEEN KILLED BY THE JOYCES!

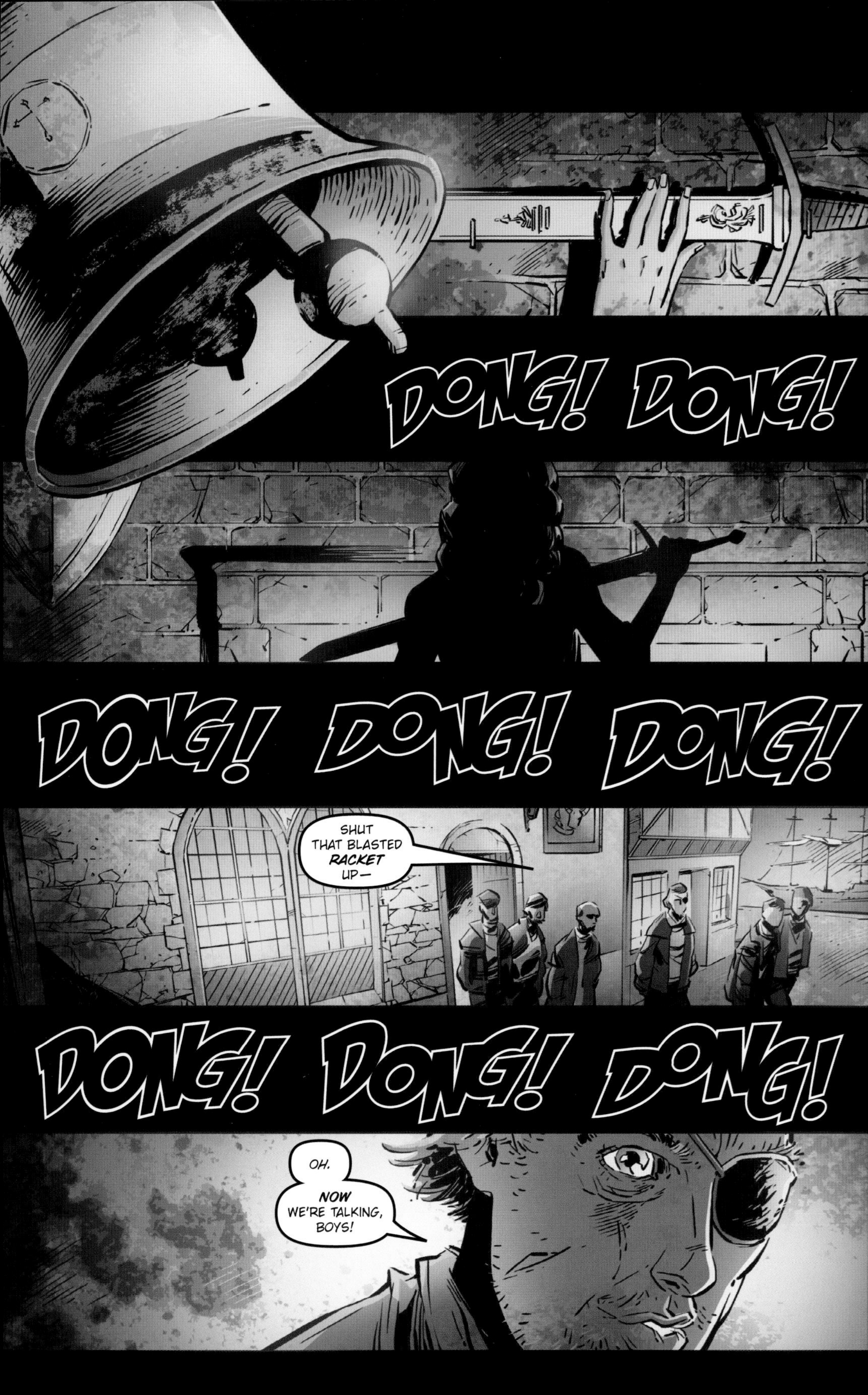
DONG! DONG!
DONG! DONG! DONG!
SHUT THAT BLASTED *RACKET* UP—
DONG! DONG! DONG!
OH.
NOW WE'RE TALKING, BOYS!

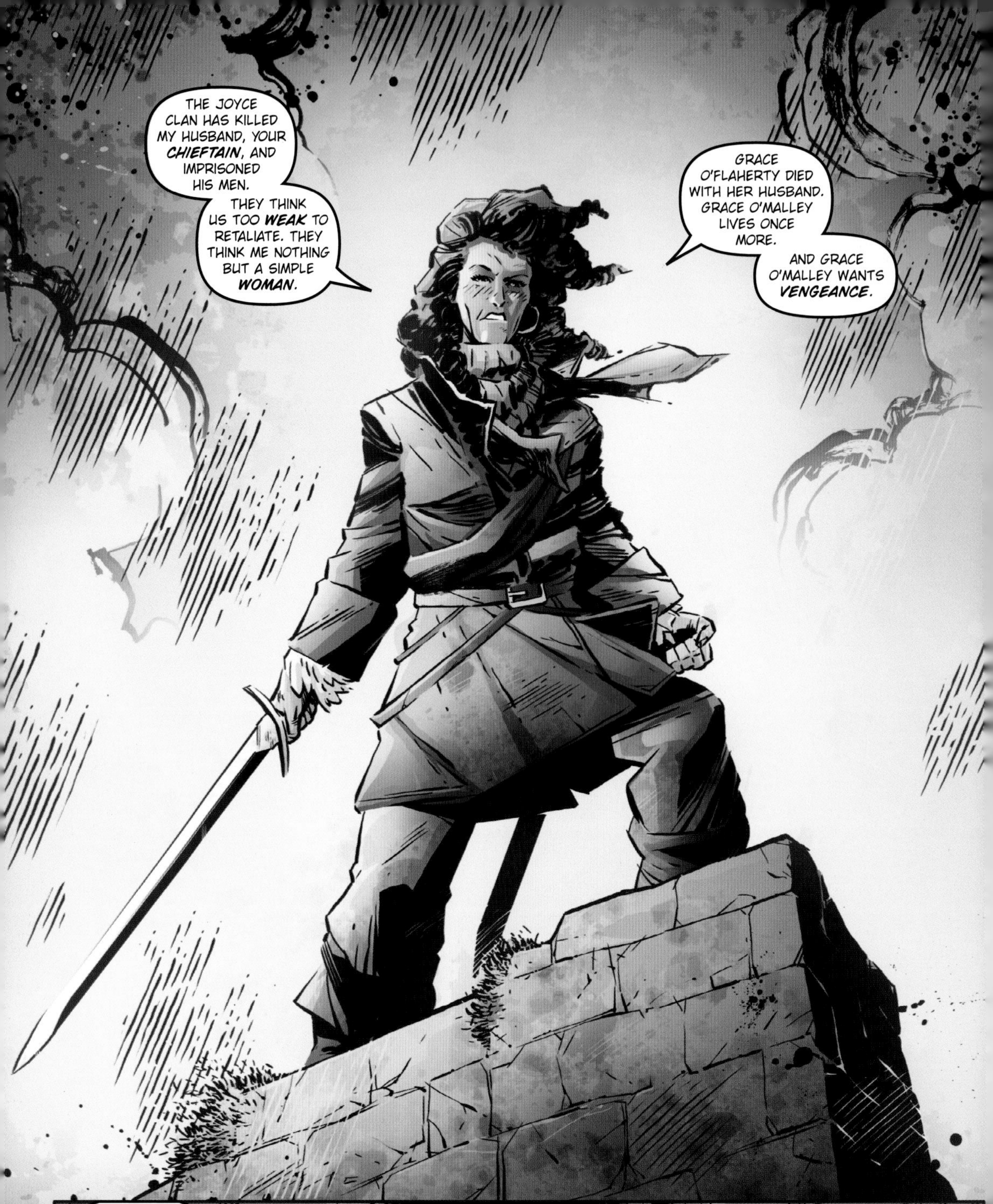
THE JOYCE CLAN HAS KILLED MY HUSBAND, YOUR CHIEFTAIN, AND IMPRISONED HIS MEN.
THEY THINK US TOO WEAK TO RETALIATE. THEY THINK ME NOTHING BUT A SIMPLE WOMAN.
GRACE O'FLAHERTY DIED WITH HER HUSBAND. GRACE O'MALLEY LIVES ONCE MORE.
AND GRACE O'MALLEY WANTS VENGEANCE.

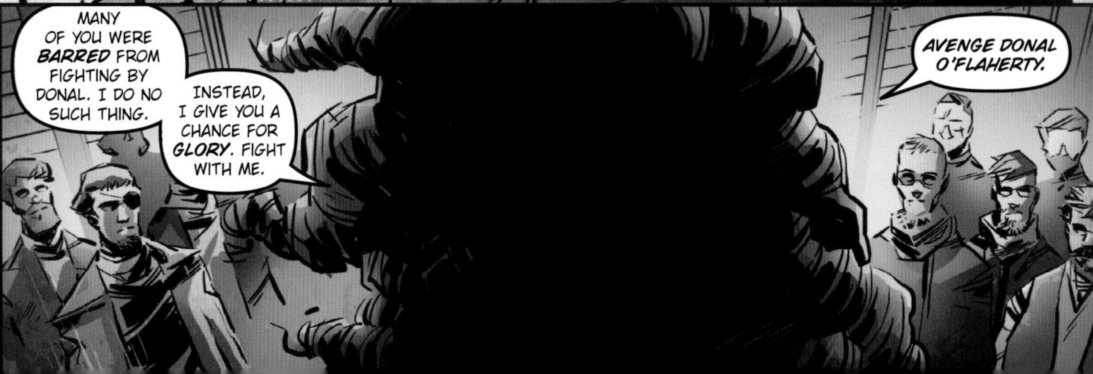
MANY OF YOU WERE BARRED FROM FIGHTING BY DONAL. I DO NO SUCH THING.
INSTEAD, I GIVE YOU A CHANCE FOR GLORY. FIGHT WITH ME.
AVENGE DONAL O'FLAHERTY.

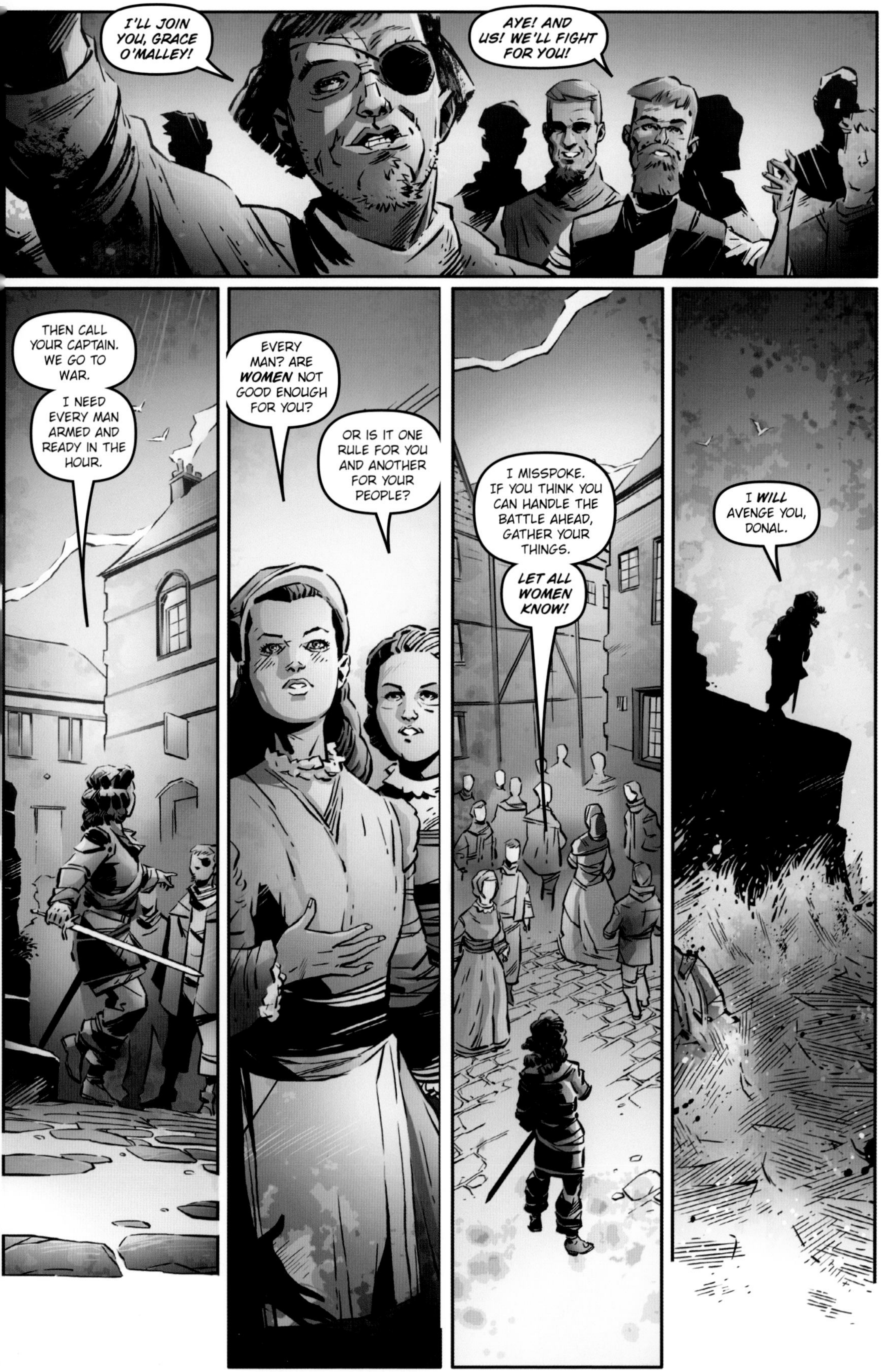
I'LL JOIN YOU, GRACE O'MALLEY!
AYE! AND US! WE'LL FIGHT FOR YOU!
THEN CALL YOUR CAPTAIN. WE GO TO WAR.
I NEED EVERY MAN ARMED AND READY IN THE HOUR.
EVERY MAN? ARE WOMEN NOT GOOD ENOUGH FOR YOU?
OR IS IT ONE RULE FOR YOU AND ANOTHER FOR YOUR PEOPLE?
I MISSPOKE. IF YOU THINK YOU CAN HANDLE THE BATTLE AHEAD, GATHER YOUR THINGS.
LET ALL WOMEN KNOW!
I WILL AVENGE YOU, DONAL.

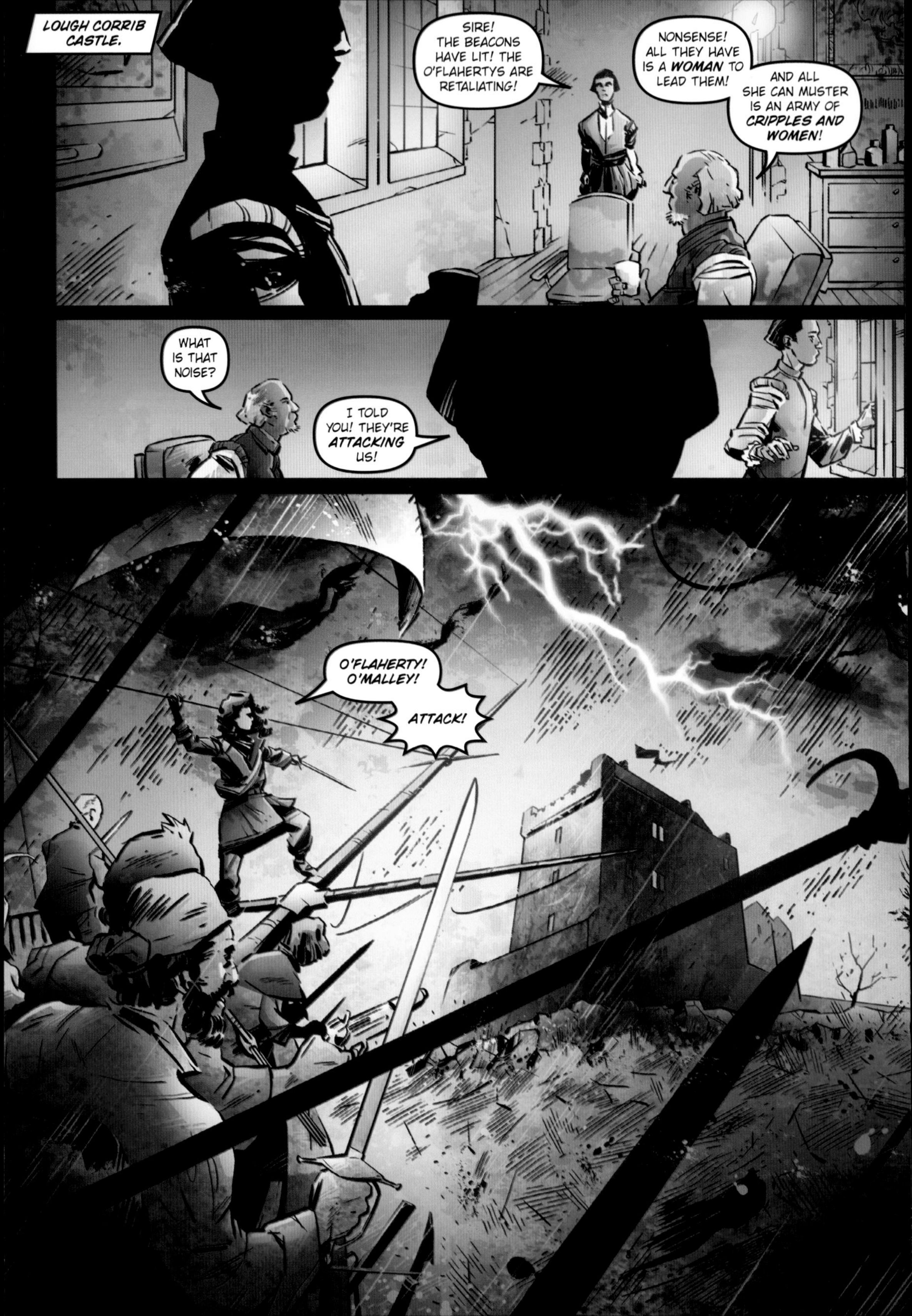
LOUGH CORRIB CASTLE.
SIRE! THE BEACONS HAVE LIT! THE O'FLAHERTYS ARE RETALIATING!
NONSENSE! ALL THEY HAVE IS A WOMAN TO LEAD THEM!
AND ALL SHE CAN MUSTER IS AN ARMY OF CRIPPLES AND WOMEN!
WHAT IS THAT NOISE?
I TOLD YOU! THEY'RE ATTACKING US!
O'FLAHERTY! O'MALLEY!
ATTACK!

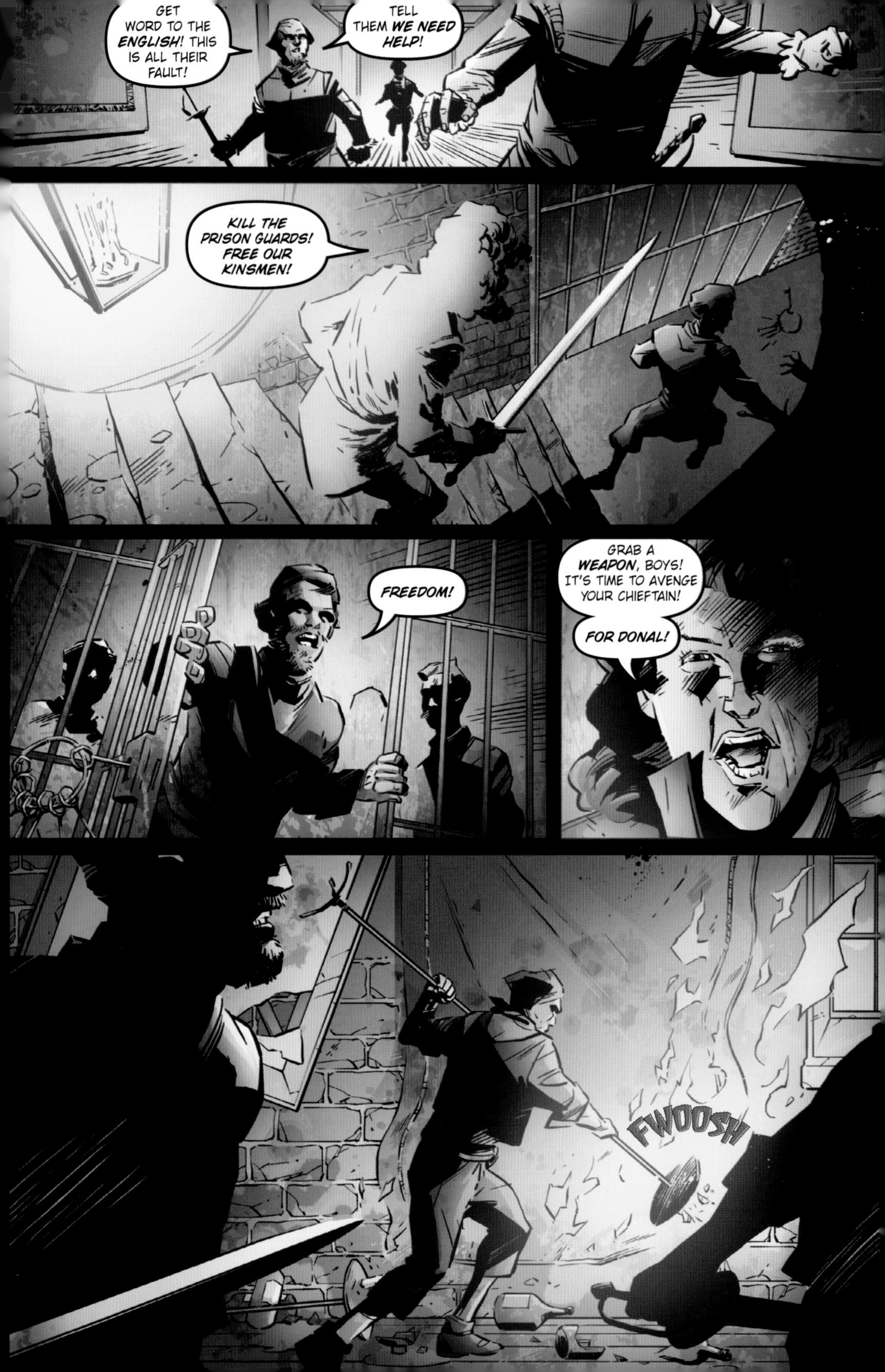
GET WORD TO THE **ENGLISH**! THIS IS ALL THEIR FAULT!
TELL THEM **WE NEED HELP**!
KILL THE PRISON GUARDS! FREE OUR KINSMEN!
FREEDOM!
GRAB A **WEAPON**, BOYS! IT'S TIME TO AVENGE YOUR CHIEFTAIN!
FOR DONAL!
FWOOSH

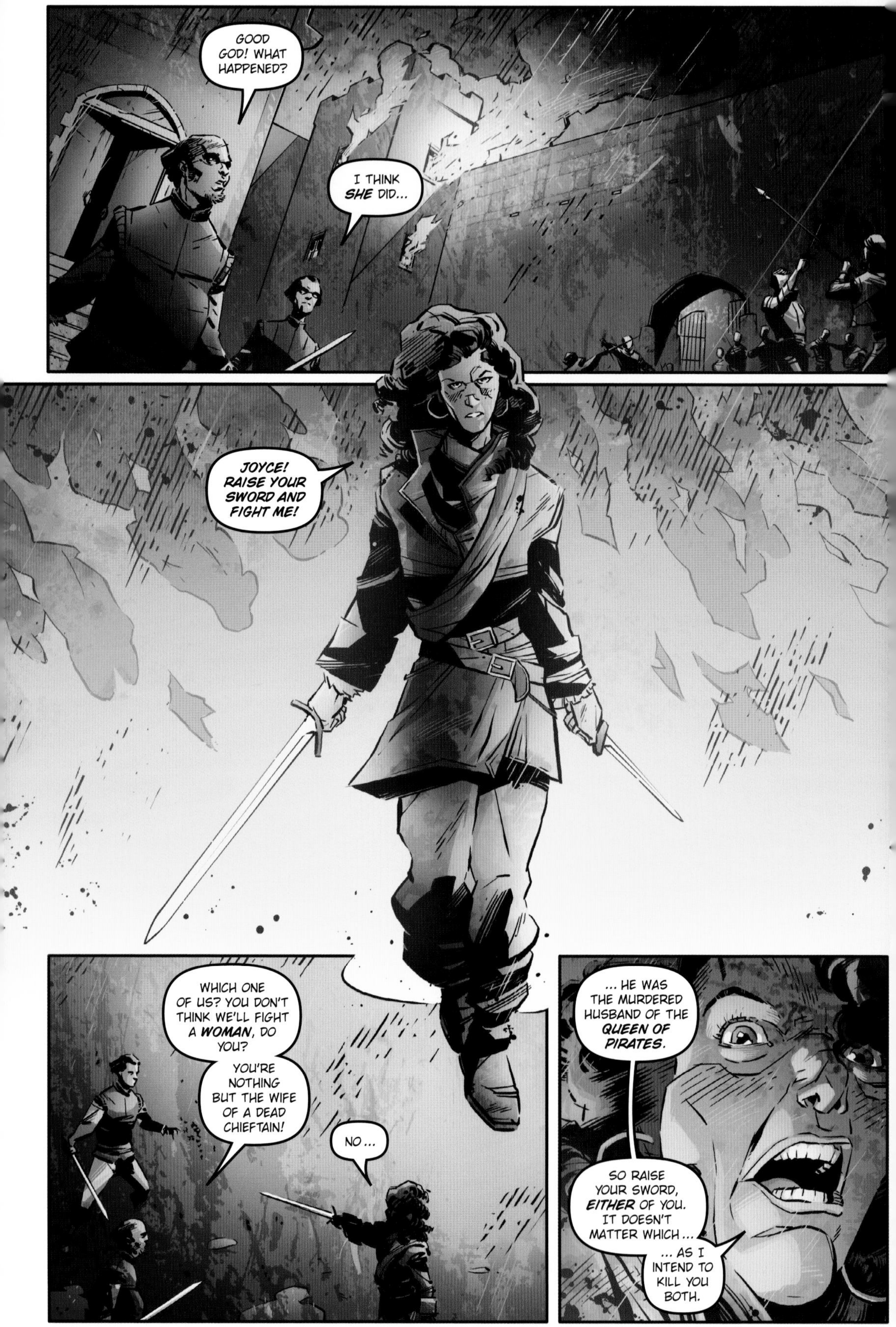

GOOD GOD! WHAT HAPPENED?
I THINK SHE DID...
JOYCE! RAISE YOUR SWORD AND FIGHT ME!
WHICH ONE OF US? YOU DON'T THINK WE'LL FIGHT A WOMAN, DO YOU?
YOU'RE NOTHING BUT THE WIFE OF A DEAD CHIEFTAIN!
NO...
... HE WAS THE MURDERED HUSBAND OF THE QUEEN OF PIRATES.
SO RAISE YOUR SWORD, EITHER OF YOU. IT DOESN'T MATTER WHICH...
... AS I INTEND TO KILL YOU BOTH.

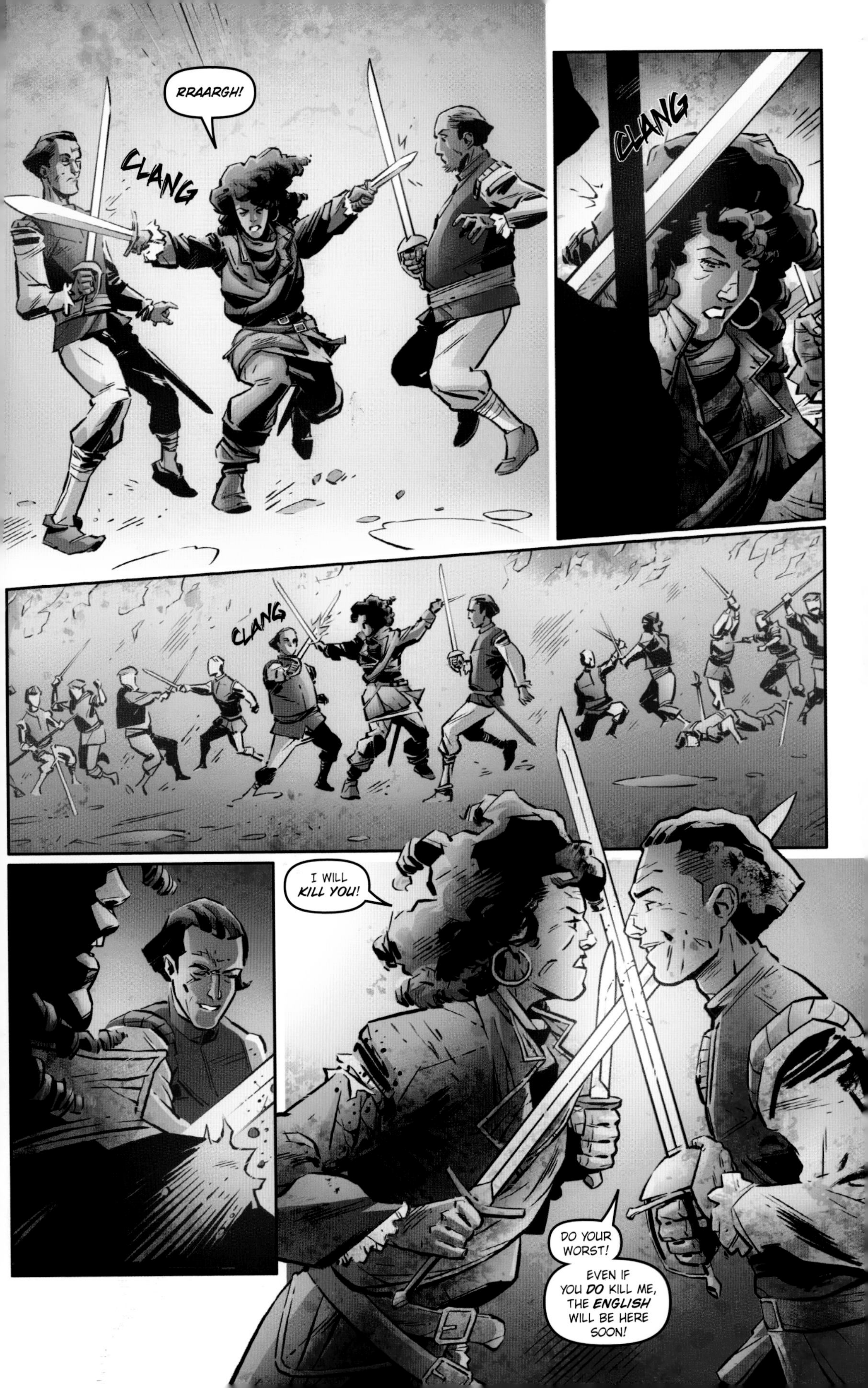
RRAARGH!
CLANG
CLANG
CLANG
I WILL KILL YOU!
DO YOUR WORST!
EVEN IF YOU DO KILL ME, THE ENGLISH WILL BE HERE SOON!

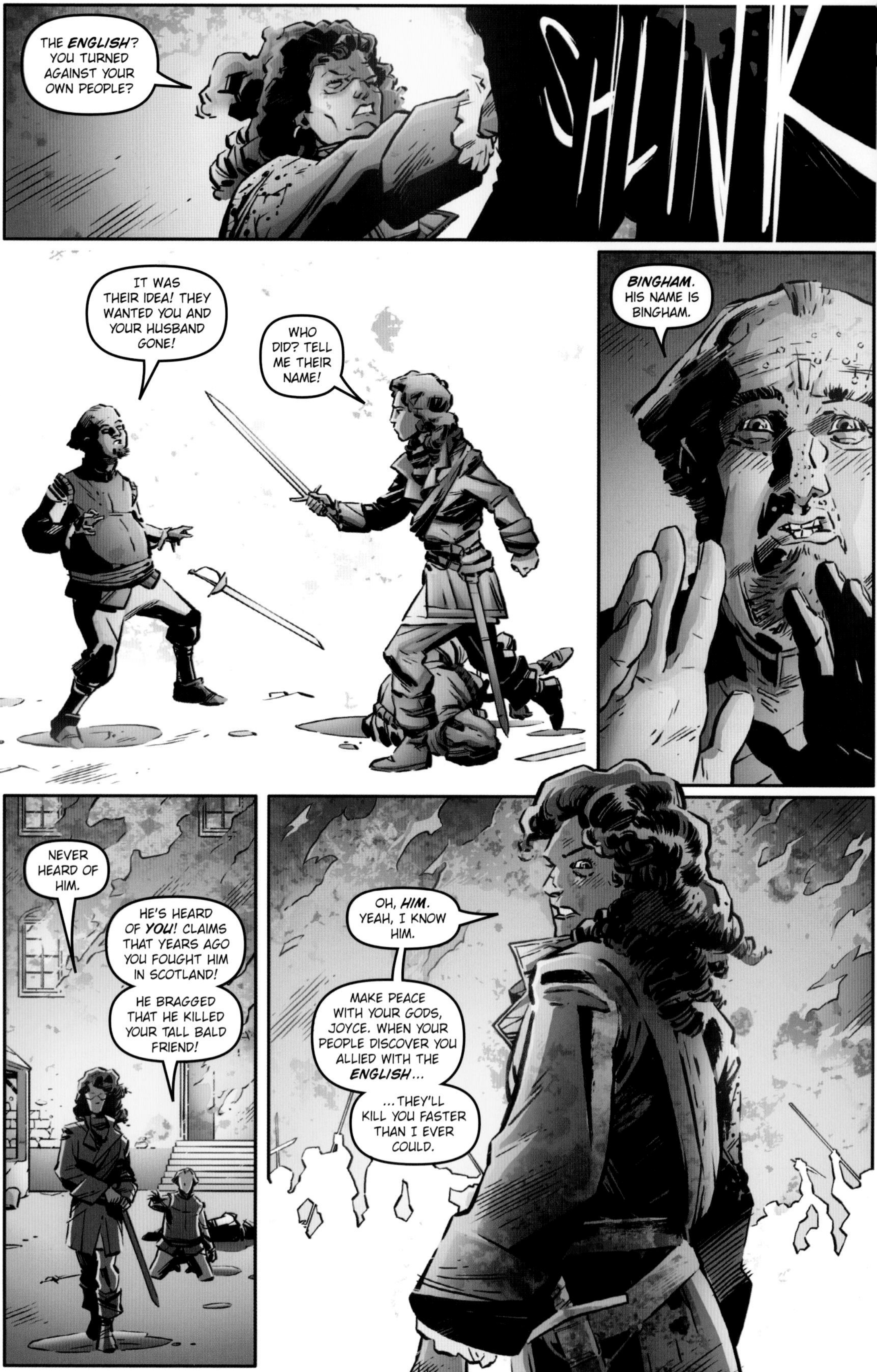
THE ENGLISH? YOU TURNED AGAINST YOUR OWN PEOPLE?
SHLINK
IT WAS THEIR IDEA! THEY WANTED YOU AND YOUR HUSBAND GONE!
WHO DID? TELL ME THEIR NAME!
BINGHAM. HIS NAME IS BINGHAM.
NEVER HEARD OF HIM.
HE'S HEARD OF YOU! CLAIMS THAT YEARS AGO YOU FOUGHT HIM IN SCOTLAND!
HE BRAGGED THAT HE KILLED YOUR TALL BALD FRIEND!
OH, HIM. YEAH, I KNOW HIM.
MAKE PEACE WITH YOUR GODS, JOYCE. WHEN YOUR PEOPLE DISCOVER YOU ALLIED WITH THE ENGLISH...
...THEY'LL KILL YOU FASTER THAN I EVER COULD.

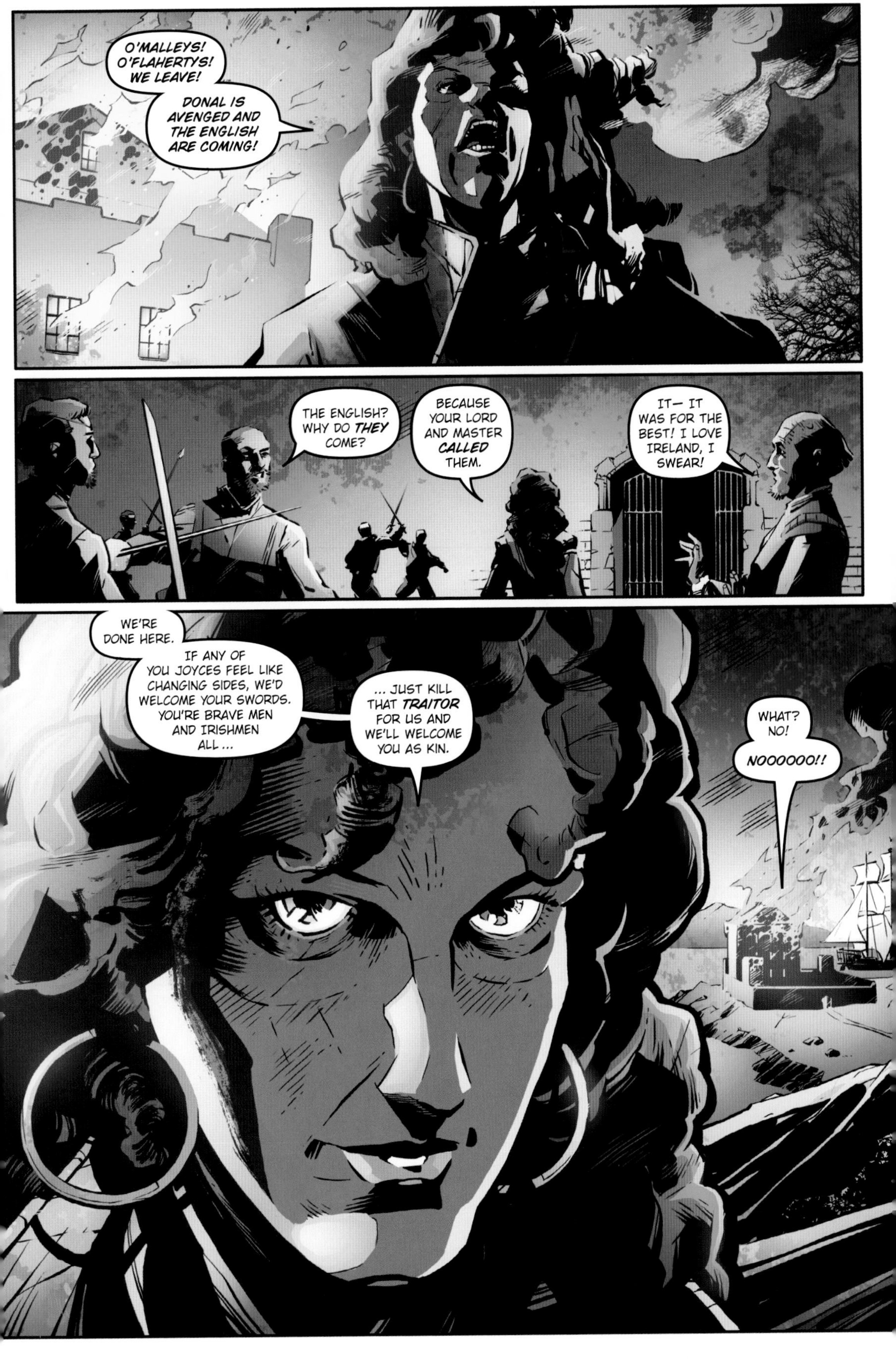
O'MALLEYS! O'FLAHERTYS! WE LEAVE!
DONAL IS AVENGED AND THE ENGLISH ARE COMING!
THE ENGLISH? WHY DO THEY COME?
BECAUSE YOUR LORD AND MASTER CALLED THEM.
IT— IT WAS FOR THE BEST! I LOVE IRELAND, I SWEAR!
WE'RE DONE HERE.
IF ANY OF YOU JOYCES FEEL LIKE CHANGING SIDES, WE'D WELCOME YOUR SWORDS. YOU'RE BRAVE MEN AND IRISHMEN ALL ...
... JUST KILL THAT TRAITOR FOR US AND WE'LL WELCOME YOU AS KIN.
WHAT? NO!
NOOOOOO!!

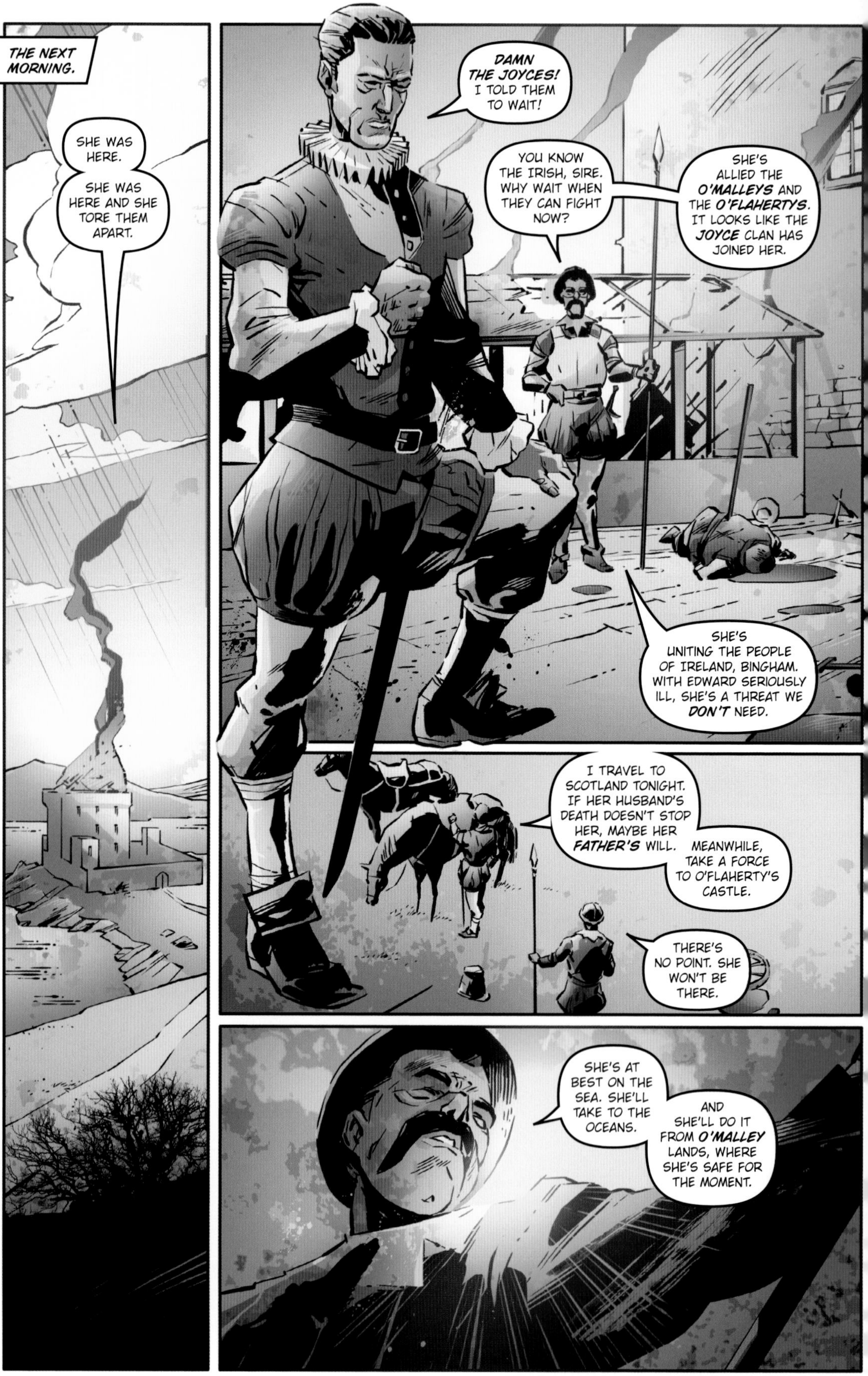
THE NEXT MORNING.
SHE WAS HERE.
SHE WAS HERE AND SHE TORE THEM APART.
DAMN THE JOYCES! I TOLD THEM TO WAIT!
YOU KNOW THE IRISH, SIRE. WHY WAIT WHEN THEY CAN FIGHT NOW?
SHE'S ALLIED THE O'MALLEYS AND THE O'FLAHERTYS. IT LOOKS LIKE THE JOYCE CLAN HAS JOINED HER.
SHE'S UNITING THE PEOPLE OF IRELAND, BINGHAM. WITH EDWARD SERIOUSLY ILL, SHE'S A THREAT WE DON'T NEED.
I TRAVEL TO SCOTLAND TONIGHT. IF HER HUSBAND'S DEATH DOESN'T STOP HER, MAYBE HER FATHER'S WILL.
MEANWHILE, TAKE A FORCE TO O'FLAHERTY'S CASTLE.
THERE'S NO POINT. SHE WON'T BE THERE.
SHE'S AT BEST ON THE SEA. SHE'LL TAKE TO THE OCEANS.
AND SHE'LL DO IT FROM O'MALLEY LANDS, WHERE SHE'S SAFE FOR THE MOMENT.

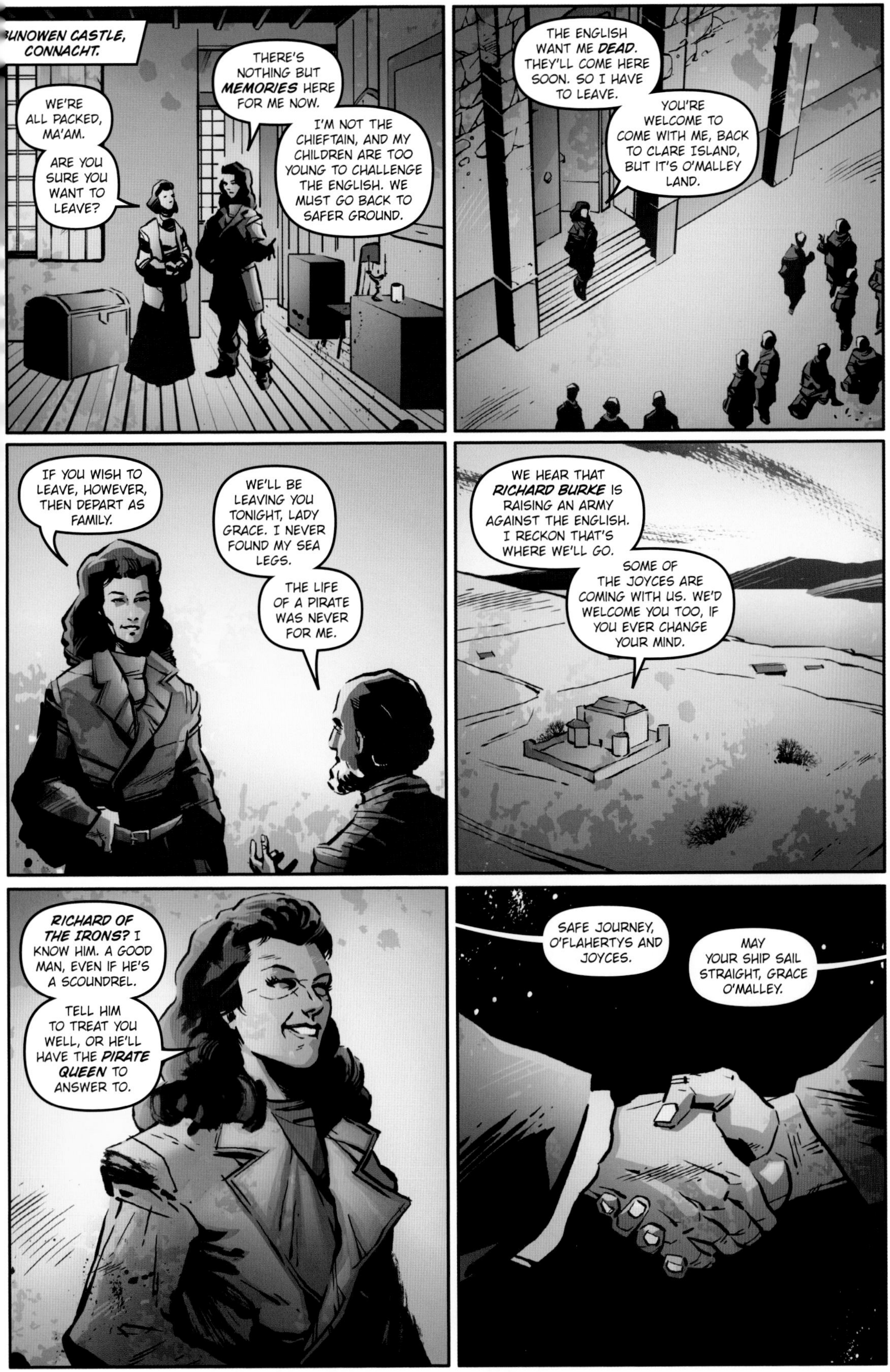
BUNOWEN CASTLE, CONNACHT.
WE'RE ALL PACKED, MA'AM.
ARE YOU SURE YOU WANT TO LEAVE?
THERE'S NOTHING BUT MEMORIES HERE FOR ME NOW.
I'M NOT THE CHIEFTAIN, AND MY CHILDREN ARE TOO YOUNG TO CHALLENGE THE ENGLISH. WE MUST GO BACK TO SAFER GROUND.
THE ENGLISH WANT ME DEAD. THEY'LL COME HERE SOON. SO I HAVE TO LEAVE.
YOU'RE WELCOME TO COME WITH ME, BACK TO CLARE ISLAND, BUT IT'S O'MALLEY LAND.
IF YOU WISH TO LEAVE, HOWEVER, THEN DEPART AS FAMILY.
WE'LL BE LEAVING YOU TONIGHT, LADY GRACE. I NEVER FOUND MY SEA LEGS.
THE LIFE OF A PIRATE WAS NEVER FOR ME.
WE HEAR THAT RICHARD BURKE IS RAISING AN ARMY AGAINST THE ENGLISH. I RECKON THAT'S WHERE WE'LL GO.
SOME OF THE JOYCES ARE COMING WITH US. WE'D WELCOME YOU TOO, IF YOU EVER CHANGE YOUR MIND.
RICHARD OF THE IRONS? I KNOW HIM. A GOOD MAN, EVEN IF HE'S A SCOUNDREL.
TELL HIM TO TREAT YOU WELL, OR HE'LL HAVE THE PIRATE QUEEN TO ANSWER TO.
SAFE JOURNEY, O'FLAHERTYS AND JOYCES.
MAY YOUR SHIP SAIL STRAIGHT, GRACE O'MALLEY.

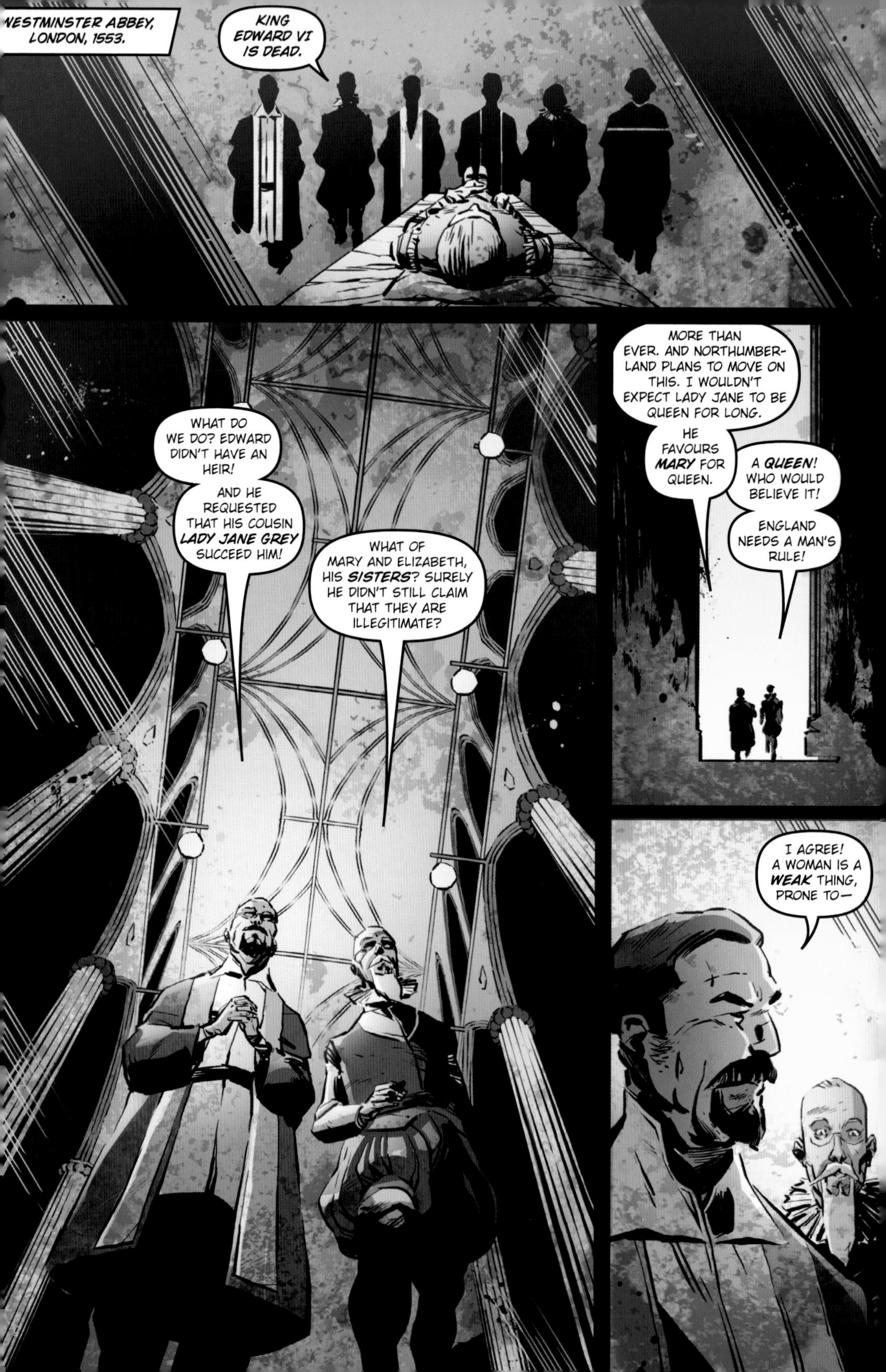

WESTMINSTER ABBEY, LONDON, 1553.
KING EDWARD VI IS DEAD.
WHAT DO WE DO? EDWARD DIDN'T HAVE AN HEIR!
AND HE REQUESTED THAT HIS COUSIN LADY JANE GREY SUCCEED HIM!
WHAT OF MARY AND ELIZABETH, HIS SISTERS? SURELY HE DIDN'T STILL CLAIM THAT THEY ARE ILLEGITIMATE?
MORE THAN EVER. AND NORTHUMBERLAND PLANS TO MOVE ON THIS. I WOULDN'T EXPECT LADY JANE TO BE QUEEN FOR LONG.
HE FAVOURS MARY FOR QUEEN.
A QUEEN! WHO WOULD BELIEVE IT!
ENGLAND NEEDS A MAN'S RULE!
I AGREE! A WOMAN IS A WEAK THING, PRONE TO—

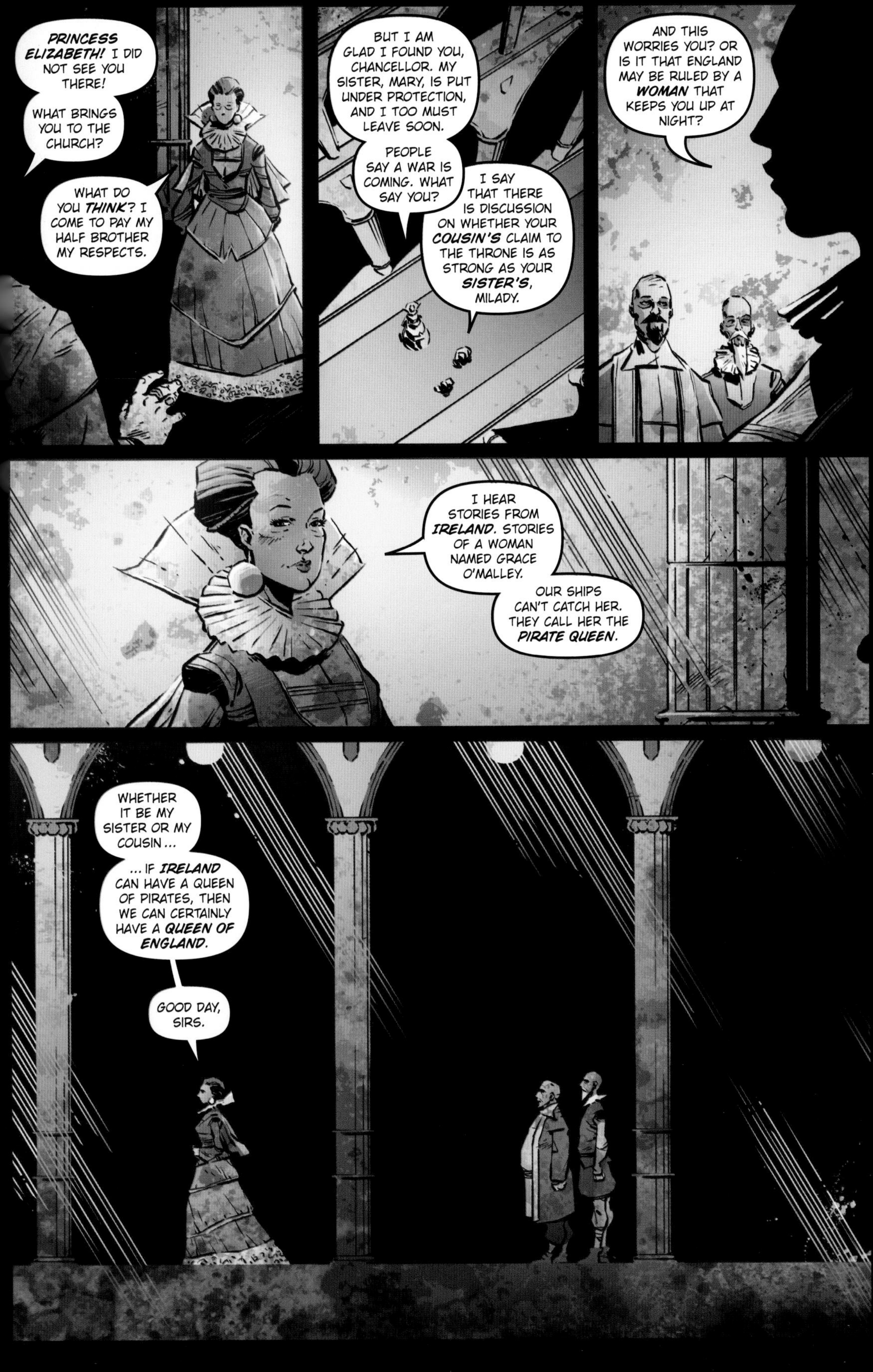
PRINCESS ELIZABETH! I DID NOT SEE YOU THERE!
WHAT BRINGS YOU TO THE CHURCH?
WHAT DO YOU THINK? I COME TO PAY MY HALF BROTHER MY RESPECTS.
BUT I AM GLAD I FOUND YOU, CHANCELLOR. MY SISTER, MARY, IS PUT UNDER PROTECTION, AND I TOO MUST LEAVE SOON.
PEOPLE SAY A WAR IS COMING. WHAT SAY YOU?
I SAY THAT THERE IS DISCUSSION ON WHETHER YOUR COUSIN'S CLAIM TO THE THRONE IS AS STRONG AS YOUR SISTER'S, MILADY.
AND THIS WORRIES YOU? OR IS IT THAT ENGLAND MAY BE RULED BY A WOMAN THAT KEEPS YOU UP AT NIGHT?
I HEAR STORIES FROM IRELAND. STORIES OF A WOMAN NAMED GRACE O'MALLEY.
OUR SHIPS CAN'T CATCH HER. THEY CALL HER THE PIRATE QUEEN.
WHETHER IT BE MY SISTER OR MY COUSIN...
...IF IRELAND CAN HAVE A QUEEN OF PIRATES, THEN WE CAN CERTAINLY HAVE A QUEEN OF ENGLAND.
GOOD DAY, SIRS.

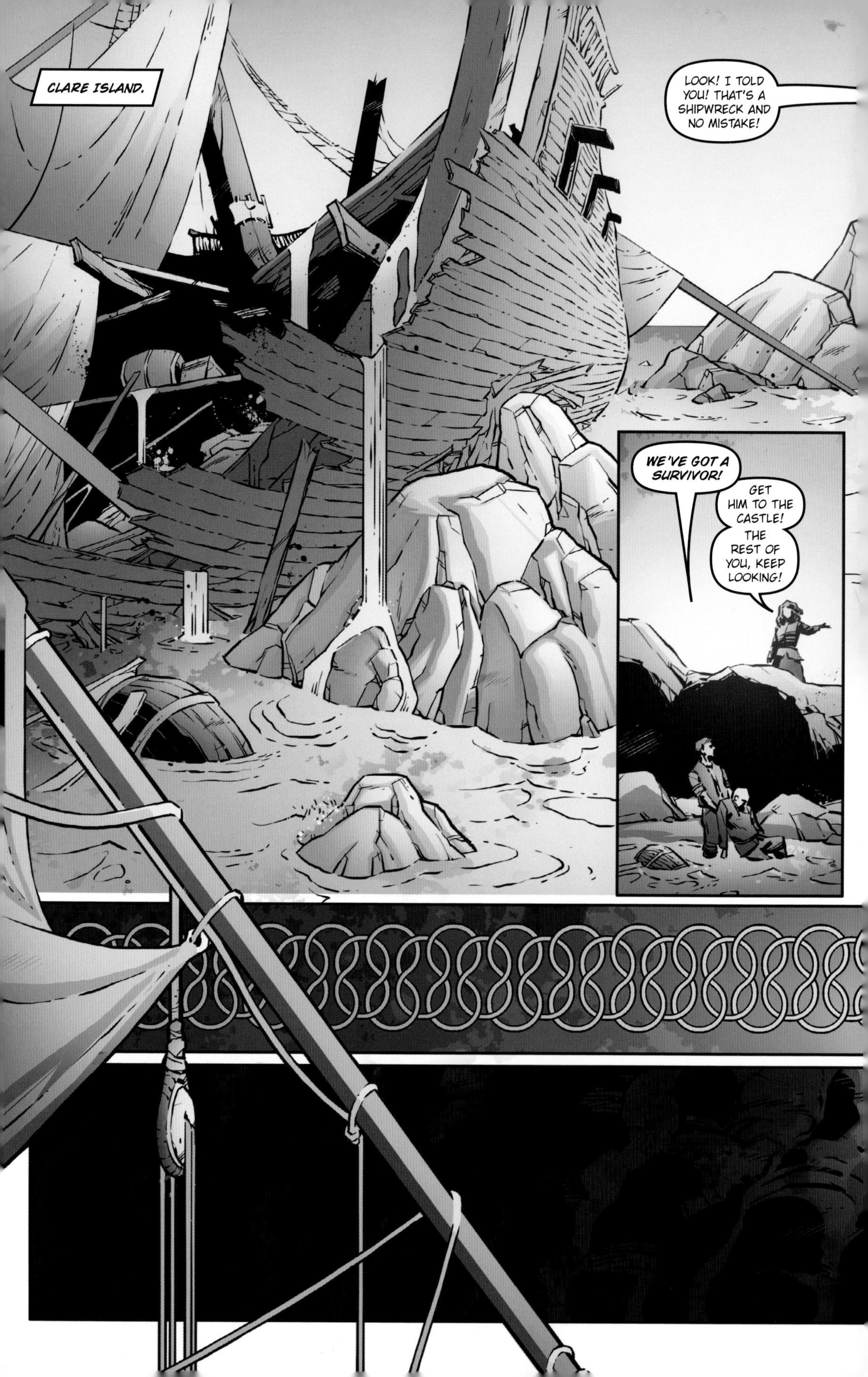
CLARE ISLAND.
LOOK! I TOLD YOU! THAT'S A SHIPWRECK AND NO MISTAKE!
WE'VE GOT A SURVIVOR!
GET HIM TO THE CASTLE!
THE REST OF YOU, KEEP LOOKING!

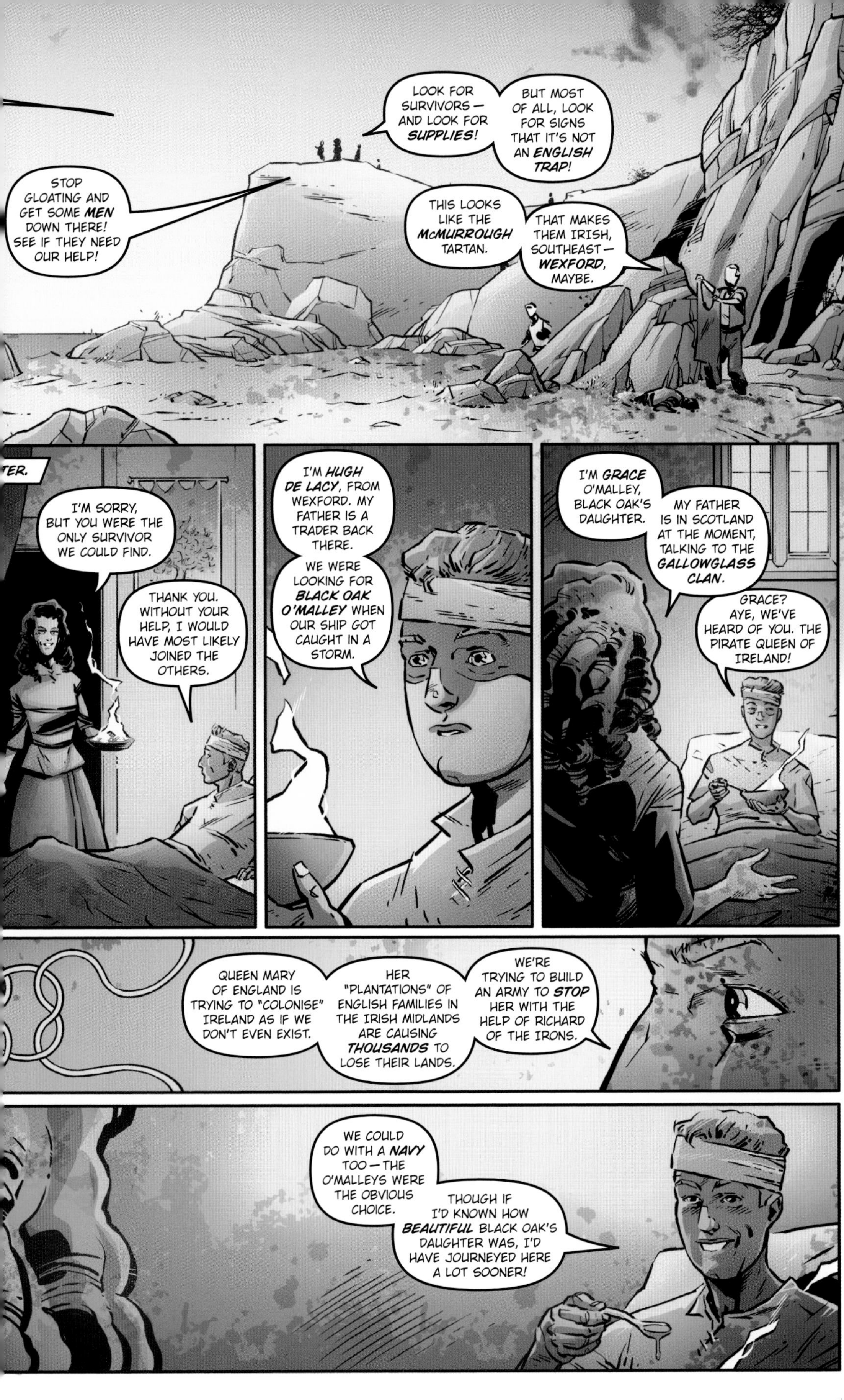

STOP GLOATING AND GET SOME MEN DOWN THERE! SEE IF THEY NEED OUR HELP!
LOOK FOR SURVIVORS — AND LOOK FOR SUPPLIES!
BUT MOST OF ALL, LOOK FOR SIGNS THAT IT'S NOT AN ENGLISH TRAP!
THIS LOOKS LIKE THE McMURROUGH TARTAN.
THAT MAKES THEM IRISH, SOUTHEAST — WEXFORD, MAYBE.
I'M SORRY, BUT YOU WERE THE ONLY SURVIVOR WE COULD FIND.
THANK YOU. WITHOUT YOUR HELP, I WOULD HAVE MOST LIKELY JOINED THE OTHERS.
I'M HUGH DE LACY, FROM WEXFORD. MY FATHER IS A TRADER BACK THERE.
WE WERE LOOKING FOR BLACK OAK O'MALLEY WHEN OUR SHIP GOT CAUGHT IN A STORM.
I'M GRACE O'MALLEY, BLACK OAK'S DAUGHTER.
MY FATHER IS IN SCOTLAND AT THE MOMENT, TALKING TO THE GALLOWGLASS CLAN.
GRACE? AYE, WE'VE HEARD OF YOU. THE PIRATE QUEEN OF IRELAND!
QUEEN MARY OF ENGLAND IS TRYING TO "COLONISE" IRELAND AS IF WE DON'T EVEN EXIST.
HER "PLANTATIONS" OF ENGLISH FAMILIES IN THE IRISH MIDLANDS ARE CAUSING THOUSANDS TO LOSE THEIR LANDS.
WE'RE TRYING TO BUILD AN ARMY TO STOP HER WITH THE HELP OF RICHARD OF THE IRONS.
WE COULD DO WITH A NAVY TOO — THE O'MALLEYS WERE THE OBVIOUS CHOICE.
THOUGH IF I'D KNOWN HOW BEAUTIFUL BLACK OAK'S DAUGHTER WAS, I'D HAVE JOURNEYED HERE A LOT SOONER!

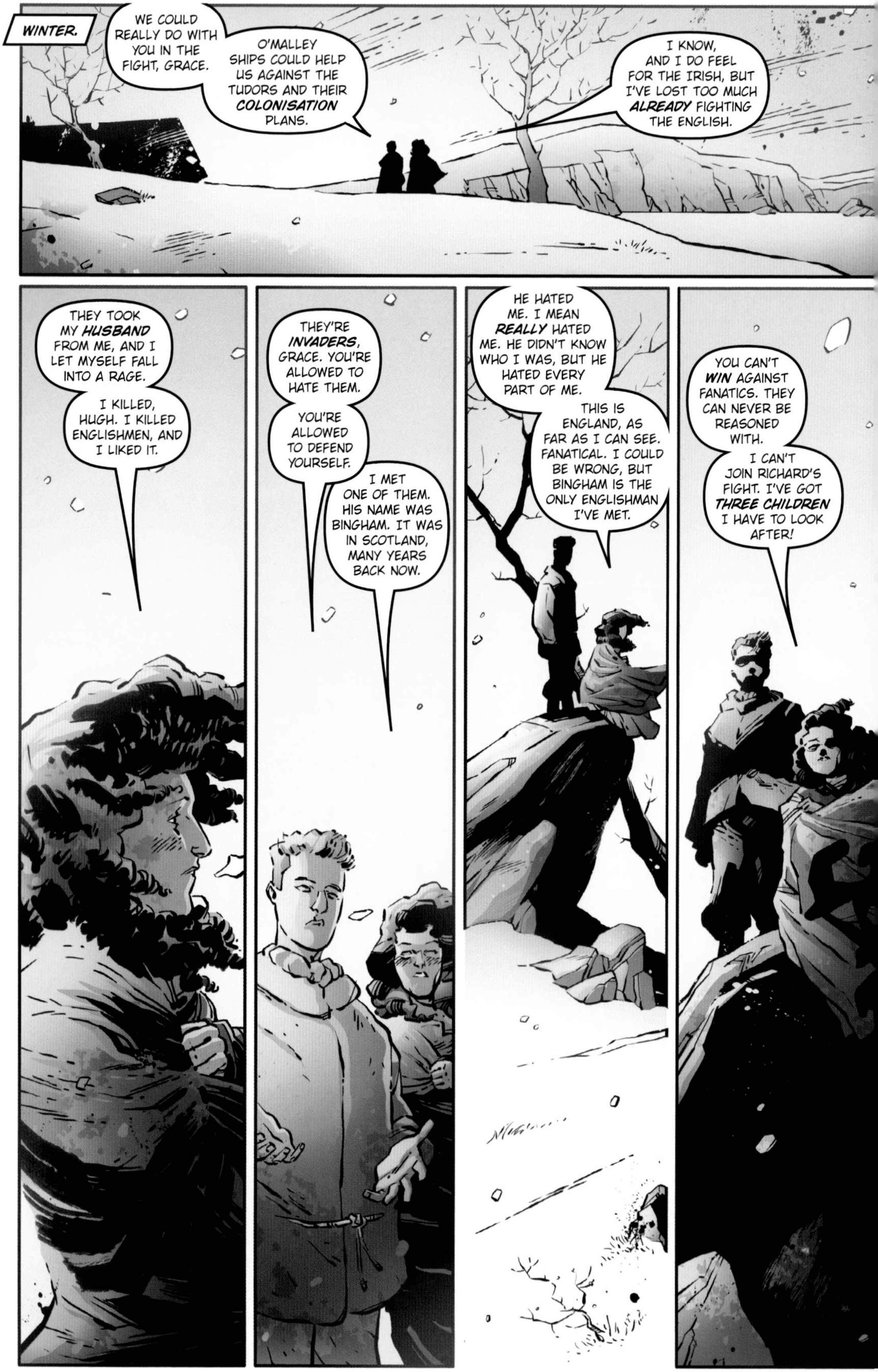

WINTER.
WE COULD REALLY DO WITH YOU IN THE FIGHT, GRACE.
O'MALLEY SHIPS COULD HELP US AGAINST THE TUDORS AND THEIR COLONISATION PLANS.
I KNOW, AND I DO FEEL FOR THE IRISH, BUT I'VE LOST TOO MUCH ALREADY FIGHTING THE ENGLISH.
THEY TOOK MY HUSBAND FROM ME, AND I LET MYSELF FALL INTO A RAGE.
I KILLED, HUGH. I KILLED ENGLISHMEN, AND I LIKED IT.
THEY'RE INVADERS, GRACE. YOU'RE ALLOWED TO HATE THEM.
YOU'RE ALLOWED TO DEFEND YOURSELF.
I MET ONE OF THEM. HIS NAME WAS BINGHAM. IT WAS IN SCOTLAND, MANY YEARS BACK NOW.
HE HATED ME. I MEAN REALLY HATED ME. HE DIDN'T KNOW WHO I WAS, BUT HE HATED EVERY PART OF ME.
THIS IS ENGLAND, AS FAR AS I CAN SEE. FANATICAL. I COULD BE WRONG, BUT BINGHAM IS THE ONLY ENGLISHMAN I'VE MET.
YOU CAN'T WIN AGAINST FANATICS. THEY CAN NEVER BE REASONED WITH.
I CAN'T JOIN RICHARD'S FIGHT. I'VE GOT THREE CHILDREN I HAVE TO LOOK AFTER!

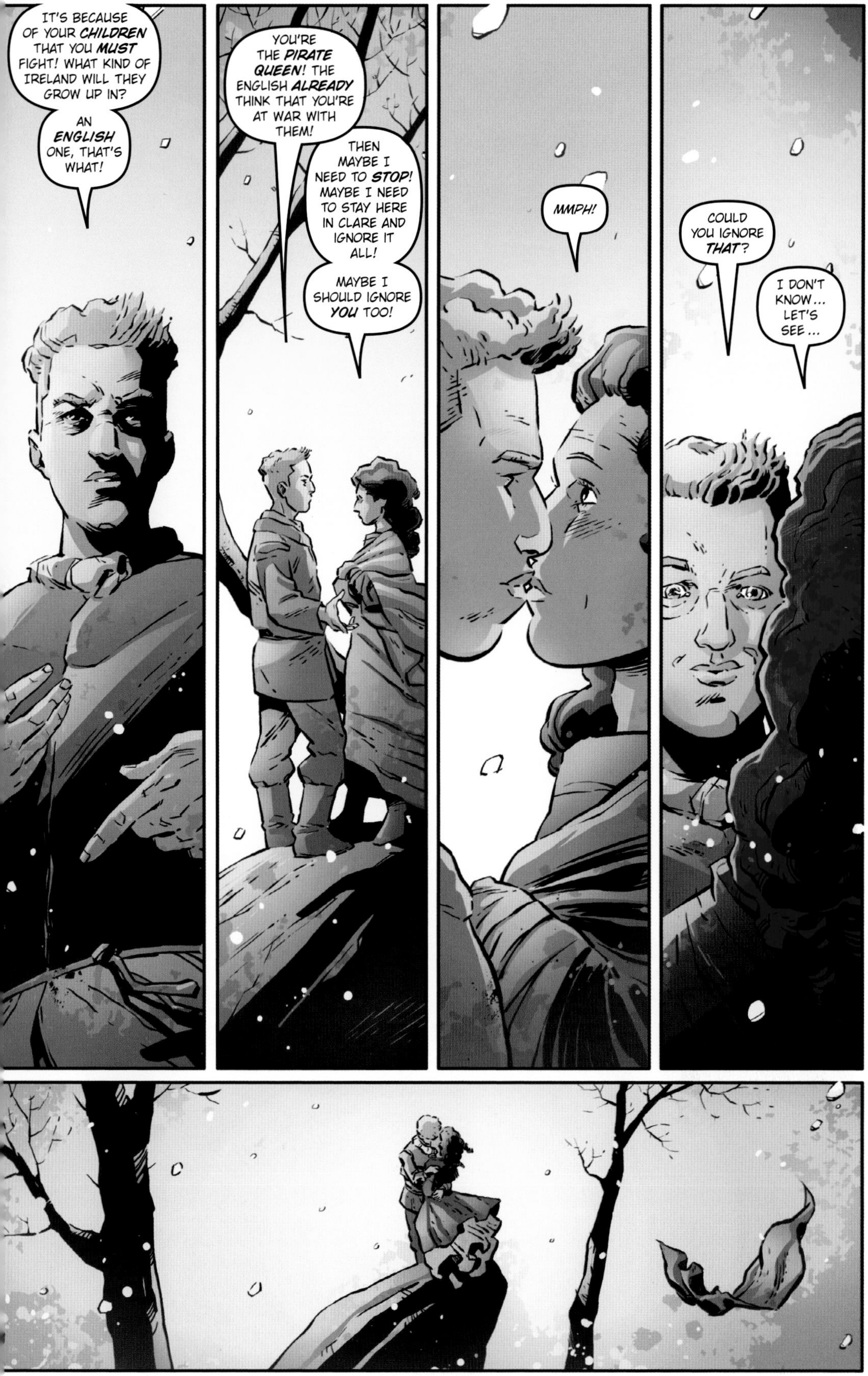
IT'S BECAUSE OF YOUR CHILDREN THAT YOU MUST FIGHT! WHAT KIND OF IRELAND WILL THEY GROW UP IN?
AN ENGLISH ONE, THAT'S WHAT!
YOU'RE THE PIRATE QUEEN! THE ENGLISH ALREADY THINK THAT YOU'RE AT WAR WITH THEM!
THEN MAYBE I NEED TO STOP! MAYBE I NEED TO STAY HERE IN CLARE AND IGNORE IT ALL!
MAYBE I SHOULD IGNORE YOU TOO!
MMPH!
COULD YOU IGNORE THAT?
I DON'T KNOW... LET'S SEE...

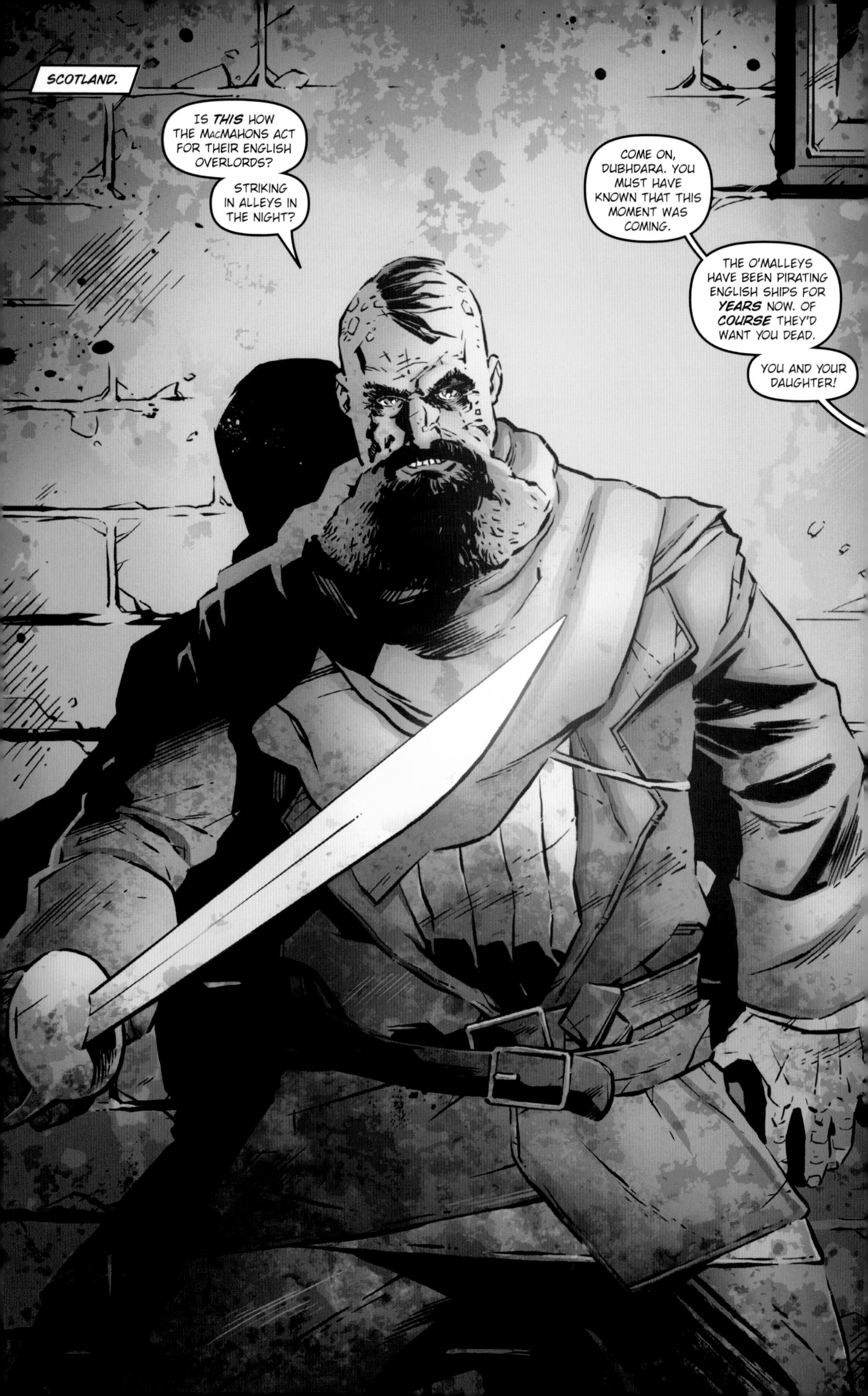
SCOTLAND.
IS *THIS* HOW THE MacMAHONS ACT FOR THEIR ENGLISH OVERLORDS?
STRIKING IN ALLEYS IN THE NIGHT?
COME ON, DUBHDARA. YOU MUST HAVE KNOWN THAT THIS MOMENT WAS COMING.
THE O'MALLEYS HAVE BEEN PIRATING ENGLISH SHIPS FOR *YEARS* NOW. OF *COURSE* THEY'D WANT YOU DEAD.
YOU AND YOUR DAUGHTER!

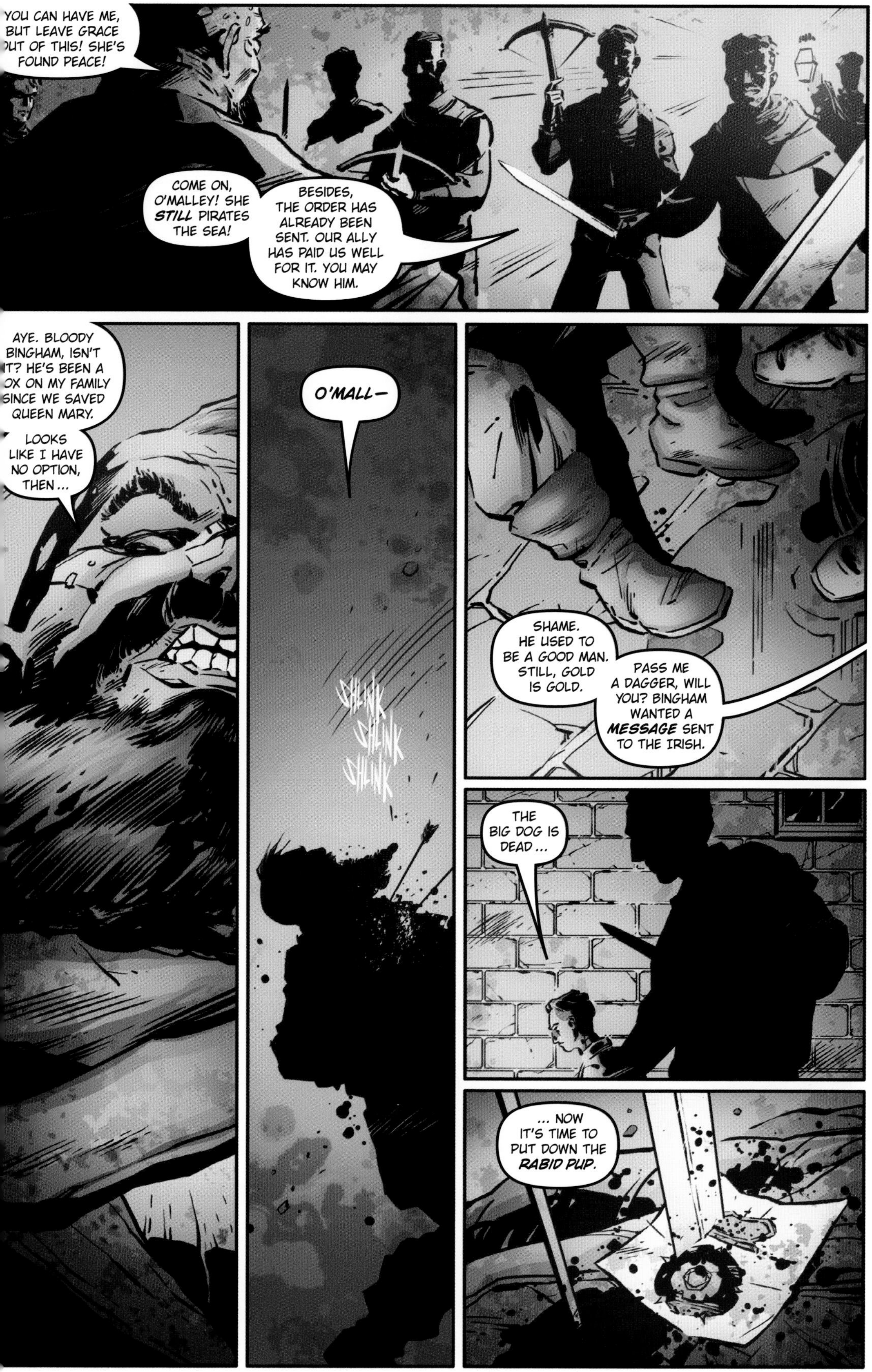
YOU CAN HAVE ME, BUT LEAVE GRACE OUT OF THIS! SHE'S FOUND PEACE!
COME ON, O'MALLEY! SHE STILL PIRATES THE SEA!
BESIDES, THE ORDER HAS ALREADY BEEN SENT. OUR ALLY HAS PAID US WELL FOR IT. YOU MAY KNOW HIM.
AYE. BLOODY BINGHAM, ISN'T IT? HE'S BEEN A POX ON MY FAMILY SINCE WE SAVED QUEEN MARY.
LOOKS LIKE I HAVE NO OPTION, THEN ...
O'MALL—
SHLINK
SHLINK
SHLINK
SHAME. HE USED TO BE A GOOD MAN. STILL, GOLD IS GOLD.
PASS ME A DAGGER, WILL YOU? BINGHAM WANTED A MESSAGE SENT TO THE IRISH.
THE BIG DOG IS DEAD ...
... NOW IT'S TIME TO PUT DOWN THE RABID PUP.

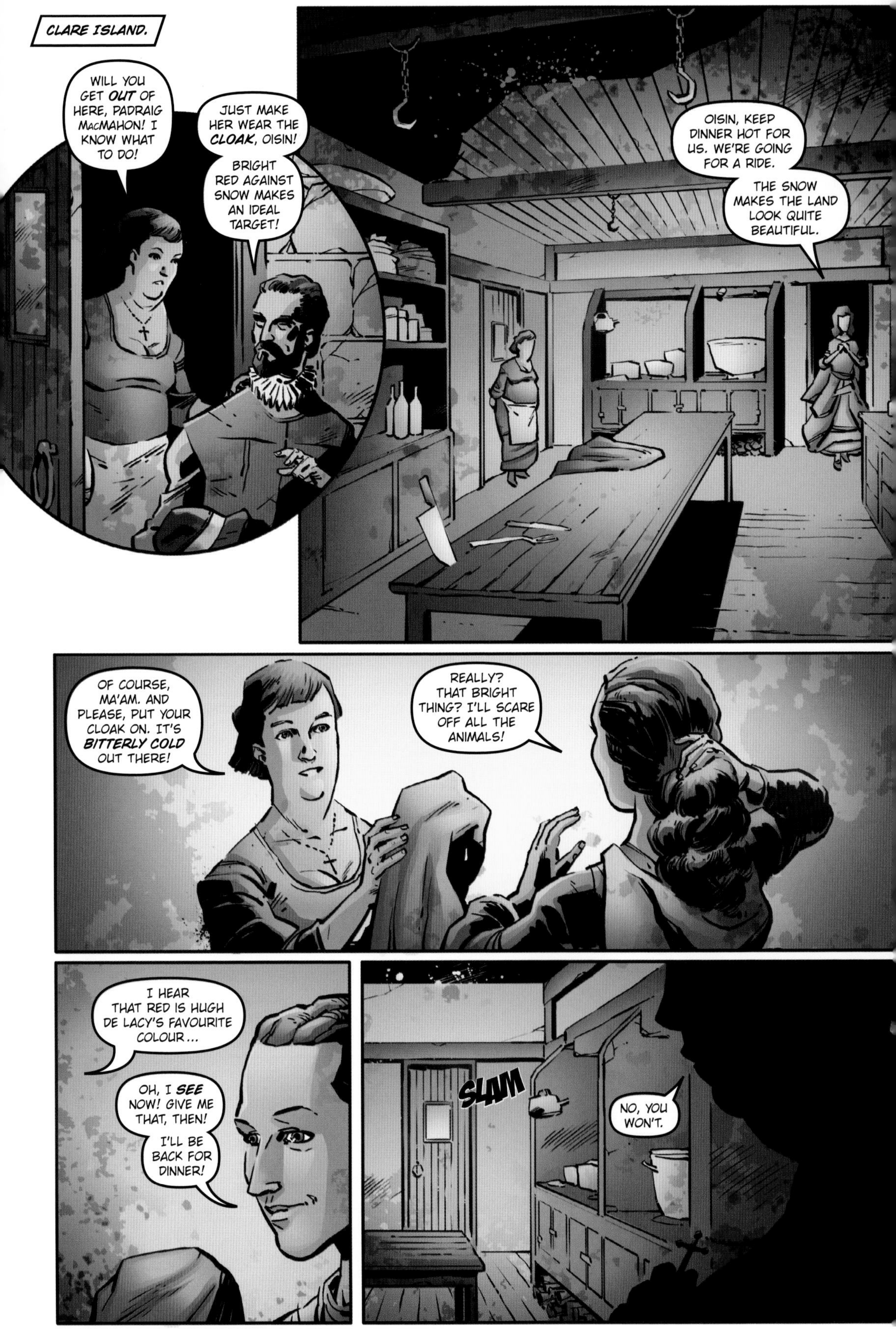
CLARE ISLAND.
WILL YOU GET OUT OF HERE, PADRAIG MacMAHON! I KNOW WHAT TO DO!
JUST MAKE HER WEAR THE CLOAK, OISIN!
BRIGHT RED AGAINST SNOW MAKES AN IDEAL TARGET!
OISIN, KEEP DINNER HOT FOR US. WE'RE GOING FOR A RIDE.
THE SNOW MAKES THE LAND LOOK QUITE BEAUTIFUL.
OF COURSE, MA'AM. AND PLEASE, PUT YOUR CLOAK ON. IT'S BITTERLY COLD OUT THERE!
REALLY? THAT BRIGHT THING? I'LL SCARE OFF ALL THE ANIMALS!
I HEAR THAT RED IS HUGH DE LACY'S FAVOURITE COLOUR...
OH, I SEE NOW! GIVE ME THAT, THEN!
I'LL BE BACK FOR DINNER!
SLAM
NO, YOU WON'T.

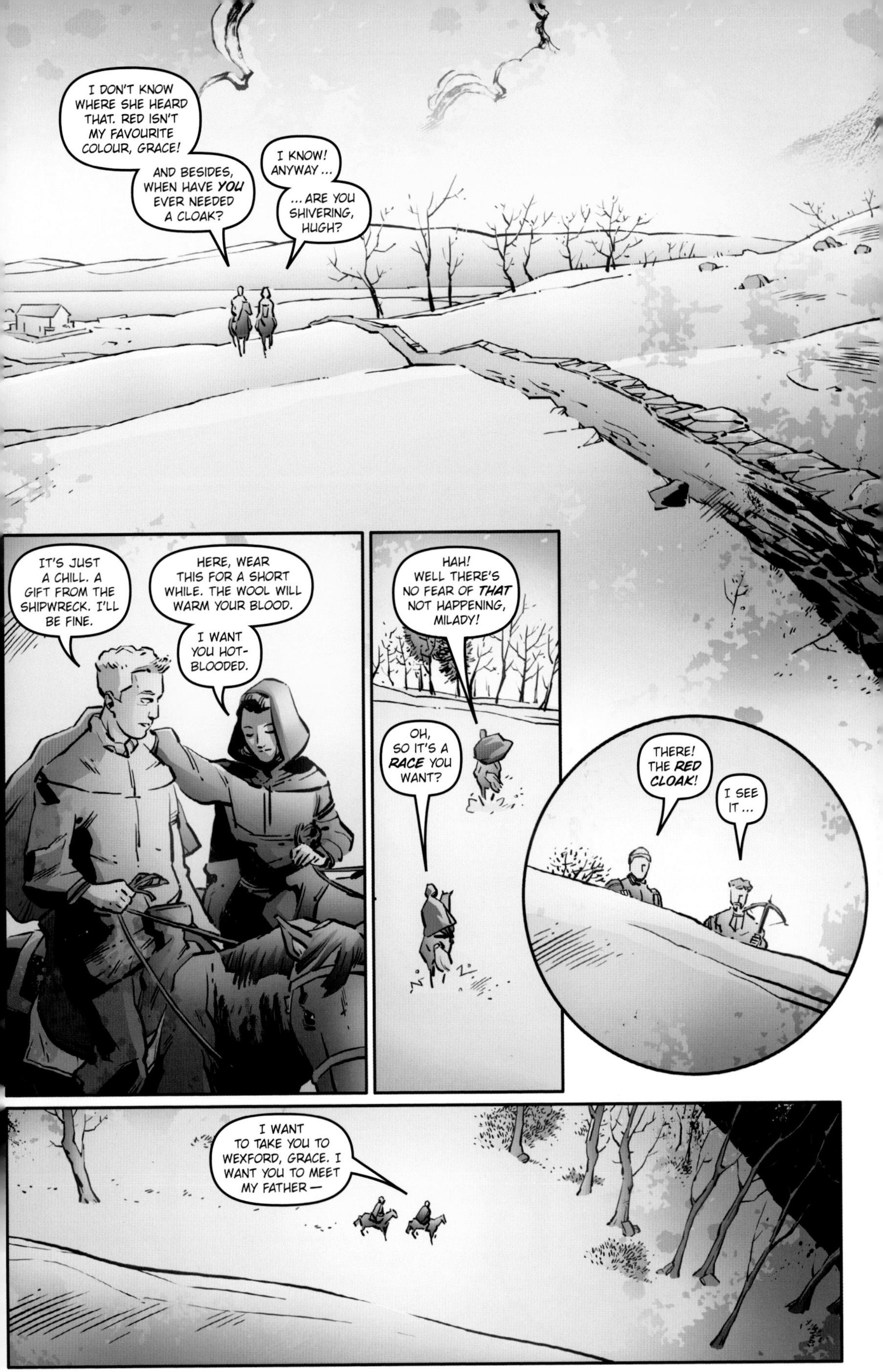
I DON'T KNOW WHERE SHE HEARD THAT. RED ISN'T MY FAVOURITE COLOUR, GRACE!
AND BESIDES, WHEN HAVE *YOU* EVER NEEDED A CLOAK?
I KNOW! ANYWAY ...
... ARE YOU SHIVERING, HUGH?
IT'S JUST A CHILL. A GIFT FROM THE SHIPWRECK. I'LL BE FINE.
HERE, WEAR THIS FOR A SHORT WHILE. THE WOOL WILL WARM YOUR BLOOD.
I WANT YOU HOT-BLOODED.
HAH! WELL THERE'S NO FEAR OF *THAT* NOT HAPPENING, MILADY!
OH, SO IT'S A *RACE* YOU WANT?
THERE! THE *RED CLOAK*!
I SEE IT ...
I WANT TO TAKE YOU TO WEXFORD, GRACE. I WANT YOU TO MEET MY FATHER —

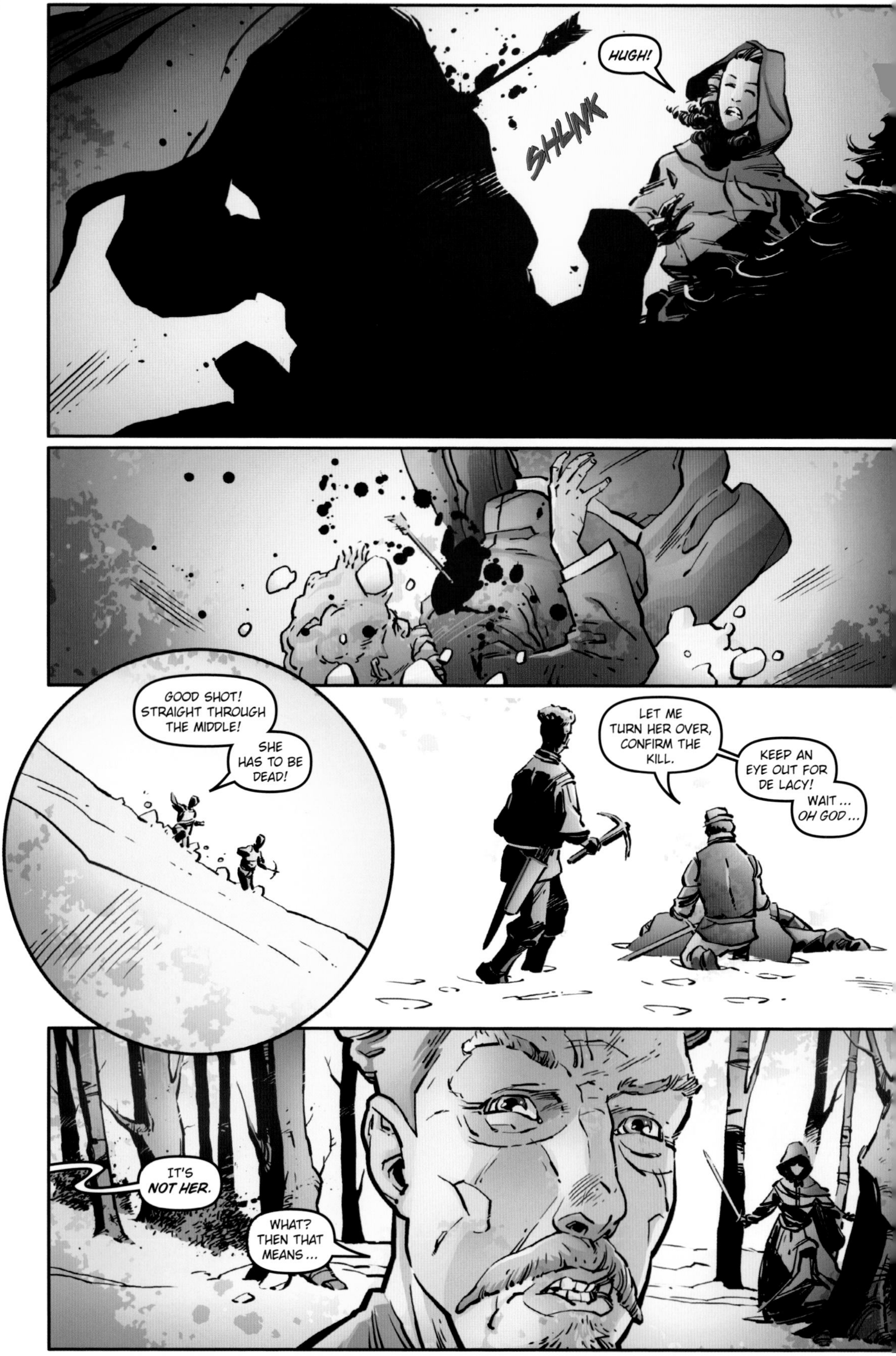
HUGH!
SHLINK
GOOD SHOT! STRAIGHT THROUGH THE MIDDLE!
SHE HAS TO BE DEAD!
LET ME TURN HER OVER, CONFIRM THE KILL.
KEEP AN EYE OUT FOR DE LACY!
WAIT ... OH GOD ...
IT'S NOT HER.
WHAT? THEN THAT MEANS ...

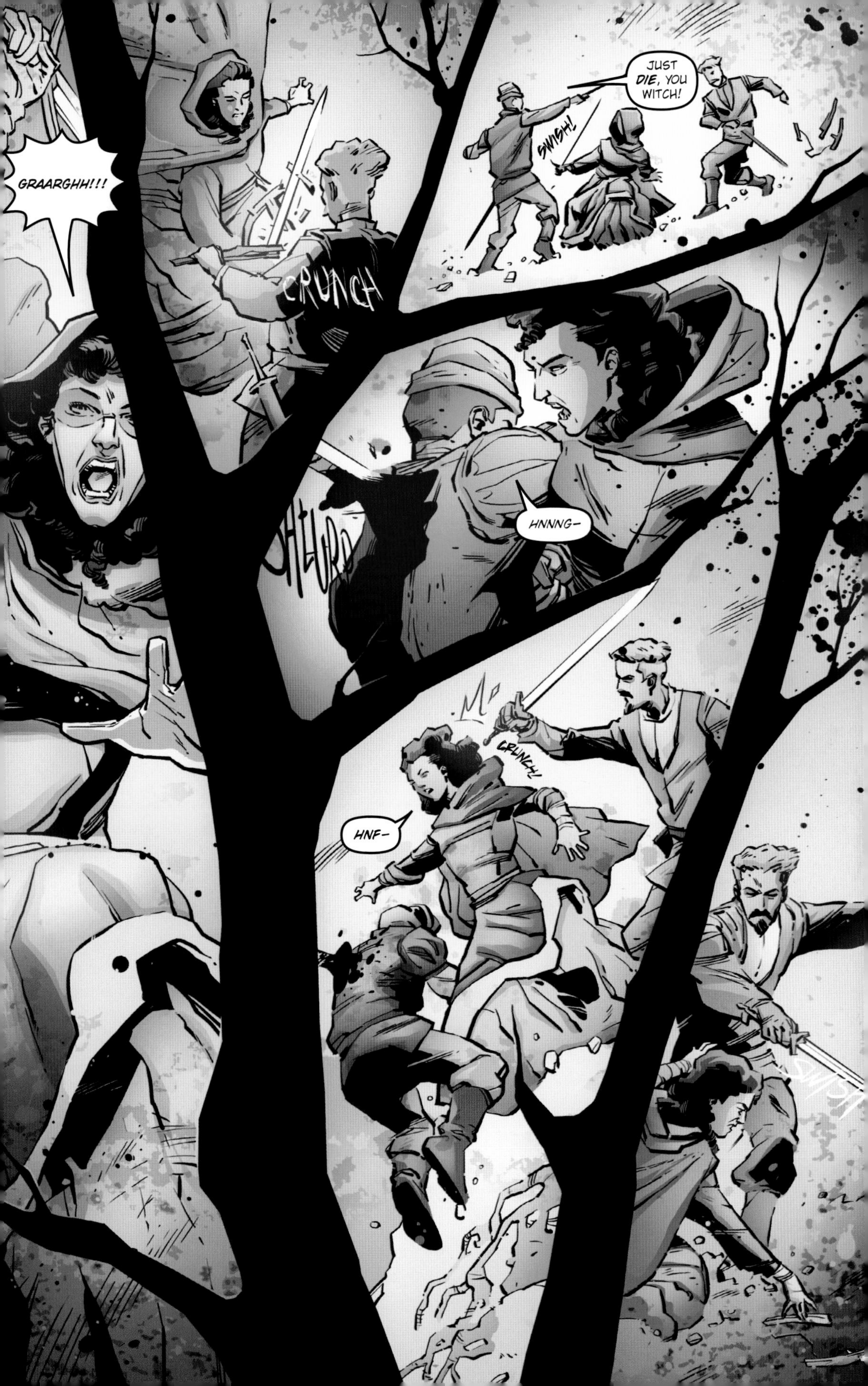
GRAARGHH!!!
CRUNCH
JUST DIE, YOU WITCH!
SWISH!
HNNNG-
SHLURP
CRUNCH!
HNF-

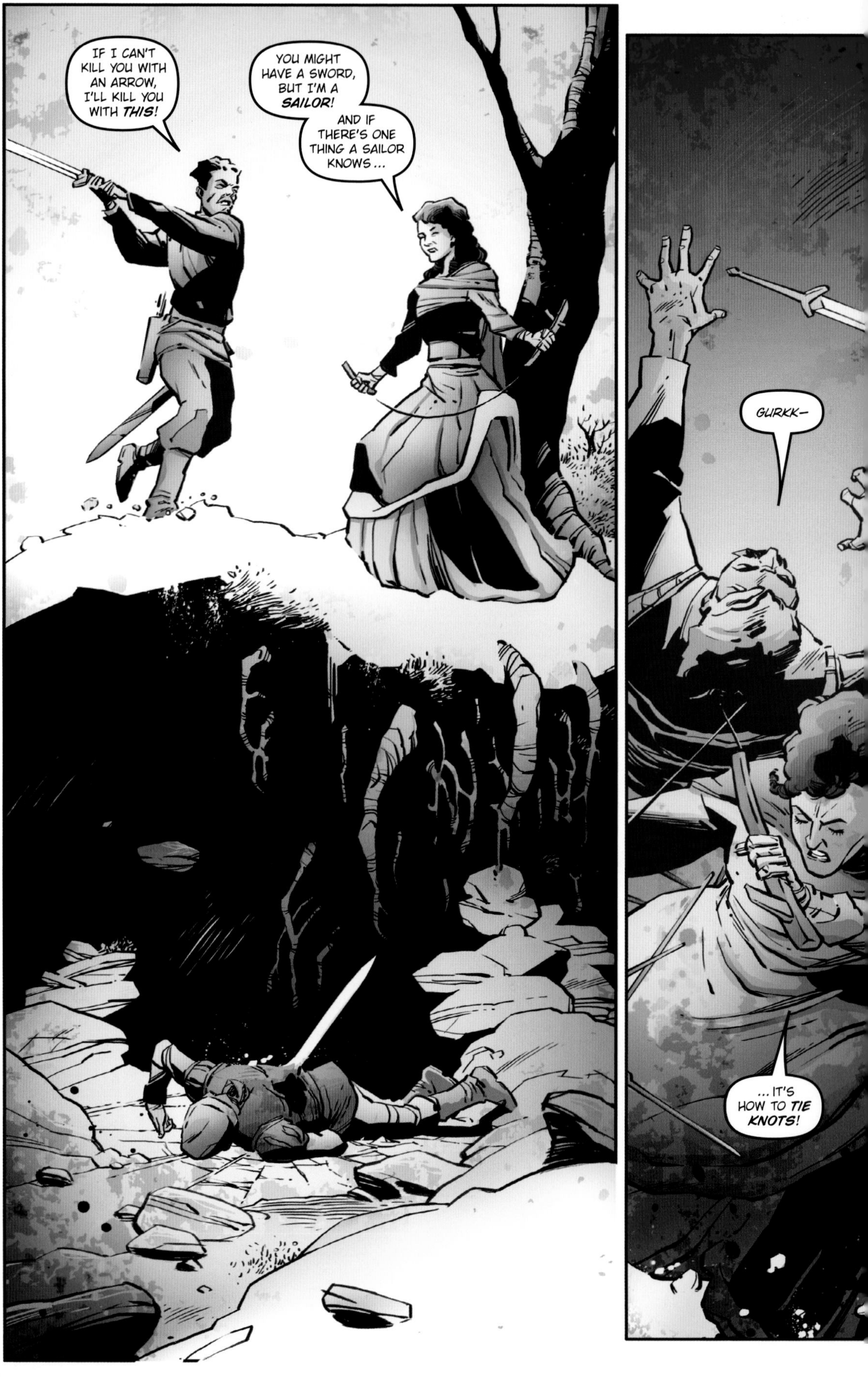
IF I CAN'T KILL YOU WITH AN ARROW, I'LL KILL YOU WITH THIS!
YOU MIGHT HAVE A SWORD, BUT I'M A SAILOR!
AND IF THERE'S ONE THING A SAILOR KNOWS...
GURKK–
...IT'S HOW TO TIE KNOTS!

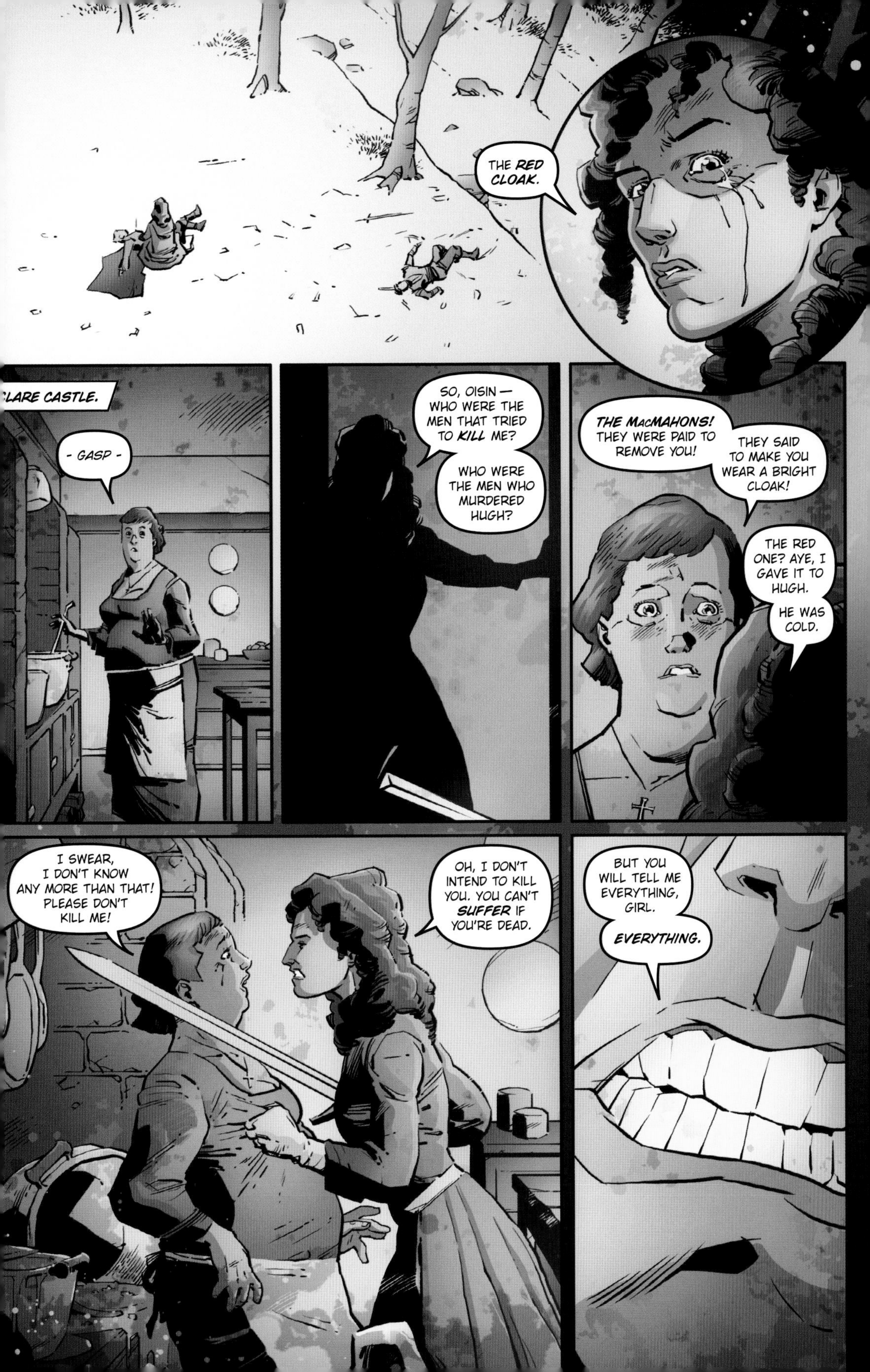
THE RED CLOAK.
CLARE CASTLE.
- GASP -
SO, OISIN — WHO WERE THE MEN THAT TRIED TO KILL ME?
WHO WERE THE MEN WHO MURDERED HUGH?
THE MacMAHONS! THEY WERE PAID TO REMOVE YOU!
THEY SAID TO MAKE YOU WEAR A BRIGHT CLOAK!
THE RED ONE? AYE, I GAVE IT TO HUGH.
HE WAS COLD.
I SWEAR, I DON'T KNOW ANY MORE THAN THAT! PLEASE DON'T KILL ME!
OH, I DON'T INTEND TO KILL YOU. YOU CAN'T SUFFER IF YOU'RE DEAD.
BUT YOU WILL TELL ME EVERYTHING, GIRL.
EVERYTHING.

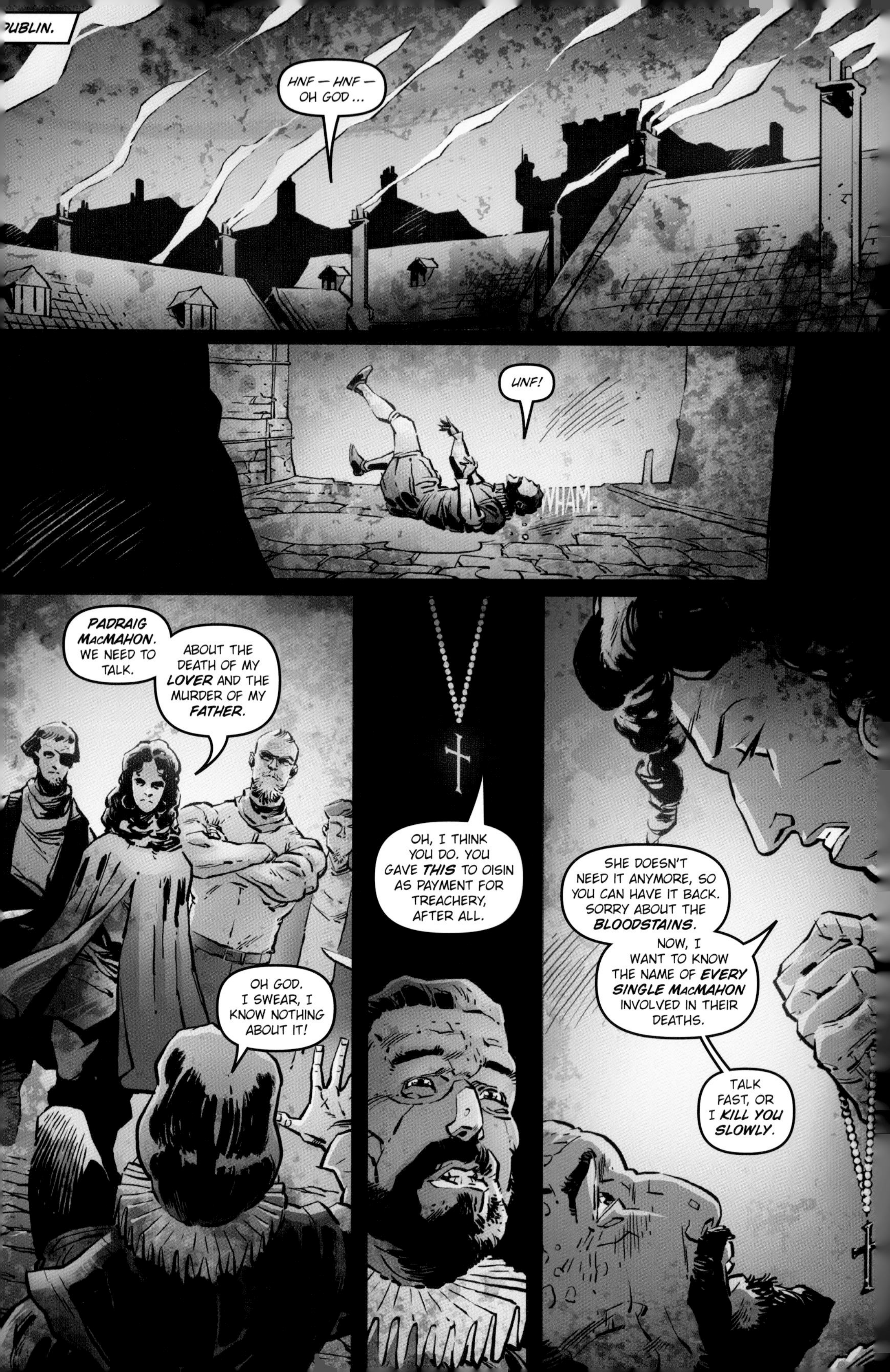

DUBLIN.
HNF — HNF — OH GOD ...
UNF!
WHAM
PADRAIG MacMAHON. WE NEED TO TALK.
ABOUT THE DEATH OF MY LOVER AND THE MURDER OF MY FATHER.
OH GOD. I SWEAR, I KNOW NOTHING ABOUT IT!
OH, I THINK YOU DO. YOU GAVE THIS TO OISIN AS PAYMENT FOR TREACHERY, AFTER ALL.
SHE DOESN'T NEED IT ANYMORE, SO YOU CAN HAVE IT BACK. SORRY ABOUT THE BLOODSTAINS.
NOW, I WANT TO KNOW THE NAME OF EVERY SINGLE MacMAHON INVOLVED IN THEIR DEATHS.
TALK FAST, OR I KILL YOU SLOWLY.

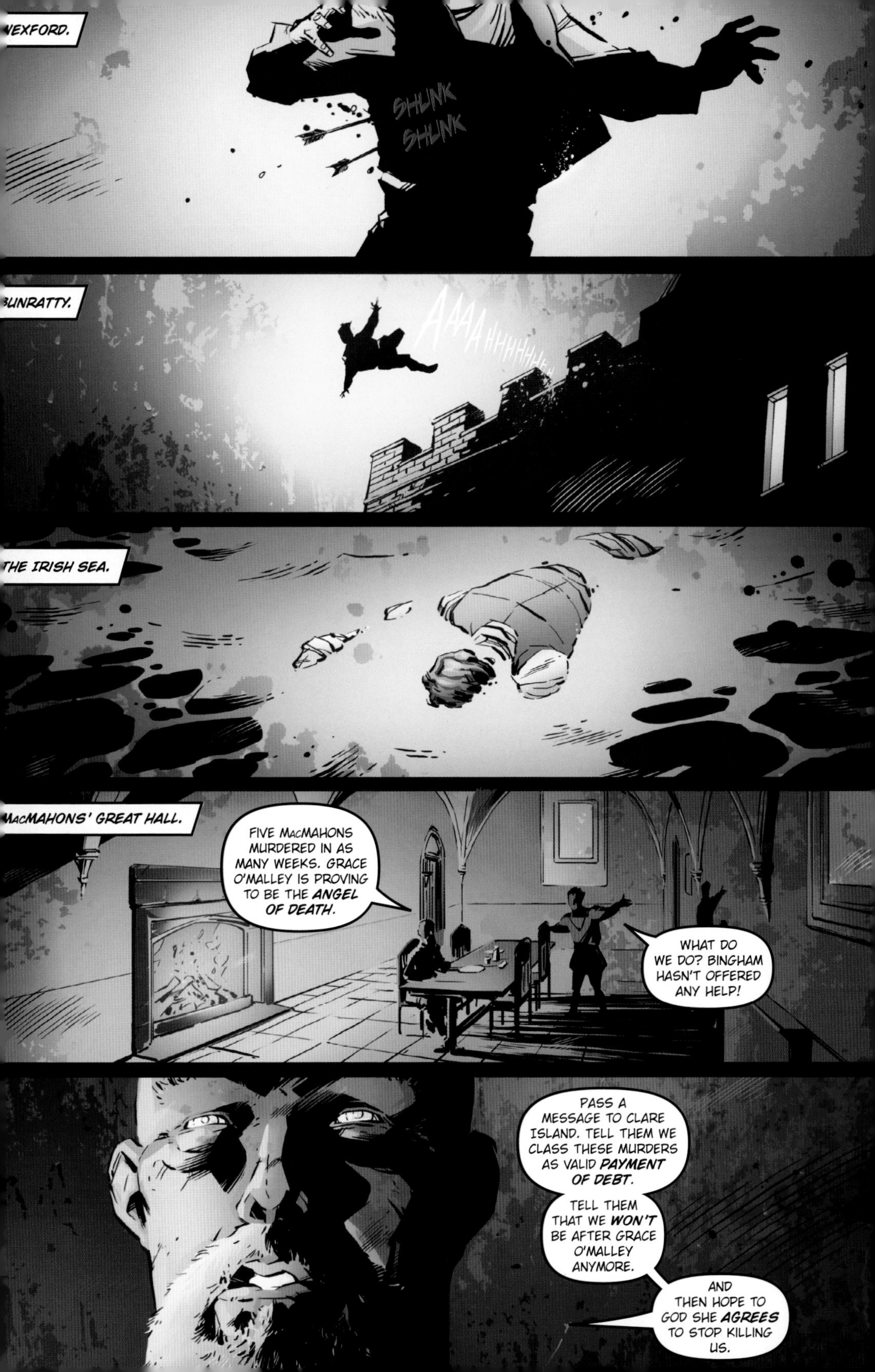
WEXFORD.
SHUNK SHUNK
BUNRATTY.
AAAAHHHHHHHH
THE IRISH SEA.
MacMAHONS' GREAT HALL.
FIVE MacMAHONS MURDERED IN AS MANY WEEKS. GRACE O'MALLEY IS PROVING TO BE THE ANGEL OF DEATH.
WHAT DO WE DO? BINGHAM HASN'T OFFERED ANY HELP!
PASS A MESSAGE TO CLARE ISLAND. TELL THEM WE CLASS THESE MURDERS AS VALID PAYMENT OF DEBT.
TELL THEM THAT WE WON'T BE AFTER GRACE O'MALLEY ANYMORE.
AND THEN HOPE TO GOD SHE AGREES TO STOP KILLING US.

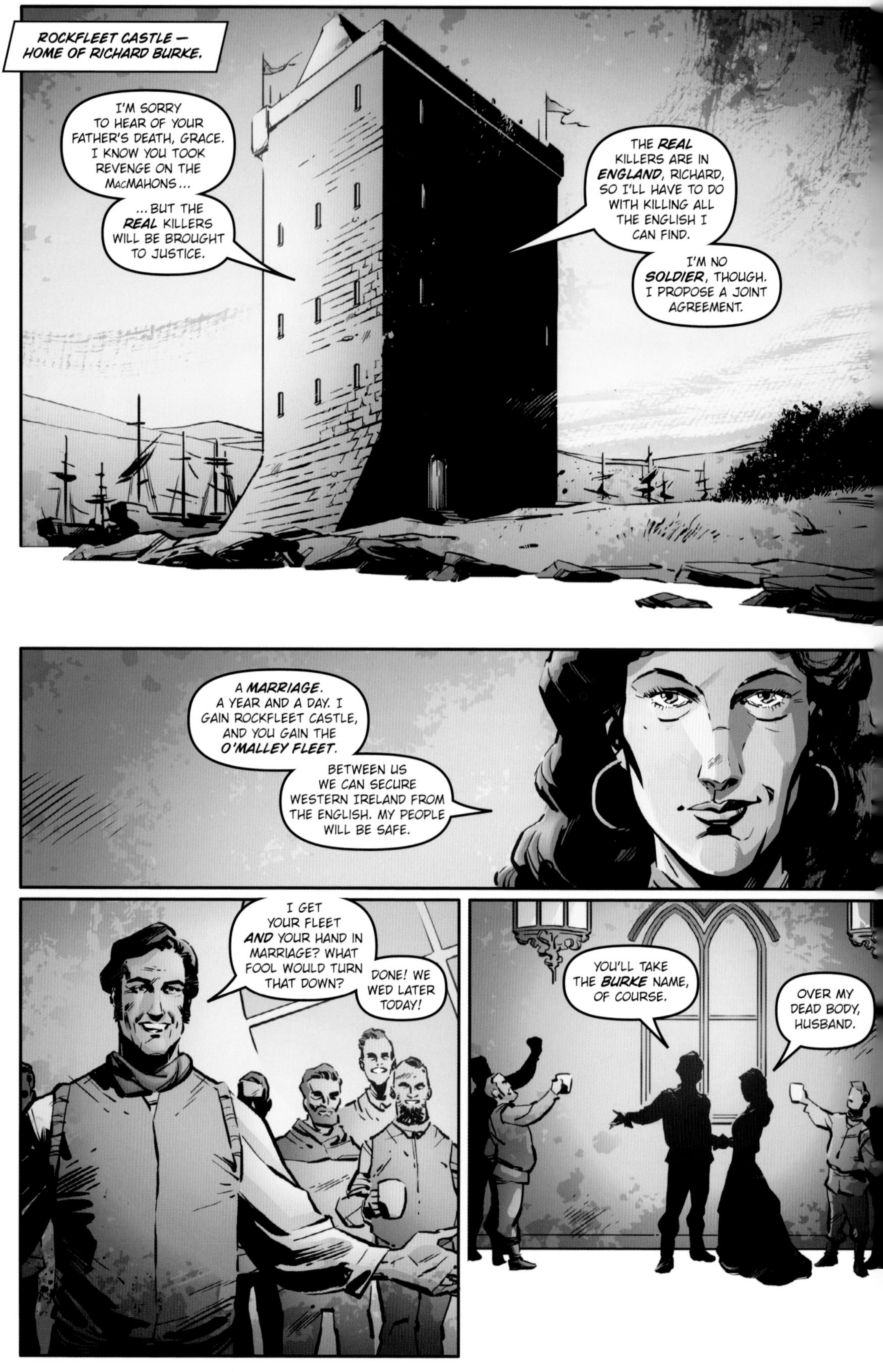
ROCKFLEET CASTLE — HOME OF RICHARD BURKE.
I'M SORRY TO HEAR OF YOUR FATHER'S DEATH, GRACE. I KNOW YOU TOOK REVENGE ON THE MacMAHONS...
...BUT THE REAL KILLERS WILL BE BROUGHT TO JUSTICE.
THE REAL KILLERS ARE IN ENGLAND, RICHARD, SO I'LL HAVE TO DO WITH KILLING ALL THE ENGLISH I CAN FIND.
I'M NO SOLDIER, THOUGH. I PROPOSE A JOINT AGREEMENT.
A MARRIAGE. A YEAR AND A DAY. I GAIN ROCKFLEET CASTLE, AND YOU GAIN THE O'MALLEY FLEET.
BETWEEN US WE CAN SECURE WESTERN IRELAND FROM THE ENGLISH. MY PEOPLE WILL BE SAFE.
I GET YOUR FLEET AND YOUR HAND IN MARRIAGE? WHAT FOOL WOULD TURN THAT DOWN?
DONE! WE WED LATER TODAY!
YOU'LL TAKE THE BURKE NAME, OF COURSE.
OVER MY DEAD BODY, HUSBAND.

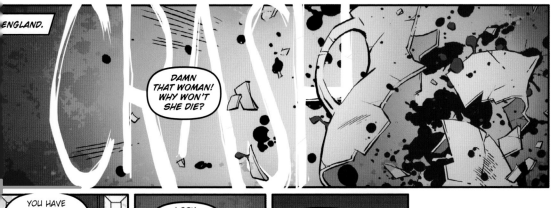

CRASH!

DAMN THAT WOMAN! WHY WON'T SHE DIE?

YOU HAVE TO GIVE HER CREDIT. SHE'S DONE WONDERFULLY SINCE YOU TRIED TO KILL HER. THE *FIRST* TIME, THAT IS.

AND NOW SHE KNOWS YOU KILLED HER FATHER...

IT WAS SUPPOSED TO *BREAK HER!* NOT *INSPIRE HER!*

AND NOW SHE'S ALLIED WITH *BURKE!* PREGNANT WITH HIS CHILD AND *STILL* PIRATING OUR SHIPS!

LOOK, RICHARD OF THE IRONS IS *NOTORIOUS* FOR HIS AFFAIRS. AFTER A YEAR AND A DAY THEY'LL SPLIT...

YOU THINK SHE *CARES?* THIS MARRIAGE IS A SHAM! SHE GIVES HIM A CHILD, HE GIVES HER WESTERN IRELAND!

THEY'LL SPLIT AT A YEAR AND A DAY, PROBABLY FOR THE REASONS YOU SAY...

... BUT IT'LL BE A *PLAY,* PERFORMED FOR AN AUDIENCE.

WE'LL THINK THEM FRACTURED, AND THAT'S WHEN THEY'LL ATTACK *HARDER.*

WE NEED TO CHANGE OUR ATTACK. WE NEED TO STOP FILLING IRELAND WITH *ENGLISH LORDS*...

... AND CONVERT THE *IRISH* CHIEFTAINS TO OUR SIDE INSTEAD.

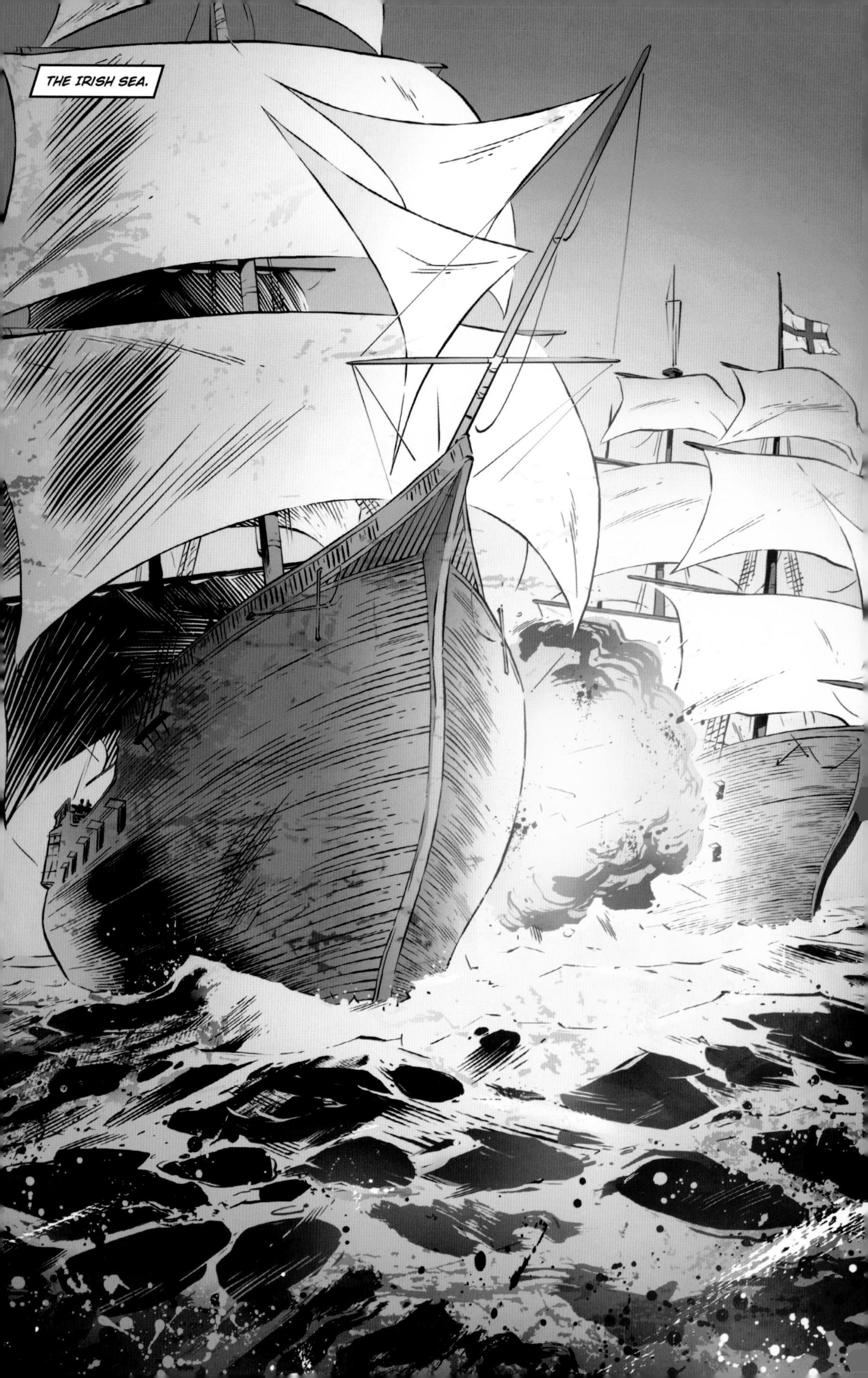
THE IRISH SEA.

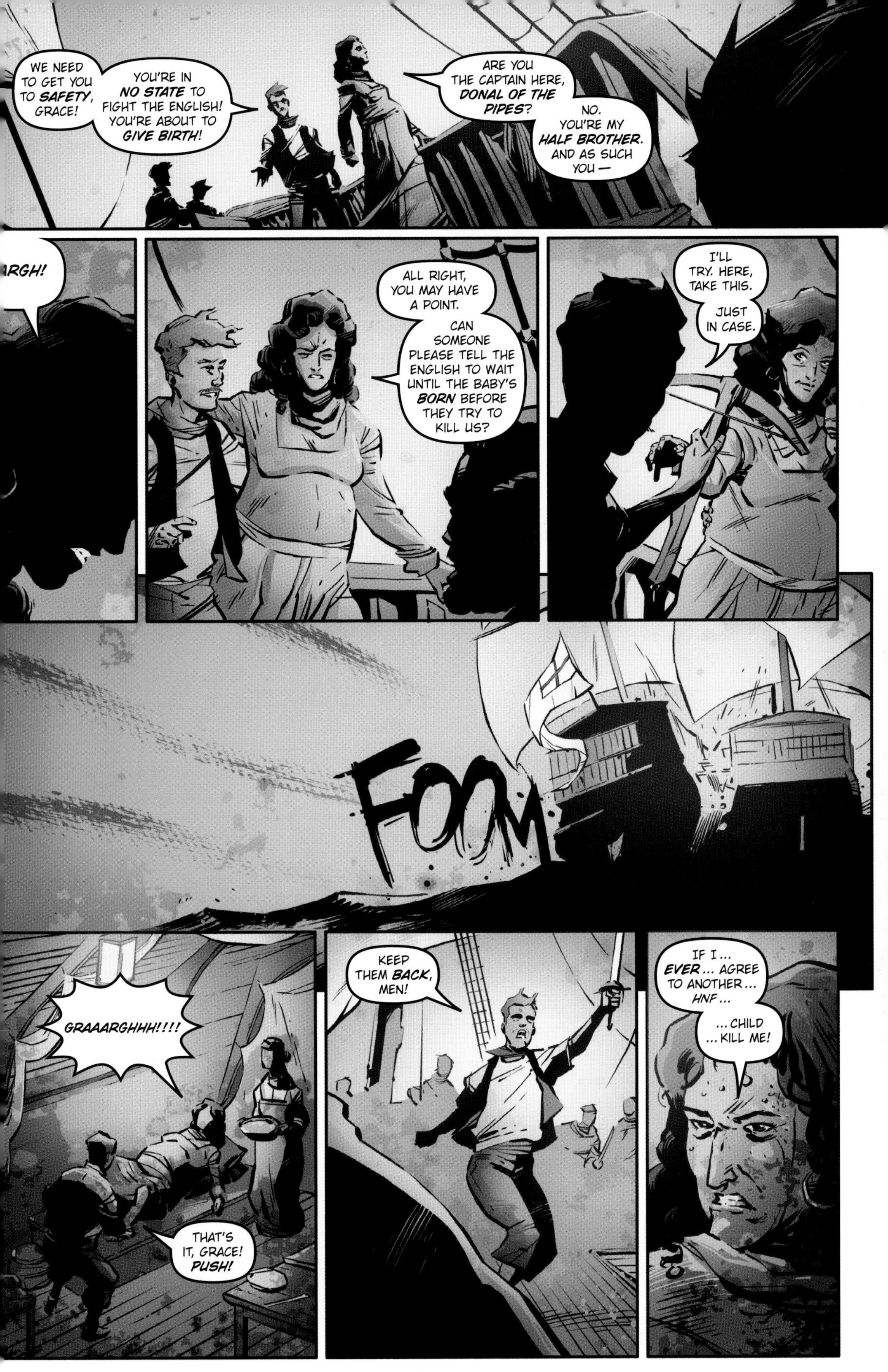
WE NEED TO GET YOU TO SAFETY, GRACE!
YOU'RE IN NO STATE TO FIGHT THE ENGLISH! YOU'RE ABOUT TO GIVE BIRTH!
ARE YOU THE CAPTAIN HERE, DONAL OF THE PIPES?
NO. YOU'RE MY HALF BROTHER. AND AS SUCH YOU —
RGH!
ALL RIGHT, YOU MAY HAVE A POINT.
CAN SOMEONE PLEASE TELL THE ENGLISH TO WAIT UNTIL THE BABY'S BORN BEFORE THEY TRY TO KILL US?
I'LL TRY. HERE, TAKE THIS.
JUST IN CASE.
FOOM
GRAAARGHHH!!!!
THAT'S IT, GRACE! PUSH!
KEEP THEM BACK, MEN!
IF I... EVER... AGREE TO ANOTHER... HNF...
... CHILD ... KILL ME!

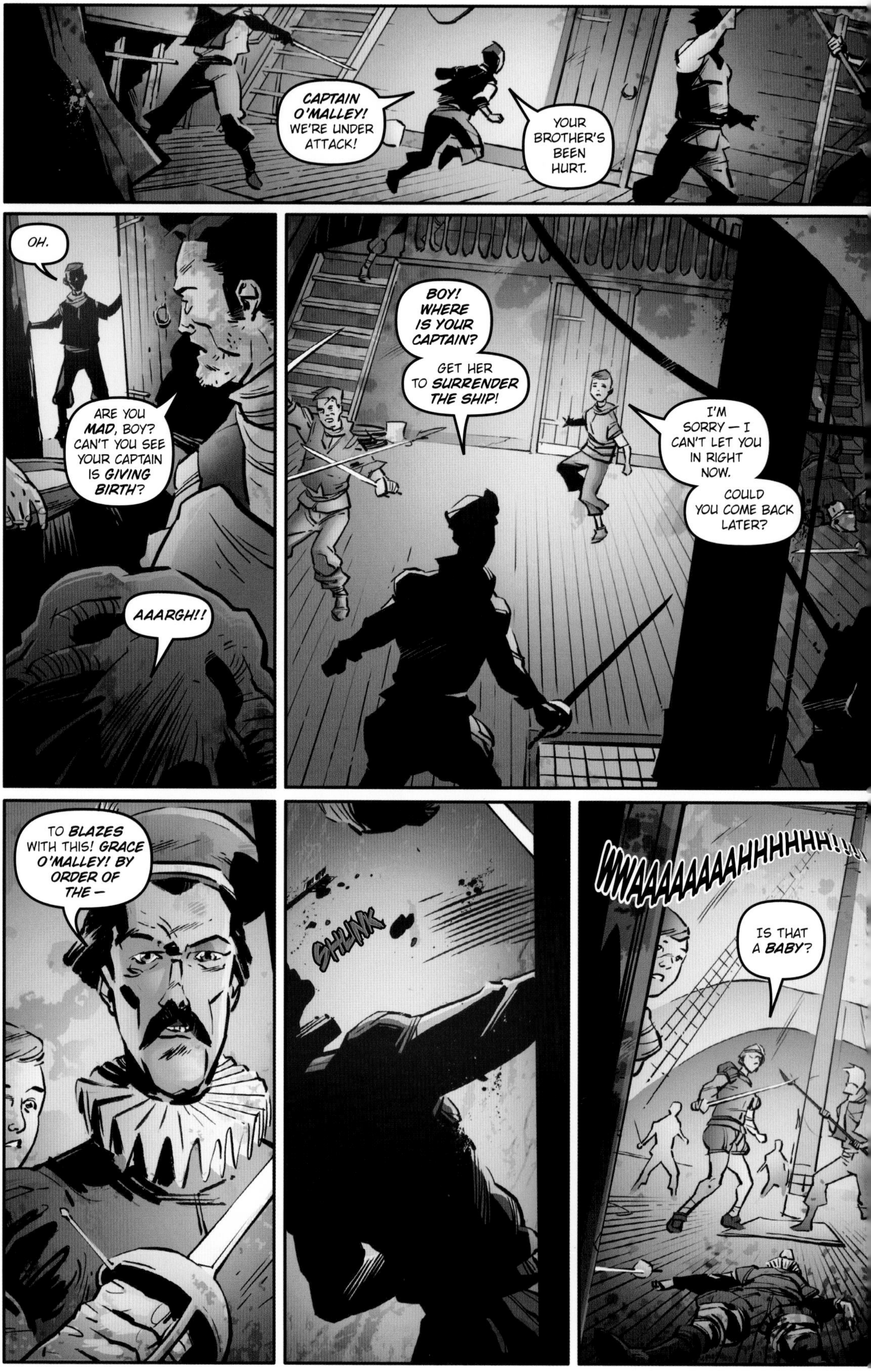

CAPTAIN O'MALLEY! WE'RE UNDER ATTACK!
YOUR BROTHER'S BEEN HURT.
OH.
ARE YOU MAD, BOY? CAN'T YOU SEE YOUR CAPTAIN IS GIVING BIRTH?
AAARGH!!
BOY! WHERE IS YOUR CAPTAIN?
GET HER TO SURRENDER THE SHIP!
I'M SORRY — I CAN'T LET YOU IN RIGHT NOW.
COULD YOU COME BACK LATER?
TO BLAZES WITH THIS! GRACE O'MALLEY! BY ORDER OF THE —
SHUNK
WWAAAAAAAAHHHHHH!!!
IS THAT A BABY?

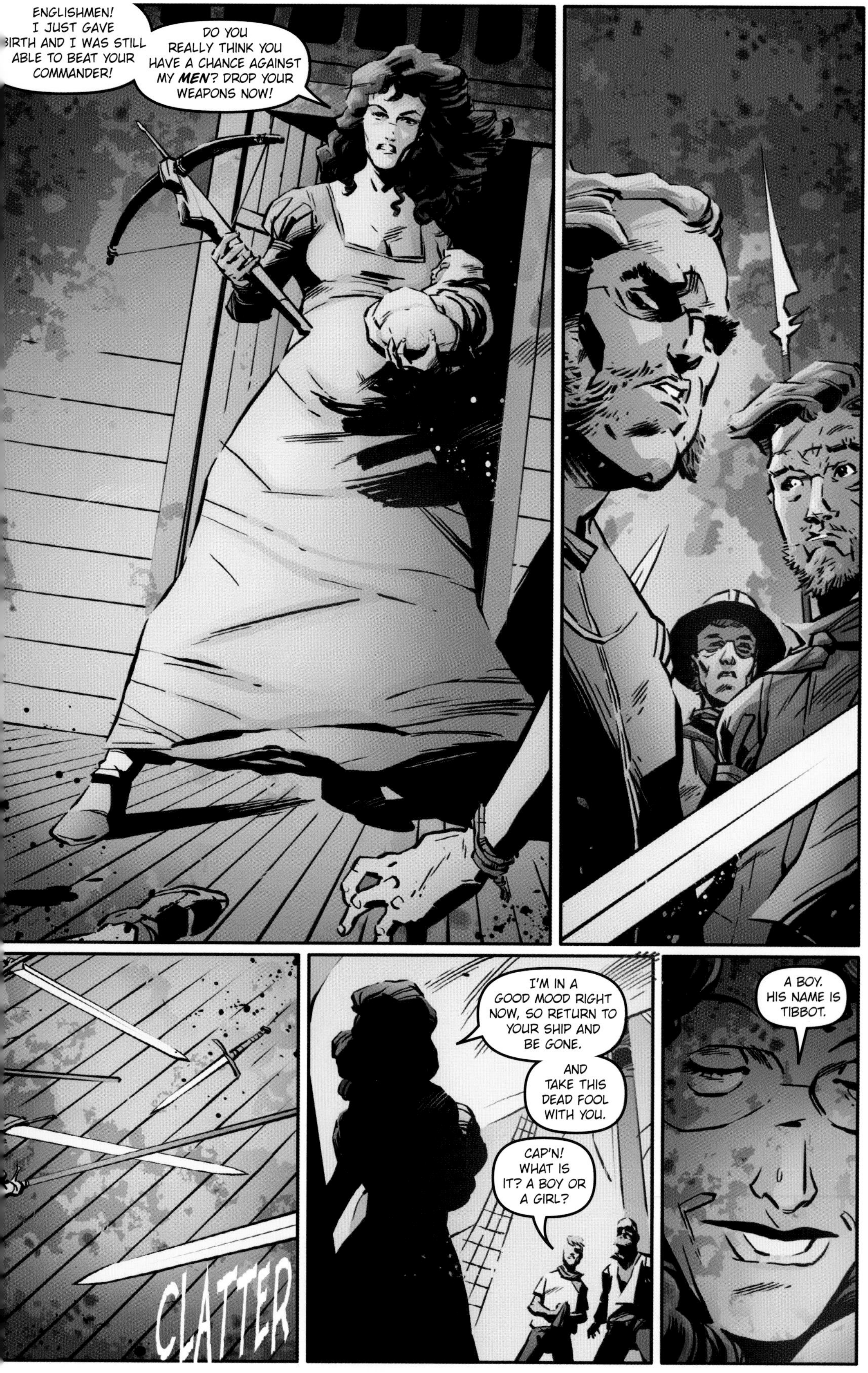

ENGLISHMEN! I JUST GAVE BIRTH AND I WAS STILL ABLE TO BEAT YOUR COMMANDER!
DO YOU REALLY THINK YOU HAVE A CHANCE AGAINST MY **MEN**? DROP YOUR WEAPONS NOW!
CLATTER
I'M IN A GOOD MOOD RIGHT NOW, SO RETURN TO YOUR SHIP AND BE GONE.
AND TAKE THIS DEAD FOOL WITH YOU.
CAP'N! WHAT IS IT? A BOY OR A GIRL?
A BOY. HIS NAME IS TIBBOT.

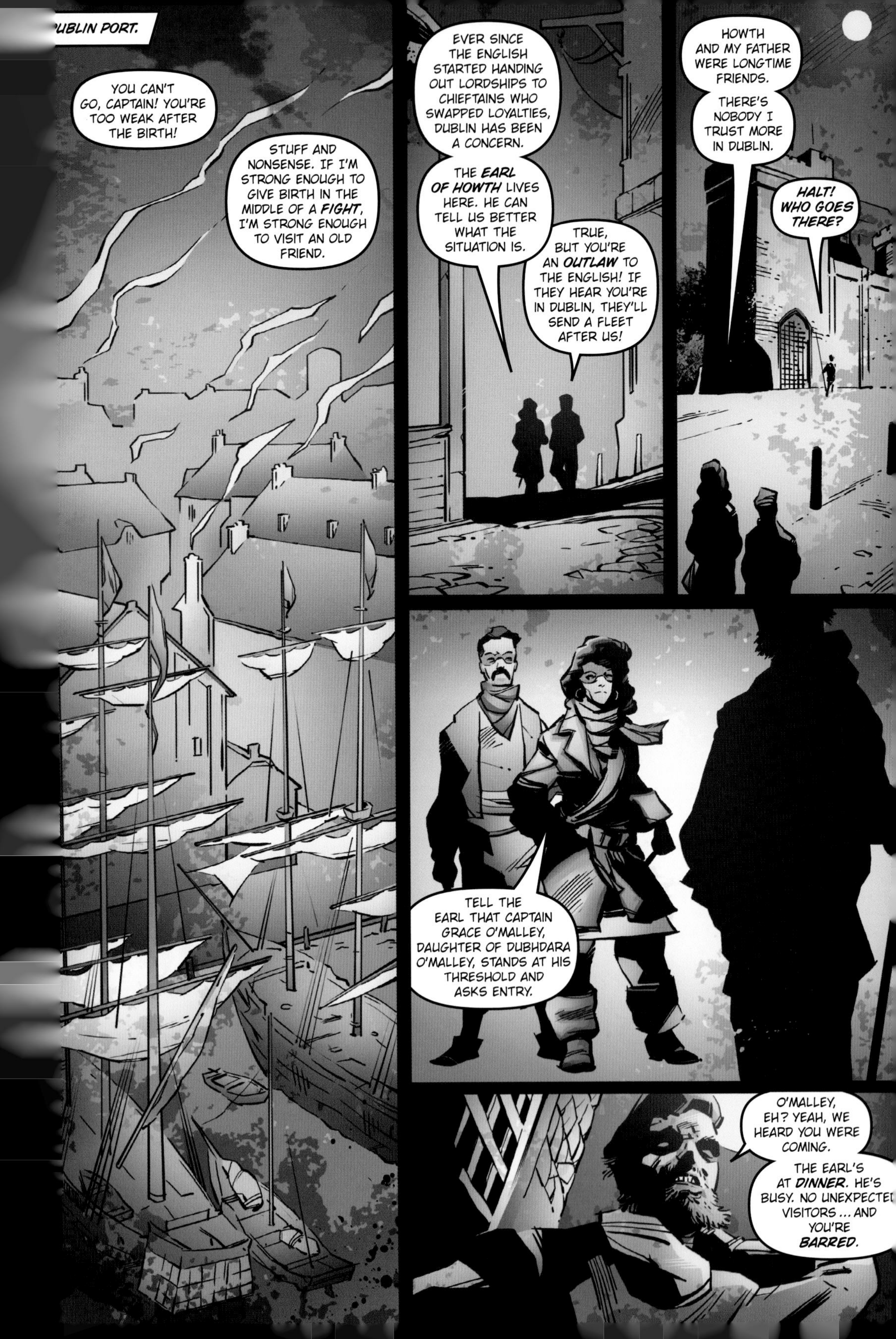
DUBLIN PORT.
YOU CAN'T GO, CAPTAIN! YOU'RE TOO WEAK AFTER THE BIRTH!
STUFF AND NONSENSE. IF I'M STRONG ENOUGH TO GIVE BIRTH IN THE MIDDLE OF A FIGHT, I'M STRONG ENOUGH TO VISIT AN OLD FRIEND.
EVER SINCE THE ENGLISH STARTED HANDING OUT LORDSHIPS TO CHIEFTAINS WHO SWAPPED LOYALTIES, DUBLIN HAS BEEN A CONCERN.
THE EARL OF HOWTH LIVES HERE. HE CAN TELL US BETTER WHAT THE SITUATION IS.
TRUE, BUT YOU'RE AN OUTLAW TO THE ENGLISH! IF THEY HEAR YOU'RE IN DUBLIN, THEY'LL SEND A FLEET AFTER US!
HOWTH AND MY FATHER WERE LONGTIME FRIENDS.
THERE'S NOBODY I TRUST MORE IN DUBLIN.
HALT! WHO GOES THERE?
TELL THE EARL THAT CAPTAIN GRACE O'MALLEY, DAUGHTER OF DUBHDARA O'MALLEY, STANDS AT HIS THRESHOLD AND ASKS ENTRY.
O'MALLEY, EH? YEAH, WE HEARD YOU WERE COMING.
THE EARL'S AT DINNER. HE'S BUSY. NO UNEXPECTED VISITORS ... AND YOU'RE BARRED.

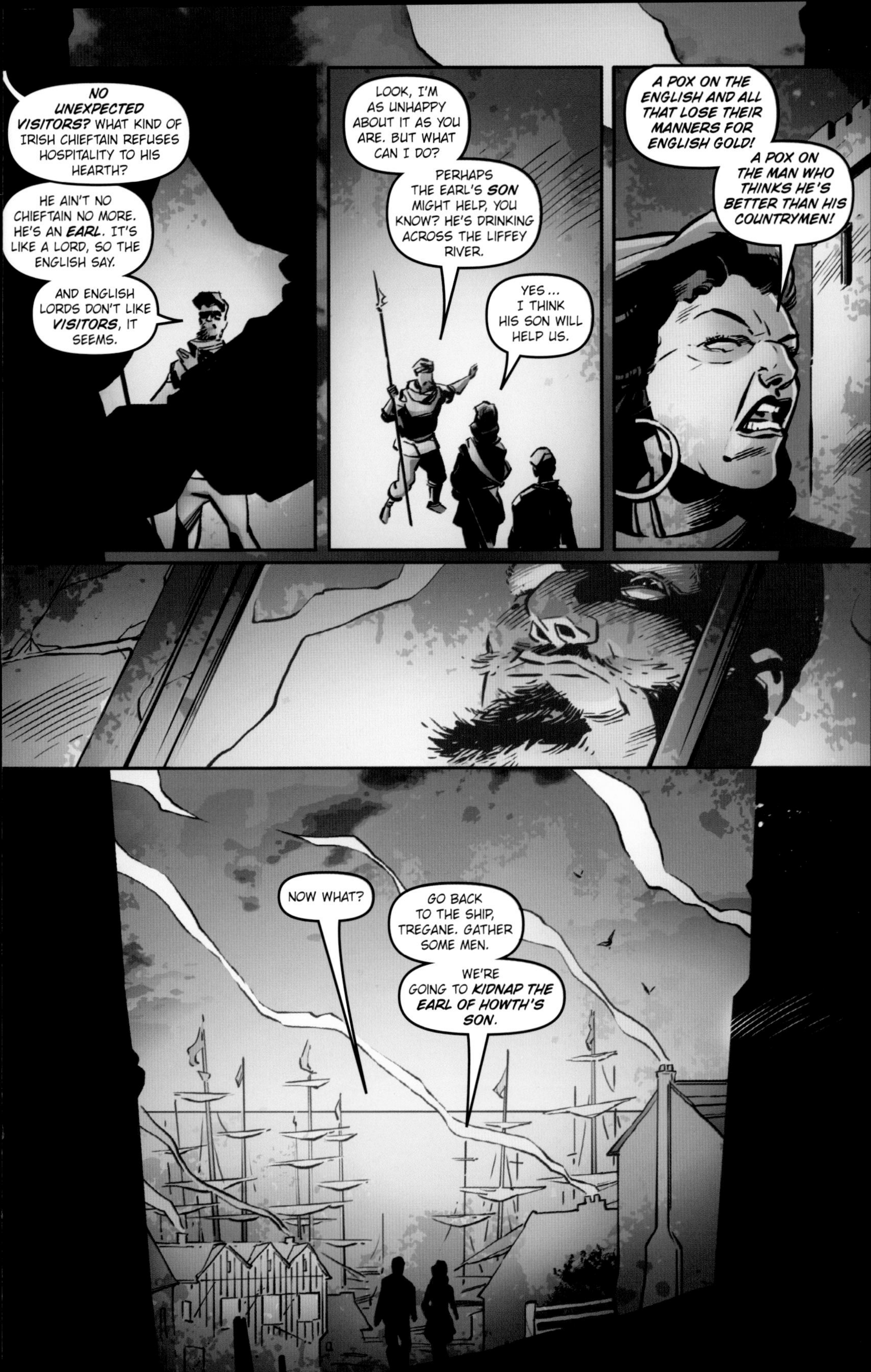
NO UNEXPECTED VISITORS? WHAT KIND OF IRISH CHIEFTAIN REFUSES HOSPITALITY TO HIS HEARTH?
HE AIN'T NO CHIEFTAIN NO MORE. HE'S AN EARL. IT'S LIKE A LORD, SO THE ENGLISH SAY.
AND ENGLISH LORDS DON'T LIKE VISITORS, IT SEEMS.
LOOK, I'M AS UNHAPPY ABOUT IT AS YOU ARE. BUT WHAT CAN I DO?
PERHAPS THE EARL'S SON MIGHT HELP, YOU KNOW? HE'S DRINKING ACROSS THE LIFFEY RIVER.
YES ... I THINK HIS SON WILL HELP US.
A POX ON THE ENGLISH AND ALL THAT LOSE THEIR MANNERS FOR ENGLISH GOLD!
A POX ON THE MAN WHO THINKS HE'S BETTER THAN HIS COUNTRYMEN!
NOW WHAT?
GO BACK TO THE SHIP, TREGANE. GATHER SOME MEN.
WE'RE GOING TO KIDNAP THE EARL OF HOWTH'S SON.

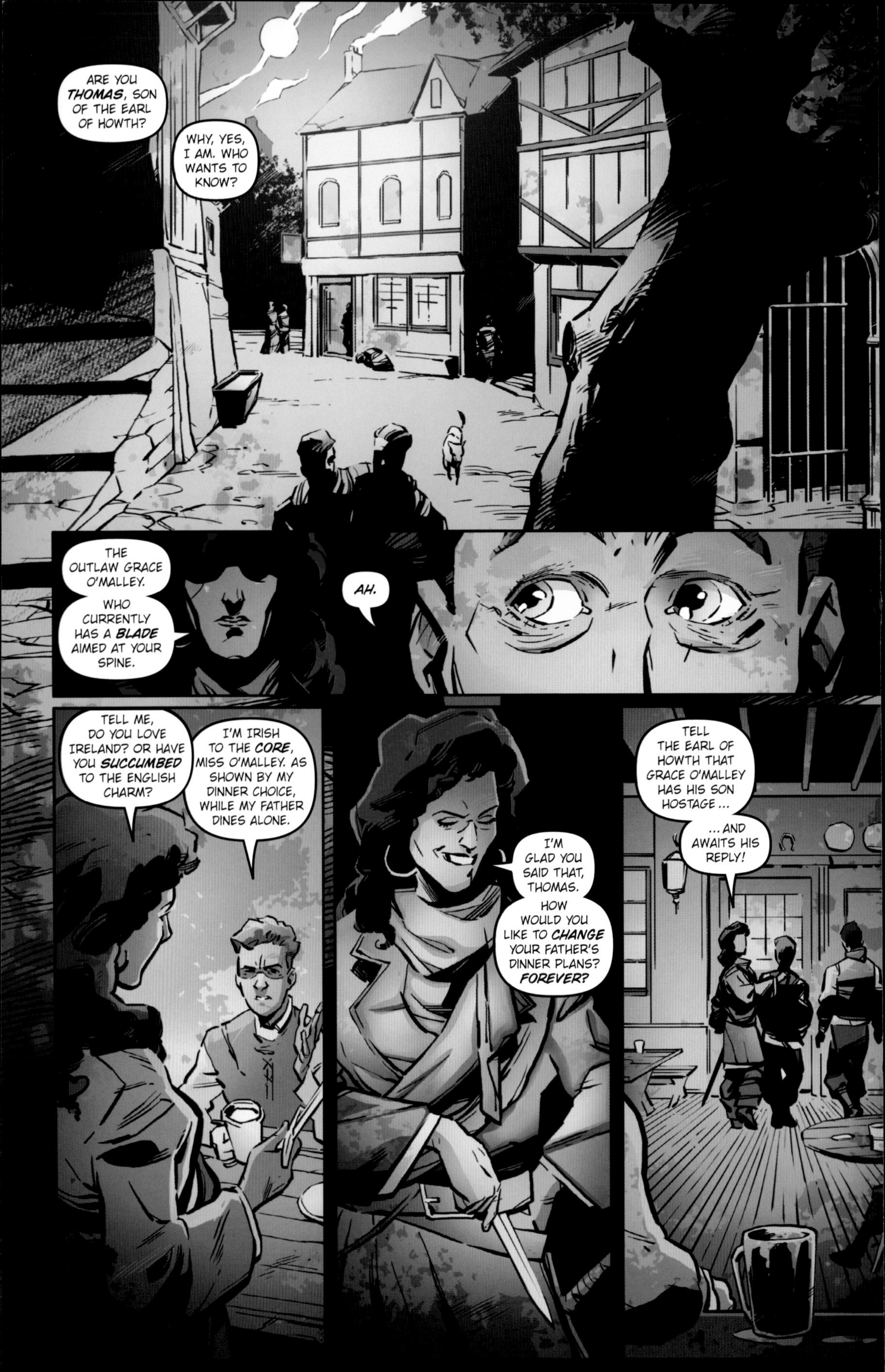

ARE YOU THOMAS, SON OF THE EARL OF HOWTH?
WHY, YES, I AM. WHO WANTS TO KNOW?
THE OUTLAW GRACE O'MALLEY.
WHO CURRENTLY HAS A BLADE AIMED AT YOUR SPINE.
AH.
TELL ME, DO YOU LOVE IRELAND? OR HAVE YOU SUCCUMBED TO THE ENGLISH CHARM?
I'M IRISH TO THE CORE, MISS O'MALLEY. AS SHOWN BY MY DINNER CHOICE, WHILE MY FATHER DINES ALONE.
I'M GLAD YOU SAID THAT, THOMAS.
HOW WOULD YOU LIKE TO CHANGE YOUR FATHER'S DINNER PLANS? FOREVER?
TELL THE EARL OF HOWTH THAT GRACE O'MALLEY HAS HIS SON HOSTAGE ...
... AND AWAITS HIS REPLY!

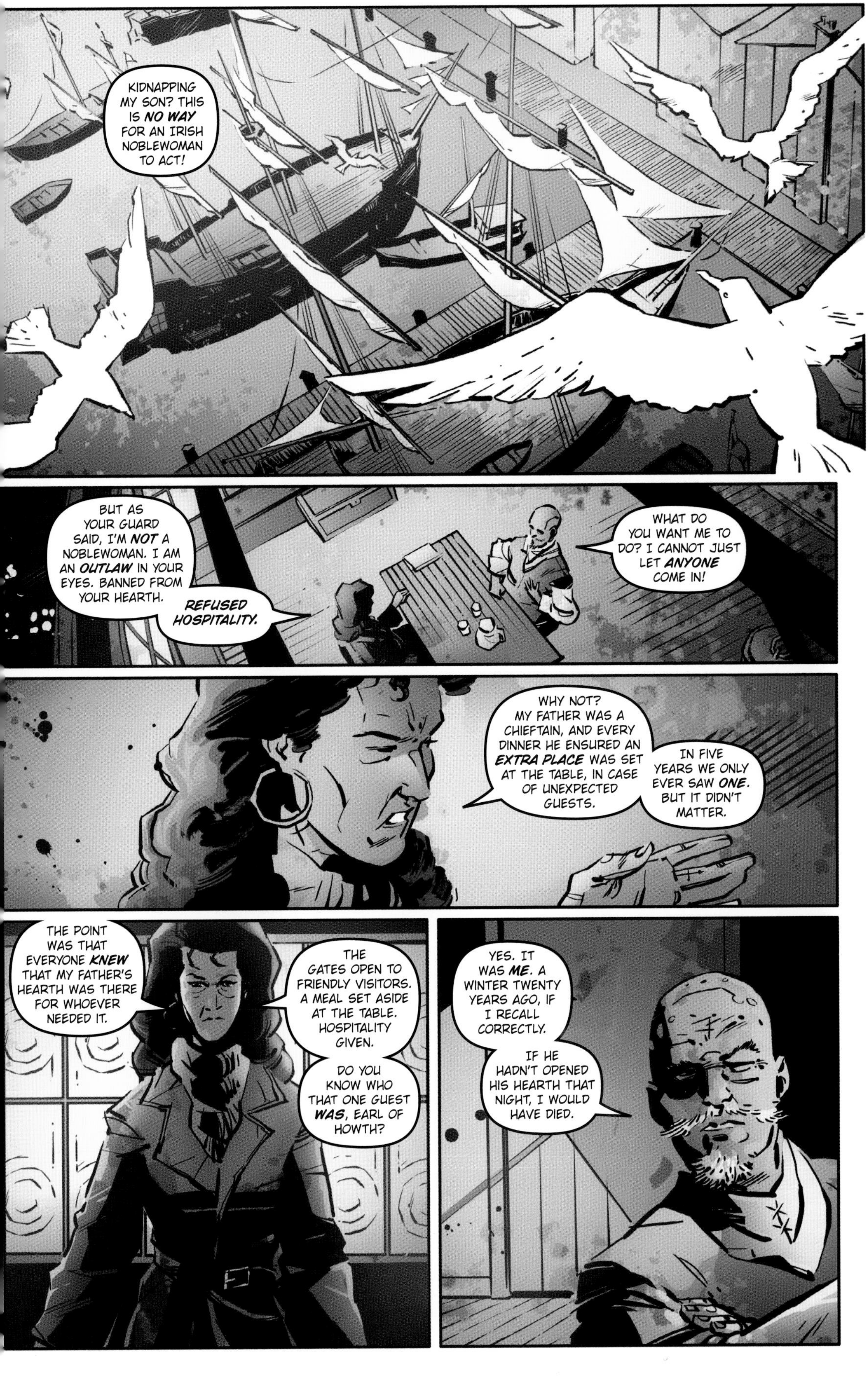

KIDNAPPING MY SON? THIS IS NO WAY FOR AN IRISH NOBLEWOMAN TO ACT!
BUT AS YOUR GUARD SAID, I'M NOT A NOBLEWOMAN. I AM AN OUTLAW IN YOUR EYES. BANNED FROM YOUR HEARTH.
REFUSED HOSPITALITY.
WHAT DO YOU WANT ME TO DO? I CANNOT JUST LET ANYONE COME IN!
WHY NOT? MY FATHER WAS A CHIEFTAIN, AND EVERY DINNER HE ENSURED AN EXTRA PLACE WAS SET AT THE TABLE, IN CASE OF UNEXPECTED GUESTS.
IN FIVE YEARS WE ONLY EVER SAW ONE. BUT IT DIDN'T MATTER.
THE POINT WAS THAT EVERYONE KNEW THAT MY FATHER'S HEARTH WAS THERE FOR WHOEVER NEEDED IT.
THE GATES OPEN TO FRIENDLY VISITORS. A MEAL SET ASIDE AT THE TABLE. HOSPITALITY GIVEN.
DO YOU KNOW WHO THAT ONE GUEST WAS, EARL OF HOWTH?
YES. IT WAS ME. A WINTER TWENTY YEARS AGO, IF I RECALL CORRECTLY.
IF HE HADN'T OPENED HIS HEARTH THAT NIGHT, I WOULD HAVE DIED.

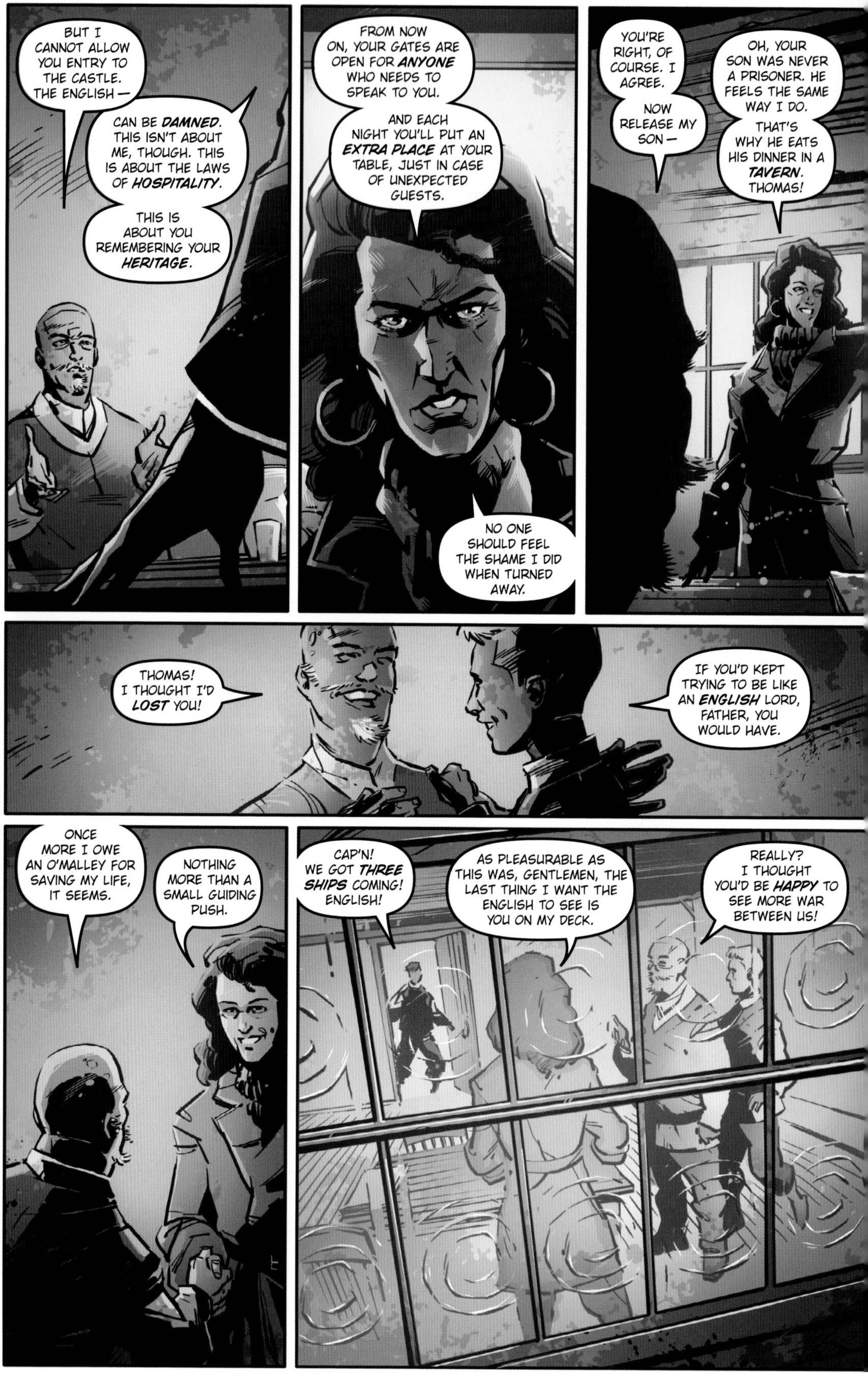
BUT I CANNOT ALLOW YOU ENTRY TO THE CASTLE. THE ENGLISH —
CAN BE DAMNED. THIS ISN'T ABOUT ME, THOUGH. THIS IS ABOUT THE LAWS OF HOSPITALITY.
THIS IS ABOUT YOU REMEMBERING YOUR HERITAGE.
FROM NOW ON, YOUR GATES ARE OPEN FOR ANYONE WHO NEEDS TO SPEAK TO YOU.
AND EACH NIGHT YOU'LL PUT AN EXTRA PLACE AT YOUR TABLE, JUST IN CASE OF UNEXPECTED GUESTS.
NO ONE SHOULD FEEL THE SHAME I DID WHEN TURNED AWAY.
YOU'RE RIGHT, OF COURSE. I AGREE.
NOW RELEASE MY SON —
OH, YOUR SON WAS NEVER A PRISONER. HE FEELS THE SAME WAY I DO.
THAT'S WHY HE EATS HIS DINNER IN A TAVERN. THOMAS!
THOMAS! I THOUGHT I'D LOST YOU!
IF YOU'D KEPT TRYING TO BE LIKE AN ENGLISH LORD, FATHER, YOU WOULD HAVE.
ONCE MORE I OWE AN O'MALLEY FOR SAVING MY LIFE, IT SEEMS.
NOTHING MORE THAN A SMALL GUIDING PUSH.
CAP'N! WE GOT THREE SHIPS COMING! ENGLISH!
AS PLEASURABLE AS THIS WAS, GENTLEMEN, THE LAST THING I WANT THE ENGLISH TO SEE IS YOU ON MY DECK.
REALLY? I THOUGHT YOU'D BE HAPPY TO SEE MORE WAR BETWEEN US!

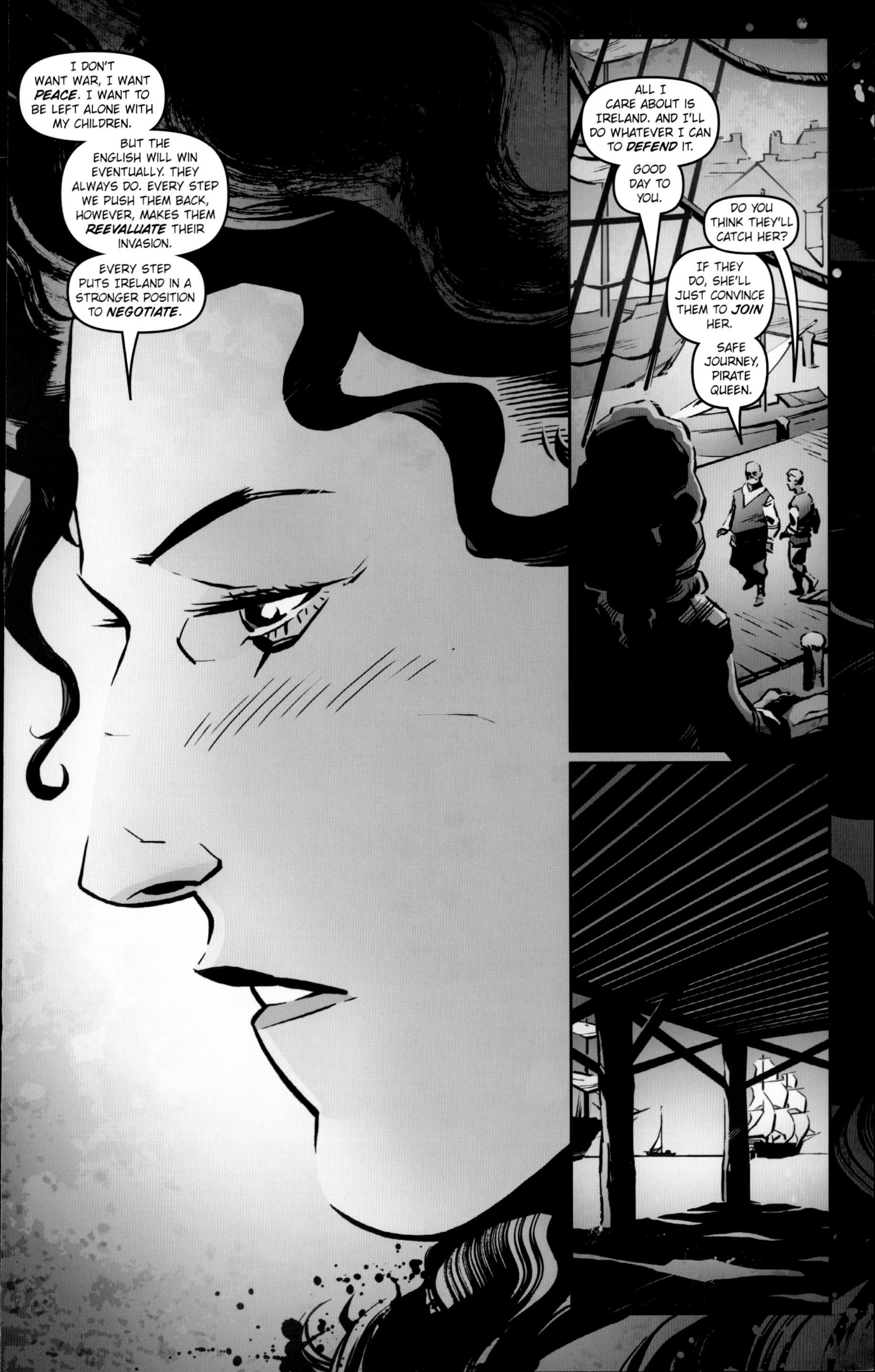
I DON'T WANT WAR, I WANT PEACE. I WANT TO BE LEFT ALONE WITH MY CHILDREN.
BUT THE ENGLISH WILL WIN EVENTUALLY. THEY ALWAYS DO. EVERY STEP WE PUSH THEM BACK, HOWEVER, MAKES THEM REEVALUATE THEIR INVASION.
EVERY STEP PUTS IRELAND IN A STRONGER POSITION TO NEGOTIATE.
ALL I CARE ABOUT IS IRELAND. AND I'LL DO WHATEVER I CAN TO DEFEND IT.
GOOD DAY TO YOU.
DO YOU THINK THEY'LL CATCH HER?
IF THEY DO, SHE'LL JUST CONVINCE THEM TO JOIN HER.
SAFE JOURNEY, PIRATE QUEEN.

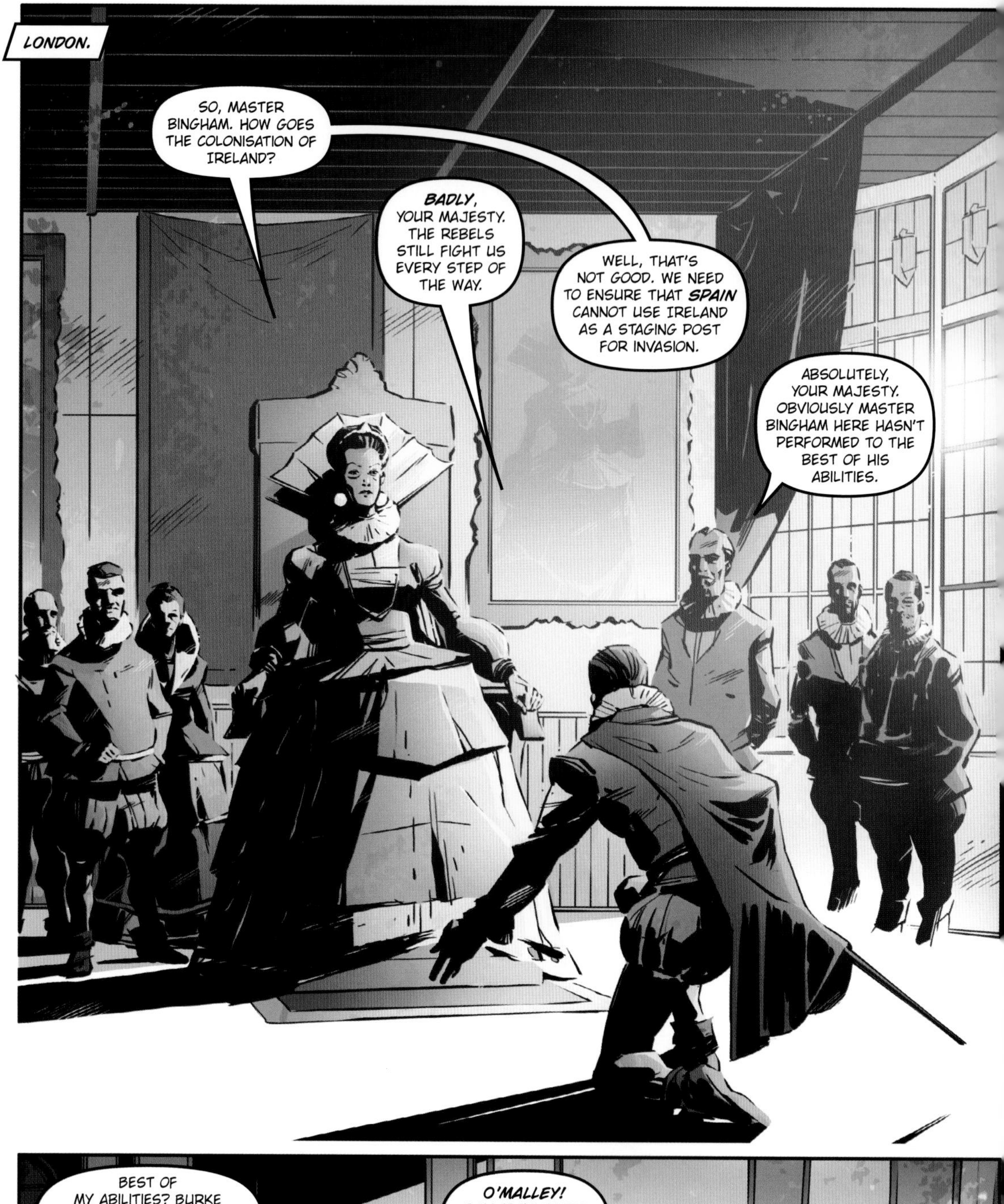
LONDON.
SO, MASTER BINGHAM. HOW GOES THE COLONISATION OF IRELAND?
BADLY, YOUR MAJESTY. THE REBELS STILL FIGHT US EVERY STEP OF THE WAY.
WELL, THAT'S NOT GOOD. WE NEED TO ENSURE THAT SPAIN CANNOT USE IRELAND AS A STAGING POST FOR INVASION.
ABSOLUTELY, YOUR MAJESTY. OBVIOUSLY MASTER BINGHAM HERE HASN'T PERFORMED TO THE BEST OF HIS ABILITIES.

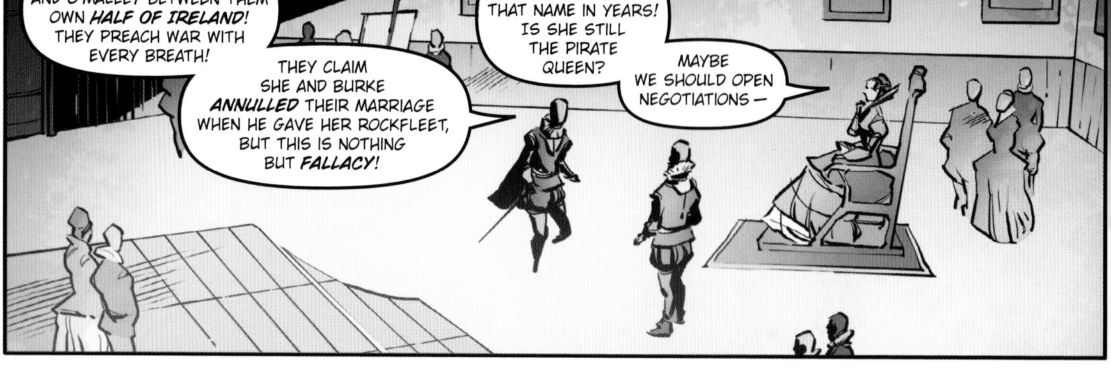
BEST OF MY ABILITIES? BURKE AND O'MALLEY BETWEEN THEM OWN HALF OF IRELAND! THEY PREACH WAR WITH EVERY BREATH!
THEY CLAIM SHE AND BURKE ANNULLED THEIR MARRIAGE WHEN HE GAVE HER ROCKFLEET, BUT THIS IS NOTHING BUT FALLACY!
O'MALLEY! I HAVEN'T HEARD THAT NAME IN YEARS! IS SHE STILL THE PIRATE QUEEN?
MAYBE WE SHOULD OPEN NEGOTIATIONS —

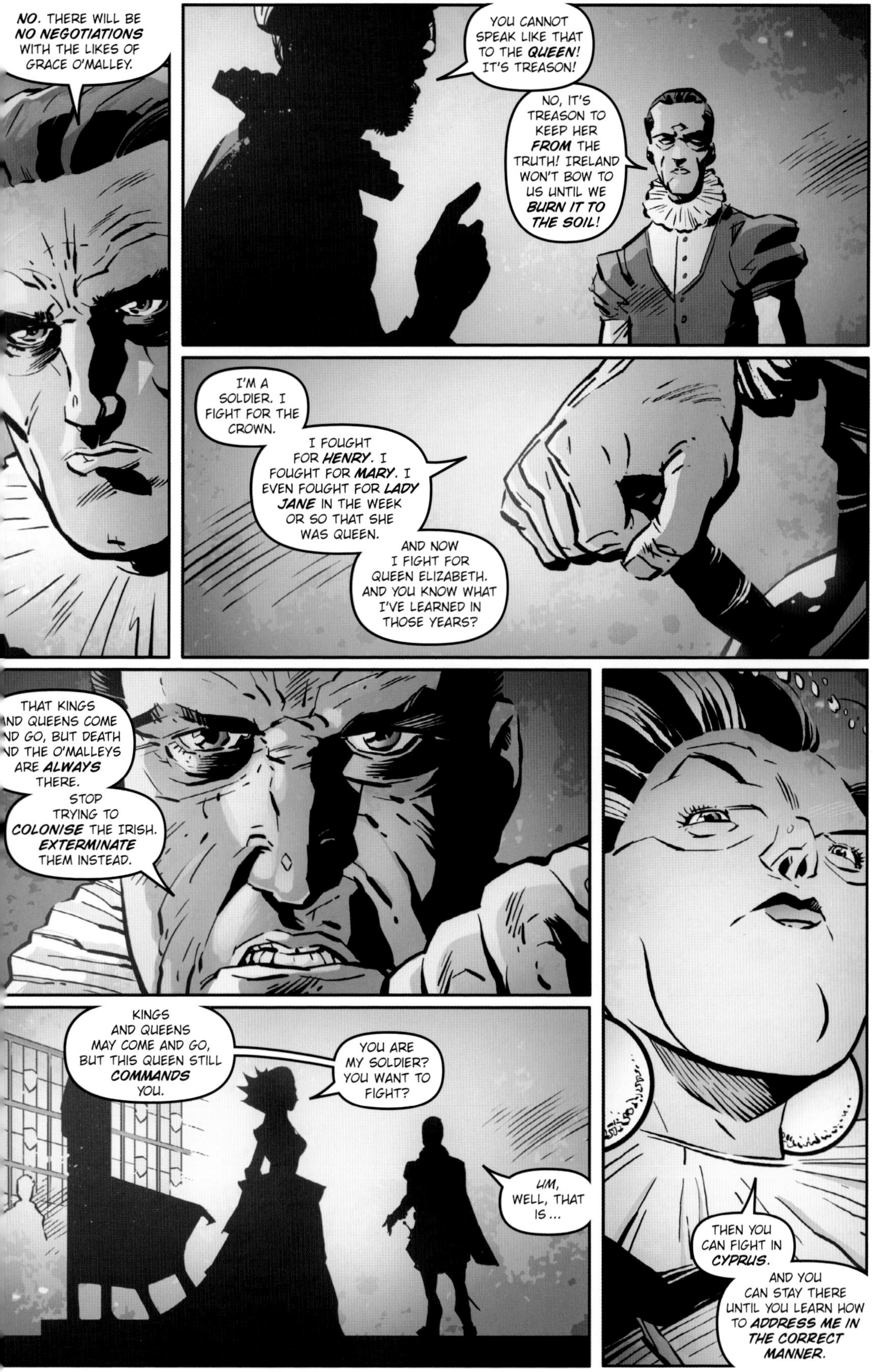
NO. THERE WILL BE NO NEGOTIATIONS WITH THE LIKES OF GRACE O'MALLEY.
YOU CANNOT SPEAK LIKE THAT TO THE QUEEN! IT'S TREASON!
NO, IT'S TREASON TO KEEP HER FROM THE TRUTH! IRELAND WON'T BOW TO US UNTIL WE BURN IT TO THE SOIL!
I'M A SOLDIER. I FIGHT FOR THE CROWN.
I FOUGHT FOR HENRY. I FOUGHT FOR MARY. I EVEN FOUGHT FOR LADY JANE IN THE WEEK OR SO THAT SHE WAS QUEEN.
AND NOW I FIGHT FOR QUEEN ELIZABETH. AND YOU KNOW WHAT I'VE LEARNED IN THOSE YEARS?
THAT KINGS AND QUEENS COME AND GO, BUT DEATH AND THE O'MALLEYS ARE ALWAYS THERE.
STOP TRYING TO COLONISE THE IRISH. EXTERMINATE THEM INSTEAD.
KINGS AND QUEENS MAY COME AND GO, BUT THIS QUEEN STILL COMMANDS YOU.
YOU ARE MY SOLDIER? YOU WANT TO FIGHT?
UM, WELL, THAT IS...
THEN YOU CAN FIGHT IN CYPRUS.
AND YOU CAN STAY THERE UNTIL YOU LEARN HOW TO ADDRESS ME IN THE CORRECT MANNER.

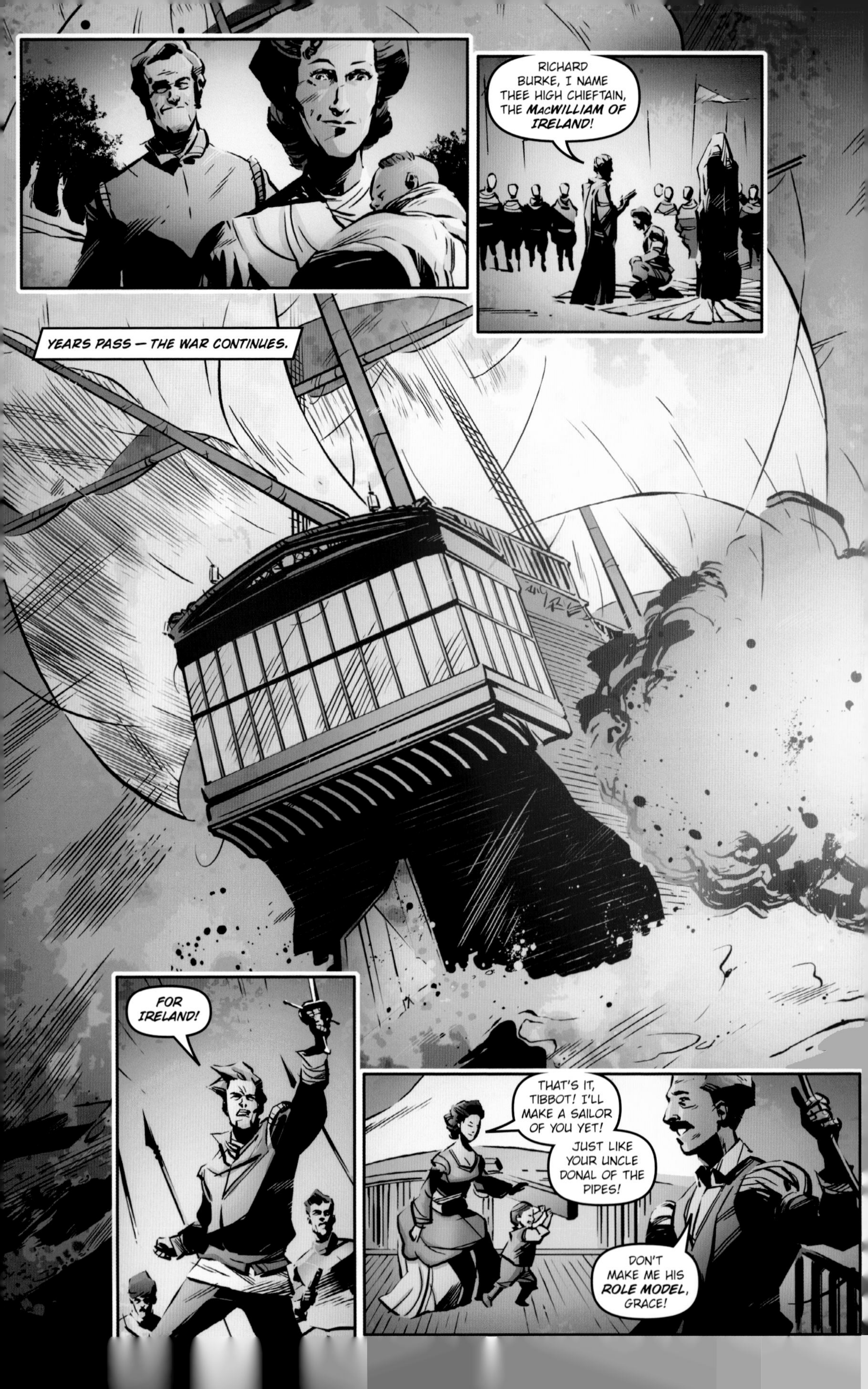
RICHARD BURKE, I NAME THEE HIGH CHIEFTAIN, THE MacWILLIAM OF IRELAND!
YEARS PASS — THE WAR CONTINUES.
FOR IRELAND!
THAT'S IT, TIBBOT! I'LL MAKE A SAILOR OF YOU YET!
JUST LIKE YOUR UNCLE DONAL OF THE PIPES!
DON'T MAKE ME HIS ROLE MODEL, GRACE!

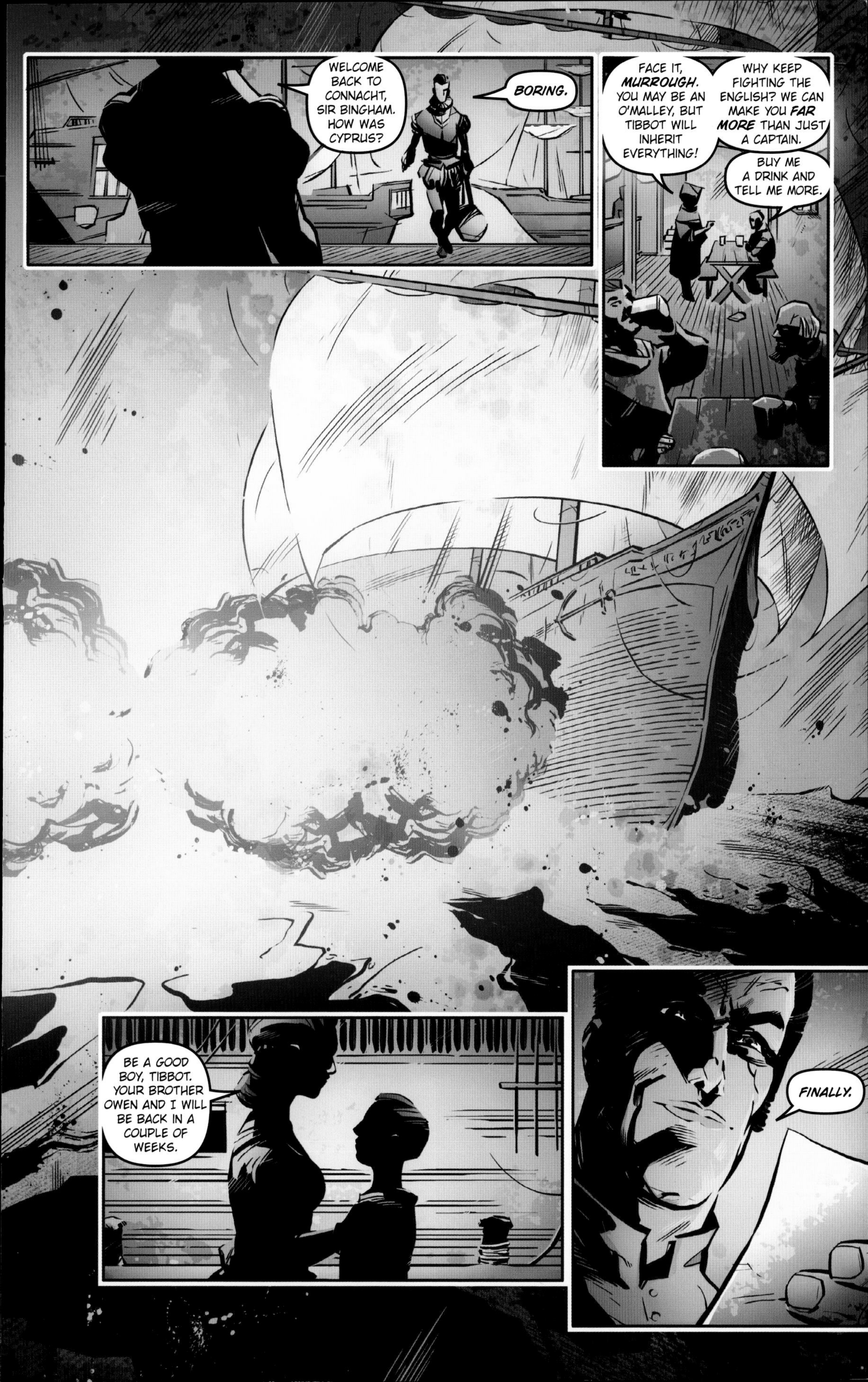
WELCOME BACK TO CONNACHT, SIR BINGHAM. HOW WAS CYPRUS?
BORING.
FACE IT, MURROUGH. YOU MAY BE AN O'MALLEY, BUT TIBBOT WILL INHERIT EVERYTHING!
WHY KEEP FIGHTING THE ENGLISH? WE CAN MAKE YOU FAR MORE THAN JUST A CAPTAIN.
BUY ME A DRINK AND TELL ME MORE.
BE A GOOD BOY, TIBBOT. YOUR BROTHER OWEN AND I WILL BE BACK IN A COUPLE OF WEEKS.
FINALLY.

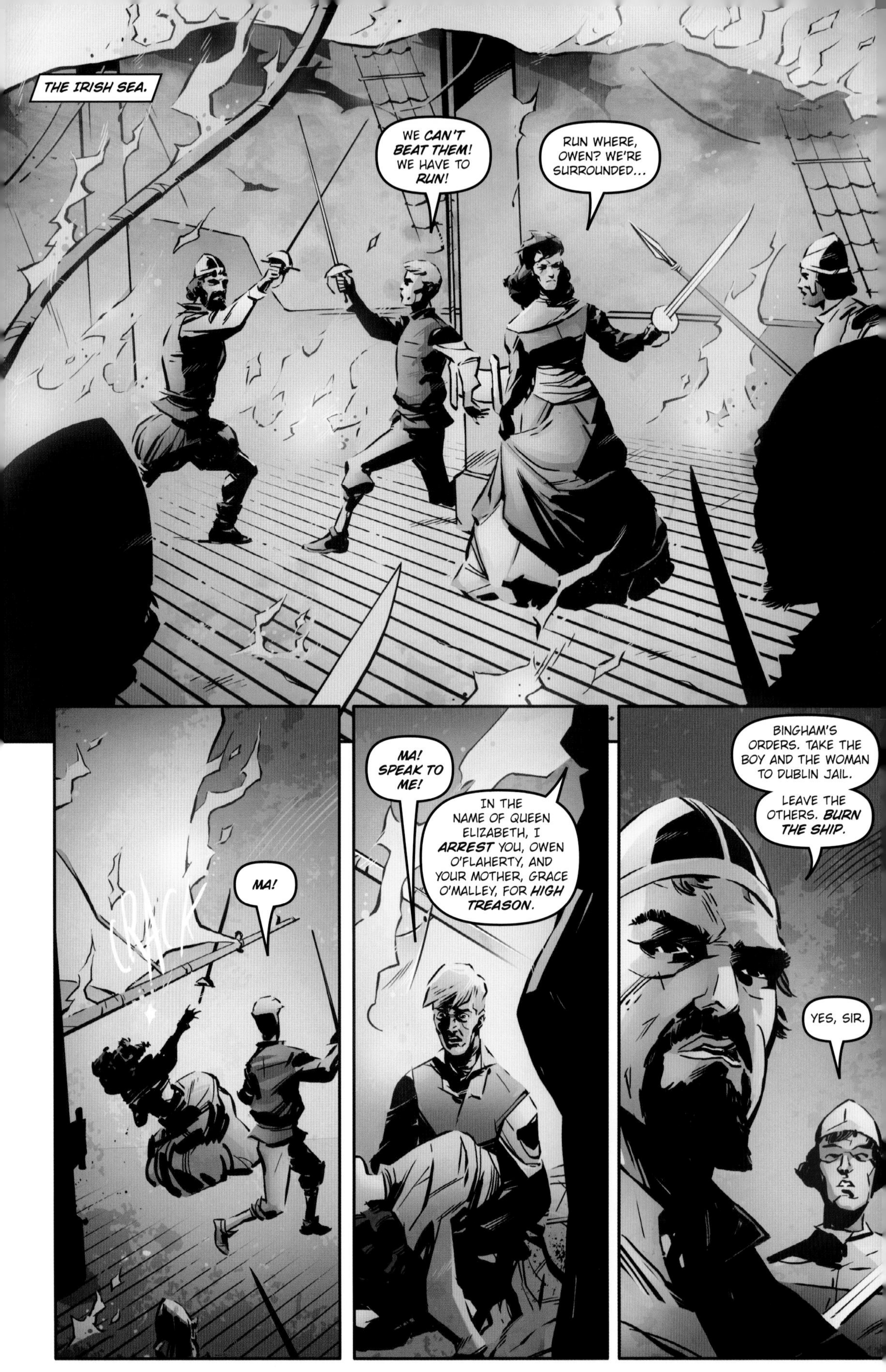
THE IRISH SEA.
WE CAN'T BEAT THEM! WE HAVE TO RUN!
RUN WHERE, OWEN? WE'RE SURROUNDED...
CRACK
MA!
MA! SPEAK TO ME!
IN THE NAME OF QUEEN ELIZABETH, I ARREST YOU, OWEN O'FLAHERTY, AND YOUR MOTHER, GRACE O'MALLEY, FOR HIGH TREASON.
BINGHAM'S ORDERS. TAKE THE BOY AND THE WOMAN TO DUBLIN JAIL.
LEAVE THE OTHERS. BURN THE SHIP.
YES, SIR.

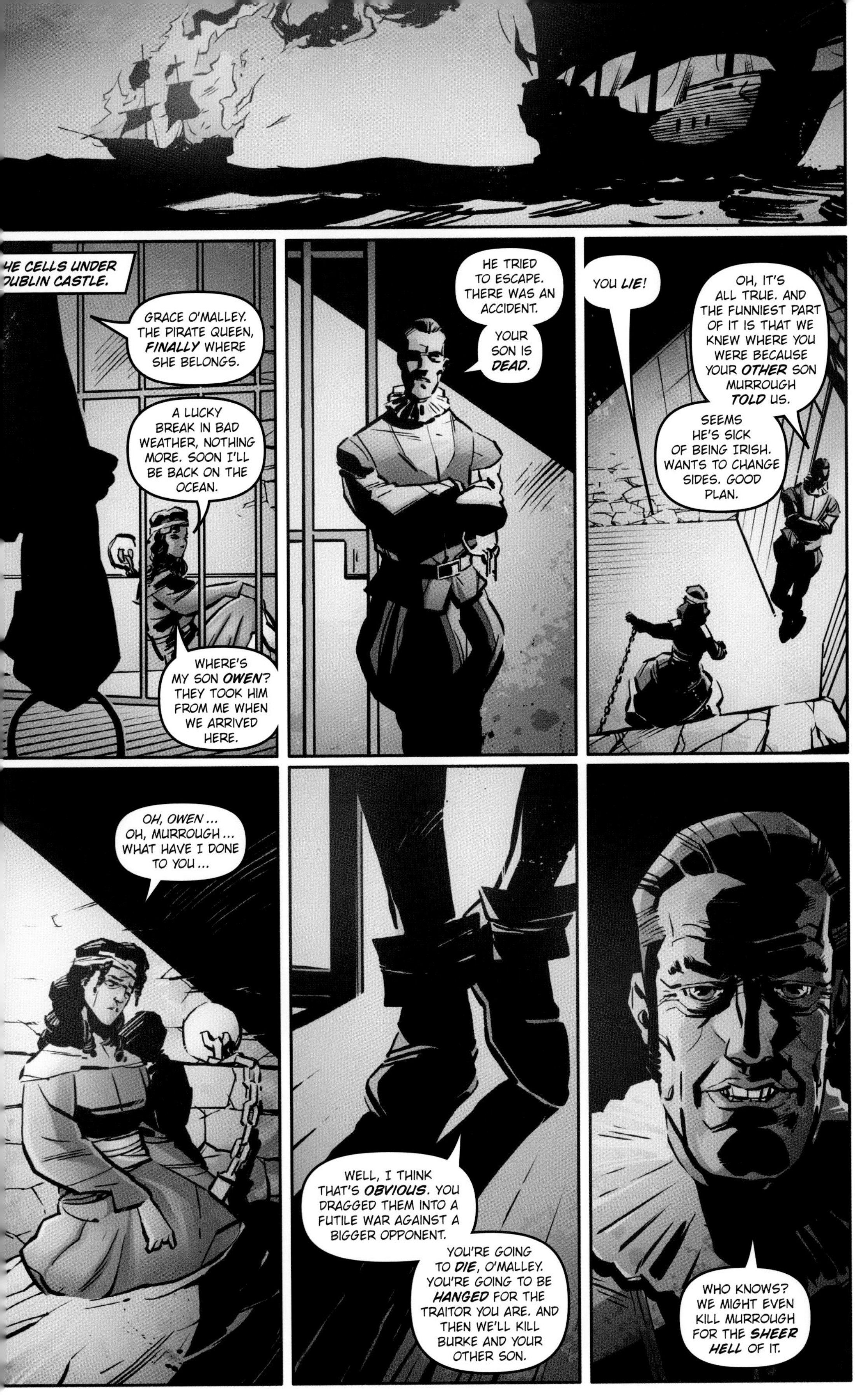

HE CELLS UNDER DUBLIN CASTLE.
GRACE O'MALLEY. THE PIRATE QUEEN, FINALLY WHERE SHE BELONGS.
A LUCKY BREAK IN BAD WEATHER, NOTHING MORE. SOON I'LL BE BACK ON THE OCEAN.
WHERE'S MY SON OWEN? THEY TOOK HIM FROM ME WHEN WE ARRIVED HERE.
HE TRIED TO ESCAPE. THERE WAS AN ACCIDENT.
YOUR SON IS DEAD.
YOU LIE!
OH, IT'S ALL TRUE. AND THE FUNNIEST PART OF IT IS THAT WE KNEW WHERE YOU WERE BECAUSE YOUR OTHER SON MURROUGH TOLD US.
SEEMS HE'S SICK OF BEING IRISH. WANTS TO CHANGE SIDES. GOOD PLAN.
OH, OWEN ... OH, MURROUGH ... WHAT HAVE I DONE TO YOU ...
WELL, I THINK THAT'S OBVIOUS. YOU DRAGGED THEM INTO A FUTILE WAR AGAINST A BIGGER OPPONENT.
YOU'RE GOING TO DIE, O'MALLEY. YOU'RE GOING TO BE HANGED FOR THE TRAITOR YOU ARE. AND THEN WE'LL KILL BURKE AND YOUR OTHER SON.
WHO KNOWS? WE MIGHT EVEN KILL MURROUGH FOR THE SHEER HELL OF IT.

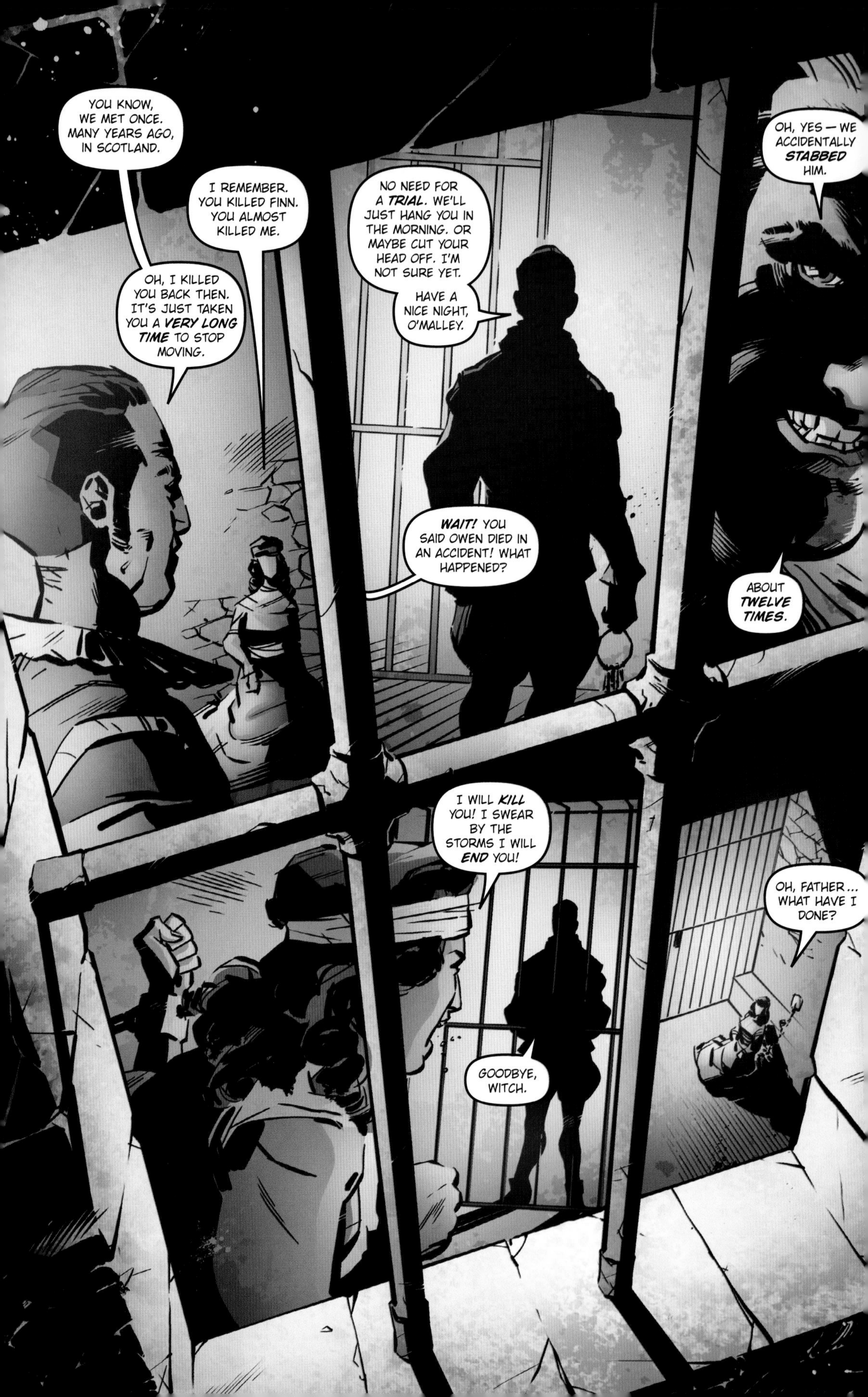
YOU KNOW, WE MET ONCE. MANY YEARS AGO, IN SCOTLAND.
I REMEMBER. YOU KILLED FINN. YOU ALMOST KILLED ME.
OH, I KILLED YOU BACK THEN. IT'S JUST TAKEN YOU A VERY LONG TIME TO STOP MOVING.
NO NEED FOR A TRIAL. WE'LL JUST HANG YOU IN THE MORNING. OR MAYBE CUT YOUR HEAD OFF. I'M NOT SURE YET.
HAVE A NICE NIGHT, O'MALLEY.
WAIT! YOU SAID OWEN DIED IN AN ACCIDENT! WHAT HAPPENED?
OH, YES — WE ACCIDENTALLY STABBED HIM.
ABOUT TWELVE TIMES.
I WILL KILL YOU! I SWEAR BY THE STORMS I WILL END YOU!
GOODBYE, WITCH.
OH, FATHER... WHAT HAVE I DONE?

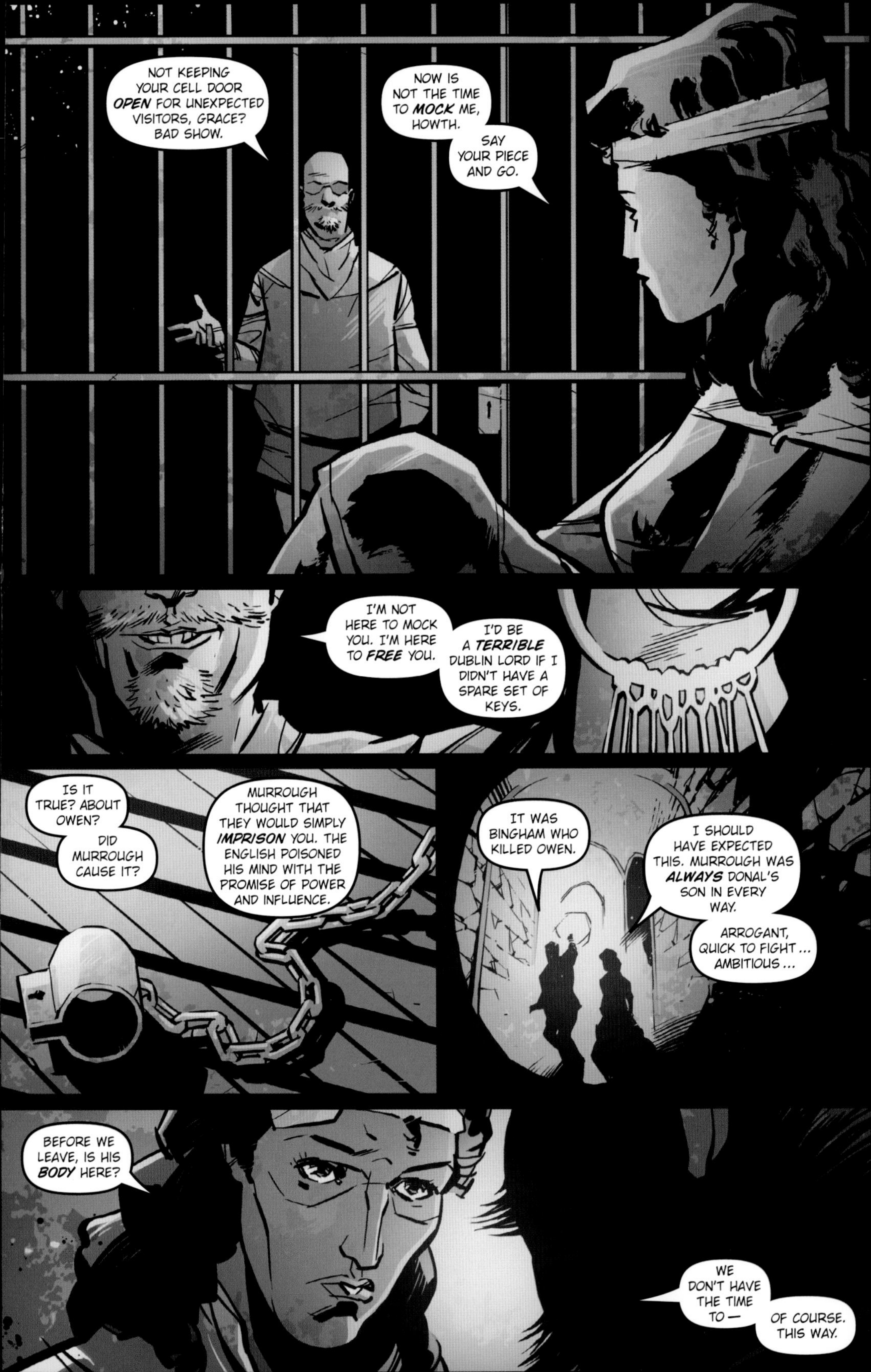
NOT KEEPING YOUR CELL DOOR OPEN FOR UNEXPECTED VISITORS, GRACE? BAD SHOW.
NOW IS NOT THE TIME TO MOCK ME, HOWTH.
SAY YOUR PIECE AND GO.
I'M NOT HERE TO MOCK YOU. I'M HERE TO FREE YOU.
I'D BE A TERRIBLE DUBLIN LORD IF I DIDN'T HAVE A SPARE SET OF KEYS.
IS IT TRUE? ABOUT OWEN?
DID MURROUGH CAUSE IT?
MURROUGH THOUGHT THAT THEY WOULD SIMPLY IMPRISON YOU. THE ENGLISH POISONED HIS MIND WITH THE PROMISE OF POWER AND INFLUENCE.
IT WAS BINGHAM WHO KILLED OWEN.
I SHOULD HAVE EXPECTED THIS. MURROUGH WAS ALWAYS DONAL'S SON IN EVERY WAY.
ARROGANT, QUICK TO FIGHT... AMBITIOUS...
BEFORE WE LEAVE, IS HIS BODY HERE?
WE DON'T HAVE THE TIME TO—
OF COURSE. THIS WAY.

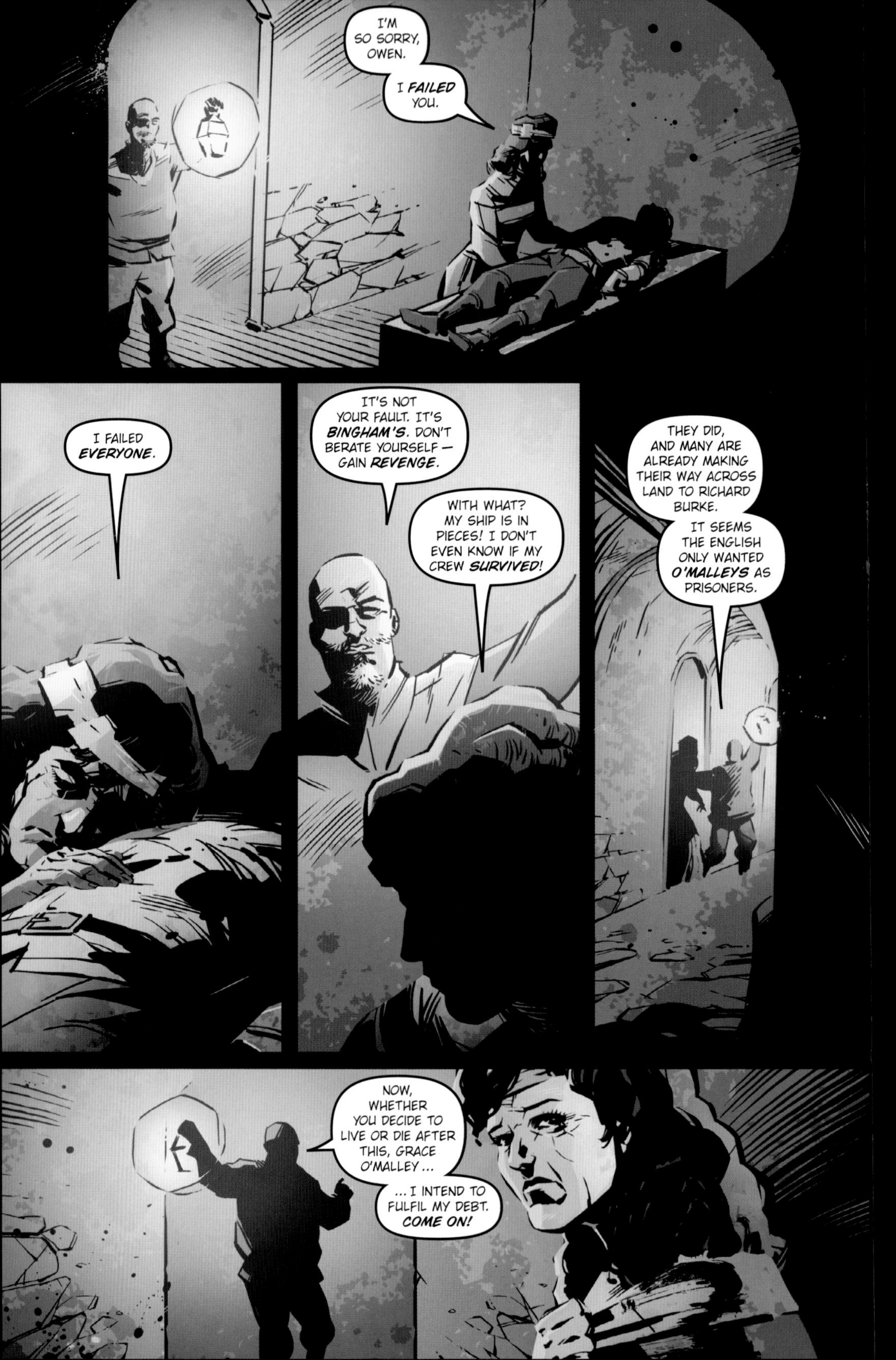
I'M SO SORRY, OWEN.
I FAILED YOU.
I FAILED EVERYONE.
IT'S NOT YOUR FAULT. IT'S BINGHAM'S. DON'T BERATE YOURSELF — GAIN REVENGE.
WITH WHAT? MY SHIP IS IN PIECES! I DON'T EVEN KNOW IF MY CREW SURVIVED!
THEY DID, AND MANY ARE ALREADY MAKING THEIR WAY ACROSS LAND TO RICHARD BURKE.
IT SEEMS THE ENGLISH ONLY WANTED O'MALLEYS AS PRISONERS.
NOW, WHETHER YOU DECIDE TO LIVE OR DIE AFTER THIS, GRACE O'MALLEY ...
... I INTEND TO FULFIL MY DEBT. COME ON!

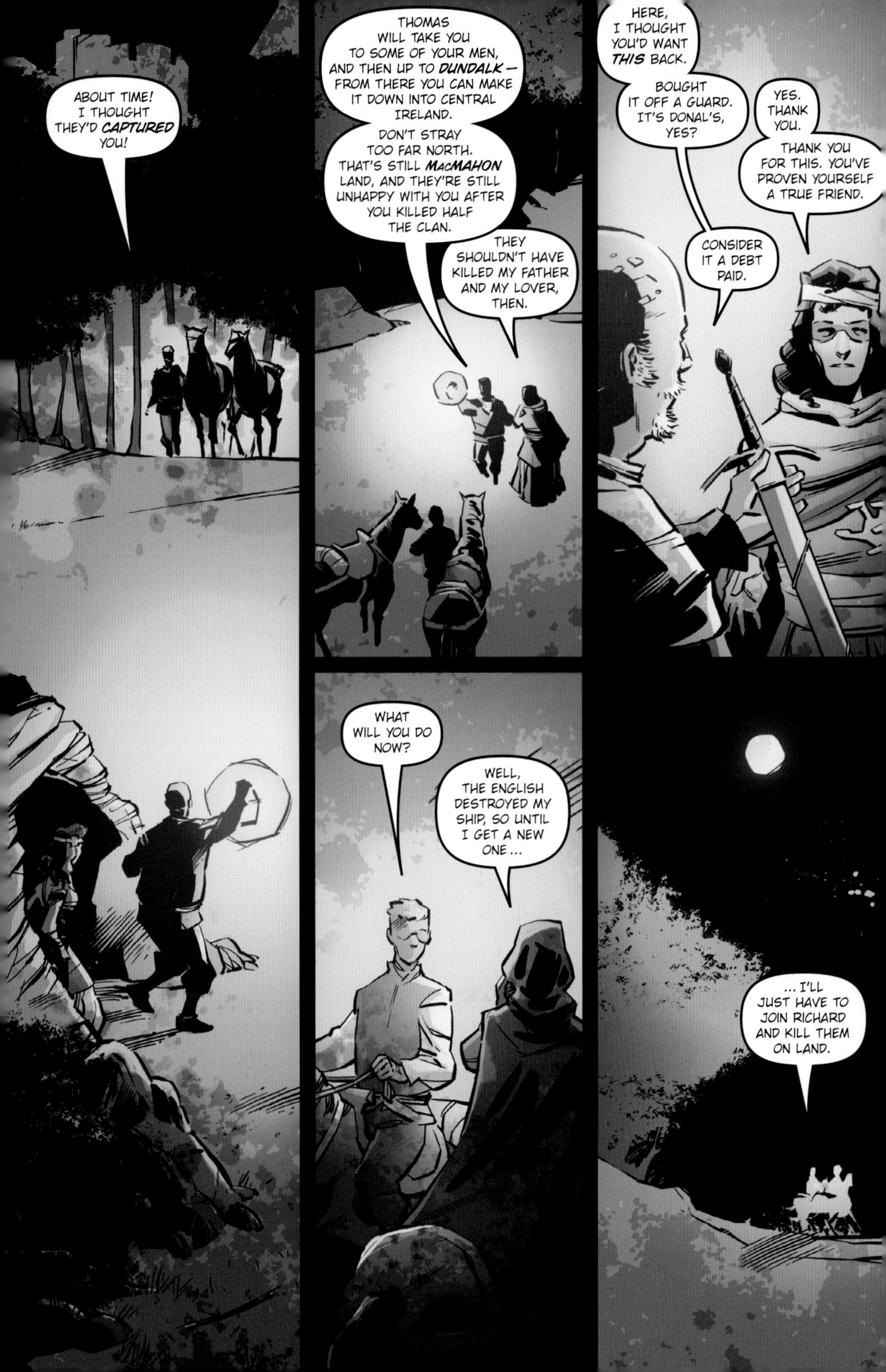
ABOUT TIME! I THOUGHT THEY'D CAPTURED YOU!
THOMAS WILL TAKE YOU TO SOME OF YOUR MEN, AND THEN UP TO DUNDALK — FROM THERE YOU CAN MAKE IT DOWN INTO CENTRAL IRELAND.
DON'T STRAY TOO FAR NORTH. THAT'S STILL MacMAHON LAND, AND THEY'RE STILL UNHAPPY WITH YOU AFTER YOU KILLED HALF THE CLAN.
THEY SHOULDN'T HAVE KILLED MY FATHER AND MY LOVER, THEN.
HERE, I THOUGHT YOU'D WANT THIS BACK.
BOUGHT IT OFF A GUARD. IT'S DONAL'S, YES?
YES. THANK YOU.
THANK YOU FOR THIS. YOU'VE PROVEN YOURSELF A TRUE FRIEND.
CONSIDER IT A DEBT PAID.
WHAT WILL YOU DO NOW?
WELL, THE ENGLISH DESTROYED MY SHIP, SO UNTIL I GET A NEW ONE ...
... I'LL JUST HAVE TO JOIN RICHARD AND KILL THEM ON LAND.

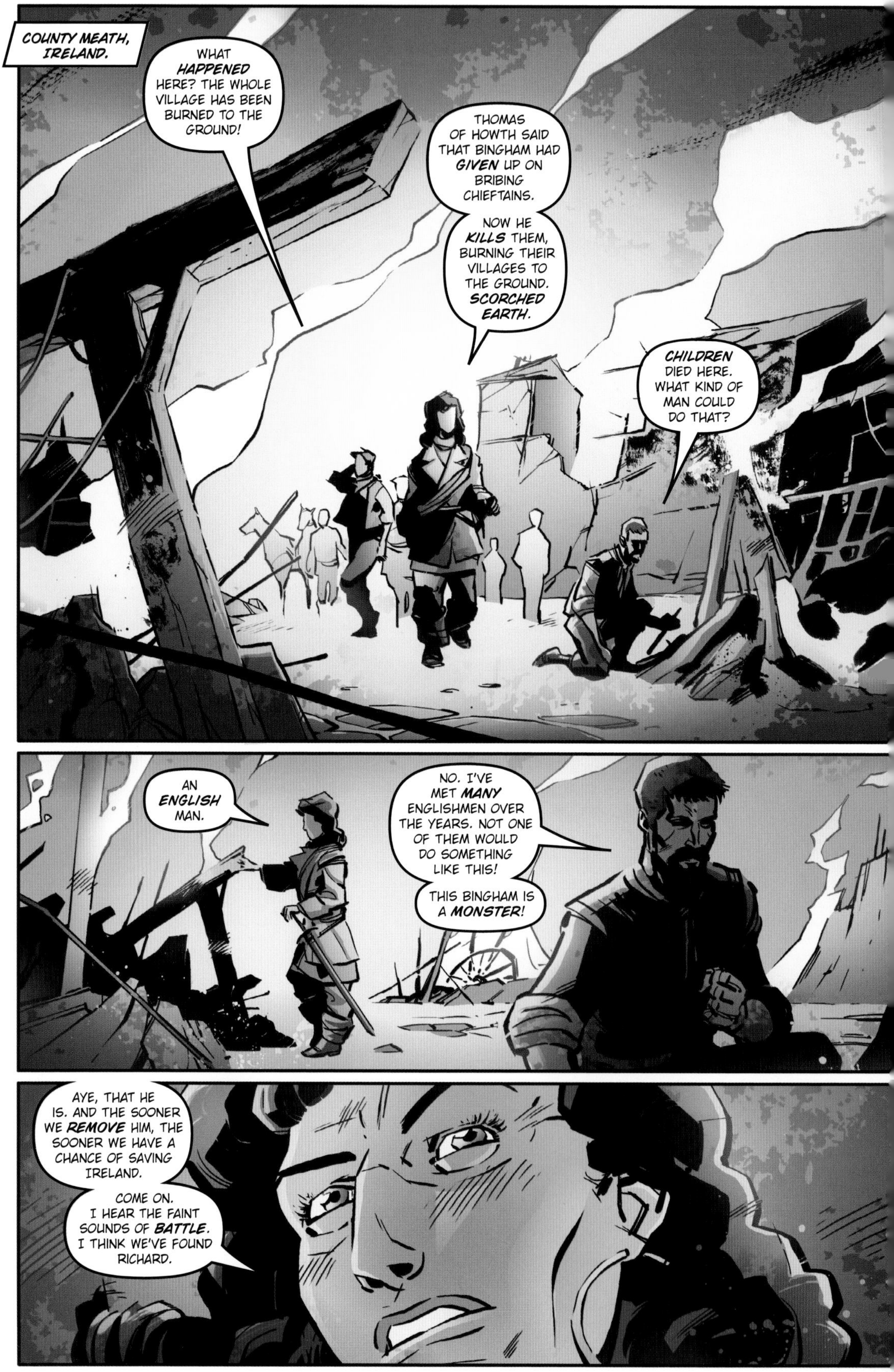
COUNTY MEATH, IRELAND.
WHAT HAPPENED HERE? THE WHOLE VILLAGE HAS BEEN BURNED TO THE GROUND!
THOMAS OF HOWTH SAID THAT BINGHAM HAD GIVEN UP ON BRIBING CHIEFTAINS.
NOW HE KILLS THEM, BURNING THEIR VILLAGES TO THE GROUND. SCORCHED EARTH.
CHILDREN DIED HERE. WHAT KIND OF MAN COULD DO THAT?
AN ENGLISH MAN.
NO. I'VE MET MANY ENGLISHMEN OVER THE YEARS. NOT ONE OF THEM WOULD DO SOMETHING LIKE THIS!
THIS BINGHAM IS A MONSTER!
AYE, THAT HE IS. AND THE SOONER WE REMOVE HIM, THE SOONER WE HAVE A CHANCE OF SAVING IRELAND.
COME ON. I HEAR THE FAINT SOUNDS OF BATTLE. I THINK WE'VE FOUND RICHARD.

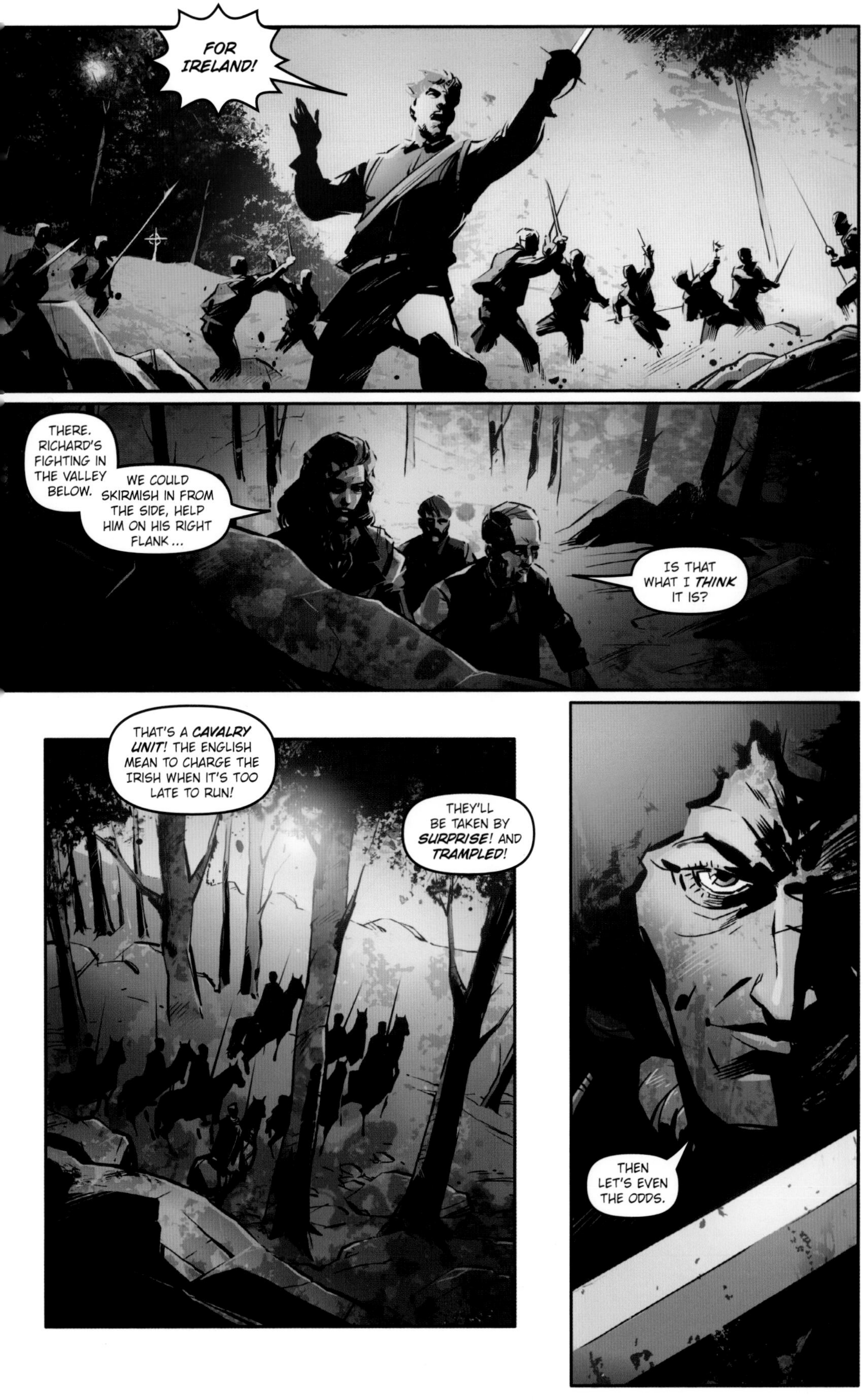
FOR IRELAND!
THERE. RICHARD'S FIGHTING IN THE VALLEY BELOW.
WE COULD SKIRMISH IN FROM THE SIDE, HELP HIM ON HIS RIGHT FLANK...
IS THAT WHAT I THINK IT IS?
THAT'S A CAVALRY UNIT! THE ENGLISH MEAN TO CHARGE THE IRISH WHEN IT'S TOO LATE TO RUN!
THEY'LL BE TAKEN BY SURPRISE! AND TRAMPLED!
THEN LET'S EVEN THE ODDS.

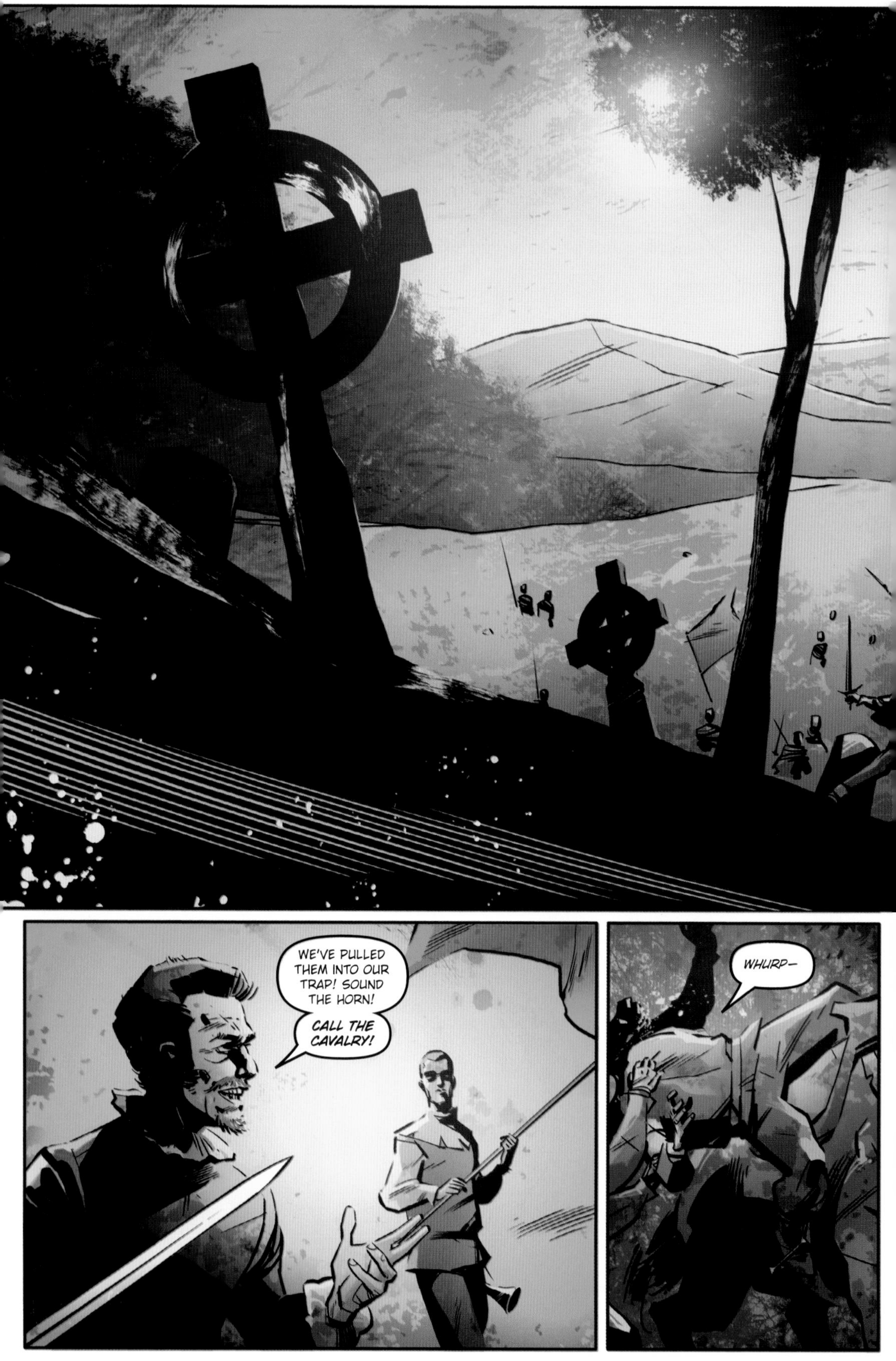
WE'VE PULLED THEM INTO OUR TRAP! SOUND THE HORN!
CALL THE CAVALRY!
WHURP—

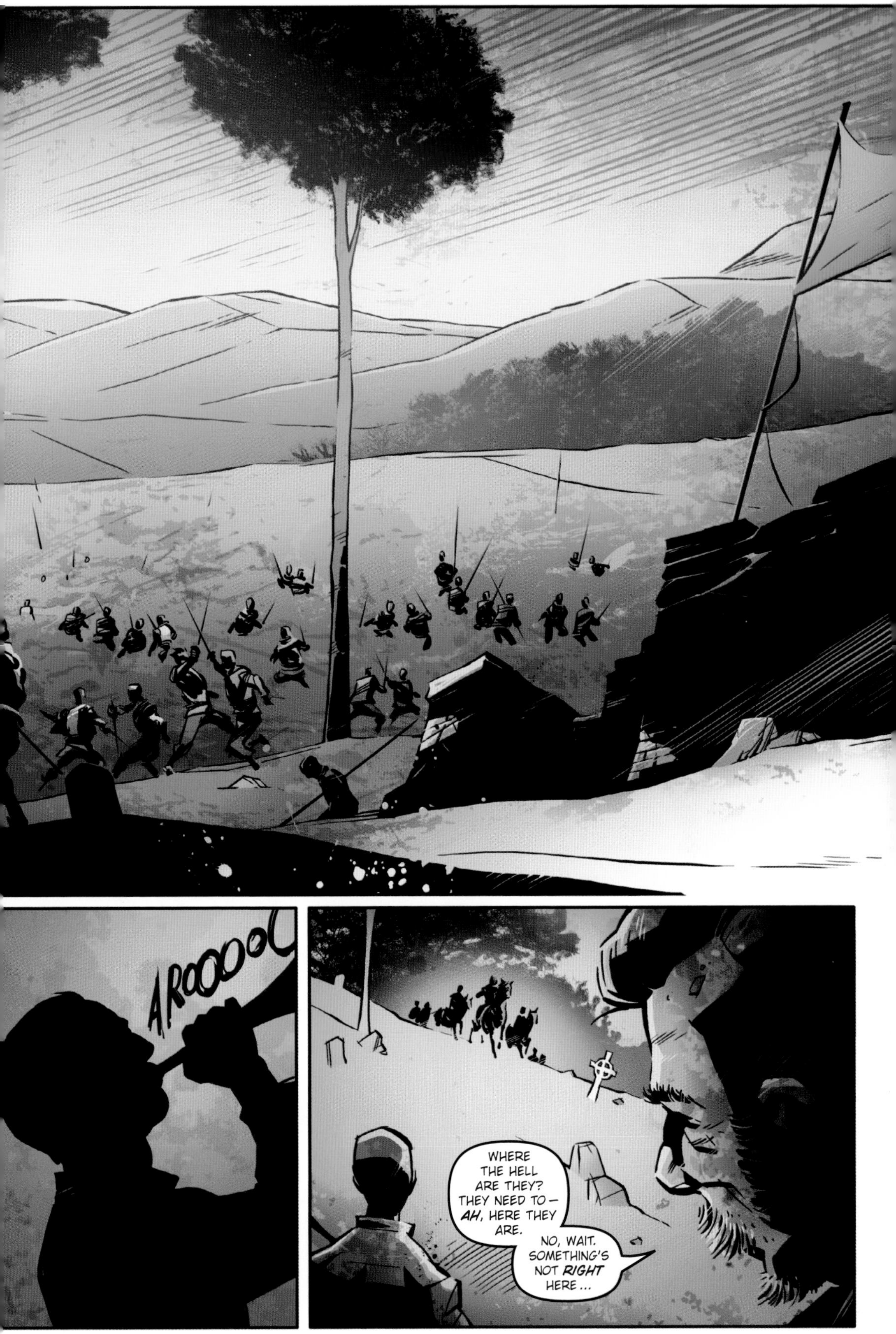
AROOOO
WHERE THE HELL ARE THEY? THEY NEED TO— AH, HERE THEY ARE.
NO, WAIT. SOMETHING'S NOT RIGHT HERE...

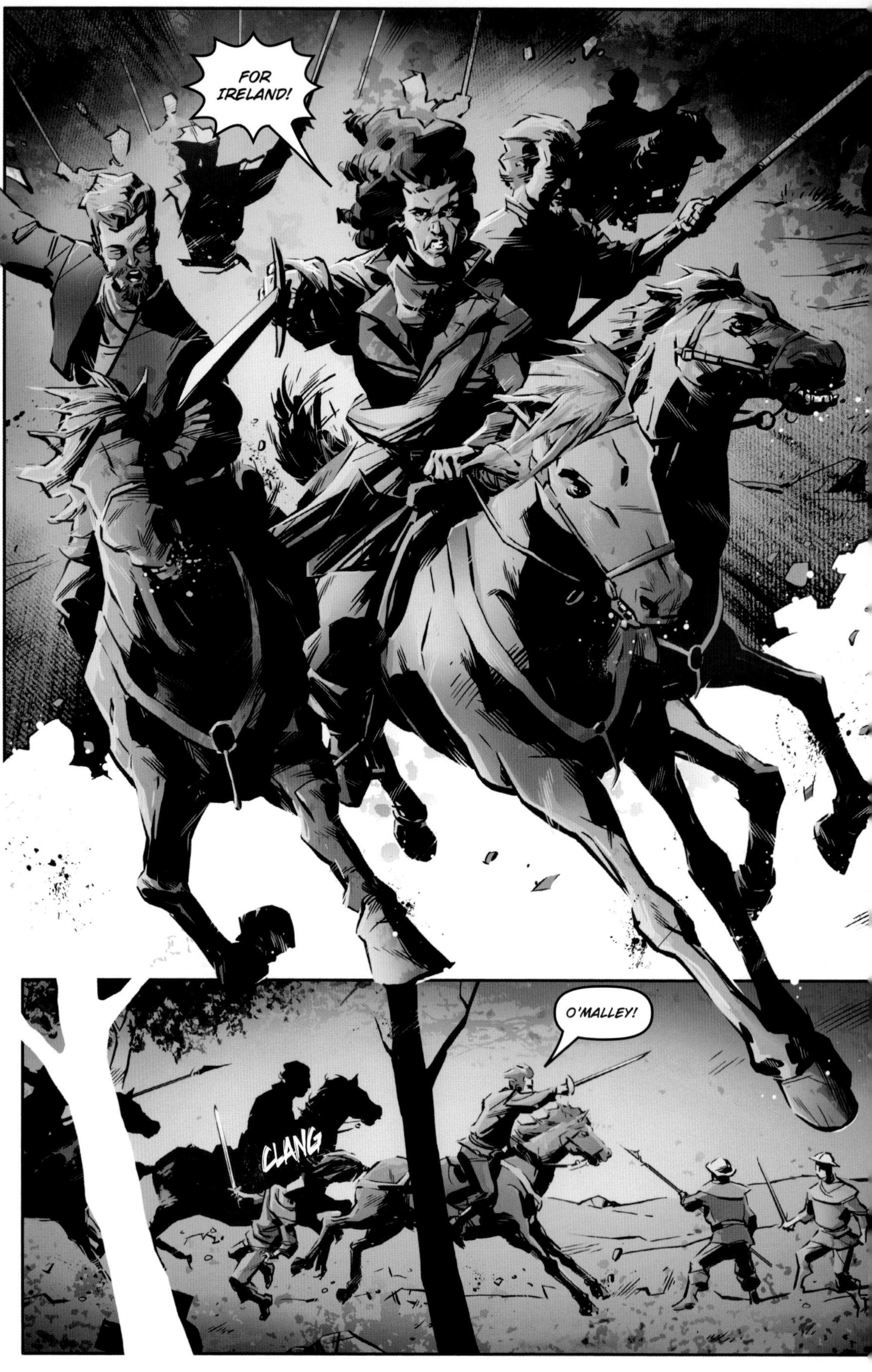
FOR IRELAND!
O'MALLEY!
CLANG

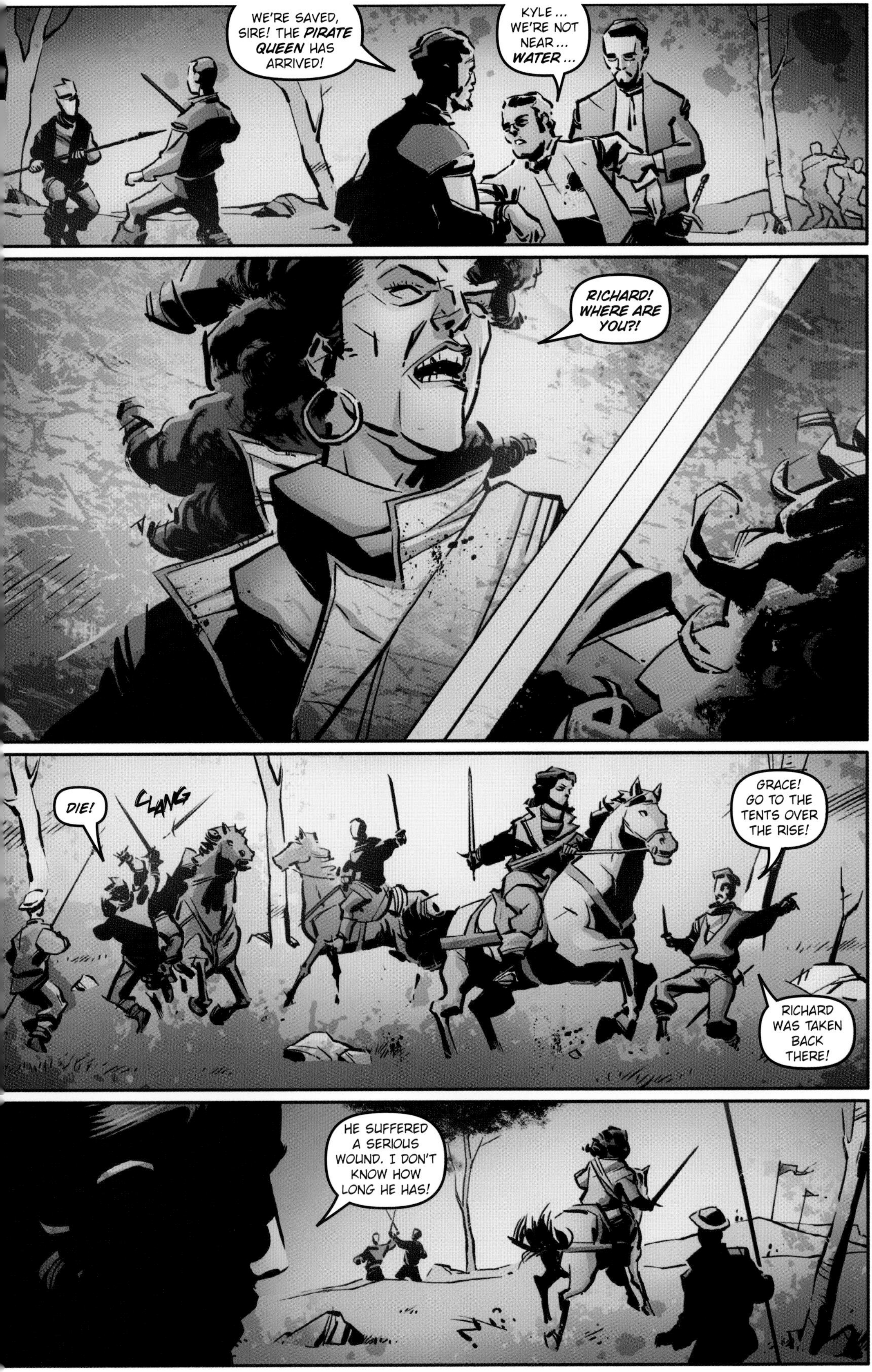

WE'RE SAVED, SIRE! THE PIRATE QUEEN HAS ARRIVED!
KYLE... WE'RE NOT NEAR... WATER...
RICHARD! WHERE ARE YOU?!
DIE!
CLANG
GRACE! GO TO THE TENTS OVER THE RISE!
RICHARD WAS TAKEN BACK THERE!
HE SUFFERED A SERIOUS WOUND. I DON'T KNOW HOW LONG HE HAS!

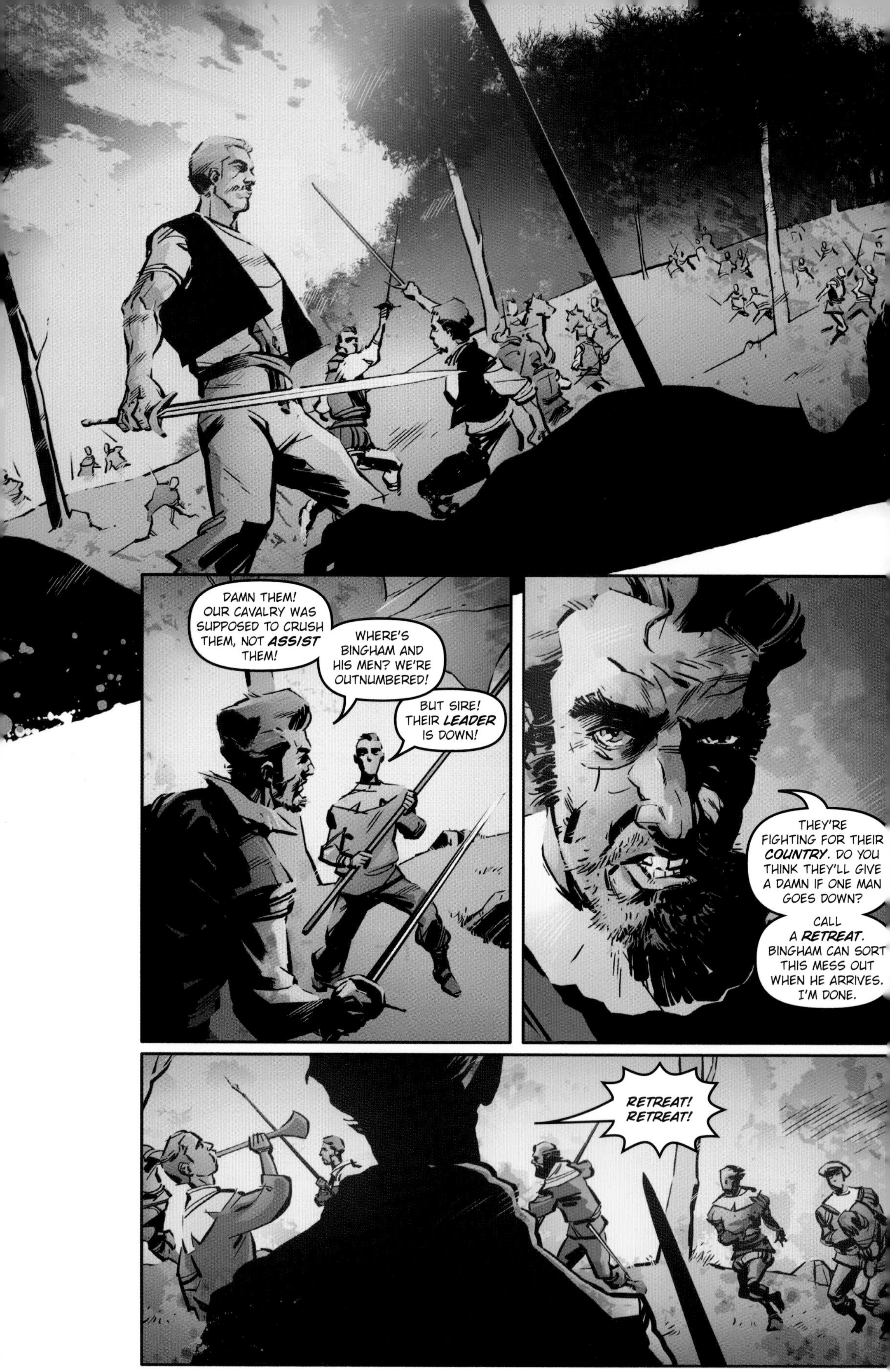
DAMN THEM! OUR CAVALRY WAS SUPPOSED TO CRUSH THEM, NOT ASSIST THEM!
WHERE'S BINGHAM AND HIS MEN? WE'RE OUTNUMBERED!
BUT SIRE! THEIR LEADER IS DOWN!
THEY'RE FIGHTING FOR THEIR COUNTRY. DO YOU THINK THEY'LL GIVE A DAMN IF ONE MAN GOES DOWN?
CALL A RETREAT. BINGHAM CAN SORT THIS MESS OUT WHEN HE ARRIVES. I'M DONE.
RETREAT! RETREAT!

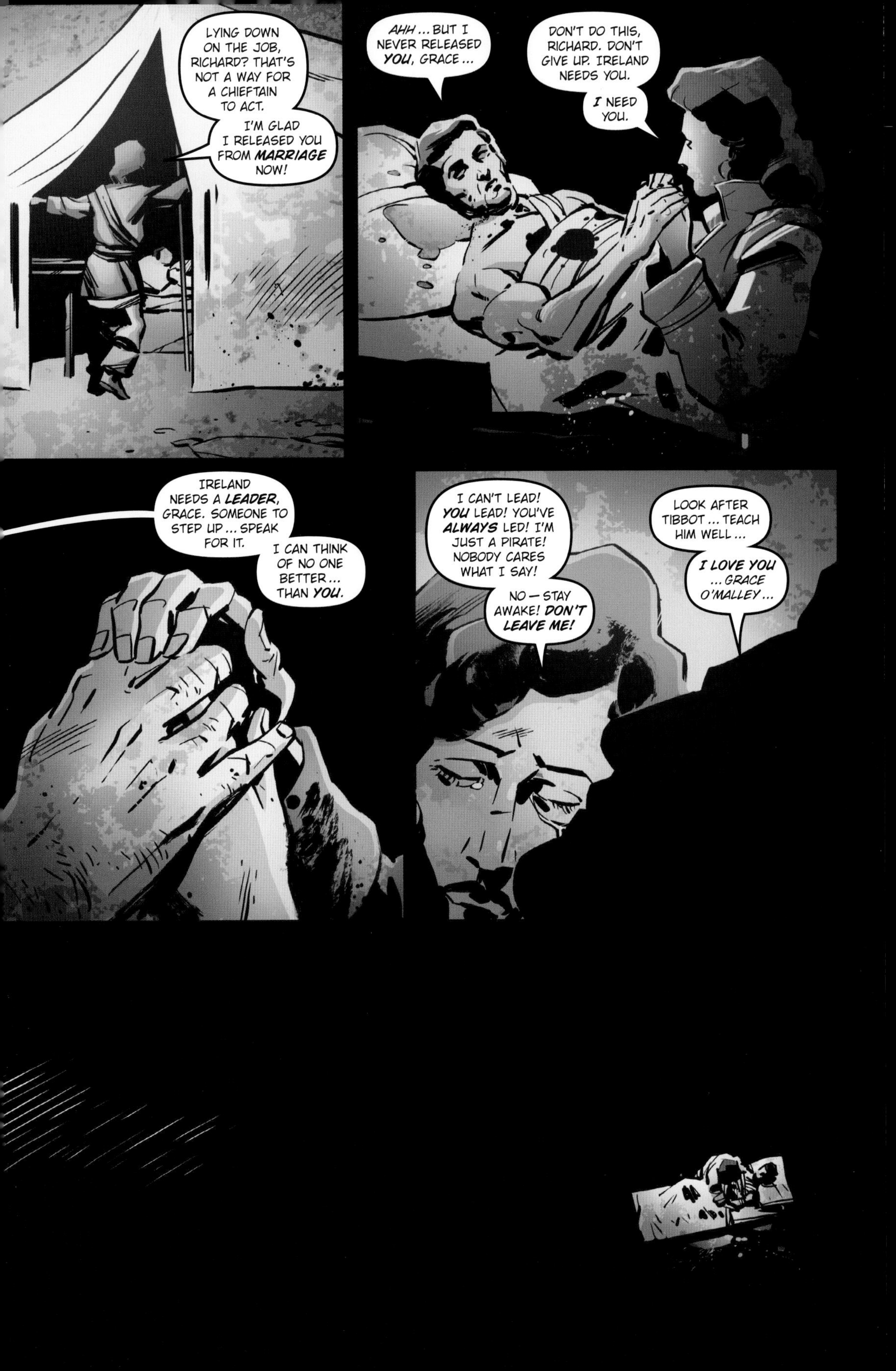
LYING DOWN ON THE JOB, RICHARD? THAT'S NOT A WAY FOR A CHIEFTAIN TO ACT.
I'M GLAD I RELEASED YOU FROM MARRIAGE NOW!
AHH ... BUT I NEVER RELEASED YOU, GRACE ...
DON'T DO THIS, RICHARD. DON'T GIVE UP. IRELAND NEEDS YOU.
I NEED YOU.
IRELAND NEEDS A LEADER, GRACE. SOMEONE TO STEP UP ... SPEAK FOR IT.
I CAN THINK OF NO ONE BETTER ... THAN YOU.
I CAN'T LEAD! YOU LEAD! YOU'VE ALWAYS LED! I'M JUST A PIRATE! NOBODY CARES WHAT I SAY!
NO — STAY AWAKE! DON'T LEAVE ME!
LOOK AFTER TIBBOT ... TEACH HIM WELL ...
I LOVE YOU ... GRACE O'MALLEY ...

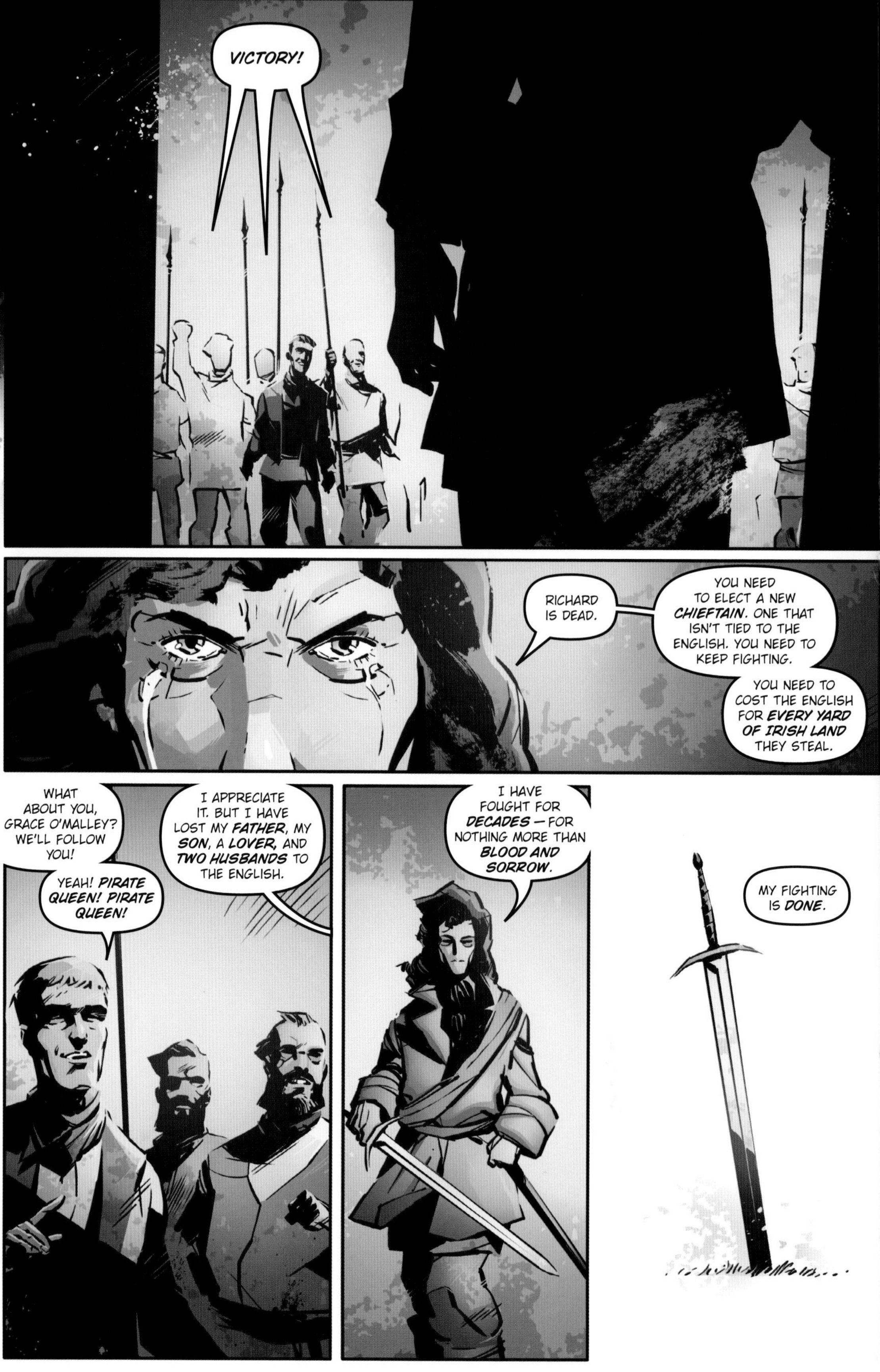
VICTORY!
RICHARD IS DEAD.
YOU NEED TO ELECT A NEW CHIEFTAIN. ONE THAT ISN'T TIED TO THE ENGLISH. YOU NEED TO KEEP FIGHTING.
YOU NEED TO COST THE ENGLISH FOR EVERY YARD OF IRISH LAND THEY STEAL.
WHAT ABOUT YOU, GRACE O'MALLEY? WE'LL FOLLOW YOU!
YEAH! PIRATE QUEEN! PIRATE QUEEN!
I APPRECIATE IT. BUT I HAVE LOST MY FATHER, MY SON, A LOVER, AND TWO HUSBANDS TO THE ENGLISH.
I HAVE FOUGHT FOR DECADES — FOR NOTHING MORE THAN BLOOD AND SORROW.
MY FIGHTING IS DONE.

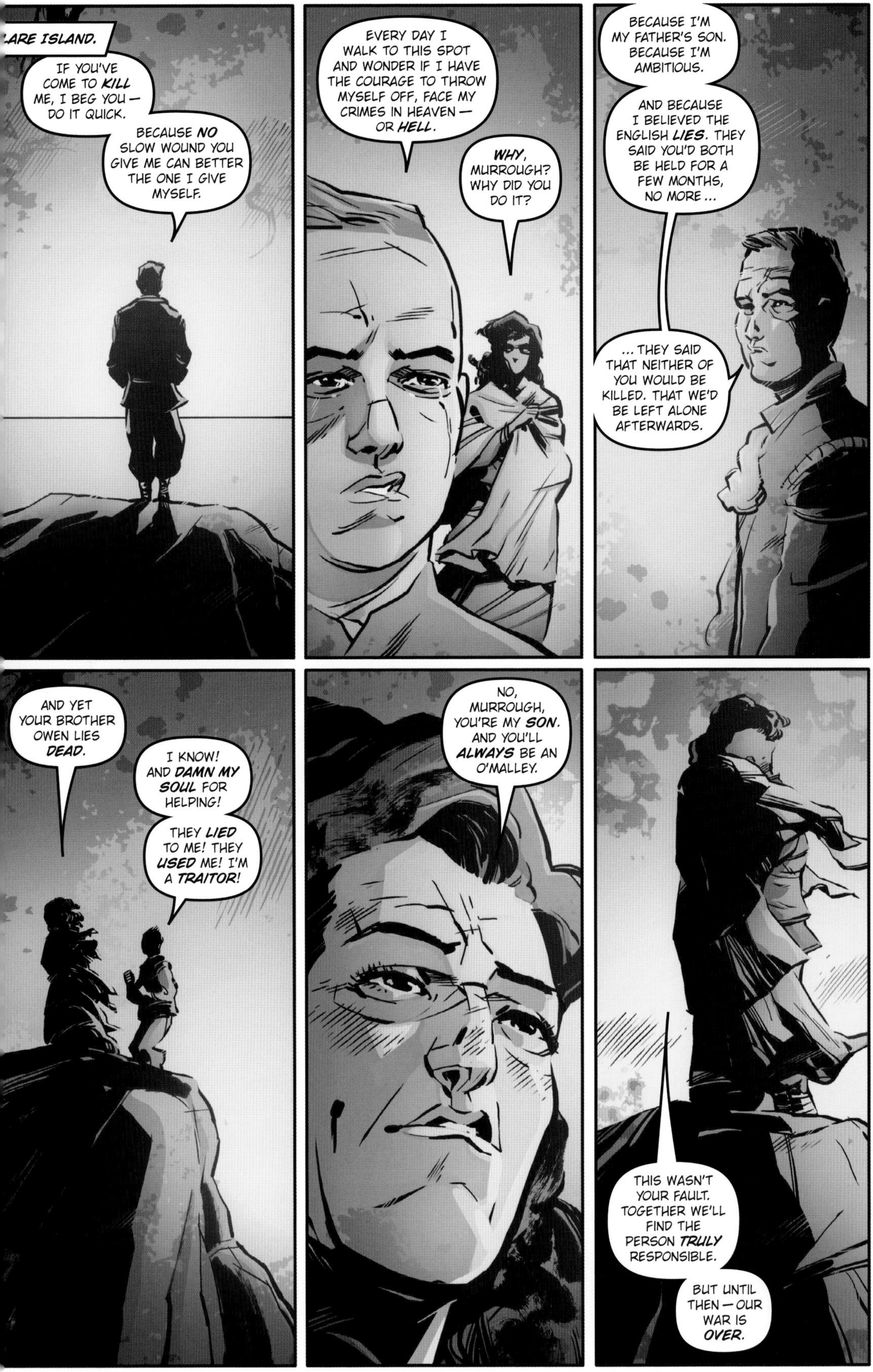

LARE ISLAND.
IF YOU'VE COME TO KILL ME, I BEG YOU — DO IT QUICK.
BECAUSE NO SLOW WOUND YOU GIVE ME CAN BETTER THE ONE I GIVE MYSELF.
EVERY DAY I WALK TO THIS SPOT AND WONDER IF I HAVE THE COURAGE TO THROW MYSELF OFF, FACE MY CRIMES IN HEAVEN — OR HELL.
WHY, MURROUGH? WHY DID YOU DO IT?
BECAUSE I'M MY FATHER'S SON. BECAUSE I'M AMBITIOUS.
AND BECAUSE I BELIEVED THE ENGLISH LIES. THEY SAID YOU'D BOTH BE HELD FOR A FEW MONTHS, NO MORE...
...THEY SAID THAT NEITHER OF YOU WOULD BE KILLED. THAT WE'D BE LEFT ALONE AFTERWARDS.
AND YET YOUR BROTHER OWEN LIES DEAD.
I KNOW! AND DAMN MY SOUL FOR HELPING!
THEY LIED TO ME! THEY USED ME! I'M A TRAITOR!
NO, MURROUGH, YOU'RE MY SON. AND YOU'LL ALWAYS BE AN O'MALLEY.
THIS WASN'T YOUR FAULT. TOGETHER WE'LL FIND THE PERSON TRULY RESPONSIBLE.
BUT UNTIL THEN — OUR WAR IS OVER.

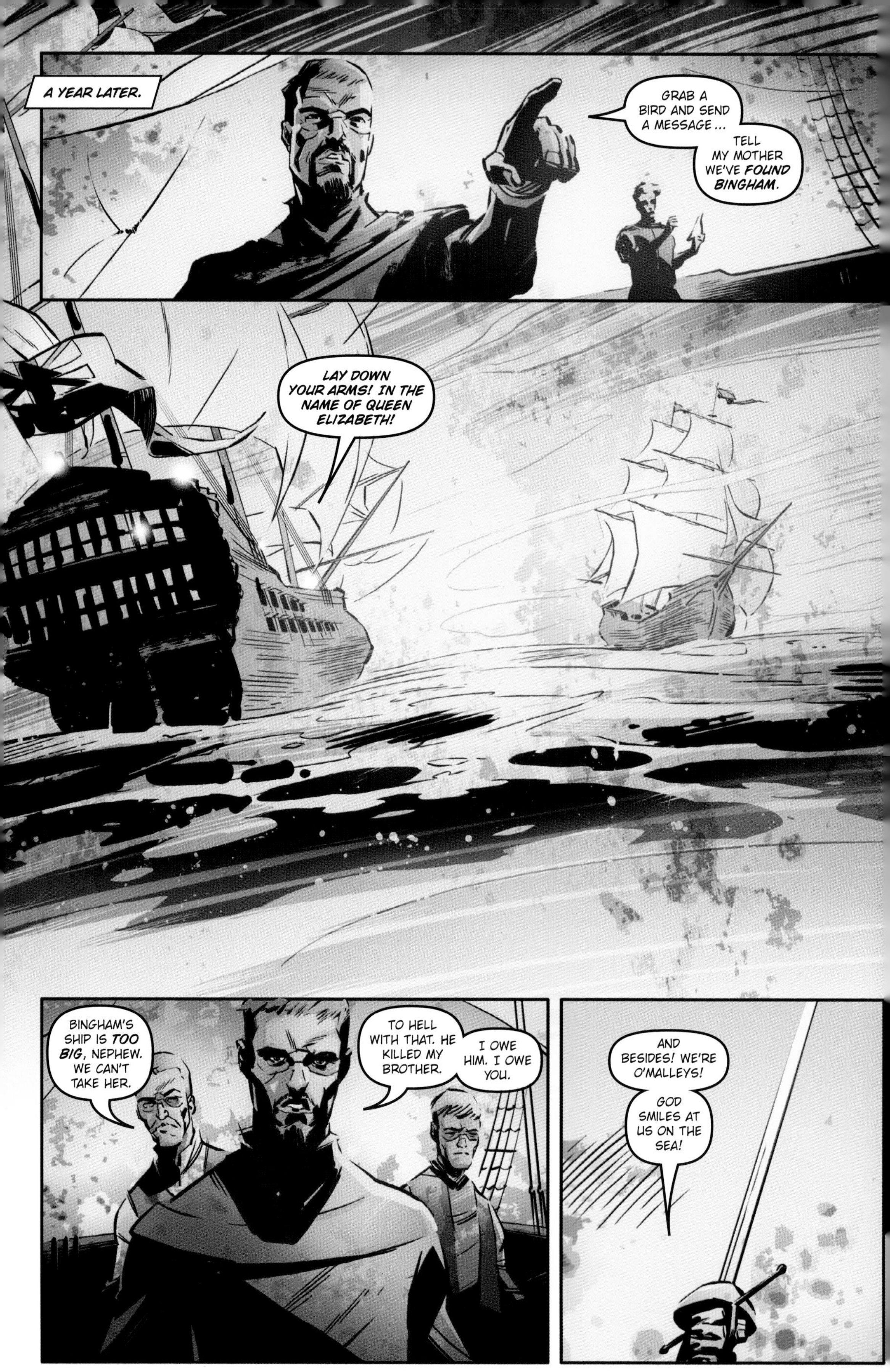
A YEAR LATER.
GRAB A BIRD AND SEND A MESSAGE...
TELL MY MOTHER WE'VE FOUND BINGHAM.
LAY DOWN YOUR ARMS! IN THE NAME OF QUEEN ELIZABETH!
BINGHAM'S SHIP IS TOO BIG, NEPHEW. WE CAN'T TAKE HER.
TO HELL WITH THAT. HE KILLED MY BROTHER.
I OWE HIM. I OWE YOU.
AND BESIDES! WE'RE O'MALLEYS!
GOD SMILES AT US ON THE SEA!

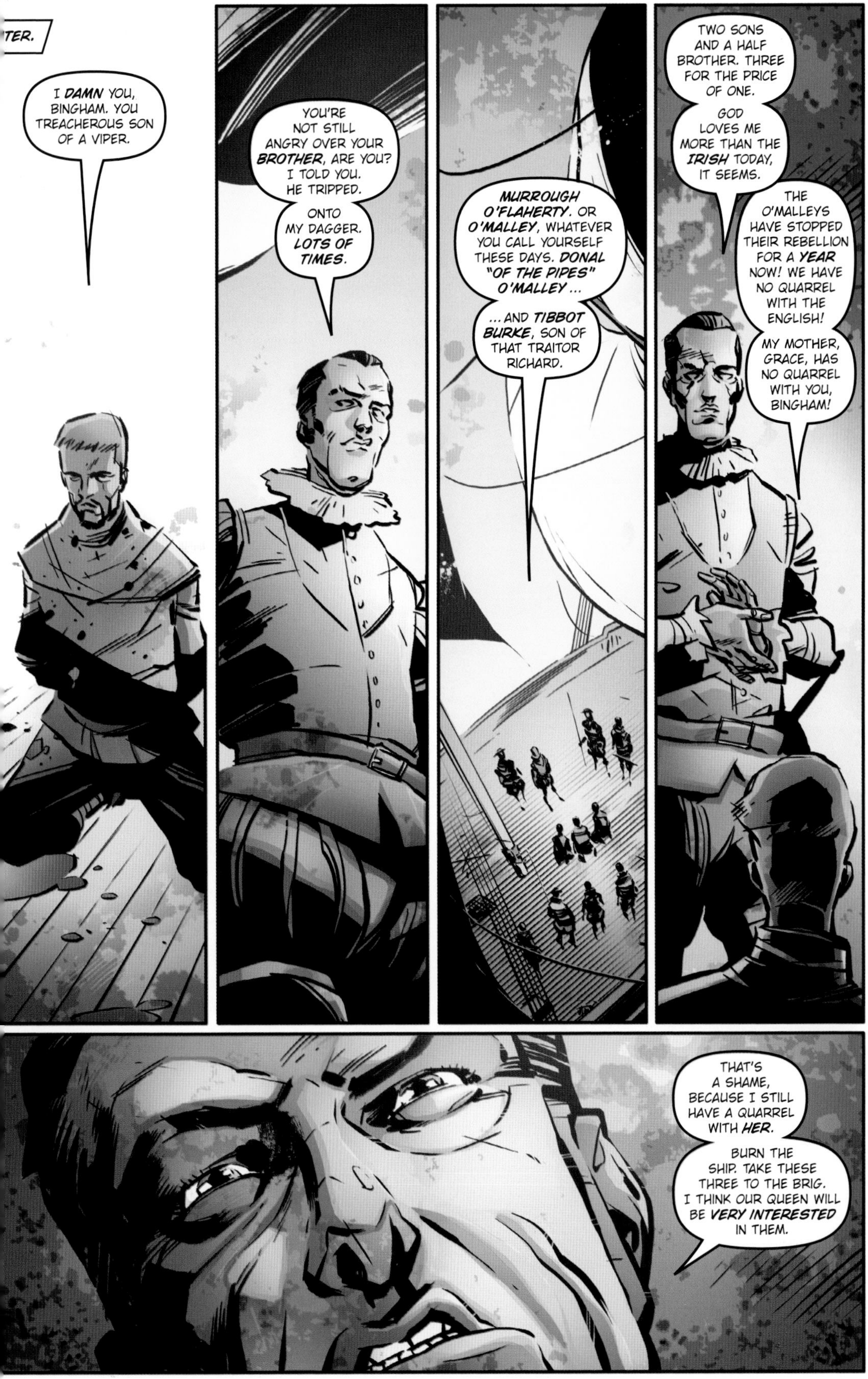
TER.
I DAMN YOU, BINGHAM. YOU TREACHEROUS SON OF A VIPER.
YOU'RE NOT STILL ANGRY OVER YOUR BROTHER, ARE YOU? I TOLD YOU. HE TRIPPED.
ONTO MY DAGGER. LOTS OF TIMES.
MURROUGH O'FLAHERTY. OR O'MALLEY, WHATEVER YOU CALL YOURSELF THESE DAYS. DONAL "OF THE PIPES" O'MALLEY...
...AND TIBBOT BURKE, SON OF THAT TRAITOR RICHARD.
TWO SONS AND A HALF BROTHER. THREE FOR THE PRICE OF ONE.
GOD LOVES ME MORE THAN THE IRISH TODAY, IT SEEMS.
THE O'MALLEYS HAVE STOPPED THEIR REBELLION FOR A YEAR NOW! WE HAVE NO QUARREL WITH THE ENGLISH!
MY MOTHER, GRACE, HAS NO QUARREL WITH YOU, BINGHAM!
THAT'S A SHAME, BECAUSE I STILL HAVE A QUARREL WITH HER.
BURN THE SHIP. TAKE THESE THREE TO THE BRIG. I THINK OUR QUEEN WILL BE VERY INTERESTED IN THEM.

CLARE ISLAND.

IT'S FROM ENGLAND. YOUR BROTHER AND YOUR SONS ARE LOCKED IN THE *TOWER OF LONDON.*

RICHARD BINGHAM HAS REQUESTED YOU GIVE YOURSELF UP AND *JOIN* THEM, OR THEY'LL BE EXECUTED.

AND IF I JOIN THEM?

IT DOESN'T SAY.

I FOUGHT FOR IRELAND FOR TWO DECADES, BUT AFTER RICHARD DIED THEY ELECTED AN *ENGLISH PUPPET* AS THE MacWILLIAM, THE HIGH CHIEFTAIN.

I WALKED AWAY FROM BATTLE AND STILL BINGHAM HOUNDS ME.

DAMN MURROUGH! I TOLD HIM *TO LEAVE IT BE!*

HE'S HUNTED FOR BINGHAM ON THE SEAS FOR A YEAR AND HE'S *NEVER* KNOWN WHAT TO DO WHEN HE FOUND HIM!

WHAT MESSAGE SHALL I SEND BACK?

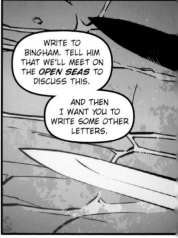

WRITE TO BINGHAM. TELL HIM THAT WE'LL MEET ON THE *OPEN SEAS* TO DISCUSS THIS.

AND THEN I WANT YOU TO WRITE SOME OTHER LETTERS.

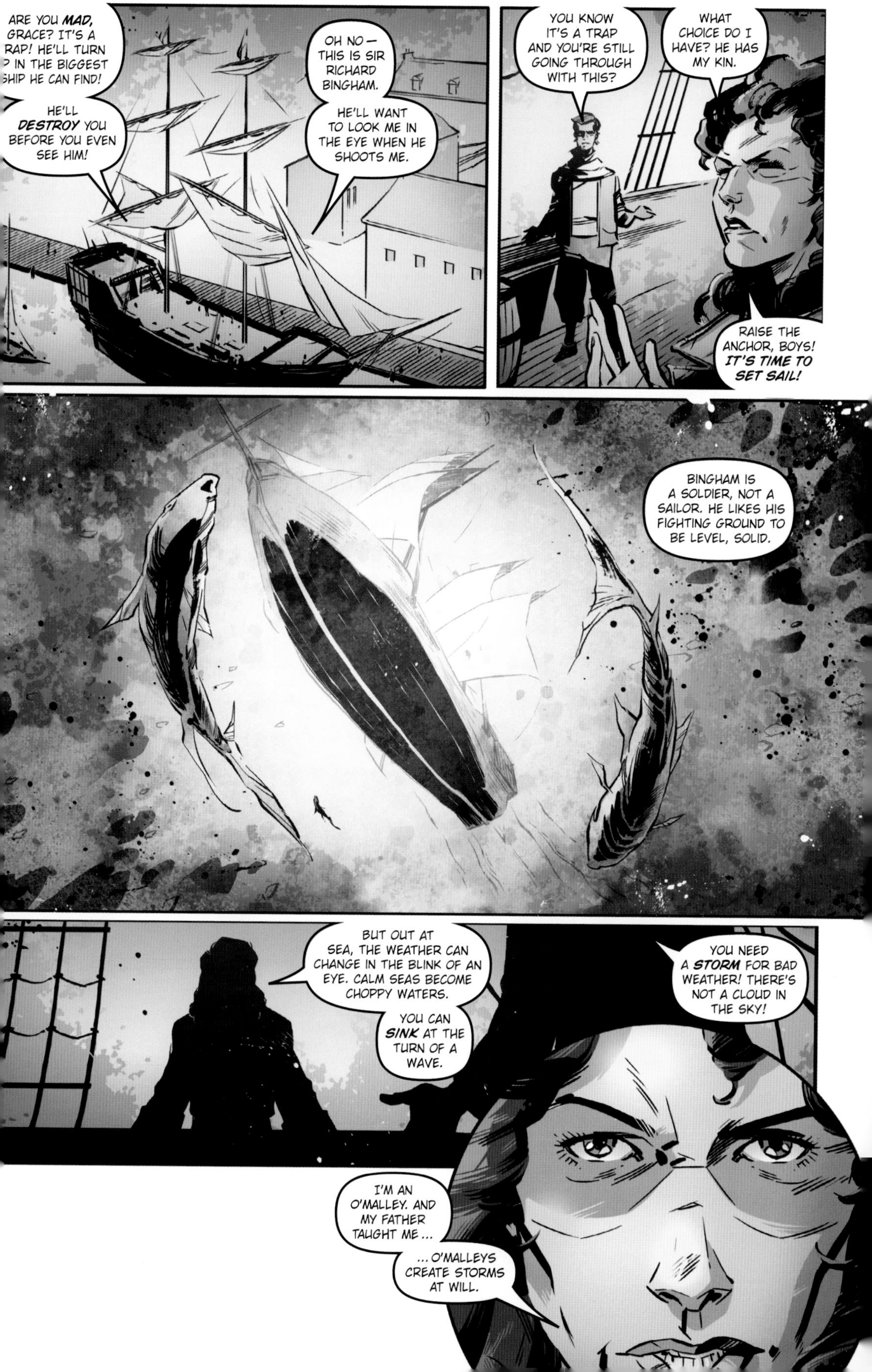
ARE YOU MAD, GRACE? IT'S A RAP! HE'LL TURN P IN THE BIGGEST SHIP HE CAN FIND!
HE'LL DESTROY YOU BEFORE YOU EVEN SEE HIM!
OH NO— THIS IS SIR RICHARD BINGHAM.
HE'LL WANT TO LOOK ME IN THE EYE WHEN HE SHOOTS ME.
YOU KNOW IT'S A TRAP AND YOU'RE STILL GOING THROUGH WITH THIS?
WHAT CHOICE DO I HAVE? HE HAS MY KIN.
RAISE THE ANCHOR, BOYS! IT'S TIME TO SET SAIL!
BINGHAM IS A SOLDIER, NOT A SAILOR. HE LIKES HIS FIGHTING GROUND TO BE LEVEL, SOLID.
BUT OUT AT SEA, THE WEATHER CAN CHANGE IN THE BLINK OF AN EYE. CALM SEAS BECOME CHOPPY WATERS.
YOU CAN SINK AT THE TURN OF A WAVE.
YOU NEED A STORM FOR BAD WEATHER! THERE'S NOT A CLOUD IN THE SKY!
I'M AN O'MALLEY. AND MY FATHER TAUGHT ME...
...O'MALLEYS CREATE STORMS AT WILL.

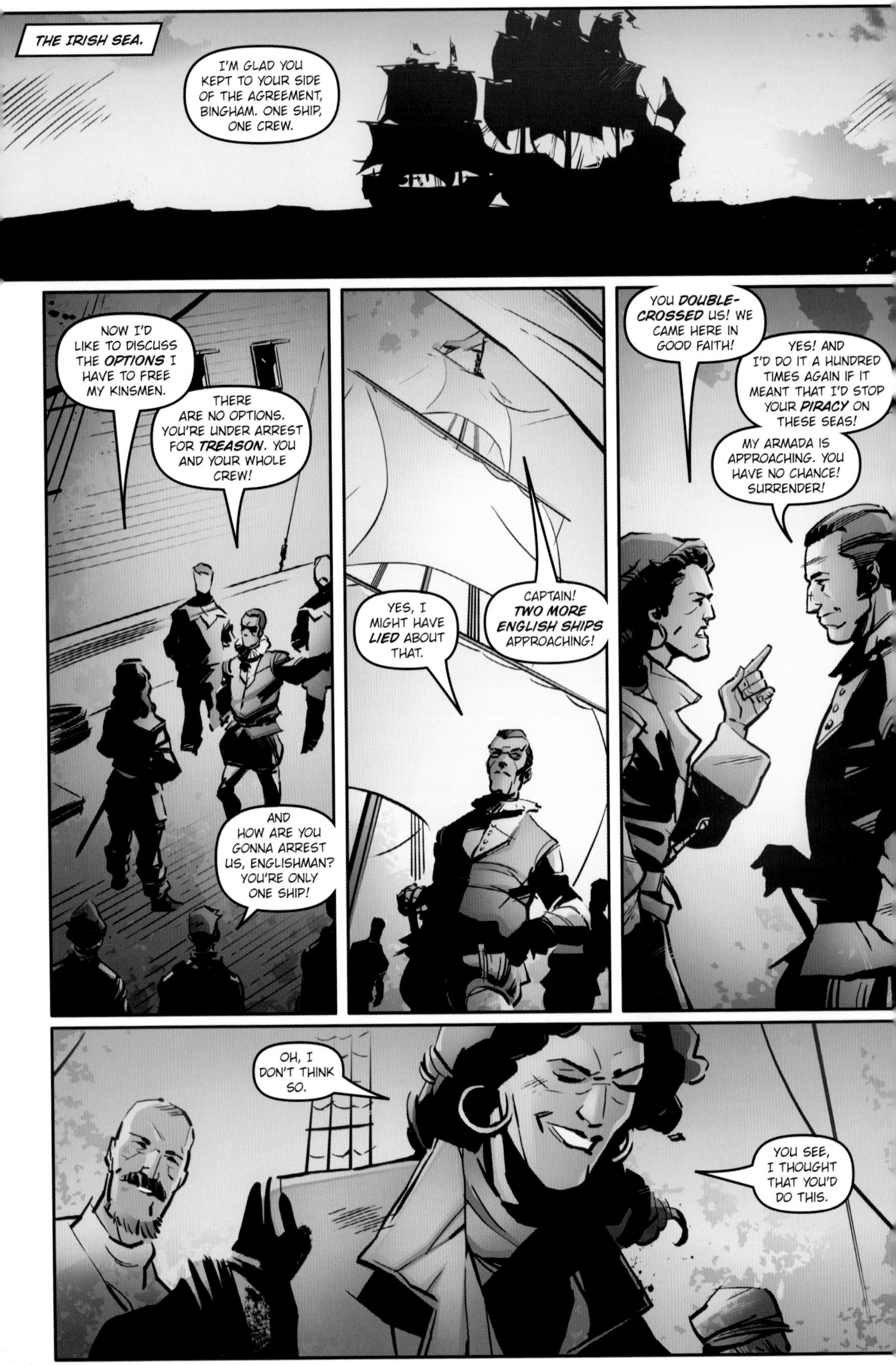
THE IRISH SEA.
I'M GLAD YOU KEPT TO YOUR SIDE OF THE AGREEMENT, BINGHAM. ONE SHIP, ONE CREW.
NOW I'D LIKE TO DISCUSS THE OPTIONS I HAVE TO FREE MY KINSMEN.
THERE ARE NO OPTIONS. YOU'RE UNDER ARREST FOR TREASON. YOU AND YOUR WHOLE CREW!
AND HOW ARE YOU GONNA ARREST US, ENGLISHMAN? YOU'RE ONLY ONE SHIP!
CAPTAIN! TWO MORE ENGLISH SHIPS APPROACHING!
YES, I MIGHT HAVE LIED ABOUT THAT.
YOU DOUBLE-CROSSED US! WE CAME HERE IN GOOD FAITH!
YES! AND I'D DO IT A HUNDRED TIMES AGAIN IF IT MEANT THAT I'D STOP YOUR PIRACY ON THESE SEAS!
MY ARMADA IS APPROACHING. YOU HAVE NO CHANCE! SURRENDER!
OH, I DON'T THINK SO.
YOU SEE, I THOUGHT THAT YOU'D DO THIS.

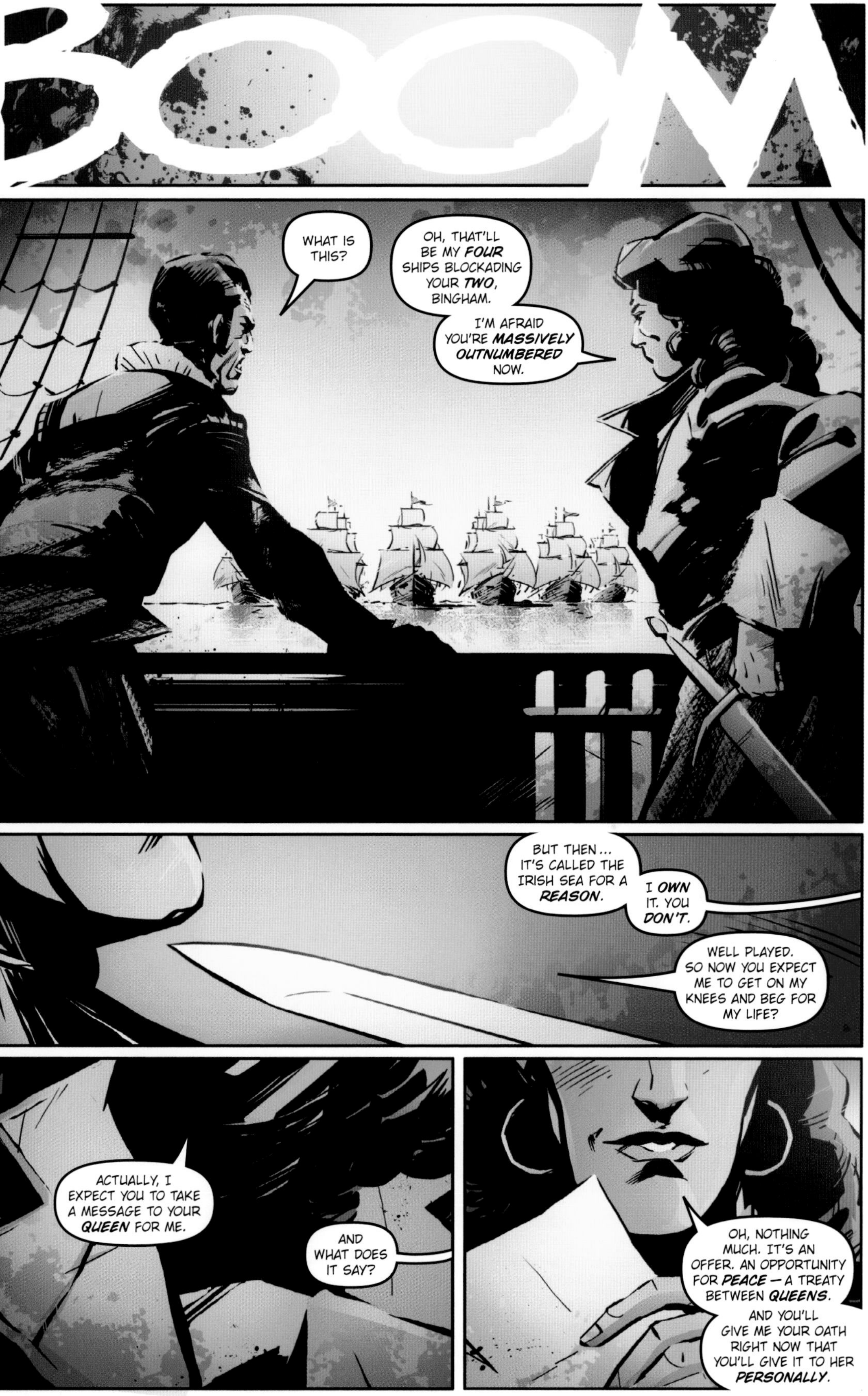
BOOM
WHAT IS THIS?
OH, THAT'LL BE MY FOUR SHIPS BLOCKADING YOUR TWO, BINGHAM.
I'M AFRAID YOU'RE MASSIVELY OUTNUMBERED NOW.
BUT THEN... IT'S CALLED THE IRISH SEA FOR A REASON.
I OWN IT. YOU DON'T.
WELL PLAYED. SO NOW YOU EXPECT ME TO GET ON MY KNEES AND BEG FOR MY LIFE?
ACTUALLY, I EXPECT YOU TO TAKE A MESSAGE TO YOUR QUEEN FOR ME.
AND WHAT DOES IT SAY?
OH, NOTHING MUCH. IT'S AN OFFER. AN OPPORTUNITY FOR PEACE — A TREATY BETWEEN QUEENS.
AND YOU'LL GIVE ME YOUR OATH RIGHT NOW THAT YOU'LL GIVE IT TO HER PERSONALLY.

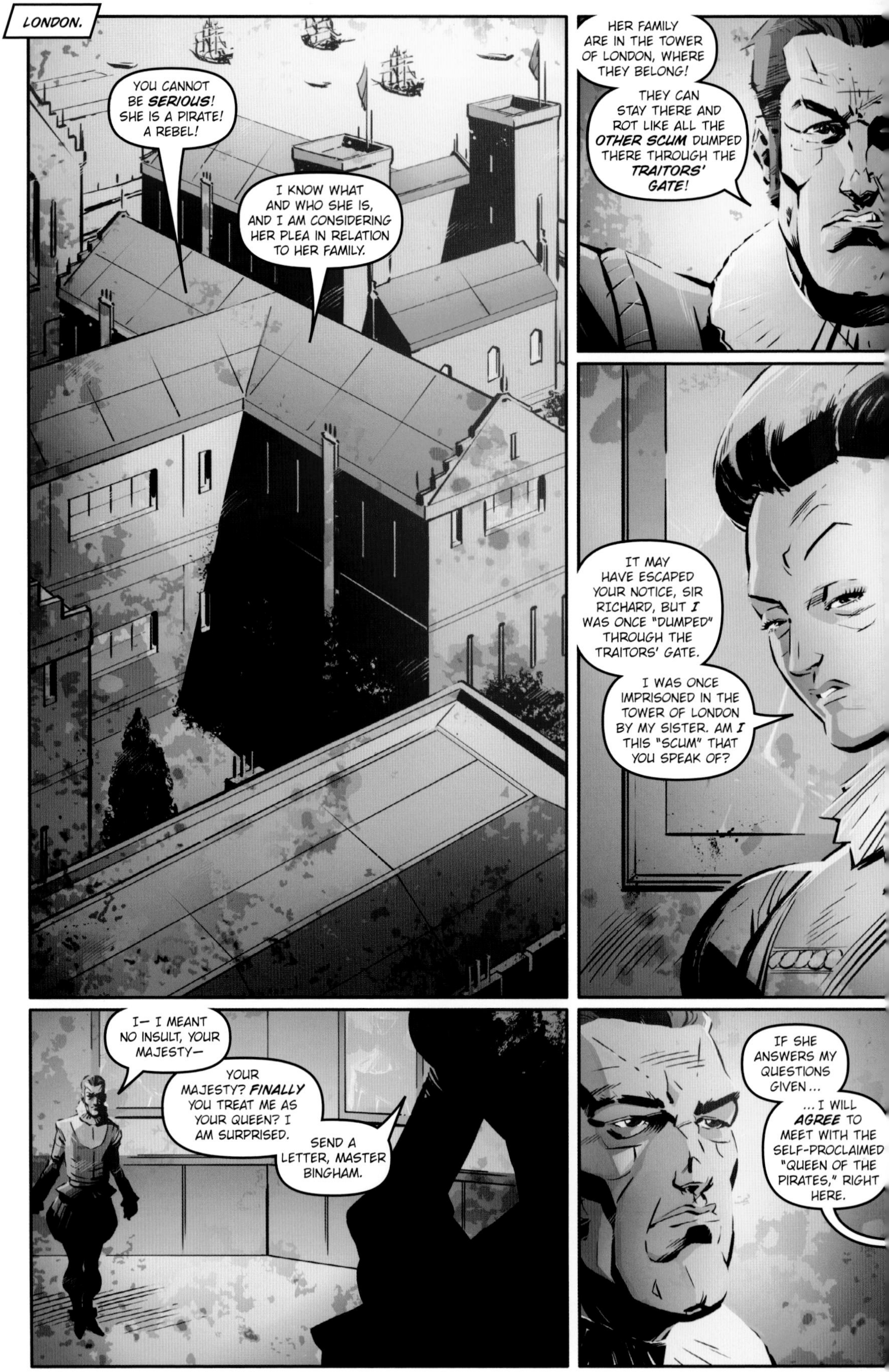
LONDON.
YOU CANNOT BE SERIOUS! SHE IS A PIRATE! A REBEL!
I KNOW WHAT AND WHO SHE IS, AND I AM CONSIDERING HER PLEA IN RELATION TO HER FAMILY.
HER FAMILY ARE IN THE TOWER OF LONDON, WHERE THEY BELONG!
THEY CAN STAY THERE AND ROT LIKE ALL THE OTHER SCUM DUMPED THERE THROUGH THE TRAITORS' GATE!
IT MAY HAVE ESCAPED YOUR NOTICE, SIR RICHARD, BUT I WAS ONCE "DUMPED" THROUGH THE TRAITORS' GATE.
I WAS ONCE IMPRISONED IN THE TOWER OF LONDON BY MY SISTER. AM I THIS "SCUM" THAT YOU SPEAK OF?
I— I MEANT NO INSULT, YOUR MAJESTY—
YOUR MAJESTY? FINALLY YOU TREAT ME AS YOUR QUEEN? I AM SURPRISED.
SEND A LETTER, MASTER BINGHAM.
IF SHE ANSWERS MY QUESTIONS GIVEN...
...I WILL AGREE TO MEET WITH THE SELF-PROCLAIMED "QUEEN OF THE PIRATES," RIGHT HERE.

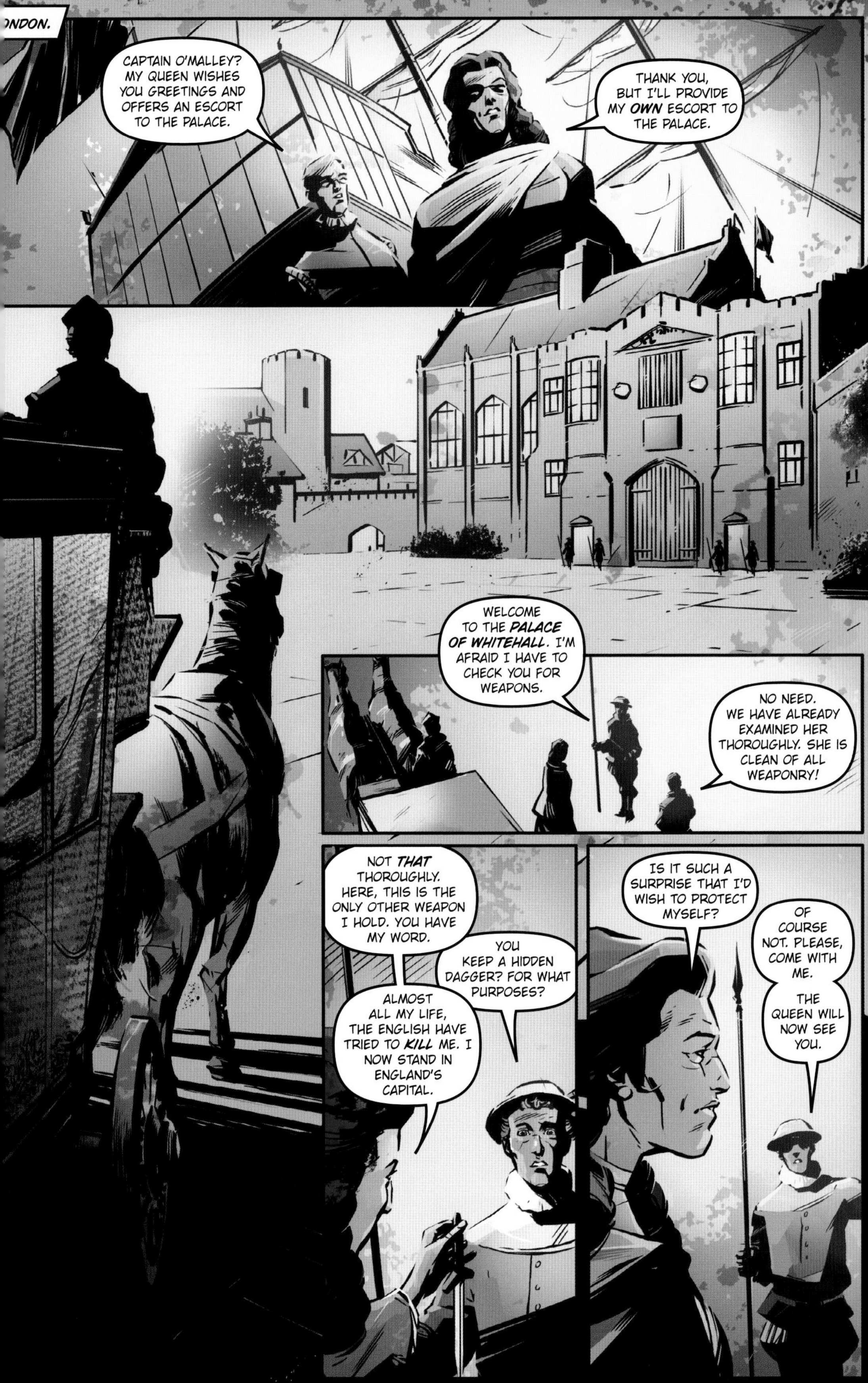
ONDON.
CAPTAIN O'MALLEY? MY QUEEN WISHES YOU GREETINGS AND OFFERS AN ESCORT TO THE PALACE.
THANK YOU, BUT I'LL PROVIDE MY OWN ESCORT TO THE PALACE.
WELCOME TO THE PALACE OF WHITEHALL. I'M AFRAID I HAVE TO CHECK YOU FOR WEAPONS.
NO NEED. WE HAVE ALREADY EXAMINED HER THOROUGHLY. SHE IS CLEAN OF ALL WEAPONRY!
NOT THAT THOROUGHLY. HERE, THIS IS THE ONLY OTHER WEAPON I HOLD. YOU HAVE MY WORD.
YOU KEEP A HIDDEN DAGGER? FOR WHAT PURPOSES?
ALMOST ALL MY LIFE, THE ENGLISH HAVE TRIED TO KILL ME. I NOW STAND IN ENGLAND'S CAPITAL.
IS IT SUCH A SURPRISE THAT I'D WISH TO PROTECT MYSELF?
OF COURSE NOT. PLEASE, COME WITH ME.
THE QUEEN WILL NOW SEE YOU.

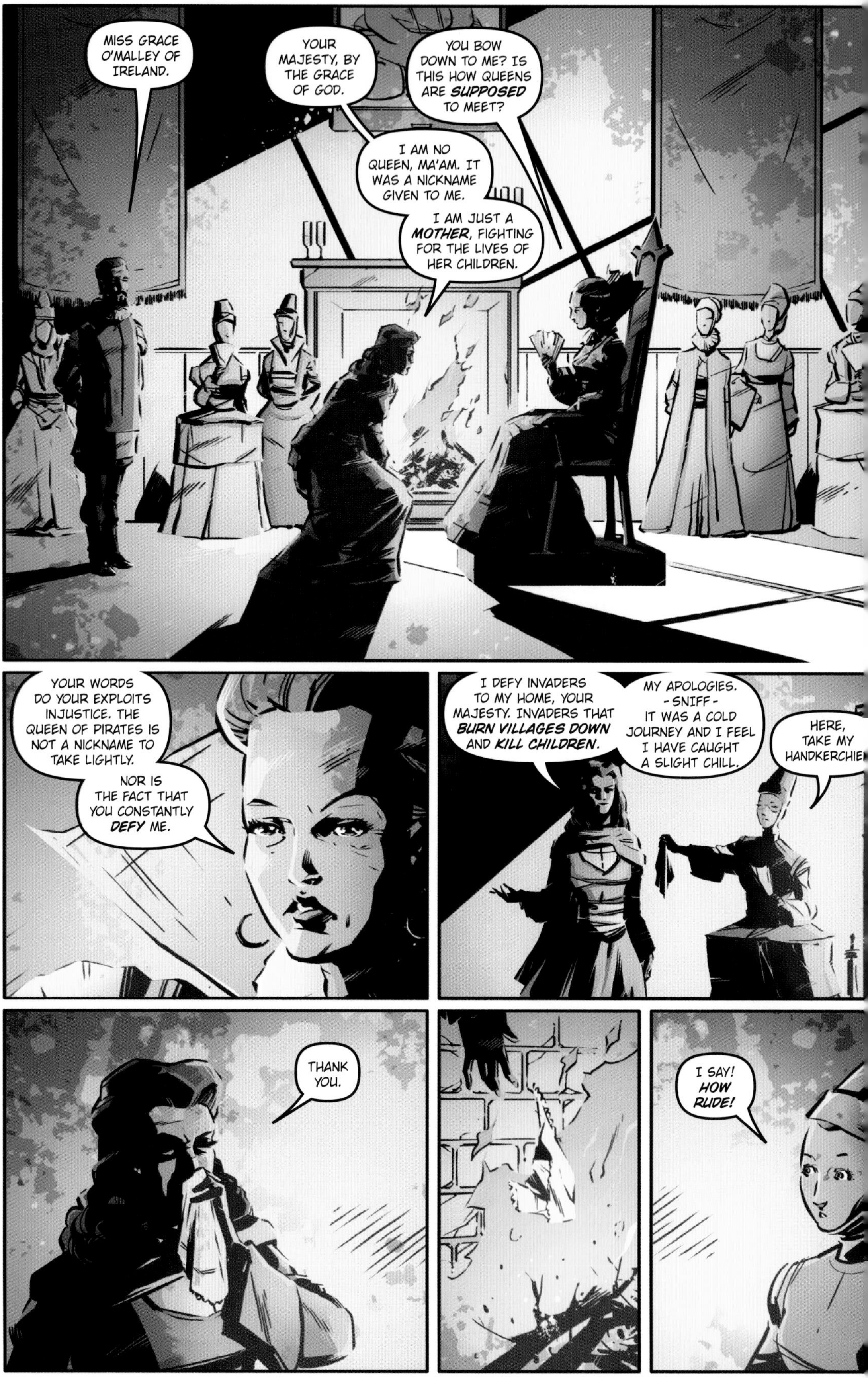
MISS GRACE O'MALLEY OF IRELAND.
YOUR MAJESTY, BY THE GRACE OF GOD.
YOU BOW DOWN TO ME? IS THIS HOW QUEENS ARE SUPPOSED TO MEET?
I AM NO QUEEN, MA'AM. IT WAS A NICKNAME GIVEN TO ME.
I AM JUST A MOTHER, FIGHTING FOR THE LIVES OF HER CHILDREN.
YOUR WORDS DO YOUR EXPLOITS INJUSTICE. THE QUEEN OF PIRATES IS NOT A NICKNAME TO TAKE LIGHTLY.
NOR IS THE FACT THAT YOU CONSTANTLY DEFY ME.
I DEFY INVADERS TO MY HOME, YOUR MAJESTY. INVADERS THAT BURN VILLAGES DOWN AND KILL CHILDREN.
MY APOLOGIES. - SNIFF - IT WAS A COLD JOURNEY AND I FEEL I HAVE CAUGHT A SLIGHT CHILL.
HERE, TAKE MY HANDKERCHIE
THANK YOU.
I SAY! HOW RUDE!

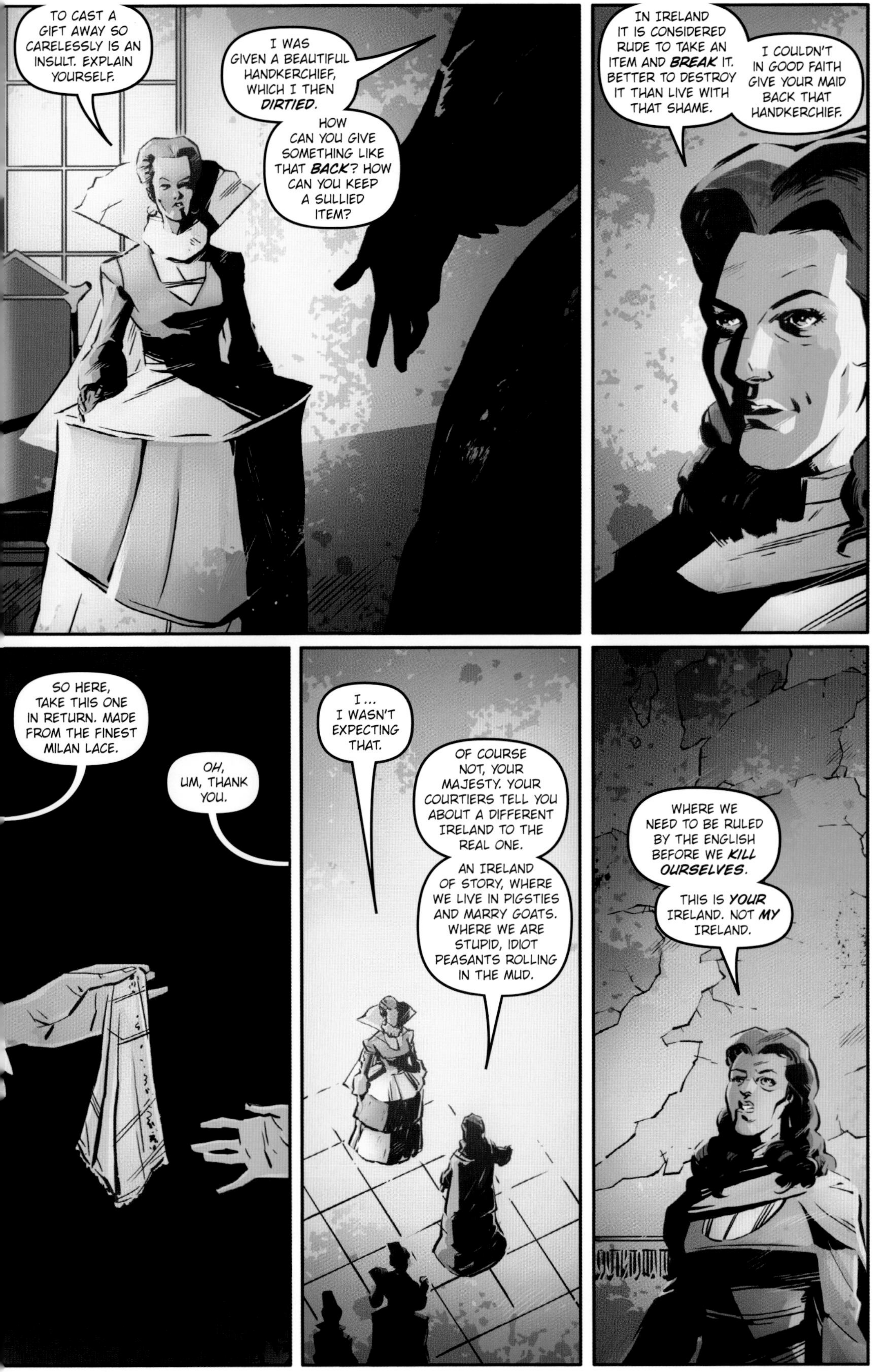
TO CAST A GIFT AWAY SO CARELESSLY IS AN INSULT. EXPLAIN YOURSELF.
I WAS GIVEN A BEAUTIFUL HANDKERCHIEF, WHICH I THEN DIRTIED.
HOW CAN YOU GIVE SOMETHING LIKE THAT BACK? HOW CAN YOU KEEP A SULLIED ITEM?
IN IRELAND IT IS CONSIDERED RUDE TO TAKE AN ITEM AND BREAK IT. BETTER TO DESTROY IT THAN LIVE WITH THAT SHAME.
I COULDN'T IN GOOD FAITH GIVE YOUR MAID BACK THAT HANDKERCHIEF.
SO HERE, TAKE THIS ONE IN RETURN. MADE FROM THE FINEST MILAN LACE.
OH, UM, THANK YOU.
I... I WASN'T EXPECTING THAT.
OF COURSE NOT, YOUR MAJESTY. YOUR COURTIERS TELL YOU ABOUT A DIFFERENT IRELAND TO THE REAL ONE.
AN IRELAND OF STORY, WHERE WE LIVE IN PIGSTIES AND MARRY GOATS. WHERE WE ARE STUPID, IDIOT PEASANTS ROLLING IN THE MUD.
WHERE WE NEED TO BE RULED BY THE ENGLISH BEFORE WE KILL OURSELVES.
THIS IS YOUR IRELAND. NOT MY IRELAND.

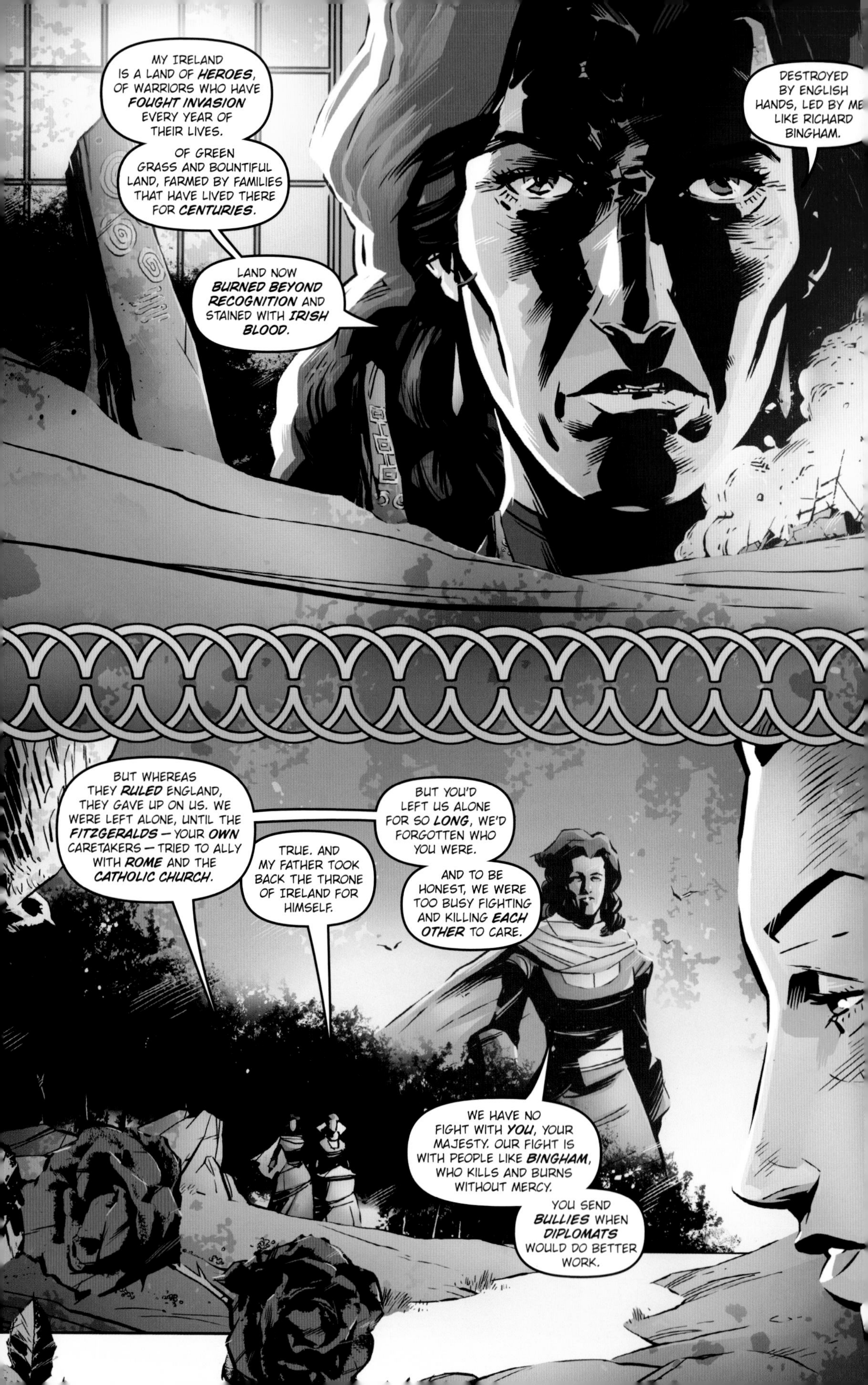
MY IRELAND IS A LAND OF HEROES, OF WARRIORS WHO HAVE FOUGHT INVASION EVERY YEAR OF THEIR LIVES.
OF GREEN GRASS AND BOUNTIFUL LAND, FARMED BY FAMILIES THAT HAVE LIVED THERE FOR CENTURIES.
LAND NOW BURNED BEYOND RECOGNITION AND STAINED WITH IRISH BLOOD.
DESTROYED BY ENGLISH HANDS, LED BY ME LIKE RICHARD BINGHAM.
BUT WHEREAS THEY RULED ENGLAND, THEY GAVE UP ON US. WE WERE LEFT ALONE, UNTIL THE FITZGERALDS — YOUR OWN CARETAKERS — TRIED TO ALLY WITH ROME AND THE CATHOLIC CHURCH.
TRUE. AND MY FATHER TOOK BACK THE THRONE OF IRELAND FOR HIMSELF.
BUT YOU'D LEFT US ALONE FOR SO LONG, WE'D FORGOTTEN WHO YOU WERE.
AND TO BE HONEST, WE WERE TOO BUSY FIGHTING AND KILLING EACH OTHER TO CARE.
WE HAVE NO FIGHT WITH YOU, YOUR MAJESTY. OUR FIGHT IS WITH PEOPLE LIKE BINGHAM, WHO KILLS AND BURNS WITHOUT MERCY.
YOU SEND BULLIES WHEN DIPLOMATS WOULD DO BETTER WORK.

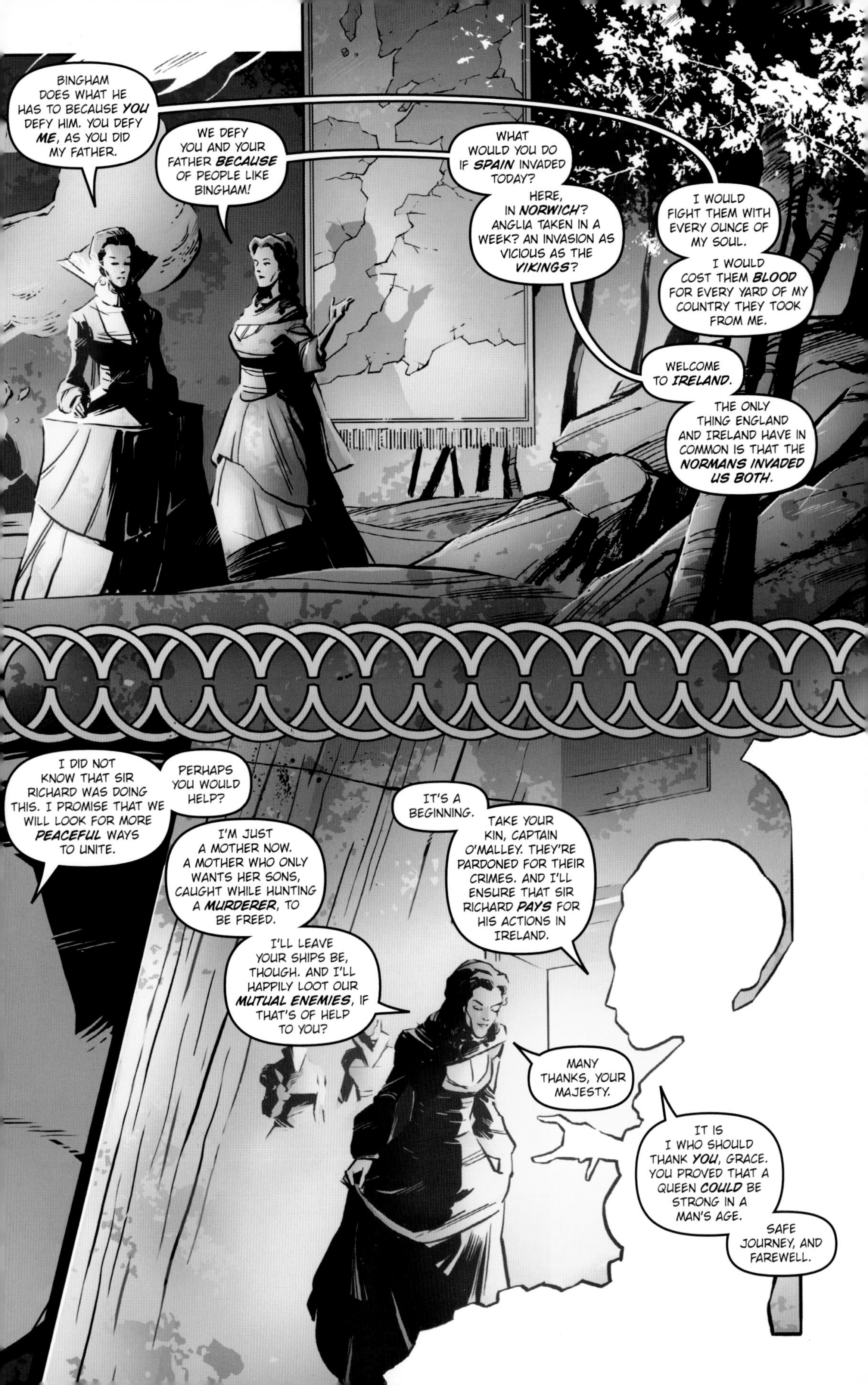

BINGHAM DOES WHAT HE HAS TO BECAUSE YOU DEFY HIM. YOU DEFY ME, AS YOU DID MY FATHER.
WE DEFY YOU AND YOUR FATHER BECAUSE OF PEOPLE LIKE BINGHAM!
WHAT WOULD YOU DO IF SPAIN INVADED TODAY?
HERE, IN NORWICH? ANGLIA TAKEN IN A WEEK? AN INVASION AS VICIOUS AS THE VIKINGS?
I WOULD FIGHT THEM WITH EVERY OUNCE OF MY SOUL.
I WOULD COST THEM BLOOD FOR EVERY YARD OF MY COUNTRY THEY TOOK FROM ME.
WELCOME TO IRELAND.
THE ONLY THING ENGLAND AND IRELAND HAVE IN COMMON IS THAT THE NORMANS INVADED US BOTH.
I DID NOT KNOW THAT SIR RICHARD WAS DOING THIS. I PROMISE THAT WE WILL LOOK FOR MORE PEACEFUL WAYS TO UNITE.
PERHAPS YOU WOULD HELP?
I'M JUST A MOTHER NOW. A MOTHER WHO ONLY WANTS HER SONS, CAUGHT WHILE HUNTING A MURDERER, TO BE FREED.
I'LL LEAVE YOUR SHIPS BE, THOUGH. AND I'LL HAPPILY LOOT OUR MUTUAL ENEMIES, IF THAT'S OF HELP TO YOU?
IT'S A BEGINNING.
TAKE YOUR KIN, CAPTAIN O'MALLEY. THEY'RE PARDONED FOR THEIR CRIMES. AND I'LL ENSURE THAT SIR RICHARD PAYS FOR HIS ACTIONS IN IRELAND.
MANY THANKS, YOUR MAJESTY.
IT IS I WHO SHOULD THANK YOU, GRACE. YOU PROVED THAT A QUEEN COULD BE STRONG IN A MAN'S AGE.
SAFE JOURNEY, AND FAREWELL.

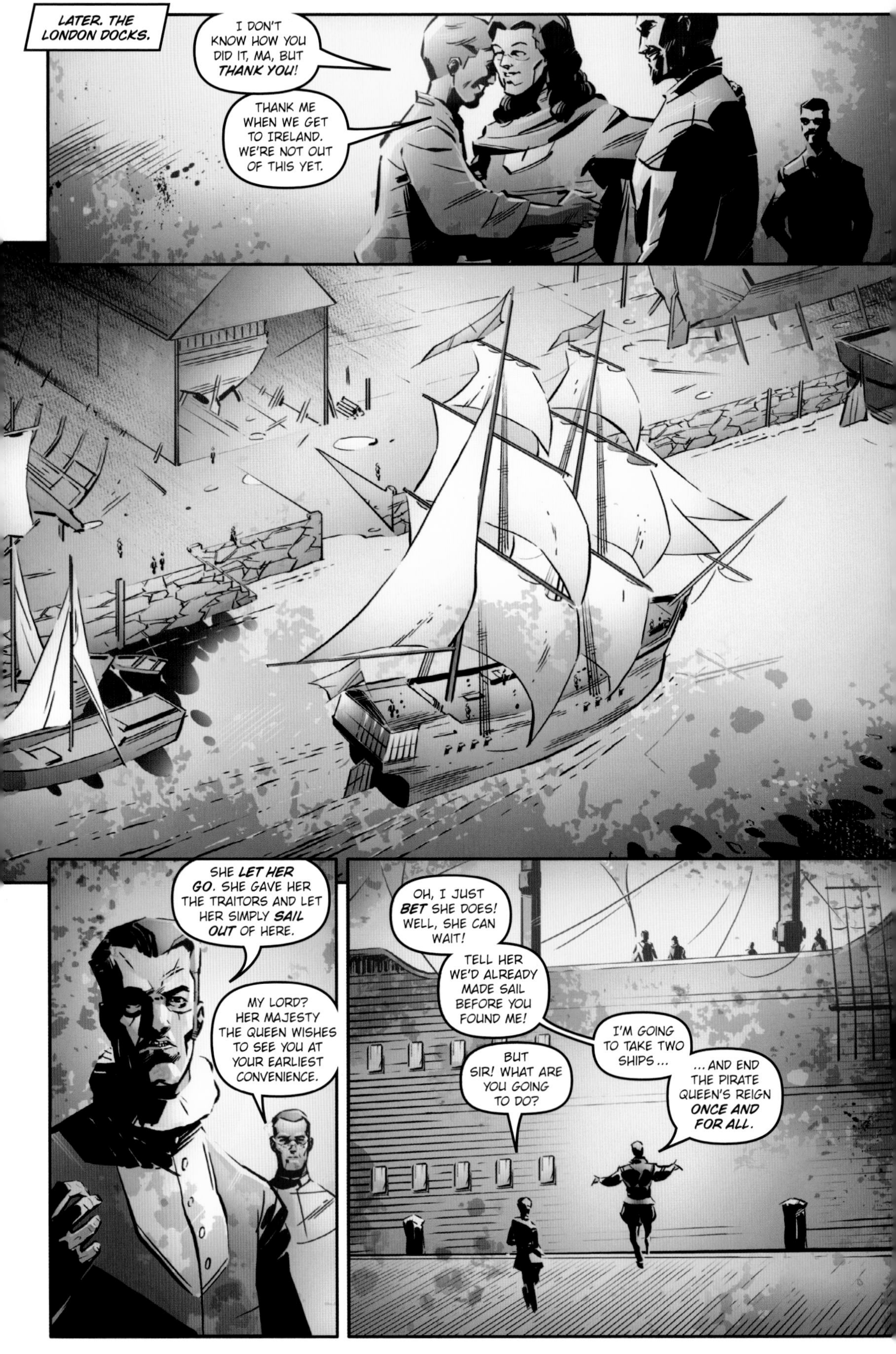
LATER. THE LONDON DOCKS.
I DON'T KNOW HOW YOU DID IT, MA, BUT THANK YOU!
THANK ME WHEN WE GET TO IRELAND. WE'RE NOT OUT OF THIS YET.
SHE LET HER GO. SHE GAVE HER THE TRAITORS AND LET HER SIMPLY SAIL OUT OF HERE.
MY LORD? HER MAJESTY THE QUEEN WISHES TO SEE YOU AT YOUR EARLIEST CONVENIENCE.
OH, I JUST BET SHE DOES! WELL, SHE CAN WAIT!
TELL HER WE'D ALREADY MADE SAIL BEFORE YOU FOUND ME!
BUT SIR! WHAT ARE YOU GOING TO DO?
I'M GOING TO TAKE TWO SHIPS...
...AND END THE PIRATE QUEEN'S REIGN ONCE AND FOR ALL.

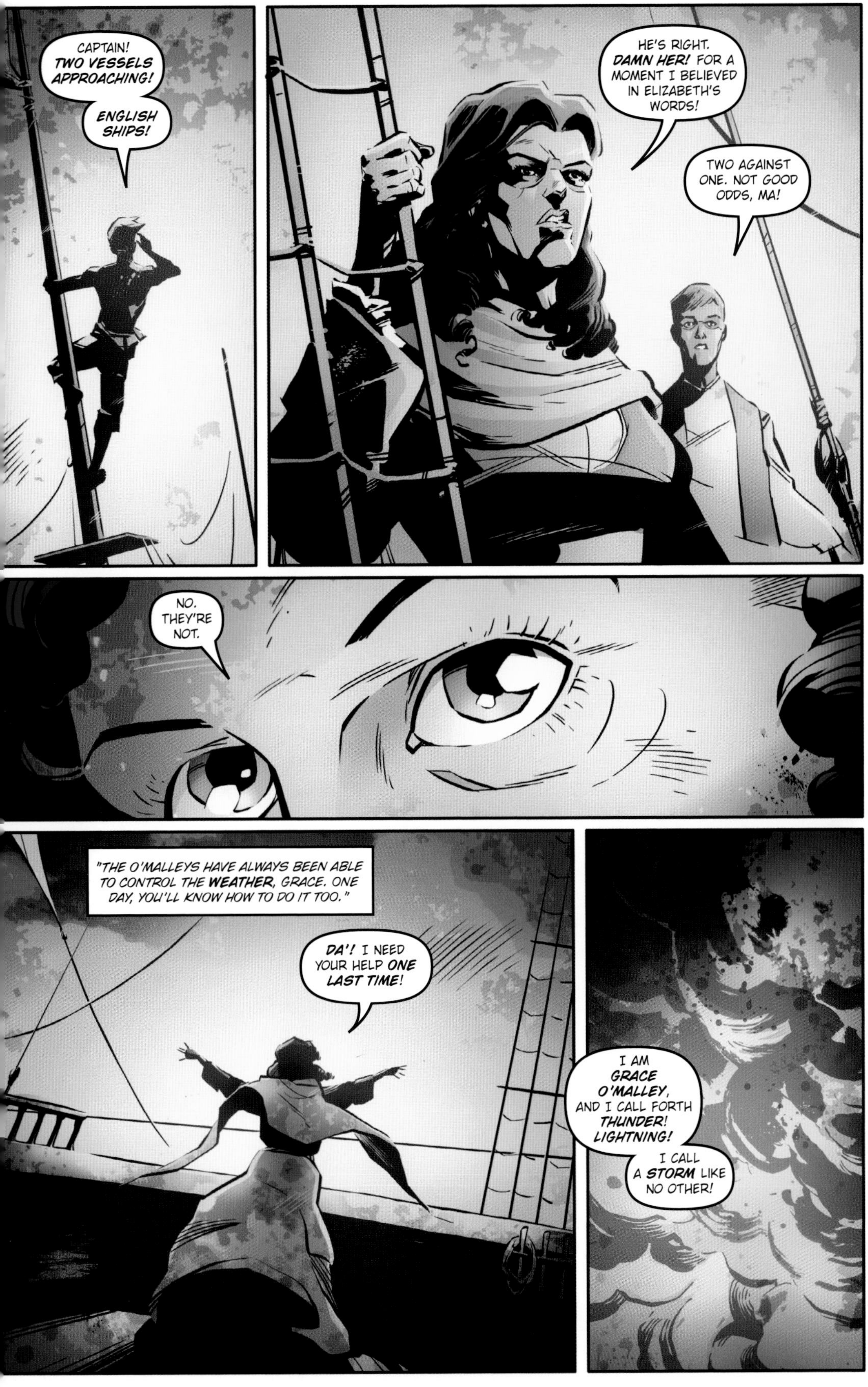
CAPTAIN! TWO VESSELS APPROACHING!
ENGLISH SHIPS!
HE'S RIGHT. DAMN HER! FOR A MOMENT I BELIEVED IN ELIZABETH'S WORDS!
TWO AGAINST ONE. NOT GOOD ODDS, MA!
NO. THEY'RE NOT.
"THE O'MALLEYS HAVE ALWAYS BEEN ABLE TO CONTROL THE WEATHER, GRACE. ONE DAY, YOU'LL KNOW HOW TO DO IT TOO."
DA'! I NEED YOUR HELP ONE LAST TIME!
I AM GRACE O'MALLEY, AND I CALL FORTH THUNDER! LIGHTNING!
I CALL A STORM LIKE NO OTHER!

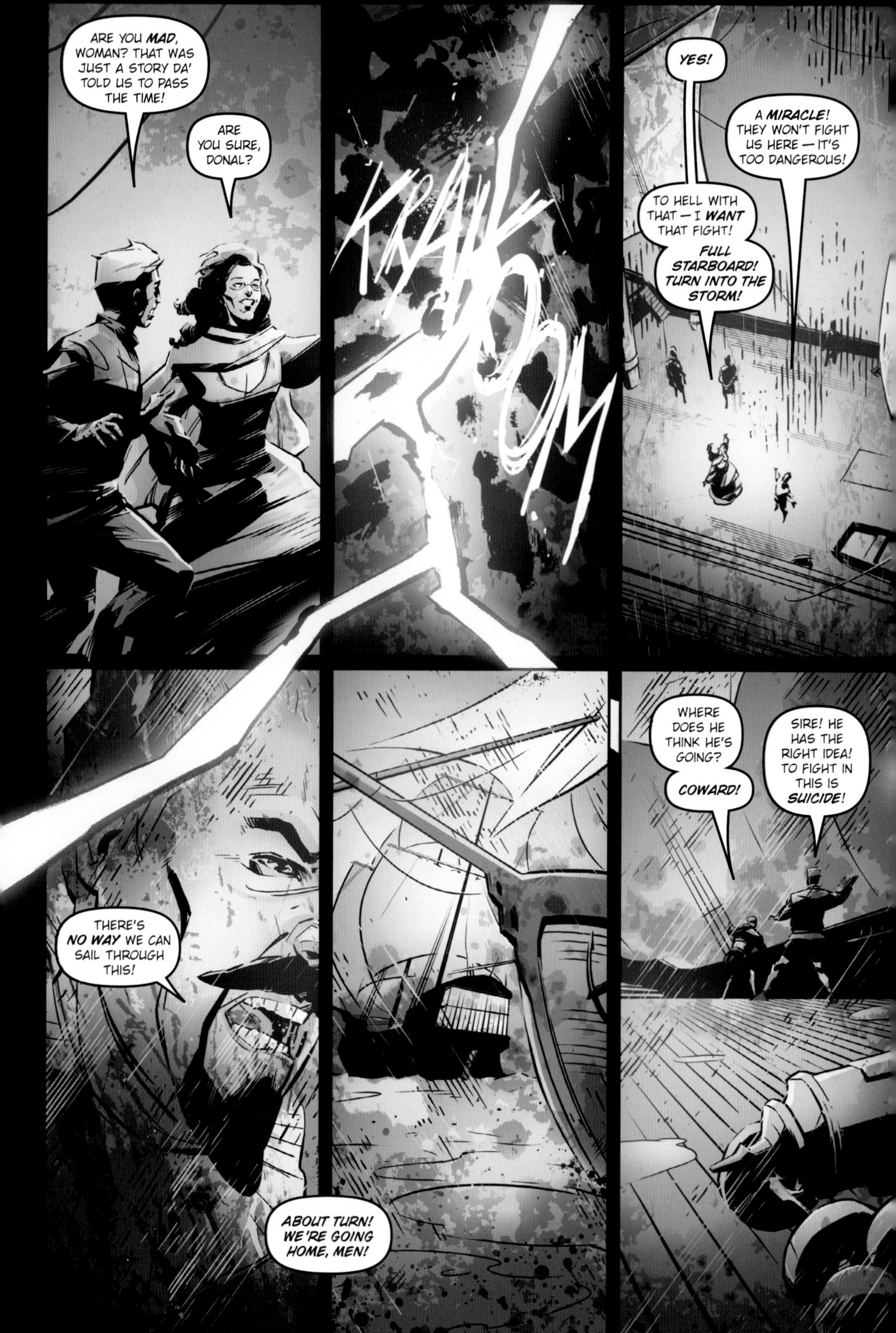
ARE YOU MAD, WOMAN? THAT WAS JUST A STORY DA' TOLD US TO PASS THE TIME!
ARE YOU SURE, DONAL?
KRAKOOM
YES!
A MIRACLE! THEY WON'T FIGHT US HERE — IT'S TOO DANGEROUS!
TO HELL WITH THAT — I WANT THAT FIGHT!
FULL STARBOARD! TURN INTO THE STORM!
THERE'S NO WAY WE CAN SAIL THROUGH THIS!
ABOUT TURN! WE'RE GOING HOME, MEN!
WHERE DOES HE THINK HE'S GOING?
COWARD!
SIRE! HE HAS THE RIGHT IDEA! TO FIGHT IN THIS IS SUICIDE!

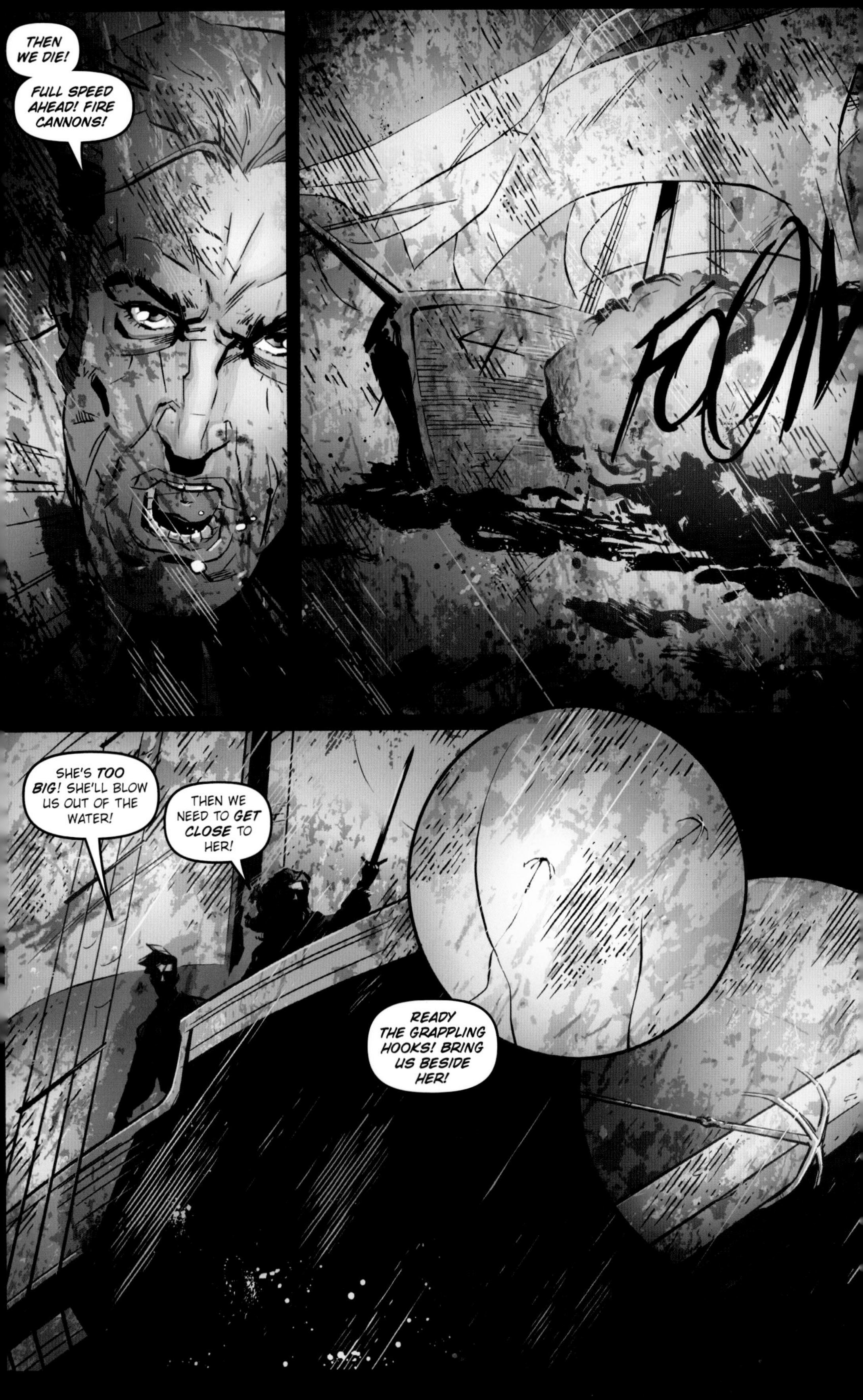
THEN WE DIE!
FULL SPEED AHEAD! FIRE CANNONS!
SHE'S TOO BIG! SHE'LL BLOW US OUT OF THE WATER!
THEN WE NEED TO GET CLOSE TO HER!
READY THE GRAPPLING HOOKS! BRING US BESIDE HER!

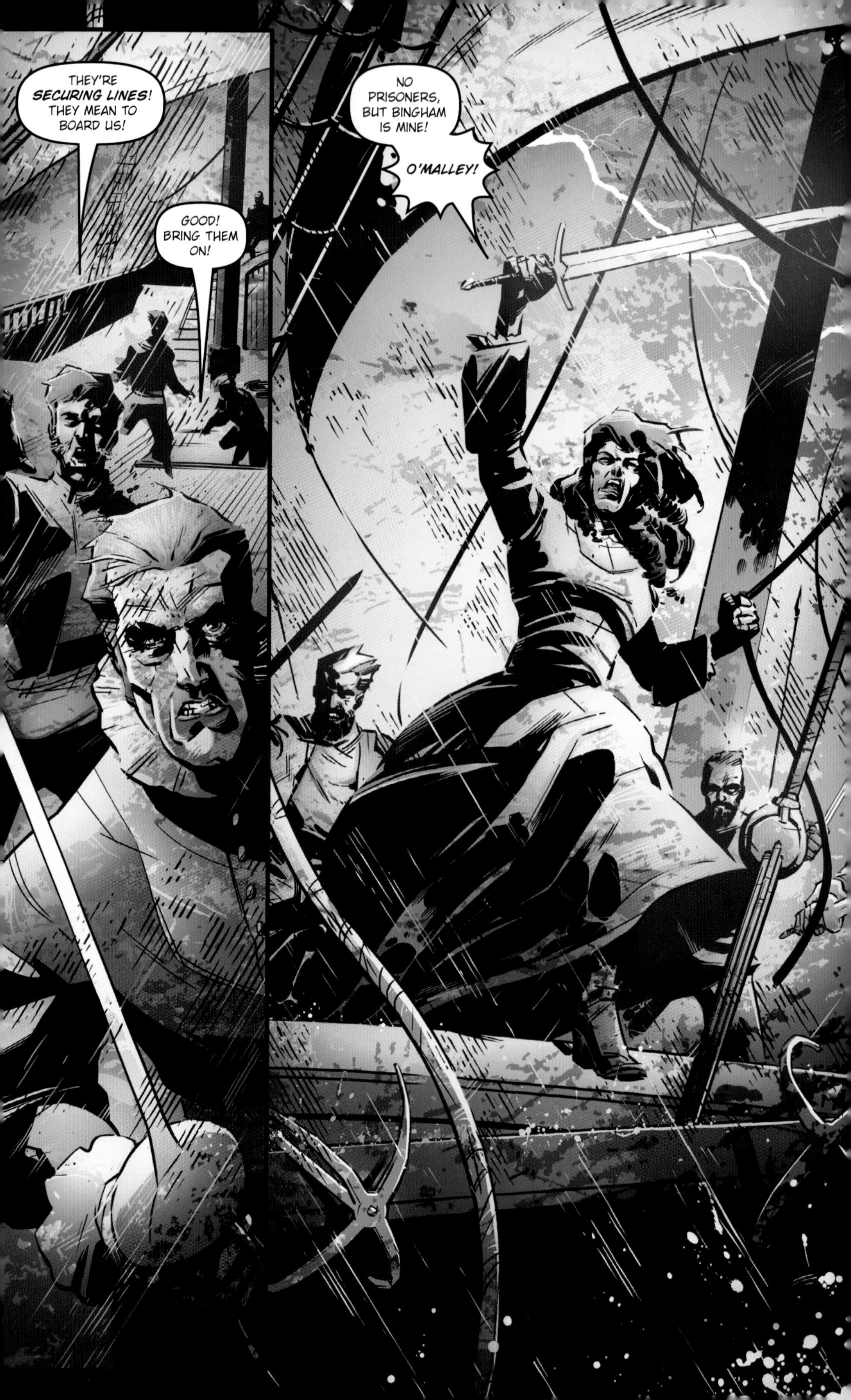
THEY'RE *SECURING LINES*! THEY MEAN TO BOARD US!
GOOD! BRING THEM ON!
NO PRISONERS, BUT BINGHAM IS MINE!
O'MALLEY!

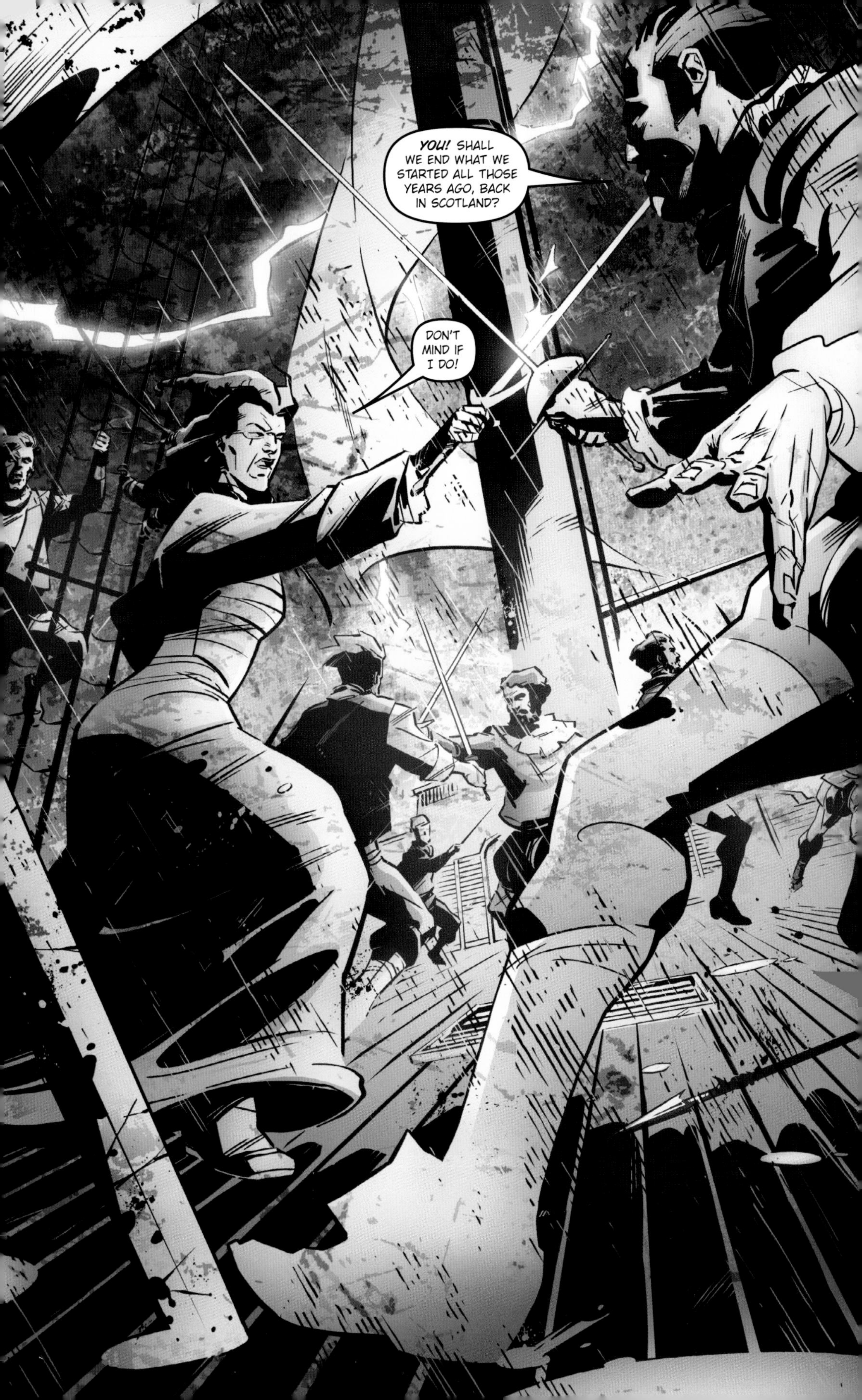
YOU! SHALL WE END WHAT WE STARTED ALL THOSE YEARS AGO, BACK IN SCOTLAND?
DON'T MIND IF I DO!

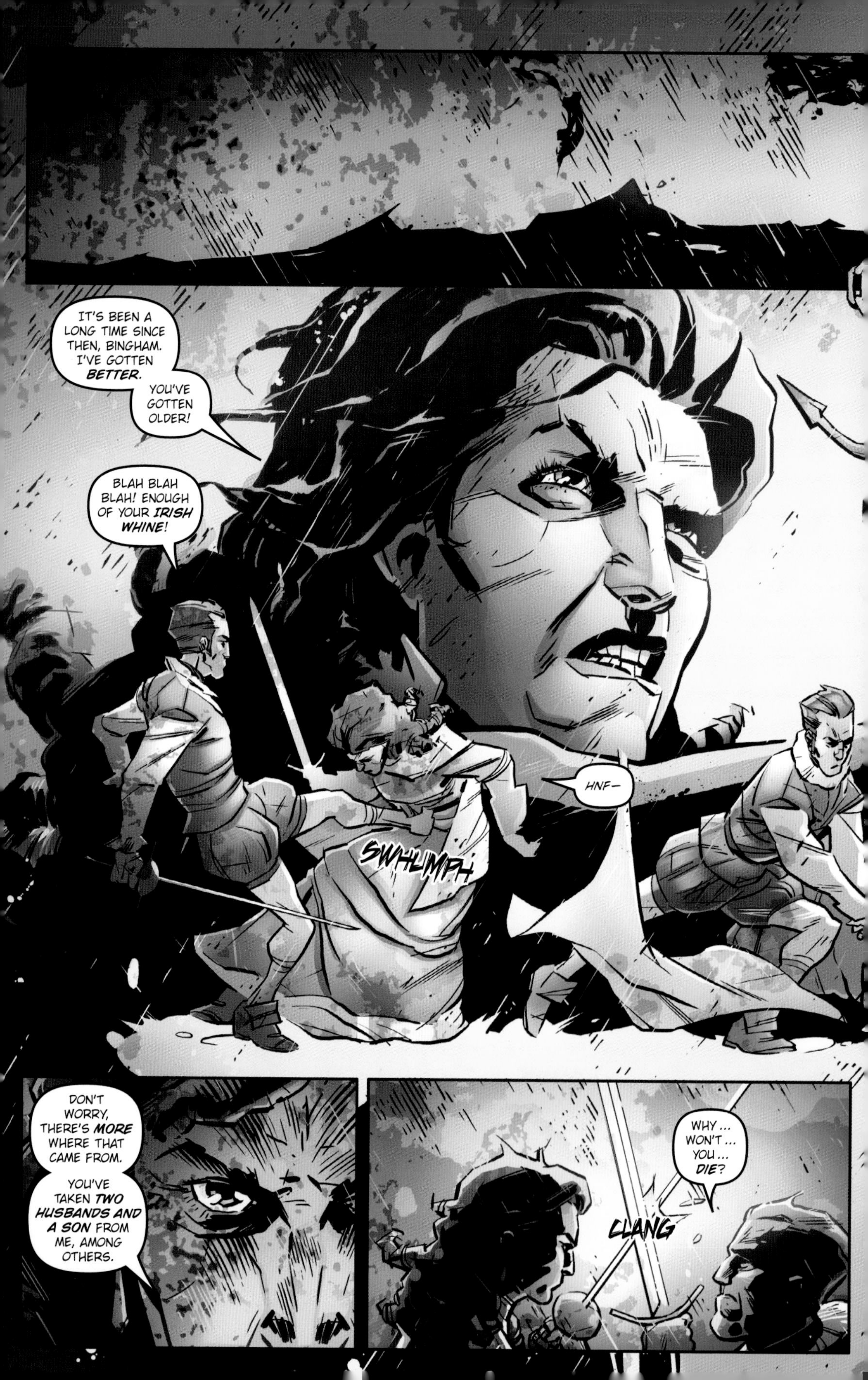
IT'S BEEN A LONG TIME SINCE THEN, BINGHAM. I'VE GOTTEN *BETTER*.
YOU'VE GOTTEN OLDER!
BLAH BLAH BLAH! ENOUGH OF YOUR *IRISH WHINE*!
HNF—
SWHUMPH
DON'T WORRY, THERE'S *MORE* WHERE THAT CAME FROM.
YOU'VE TAKEN *TWO HUSBANDS AND A SON* FROM ME, AMONG OTHERS.
WHY... WON'T... YOU... *DIE*?
CLANG

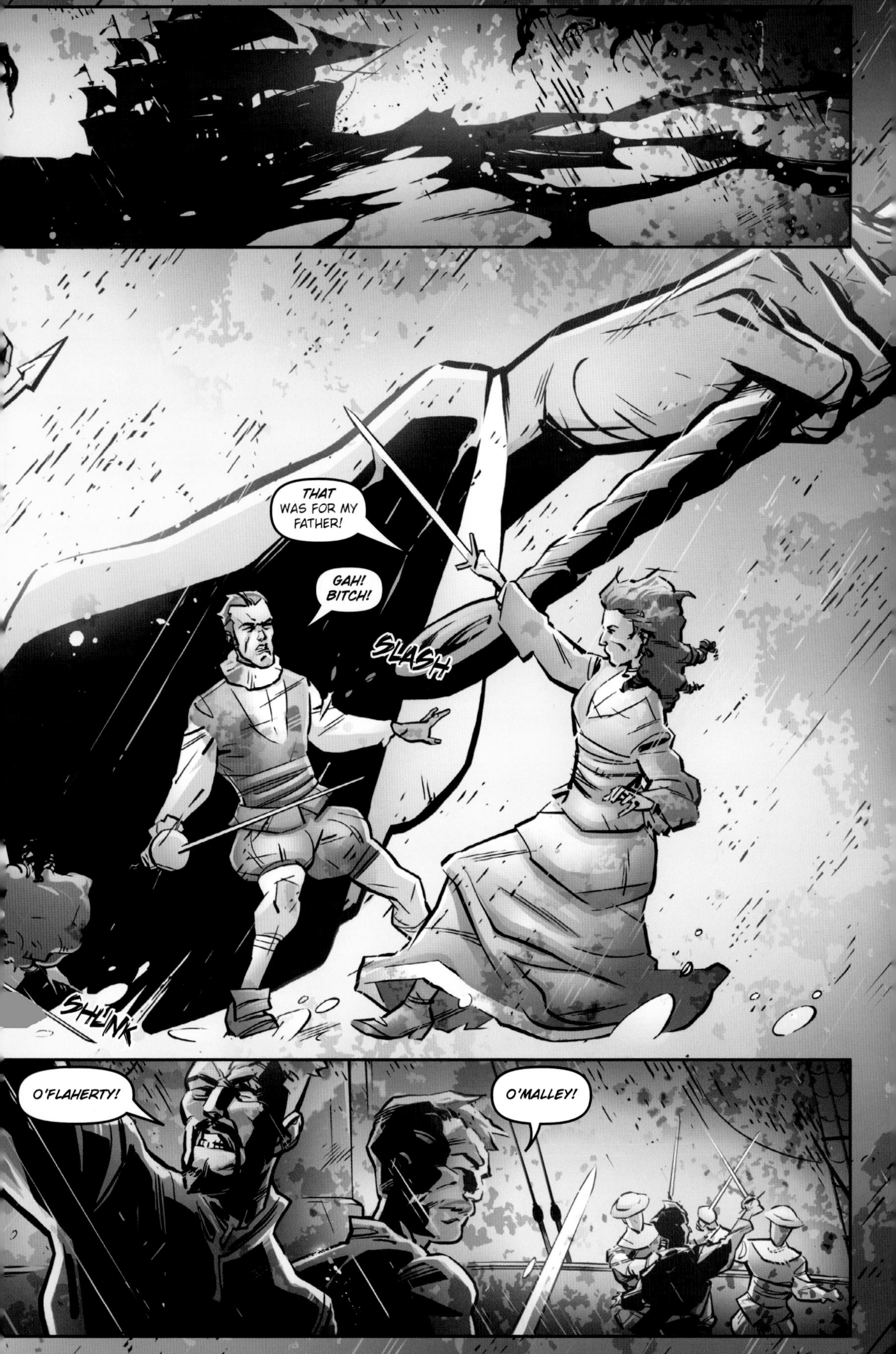
THAT WAS FOR MY FATHER!
GAH! BITCH!
SLASH
SHLINK
O'FLAHERTY!
O'MALLEY!

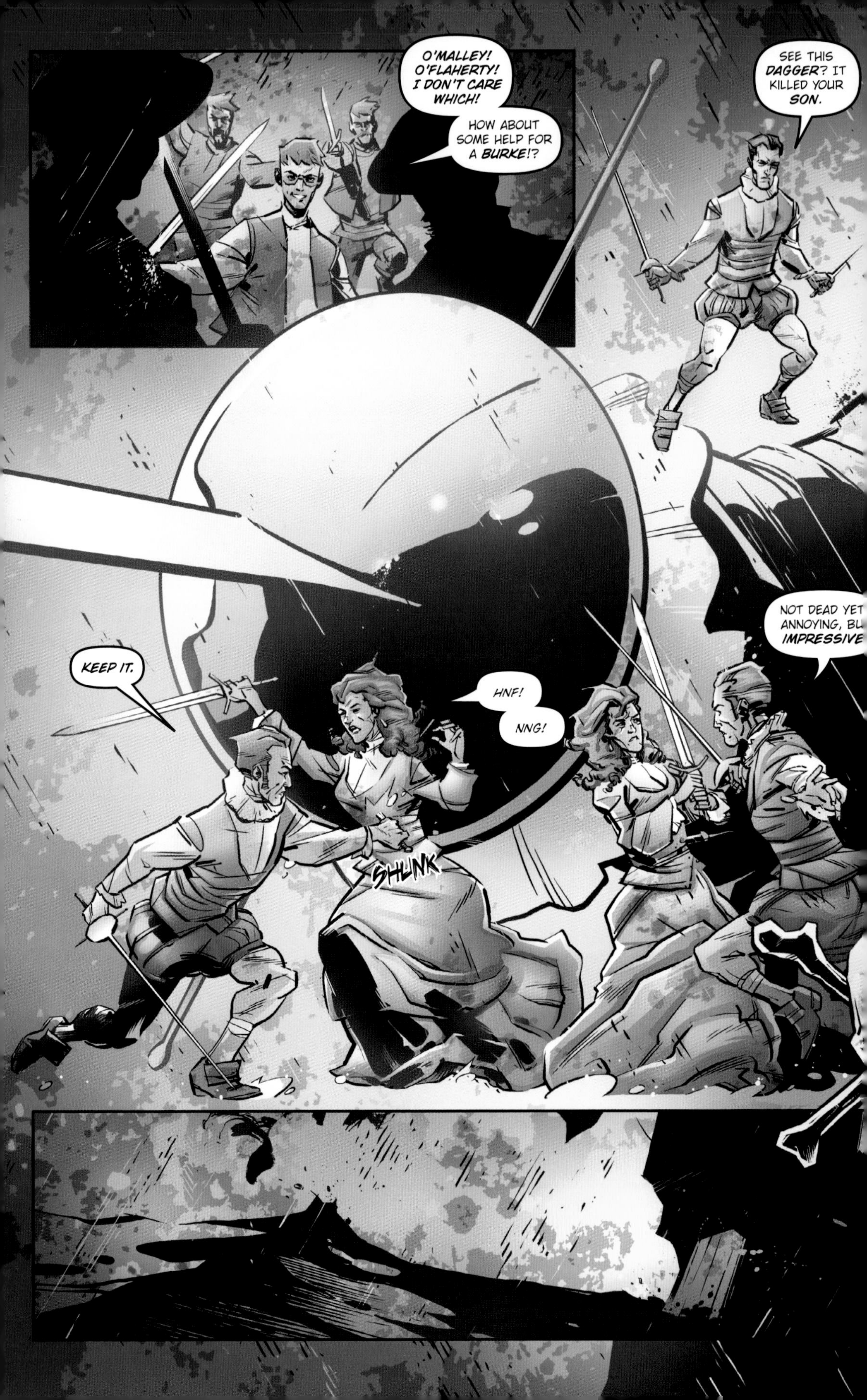
O'MALLEY! O'FLAHERTY! I DON'T CARE WHICH!
HOW ABOUT SOME HELP FOR A BURKE!?
SEE THIS DAGGER? IT KILLED YOUR SON.
KEEP IT.
SHLINK
HNF!
NNG!
NOT DEAD YET
ANNOYING, BU
IMPRESSIVE

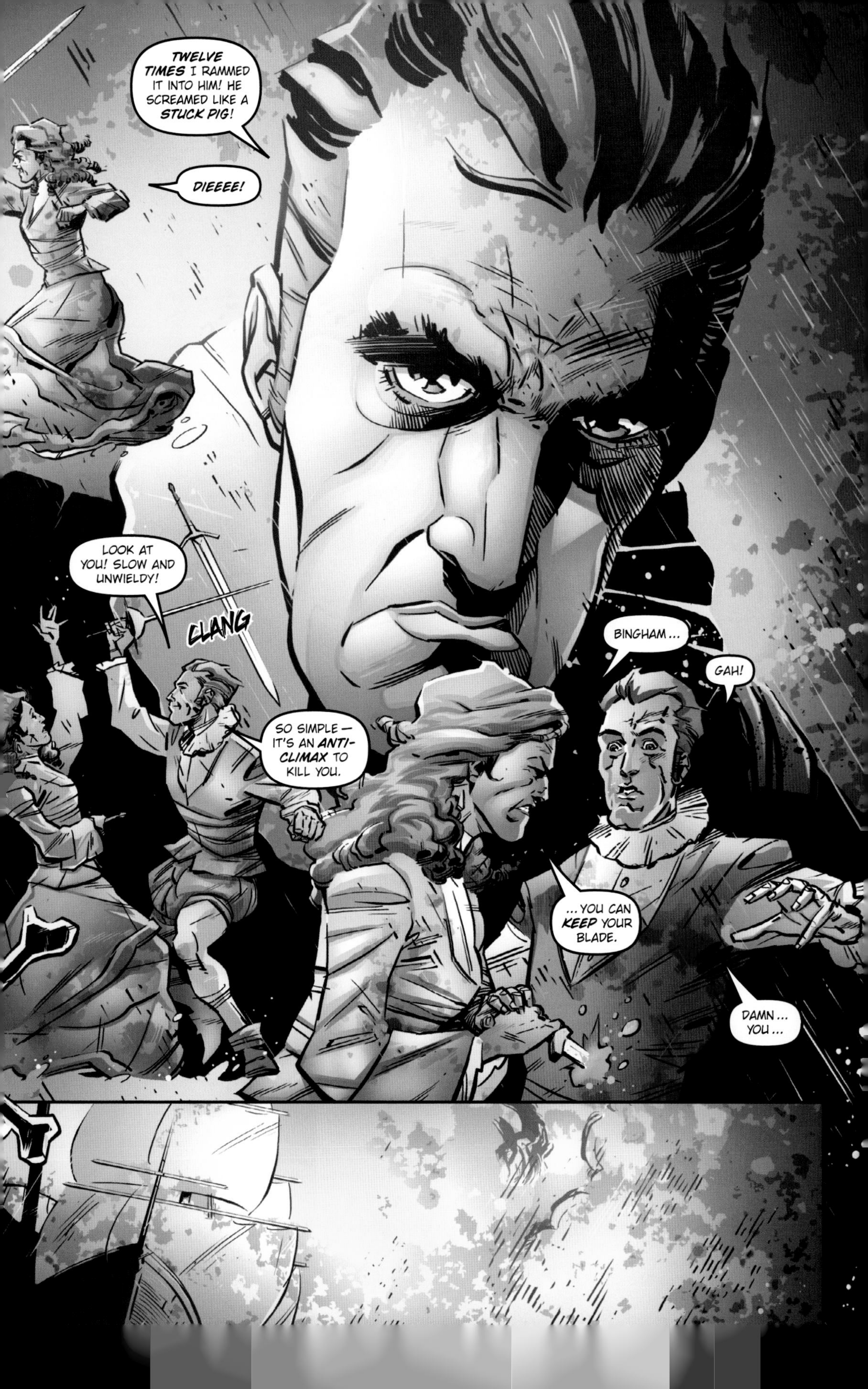
TWELVE TIMES I RAMMED IT INTO HIM! HE SCREAMED LIKE A STUCK PIG!
DIEEEE!
LOOK AT YOU! SLOW AND UNWIELDY!
CLANG
SO SIMPLE — IT'S AN ANTI-CLIMAX TO KILL YOU.
BINGHAM ...
GAH!
... YOU CAN KEEP YOUR BLADE.
DAMN ... YOU ...

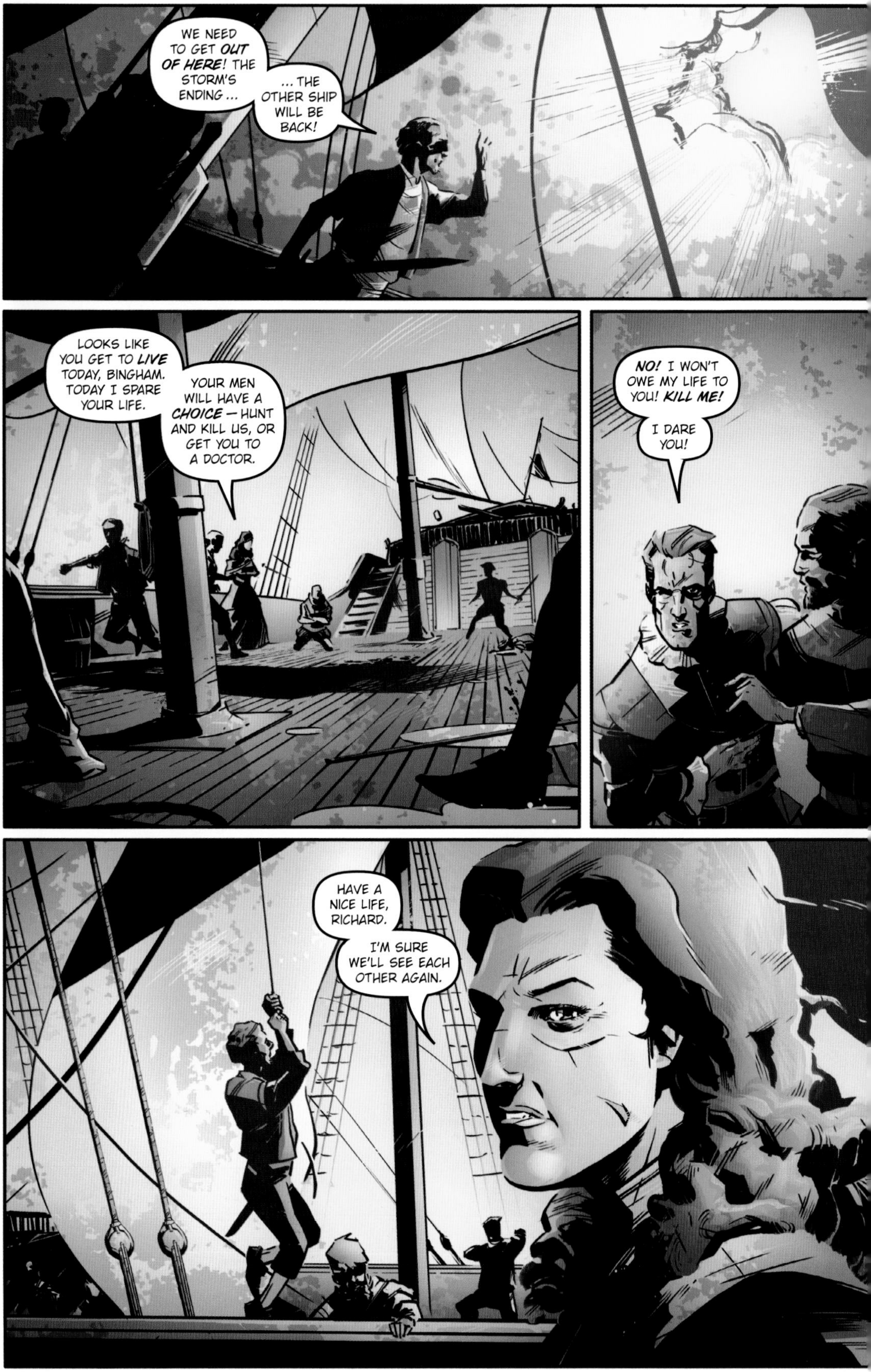
WE NEED TO GET OUT OF HERE! THE STORM'S ENDING ...
... THE OTHER SHIP WILL BE BACK!
LOOKS LIKE YOU GET TO LIVE TODAY, BINGHAM. TODAY I SPARE YOUR LIFE.
YOUR MEN WILL HAVE A CHOICE — HUNT AND KILL US, OR GET YOU TO A DOCTOR.
NO! I WON'T OWE MY LIFE TO YOU! KILL ME!
I DARE YOU!
HAVE A NICE LIFE, RICHARD.
I'M SURE WE'LL SEE EACH OTHER AGAIN.

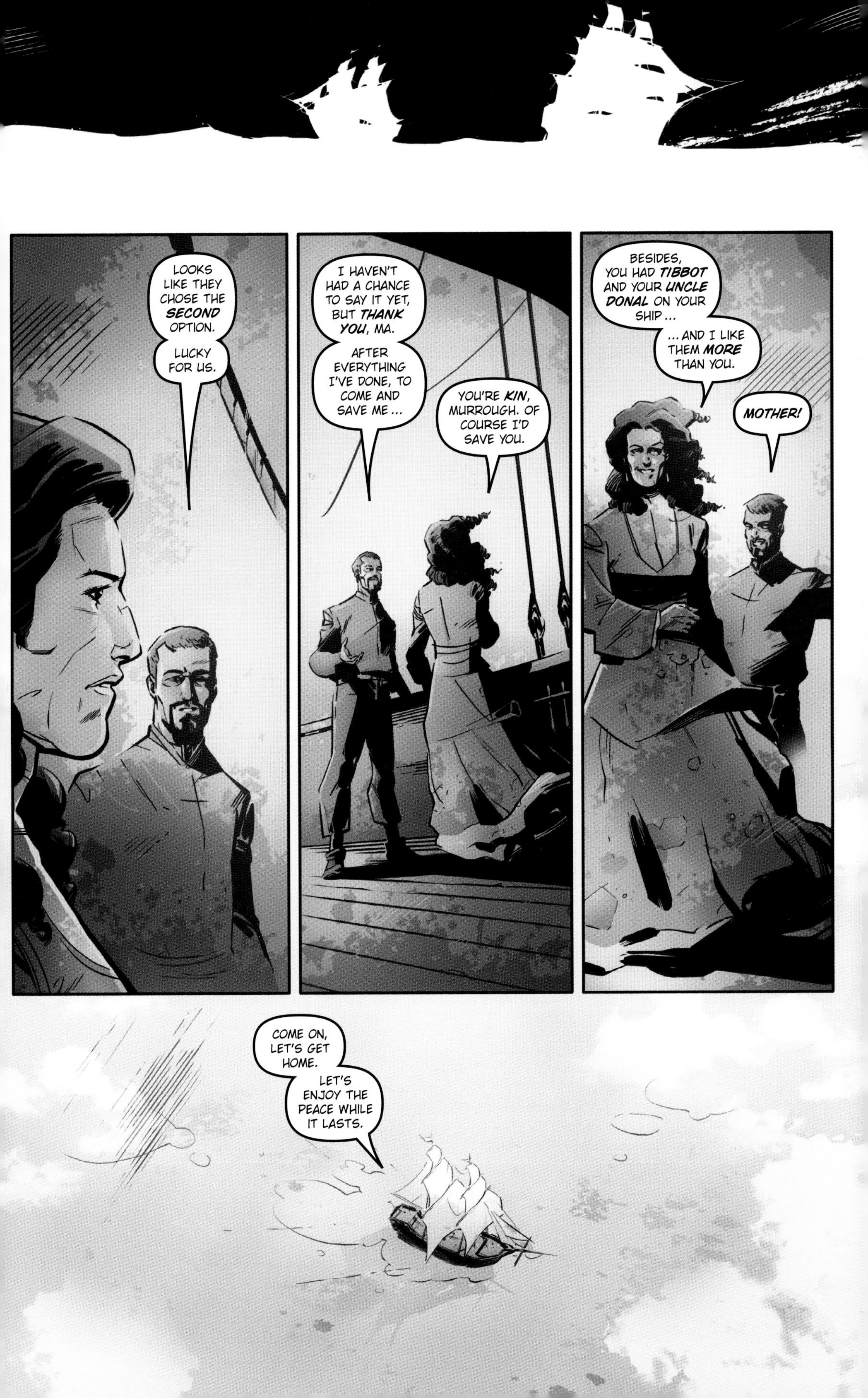
LOOKS LIKE THEY CHOSE THE SECOND OPTION.
LUCKY FOR US.
I HAVEN'T HAD A CHANCE TO SAY IT YET, BUT THANK YOU, MA.
AFTER EVERYTHING I'VE DONE, TO COME AND SAVE ME ...
YOU'RE KIN, MURROUGH. OF COURSE I'D SAVE YOU.
BESIDES, YOU HAD TIBBOT AND YOUR UNCLE DONAL ON YOUR SHIP ...
... AND I LIKE THEM MORE THAN YOU.
MOTHER!
COME ON, LET'S GET HOME.
LET'S ENJOY THE PEACE WHILE IT LASTS.

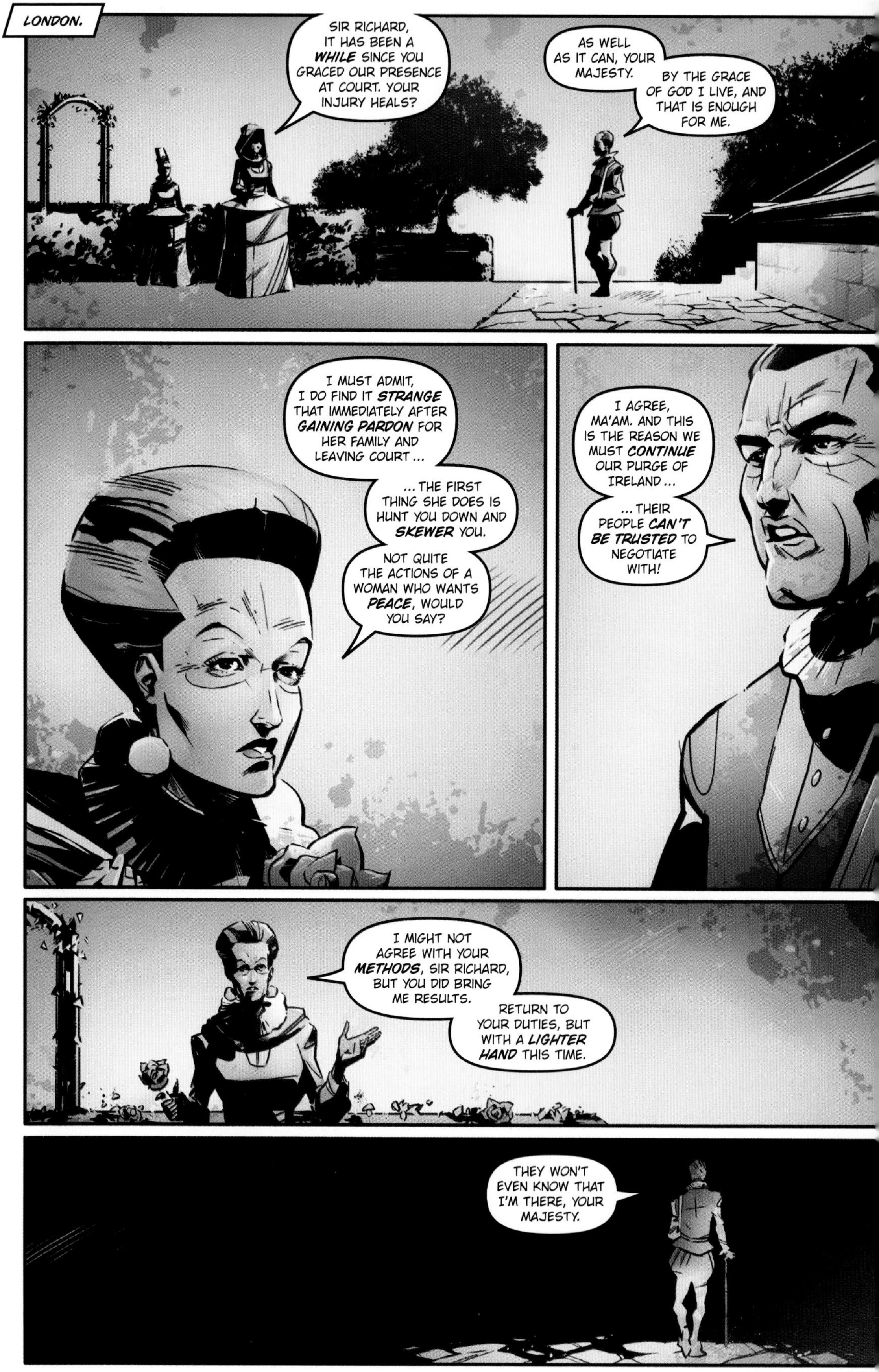
LONDON.
SIR RICHARD, IT HAS BEEN A WHILE SINCE YOU GRACED OUR PRESENCE AT COURT. YOUR INJURY HEALS?
AS WELL AS IT CAN, YOUR MAJESTY.
BY THE GRACE OF GOD I LIVE, AND THAT IS ENOUGH FOR ME.
I MUST ADMIT, I DO FIND IT STRANGE THAT IMMEDIATELY AFTER GAINING PARDON FOR HER FAMILY AND LEAVING COURT ...
... THE FIRST THING SHE DOES IS HUNT YOU DOWN AND SKEWER YOU.
NOT QUITE THE ACTIONS OF A WOMAN WHO WANTS PEACE, WOULD YOU SAY?
I AGREE, MA'AM. AND THIS IS THE REASON WE MUST CONTINUE OUR PURGE OF IRELAND ...
... THEIR PEOPLE CAN'T BE TRUSTED TO NEGOTIATE WITH!
I MIGHT NOT AGREE WITH YOUR METHODS, SIR RICHARD, BUT YOU DID BRING ME RESULTS.
RETURN TO YOUR DUTIES, BUT WITH A LIGHTER HAND THIS TIME.
THEY WON'T EVEN KNOW THAT I'M THERE, YOUR MAJESTY.

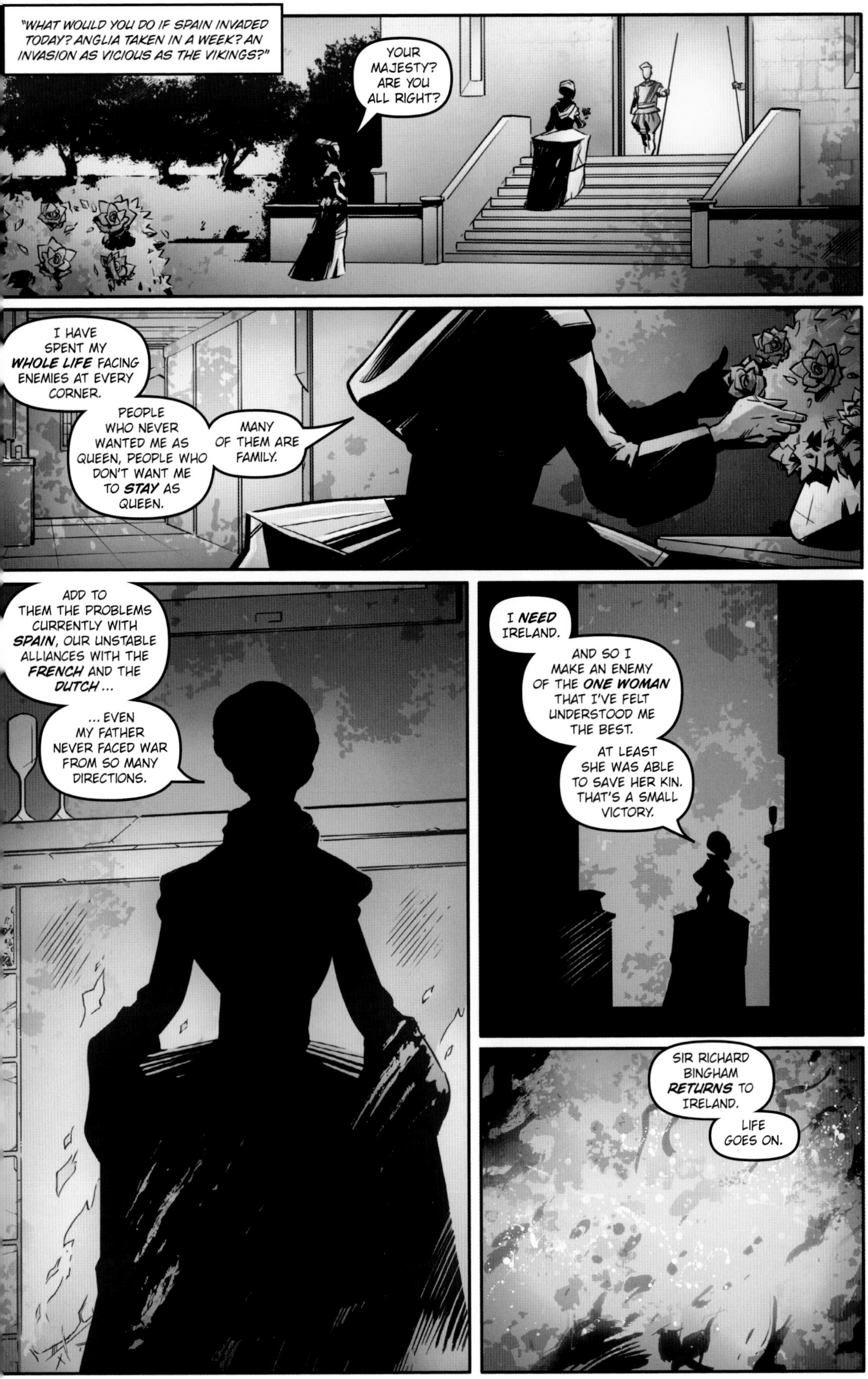
"WHAT WOULD YOU DO IF SPAIN INVADED TODAY? ANGLIA TAKEN IN A WEEK? AN INVASION AS VICIOUS AS THE VIKINGS?"
YOUR MAJESTY? ARE YOU ALL RIGHT?
I HAVE SPENT MY **WHOLE LIFE** FACING ENEMIES AT EVERY CORNER.
PEOPLE WHO NEVER WANTED ME AS QUEEN, PEOPLE WHO DON'T WANT ME TO **STAY** AS QUEEN.
MANY OF THEM ARE FAMILY.
ADD TO THEM THE PROBLEMS CURRENTLY WITH **SPAIN**, OUR UNSTABLE ALLIANCES WITH THE **FRENCH** AND THE **DUTCH** ...
... EVEN MY FATHER NEVER FACED WAR FROM SO MANY DIRECTIONS.
I **NEED** IRELAND.
AND SO I MAKE AN ENEMY OF THE **ONE WOMAN** THAT I'VE FELT UNDERSTOOD ME THE BEST.
AT LEAST SHE WAS ABLE TO SAVE HER KIN. THAT'S A SMALL VICTORY.
SIR RICHARD BINGHAM **RETURNS** TO IRELAND.
LIFE GOES ON.

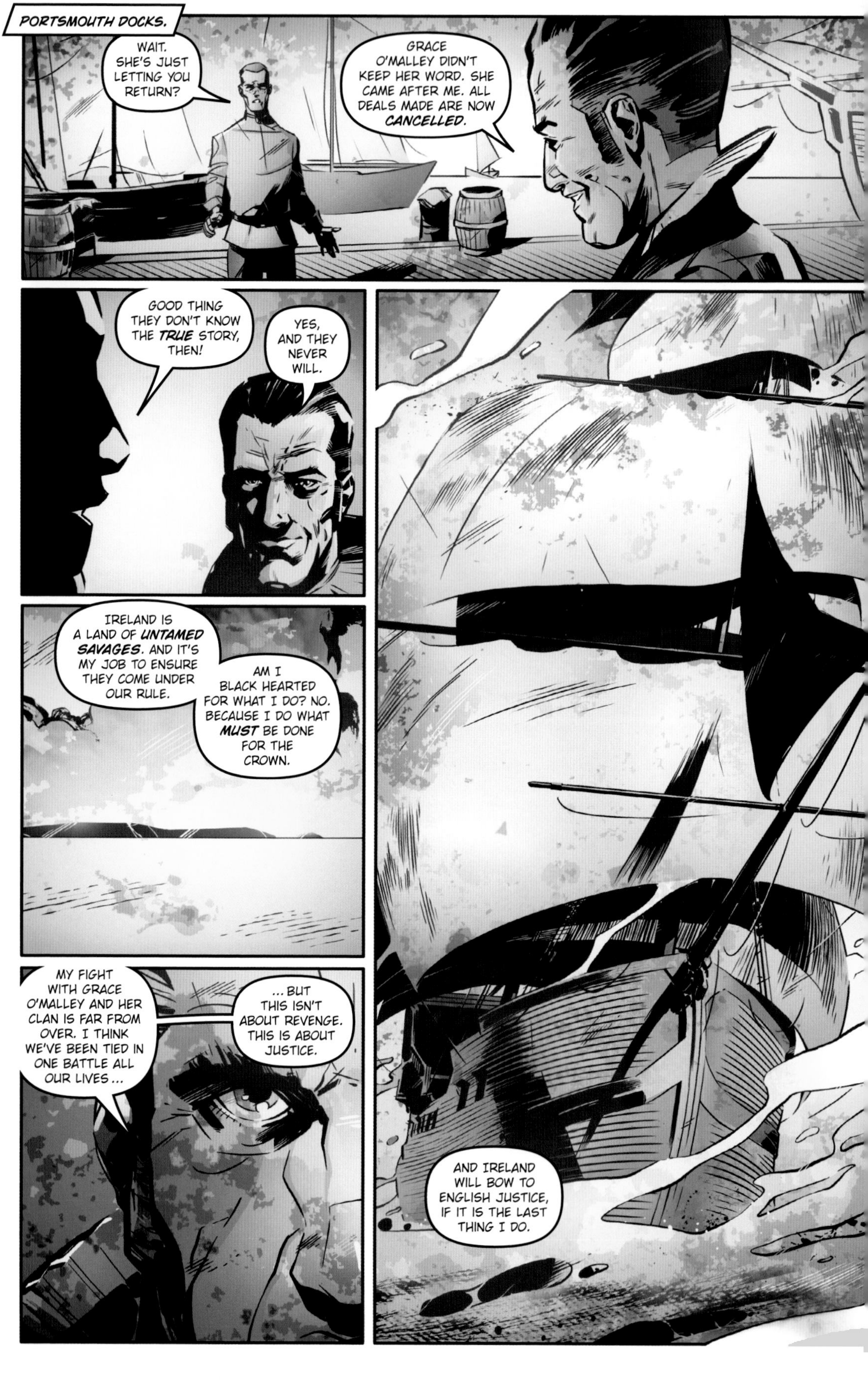
PORTSMOUTH DOCKS.
WAIT. SHE'S JUST LETTING YOU RETURN?
GRACE O'MALLEY DIDN'T KEEP HER WORD. SHE CAME AFTER ME. ALL DEALS MADE ARE NOW CANCELLED.
GOOD THING THEY DON'T KNOW THE TRUE STORY, THEN!
YES, AND THEY NEVER WILL.
IRELAND IS A LAND OF UNTAMED SAVAGES. AND IT'S MY JOB TO ENSURE THEY COME UNDER OUR RULE.
AM I BLACK HEARTED FOR WHAT I DO? NO. BECAUSE I DO WHAT MUST BE DONE FOR THE CROWN.
MY FIGHT WITH GRACE O'MALLEY AND HER CLAN IS FAR FROM OVER. I THINK WE'VE BEEN TIED IN ONE BATTLE ALL OUR LIVES...
...BUT THIS ISN'T ABOUT REVENGE. THIS IS ABOUT JUSTICE.
AND IRELAND WILL BOW TO ENGLISH JUSTICE, IF IT IS THE LAST THING I DO.

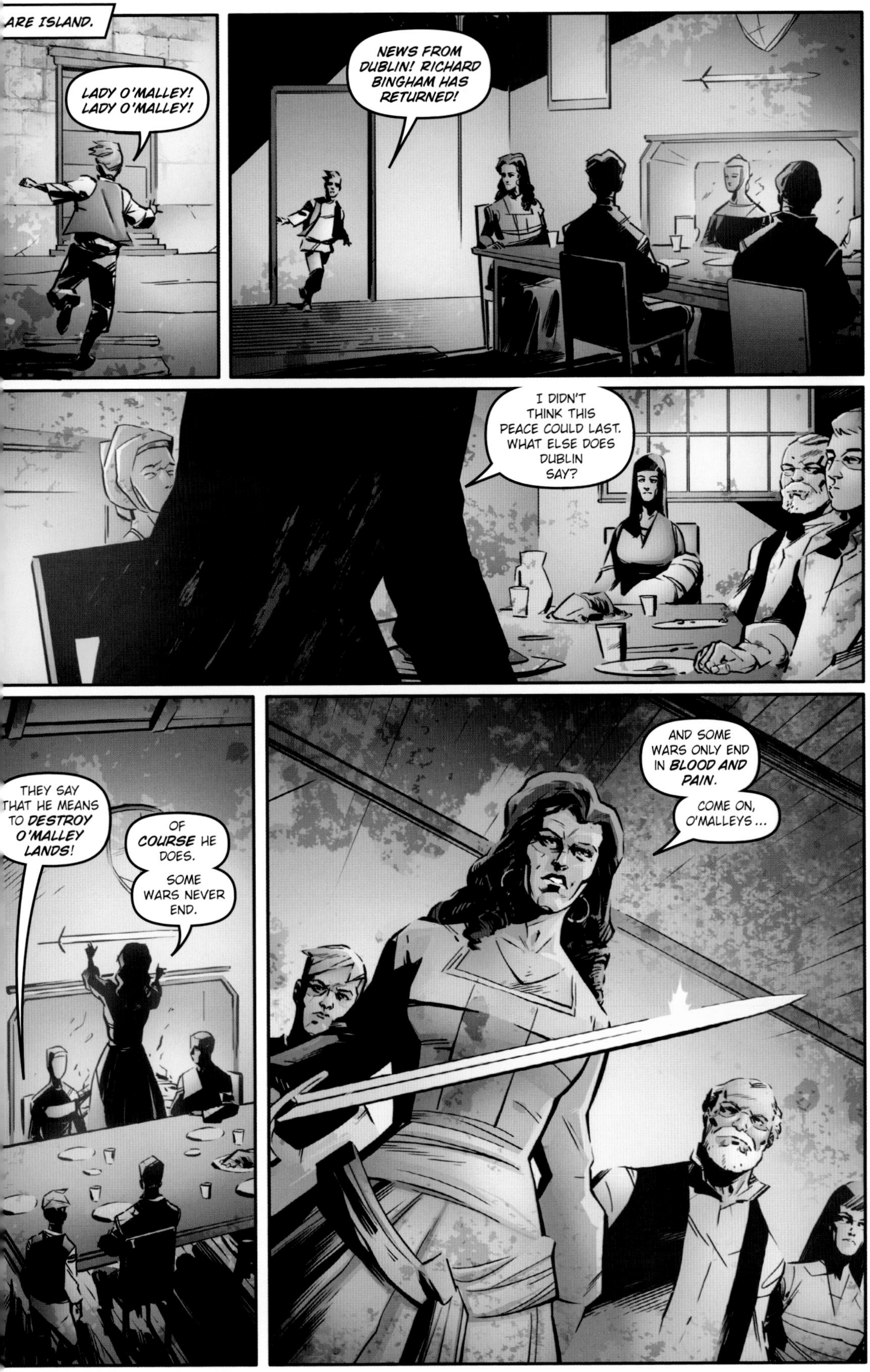

ARE ISLAND.
LADY O'MALLEY! LADY O'MALLEY!
NEWS FROM DUBLIN! RICHARD BINGHAM HAS RETURNED!
I DIDN'T THINK THIS PEACE COULD LAST. WHAT ELSE DOES DUBLIN SAY?
THEY SAY THAT HE MEANS TO DESTROY O'MALLEY LANDS!
OF COURSE HE DOES.
SOME WARS NEVER END.
AND SOME WARS ONLY END IN BLOOD AND PAIN.
COME ON, O'MALLEYS ...

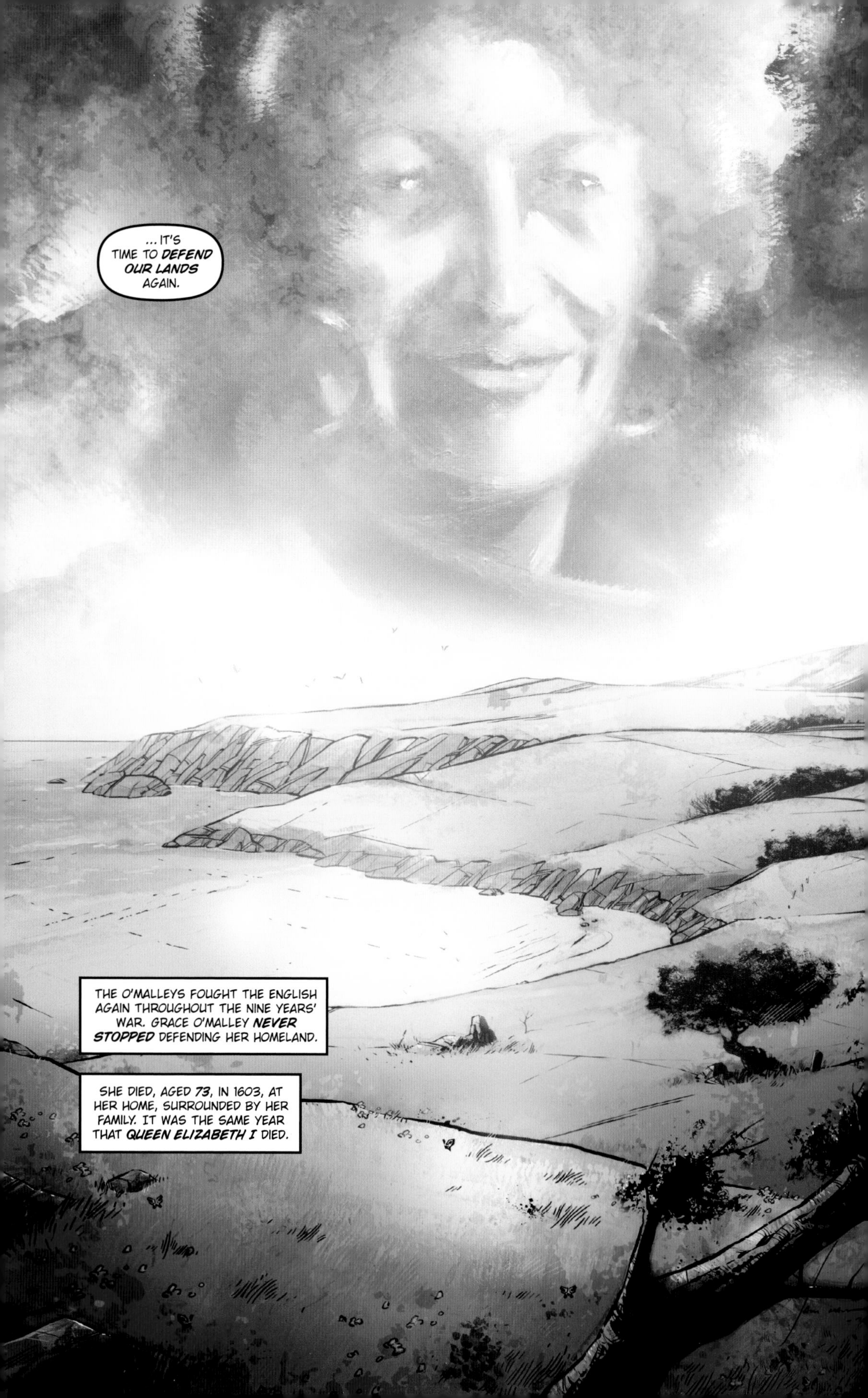
... IT'S TIME TO DEFEND OUR LANDS AGAIN.
THE O'MALLEYS FOUGHT THE ENGLISH AGAIN THROUGHOUT THE NINE YEARS' WAR. GRACE O'MALLEY NEVER STOPPED DEFENDING HER HOMELAND.
SHE DIED, AGED 73, IN 1603, AT HER HOME, SURROUNDED BY HER FAMILY. IT WAS THE SAME YEAR THAT QUEEN ELIZABETH I DIED.

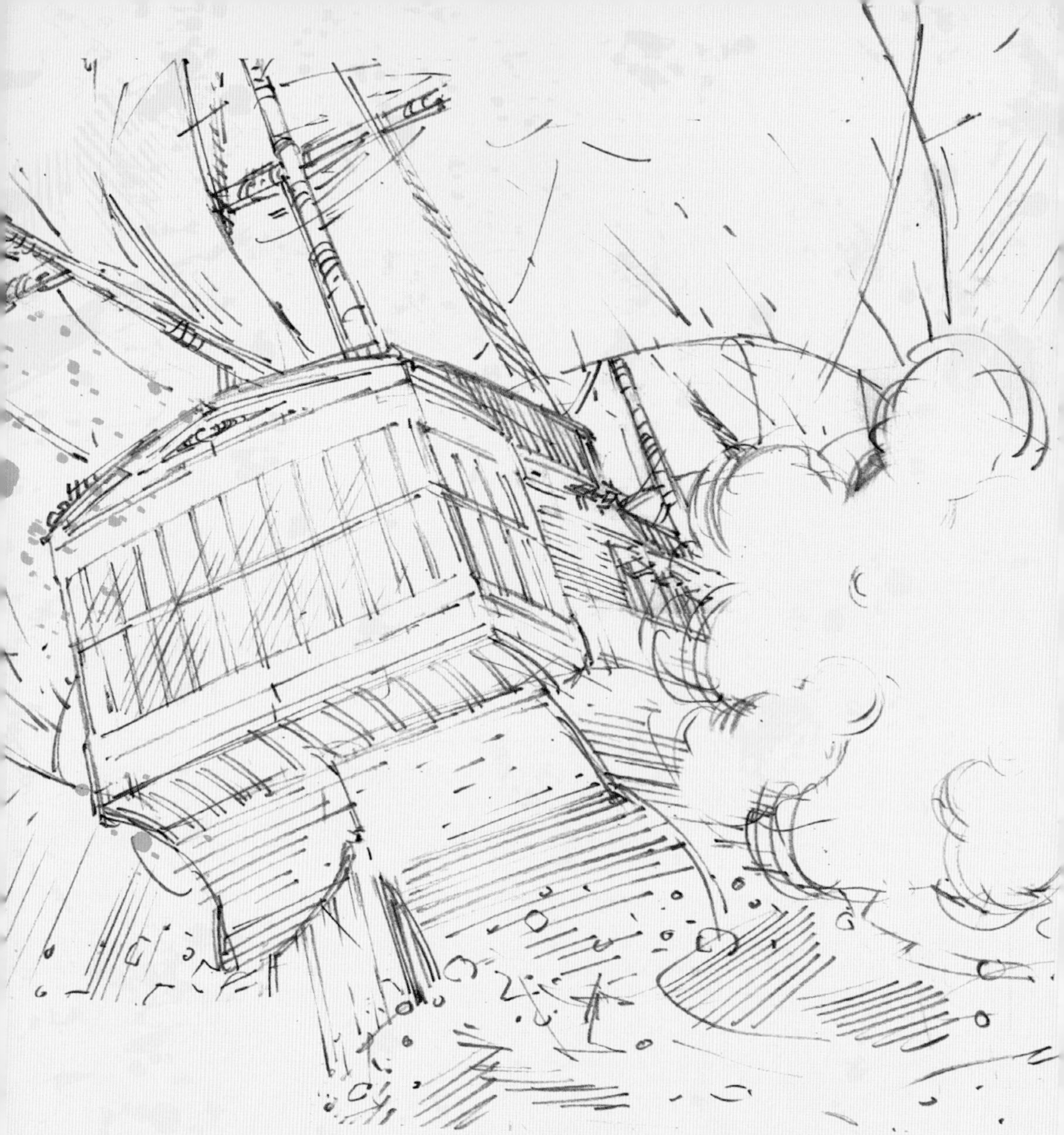

TONY LEE

Tony Lee has written for many popular comic books, including *X-Men*, *Doctor Who*, *Spider Man*, *Starship Troopers*, *Wallace & Gromit*, and *Shrek*. His adaptation of *Pride & Prejudice & Zombies: The Graphic Novel* was a #1 *New York Times* bestseller. He is also the author of the graphic novels *Outlaw: The Legend of Robin Hood*, *Excalibur: The Legend of King Arthur*, and *Messenger: The Legend of Joan of Arc*. He has also adapted Anthony Horowitz's bestselling series *The Power of Five* into graphic novels. Tony Lee lives in London.

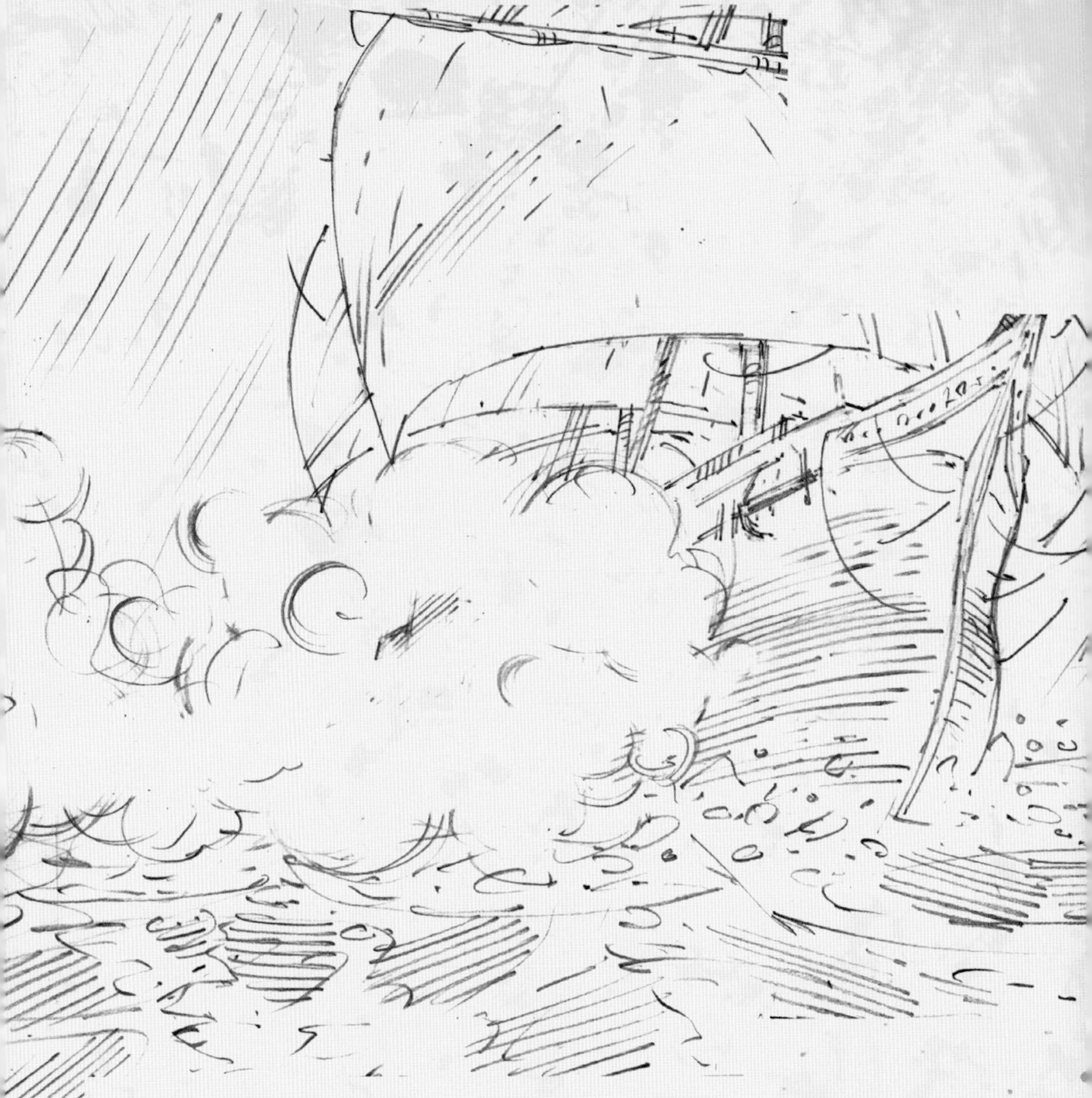

SAM HART

Sam Hart is an illustrator of comic books and graphic novels, including *Judge Dredd* and *Starship Troopers*. He is the illustrator of Tony Lee's *Outlaw: The Legend of Robin Hood*, *Excalibur: The Legend of King Arthur*, and *Messenger: The Legend of Joan of Arc*. Sam Hart lives and teaches comic art in Brazil.

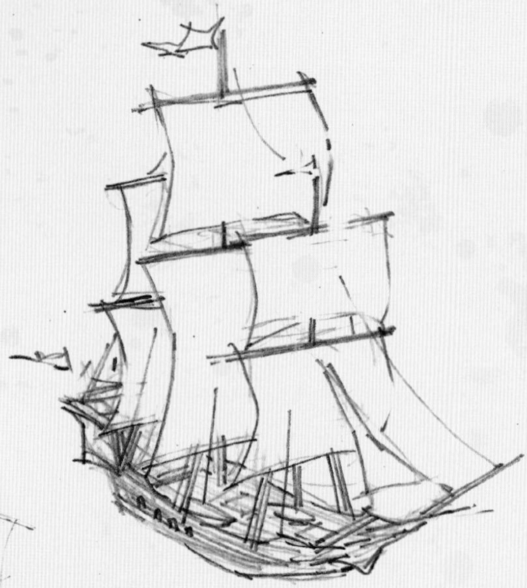

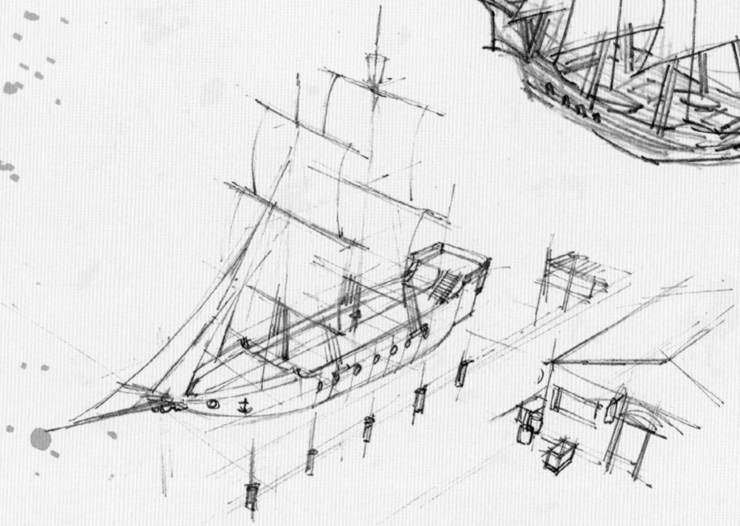

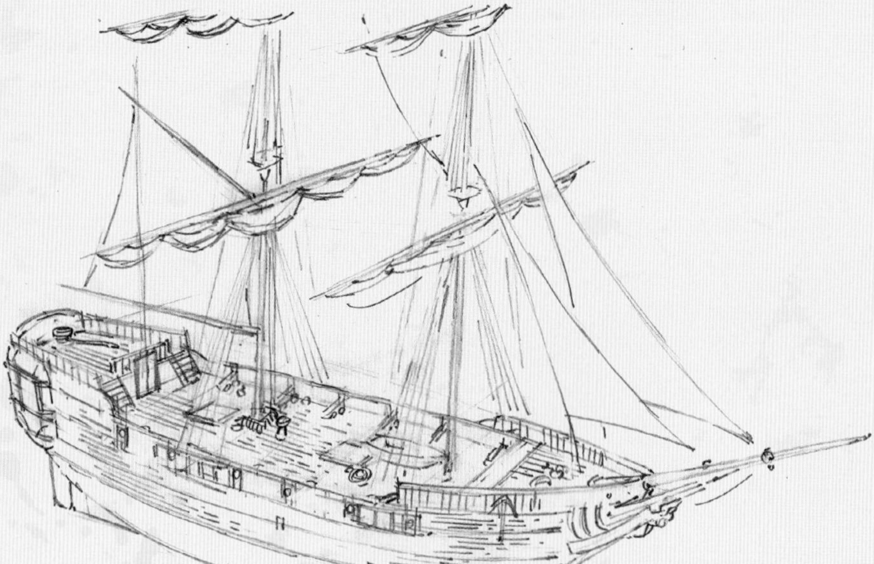

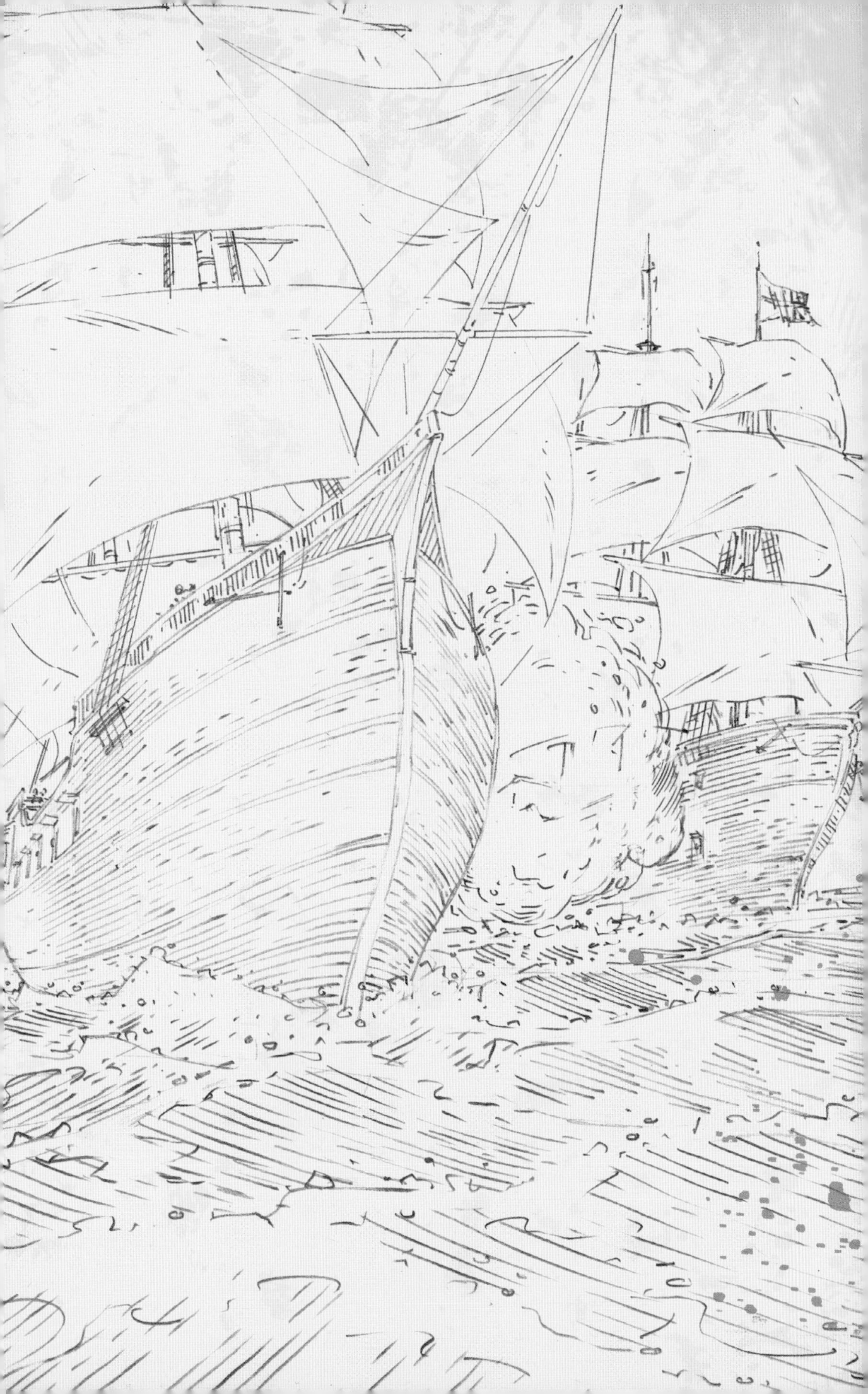

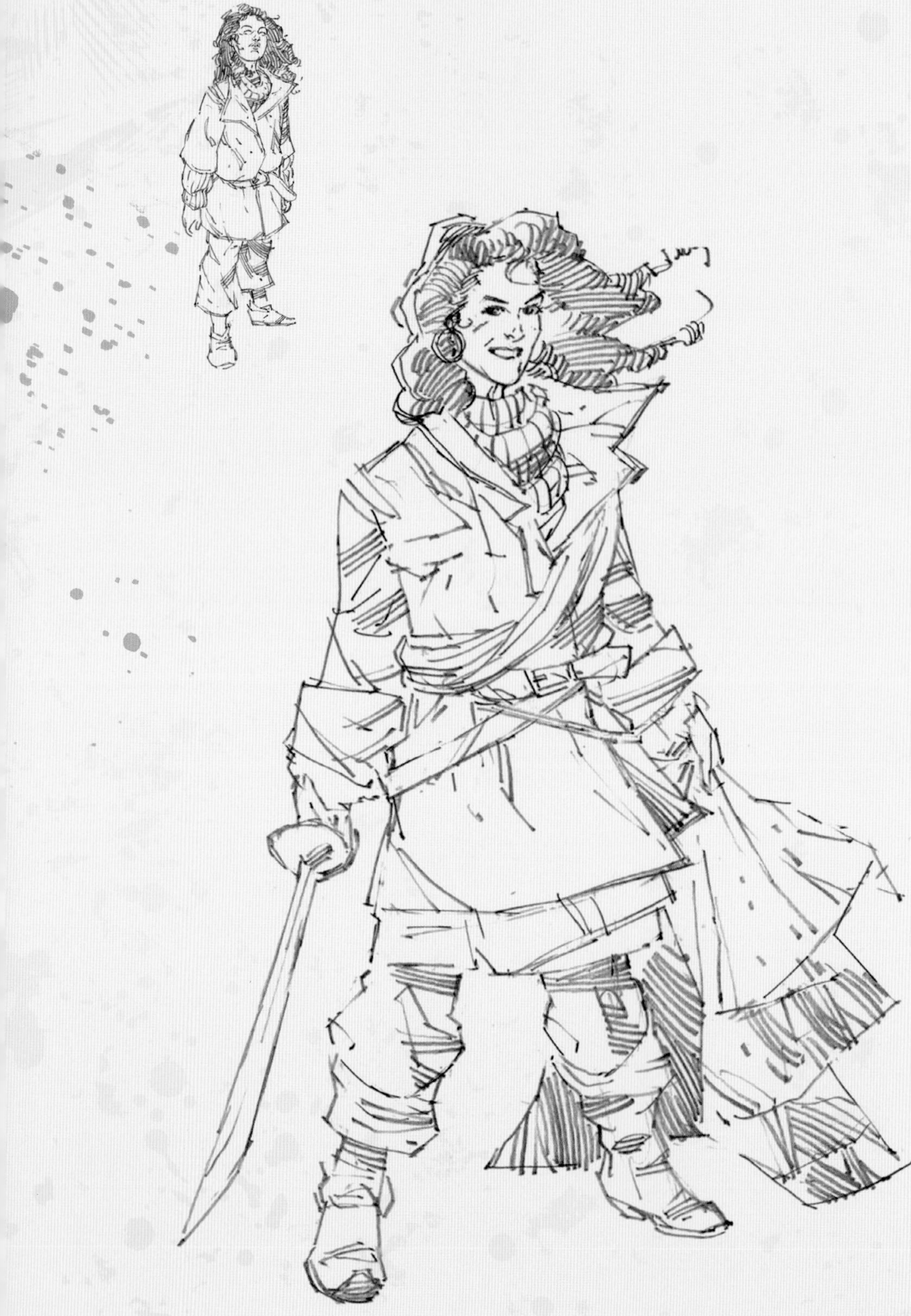

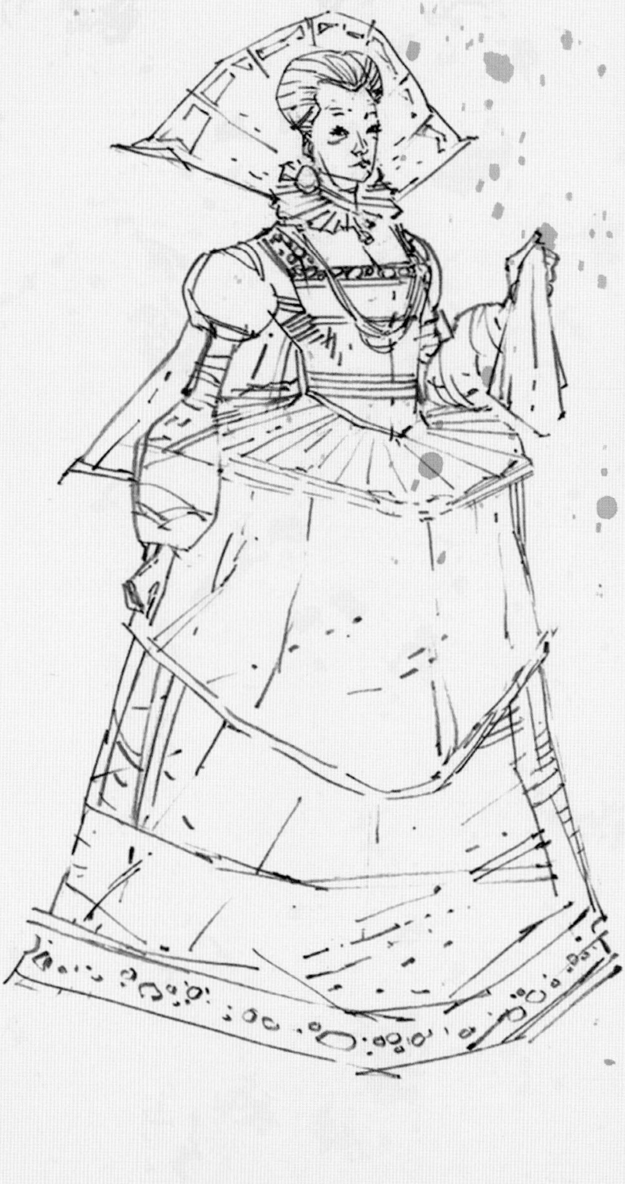

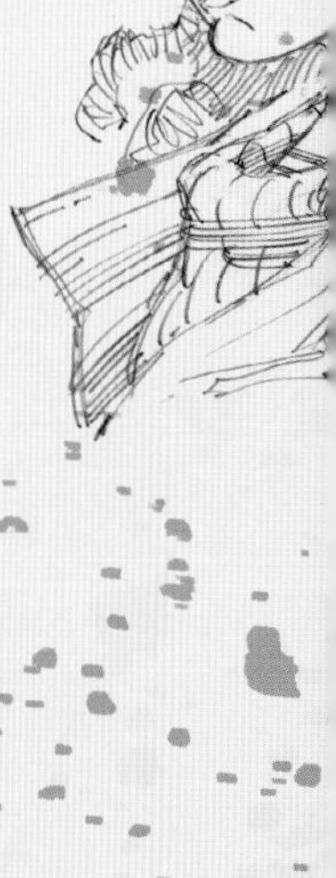

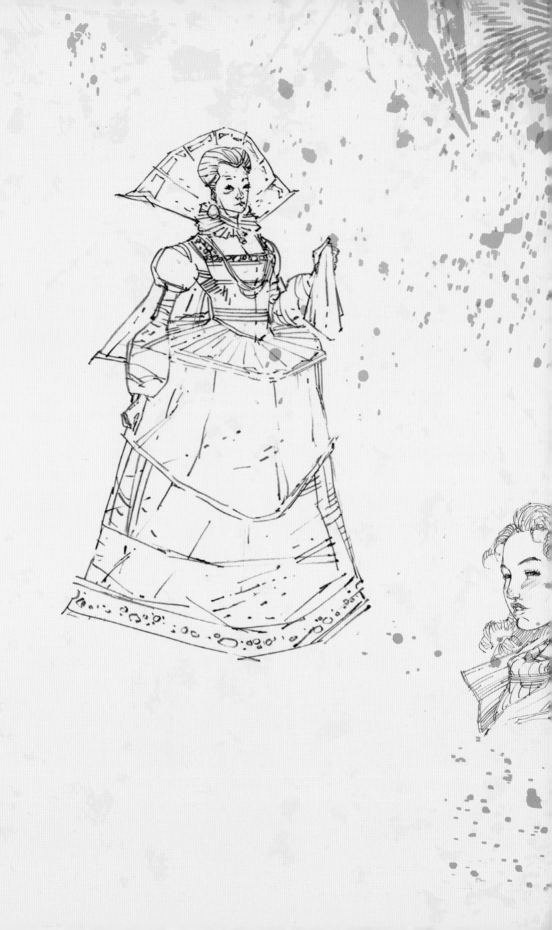